OWLSIGHT

MERCEDES LACKEY
& LARRY DIXON

OWLSIGHT

MERCEDES LACKEY
& LARRY DIXON

DAW BOOKS, INC.
DONALD A. WOLLHEIM, FOUNDER
375 Hudson Street, New York, NY 10014

www.dawbooks.com

**ELIZABETH R. WOLLHEIM
SHEILA E. GILBERT
PUBLISHERS**

To Betsy,
without whom this would not be possible.

OFFICIAL TIMELINE FOR THE

by Mercedes Lackey

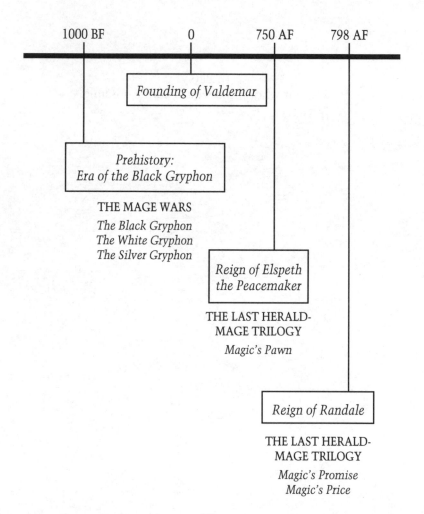

| 1000 BF | 0 | 750 AF | 798 AF |

Founding of Valdemar

Prehistory:
Era of the Black Gryphon

THE MAGE WARS

The Black Gryphon
The White Gryphon
The Silver Gryphon

Reign of Elspeth
the Peacemaker

THE LAST HERALD-
MAGE TRILOGY

Magic's Pawn

Reign of Randale

THE LAST HERALD-
MAGE TRILOGY

Magic's Promise
Magic's Price

BF *Before the Founding*
AF *After the Founding*

*Coming from DAW Books in hardcover

HERALDS OF VALDEMAR SERIES

Sequence of events by Valdemar reckoning

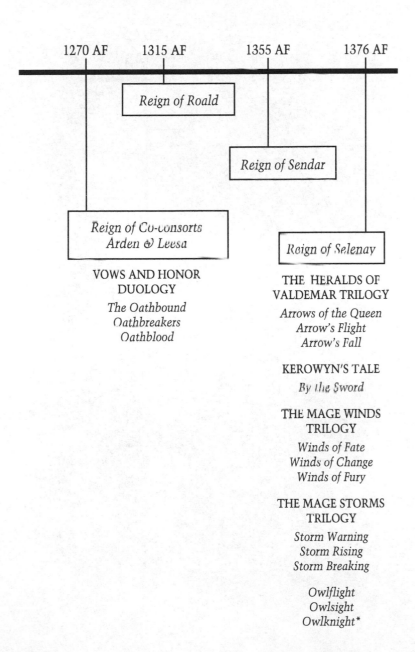

1270 AF   1315 AF   1355 AF   1376 AF

Reign of Roald

Reign of Sendar

Reign of Co-consorts
Arden & Leesa

Reign of Selenay

**VOWS AND HONOR
DUOLOGY**

*The Oathbound
Oathbreakers
Oathblood*

**THE HERALDS OF
VALDEMAR TRILOGY**

*Arrows of the Queen
Arrow's Flight
Arrow's Fall*

KEROWYN'S TALE

By the Sword

**THE MAGE WINDS
TRILOGY**

*Winds of Fate
Winds of Change
Winds of Fury*

**THE MAGE STORMS
TRILOGY**

*Storm Warning
Storm Rising
Storm Breaking*

*Owlflight
Owlsight
Owlknight**

Keisha

One

"Keisha?" When Keisha didn't answer, the fluting voice calling her name in the distance grew noticeably impatient. *"Keisha!"*

Keisha Alder ignored her sister Shandi's continued calls; she was in the middle of a job she had no intention of cutting short. The sharp smell of vinegar filled Keisha's workshop, but she was so inured to it that it hardly even stung her nose. Shandi could wait long enough for Keisha to finish decanting her bruise potion, straining out the bits of wormwood with a fine net of cheesecloth. Keisha wrinkled her nose a little as the smell of vinegar intensified; the books said to use wine for the potion, but she had found that vinegar worked just as well, and there was no mistaking it for something drinkable—unless your taste in wine was really wretched. A cloth steeped in this dark-brown liquid and bandaged against a bruise eased the pain and made the bruise itself heal much faster than it would on its own, so despite the odor the potion was much in demand. She needed so much of it that she always had several jugs or bottles of the finished potion in storage, and more jars of it in various states of preparation. It had to steep for six weeks at a minimum, so she tried to empty one jar and start another once a week.

Keisha held her hands steady; she didn't want to waste any of it in spillage. She even wrung the cheesecloth dry, then reached for a stopper whittled from a birch branch and her pot of warm paraffin. As soon as the last drop was sealed into its special dark-brown pottery jug, and the jug itself placed safely on a high shelf, she knocked the soggy fragments of herb out of the wide-mouthed jar, added two handfuls of freshly crumbled dry wormwood, and poured in vinegar to the top. Footsteps behind her warned her that Shandi had come to the workshop looking for her, so she wasted no time in tying a square of waxed linen over the top of the jar and setting it at the end of the row of nine more identical jars.

She turned to face the door, just as Shandi stepped across the threshold into the cool gloom of the workshop, blinking eyes still dazzled by the bright sun outside. Although not dressed in her festival best, Shandi was, as always, so neat and spotless that Keisha became uncomfortably aware of the state of her own stained brown breeches and far-from-immaculate, too-large tunic. Shandi wore a white apron embroidered with dark blue thread, a neat brown skirt, and a pristine white blouse with the blue embroidery matching the apron, all the work of her own hands. Keisha's tunic and breeches were hand-me-downs from her brothers, plain as a board, indifferently shortened, and both had seen their best days many years ago.

But what else am I supposed to wear for working with messy potions, dosing sick babies, and sewing up bloody gashes? she asked herself crossly, annoyed at herself for feeling embarrassed. *This isn't some tale where everyone wears cloth-of-gold and tunics with silk embroidery! Shandi would look pretty sad after a half day of* my *work!*

"Keisha, are we going to the market or not?" Shandi asked impatiently, then screwed up her face in a grimace as a whiff of vinegar reached her.

"We're going, though I don't know why *you* want to go so badly," Keisha replied, hoping she didn't sound as irritated as she felt.

"Dye," Shandi replied promptly.

"No, thank you, I have too much to do right now," Keisha said impishly, grinning as Shandi first looked puzzled, then mimed a blow at her for the pun.

"You know what I mean!" Shandi giggled. "You never know what the hunters are going to bring in, and I'm still looking for a decent red, one that won't fade the first time someone looks too long at it." She smiled. "You *know* I need to have you along. After all, you know so much more about these things than I do. *And* you're better at bargaining; I'd be sure to get cheated, and then you'd be annoyed because you weren't with me to save me from a sharp trader!"

Keisha's irritation had vanished, as it always did around Shandi. No one could stay irritated with her sister for long; Shandi's nature was as sweet as her innocent face, and she played peacemaker to the entire village of Errold's Grove. Keisha and Shandi were almost the same height, with the same willowy figures, same golden-brown hair and eyes, and almost the same features, but in all other ways they were as different as if they had come from opposite sides of the world. *Sometimes I think when the gods gave out tempers, they gave me all of the thorns and her all the rose petals.* "You're right, of course, I would be annoyed." She rinsed her hands in lemon-balm water to remove the vinegar smell and any lingering trace of wormwood—poison, if ingested—and dried them on a clean rag. "And I should have remembered about the red. How many of the girls have you promised embroidery thread to?"

"Only three—Hydee, Jenna, and Sari. I wouldn't trust the rest with red. They'd be sure to do something tasteless with it." Shandi's bright brown eyes glowed with suppressed laughter. "Ugh! Can't you imagine it? Roses the size of cabbages all around the hems of their skirts!"

"Or worse," Keisha said dryly. "Roses the size of cabbages over each breast. Lallis is not exactly subtle." *And she's always looking for a way to bring attention to her "assets." Not that anyone needs help in seeing them. You could hide half the village in that cleavage, and a quarter of the village would be oh-so-happy to stay there!* "I'm all done for now, let's go before someone decides they have a bellyache and comes looking for a posset."

Side by side, Keisha and her sister strolled down a neat, stone-edged path between the houses, heading toward the village square. Once a week, the village of Errold's Grove held a market day, and those from outside the village and no particular interest in seeking further—and possibly more lucrative— venues took full advantage of it. For some people, it simply wasn't worth the effort to travel long distances just to make more money from their goods; they'd rather that other folk did the traveling and took the extra profit. As had been the case in the past, there were plenty of traders willing to do just that, so the weekly market was usually visited by at least one far traveler from spring to early winter. And three of the quarterly Faires—Spring Equinox, Midsummer, and Harvest—brought traders in their dozens.

Errold's Grove was more prosperous now than it had been in its earlier heyday, with dozens of trappers and dye-hunters working the forest and hills. None of them was actually *from* Errold's Grove; the villagers were still far too wary of the forest to be tempted by the possibility of profit hidden in its depths. But the Hawkbrothers were here now, and to some people, their presence meant increased safety or, at least, a smaller likelihood of being eaten by misshapen monsters. So the dye-hunters and all the people who supported and profited by them were back, as well as a new class of folk who actually specialized in trapping the strange new creatures created by the Change-Circles. The population of Errold's Grove had swelled to half again more than the village had ever held before.

They even had their own temple and priest, so now the children of the village got proper lessons in the winter, instead of being home-schooled or taught by one of the old women. For most of the children, that was a mixed blessing, as the priest took his duty seriously and wasn't as easily distracted as a mother or as prone to doze off as an old granny.

They still didn't have a fully trained "official" Healer, though, and Kcisha served in place of one, wearing her ordinary clothing rather than even the pale-green robes of a Trainee. Healers were in short supply still, and so far, there hadn't been a real need to have one posted to Errold's Grove. Lord Breon had a Healer, and according to Healer's Collegium, he could take care of anything here that Keisha couldn't.

Though never selected for her Gift by a fully trained Healer in the approved and official manner, Keisha had begun showing her talents at the age of five, by taking care of the ills of the stock on the farm, then moving on to patching up the childhood hurts and illnesses of her brothers and sisters. It got to the point where they came to *her* instead of their mother, since Keisha's remedies were far more likely to set things right and taste better than their mother's book of recipes from her granny.

Things might never have gone any further, but fear of the Changebeasts and longing for other human company together drove Keisha's parents to resettle in the village. That had happened a few months after the barbarian invasion when one family decided they'd had enough of Errold's Grove and a house fortuitously fell vacant. Not long after that, once she widened her circle of "patching up" to the rest of the children and their pets, the villagers discovered Keisha's talent, and a concerted effort began to turn their new citizen into a fully educated, fully stocked, fully prepared Healer.

As she and her sister passed the home that had drawn them here—now silent, with the rest of the family out working the fields and tending the stock—Keisha grinned a little. Maybe if her parents had known what was going to happen, they wouldn't have been so quick to leave the farmstead! Her mother and father hadn't stood a chance against the will of the village, and they'd lost Keisha's labor at the farm before they knew what had happened. They might have tried to fight to keep Keisha (and her two sturdy hands) theirs alone, but the arrival of a Herald on circuit put an end to any thoughts of making the attempt.

That golden moment was a cherished memory, the point when Keisha became something other than "ordinary" in her parents' eyes. *The Herald—oh, he was fine to look at, all white and tall on his silver Companion. . . . He took one look at me that went right down to my bones and declared, in a voice like a trumpet, "This girl has the Healer's Gift."* Much to Keisha's bemusement, before he left for the rest of his circuit, he had arranged for Lord Breon's Healer, Gil Jarad, to give Keisha instruction. Several weeks later a trader delivered into her hands copies of every book used by the trainees at Healer's Collegium, courtesy of that august body, and a polite note reminding everyone that the books were worth, not a small fortune, but a rather large one. *Enough to buy half the town, and theft or harm to the books counted as a crime against the Crown!* With the books had come three sets of the pale-green robes of a Healer Trainee, lest anyone doubt her acceptance. Keisha still preferred not to wear them, though; it seemed a pity to get them as stained and dirty as they *would* be if she donned them for her regular work.

No more weeding and mowing for her; the letter that came with this library told her that she was expected to study those books any time that she wasn't tending the ailments of man or beast, or brewing medicines for same. She already had the skills needed to make most medications and had lacked only the knowledge of what herbs were needed—the books supplied that, with good pictures to guide her when she went hunting for them in the forest and fields, and detailed instructions for each preparation. Along with the books came a box of seeds for those herbs that did well under cultivation, all carefully labeled with planting and growing instructions. It was obvious that she was expected to become self-sufficient, and quickly.

For a while, Keisha had used the kitchen of the family home for her workroom—and her mother had seen that as a possible way to discourage this new career.

Mother should never have complained about my "green messes" in her kitchen, telling everyone she was afraid I was going to poison the family, Keisha thought, with just a touch of self-satisfaction. *I know she thought that the Council would agree that I should stop, but it had the opposite effect!*

In fact, the Council didn't wait for her to complain directly to them; the moment the Village Council got wind of the complaints, they assigned Keisha her own workshop, a sturdy little stone building that had once been the home of the village savior and hero, Wizard Justyn. They even went so far as to make a special day of preparing it for her, organizing a village-wide cleanup and repair of the place, presenting her with a cottage scoured inside and out, roof newly thatched, all the bits and pieces still littering the interior taken out and broken into kindling. She had only to say where she wanted workbenches and shelves, and they appeared; had only to ask for a place to lie down and a fine feather bed and a pile of pillows and quilts showed up in the sleeping-loft. The people of Errold's Grove had learned their lesson about treating a Healer right, having had to do without a Healer of any kind for so long after Wizard Justyn died.

Heady stuff for a fourteen-year-old youngster, she thought wryly, from her distant vantage of eighteen. *I'm surprised my head didn't get too big to fit a hat.* She waved at the blacksmith's oldest apprentice as they passed the forge; he waved absently back, but his eyes—as all the eyes of any male over the age of thirteen—were on Shandi. *I suppose the only reason it didn't was that I was too busy to get a swelled head.*

She had been busy every waking moment, in fact; when she wasn't studying her books, she was out in the forest gathering medicinal plants, on her knees in her new garden cultivating herbs, or making preparations for Healer Gil to examine. At last, when Gil was satisfied that her skill at producing medicines was the equal of his, he stopped inspecting her results before allowing her to use them and started teaching her how to use the knife and the needle, how to set bones and restore dislocated joints as he did.

Unfortunately, the one thing he can't teach me is how to use my Gift, and the books are not very useful there either. Healer Gil's Gift was not very strong, and he relied on his skill with the knife and his truly amazing knowledge of herbalism for most of his cures. Keisha would have been perfectly happy to do the same, but Healer Gil kept insisting that she make use of this Gift that she didn't understand. . . .

Gradually, though, what with all Gil had to do, his visits had shortened, and the intervals between them lengthened, until now he came to Errold's Grove no more than once every moon and never stayed longer than half a day. He even trusted her now to experiment with new preparations, something that made her so proud she practically glowed every time she thought about it!

That was why Shandi wanted her to come along on this hunt for the elusive true red dye. Her knowledge of herbs and other plants extended into dyes, and she had a knack for telling which ones would fade, which would need too much mordant to be practical, and which would turn some other, less desirable color with age. Some dyes could even be used as medicine, so Keisha never lost a chance to explore their possibilities. In a village where every person had some specialty, however small, Shandi was the one who supplied everyone else with common embroidery thread the equal of anything a trader could bring in. Her threads, whether spun from wool, linen, or raime, were strong, hair-fine, and even; her colors were true and fast. So even as the villagers gladly paid Keisha for tending their ills (knowing that she had to *pay* for the medicines and supplies she couldn't make, grow, or find for herself), they even more gladly told over their copper coins for a hank of Shandi's thread.

The village square was the site of the weekly market, with the square closed to all but foot traffic, and stalls set up along all four sides. Besides the usual things found in a village market—produce and foodstuffs—Errold's Grove had specialties of its own to boast of. Along with the dye-hunters had come dye-traders and dye-buyers, who purchased bundles of plants and fungus and things that defied description, then leeched or cooked out the pigments and pressed them into little cakes for sale. The buyers seldom left Errold's Grove, preferring to act as middlemen and sell their dye-cakes to traders, but they were by no means reluctant to sell a cake or two to their neighbors. The tanner also put some of his unusual furs on offer at this weekly market, giving villagers first choice of what the hunters brought him.

In addition, now Errold's Grove had its own potter, who was an artist in his own right, using some of the new and strange pigments and foreign earths from the Change-Circles and a variety of modeling and carving techniques to make ordinary clay pots into things almost too beautiful for use. There was, alas, no glass blower as yet, though there were rumors that one might be coming soon; most glass came from the Hawkbrothers or from traders.

The miller's son had begun experimenting with paper making a year ago, and now his efforts were on sale roughly every other market day, alongside inks Keisha had taught him to make from oak galls and soot, small brushes he made from badger hair, and pens he cut himself from goose quills. So now it was possible for lovers to exchange silent vows, for thrifty wives to keep account books, for those with artistic pretensions to inflict their work on their relatives, and for everyone to write to relatives far and near. That last item alone, that tiny token of civilization, made Errold's Grove seem less like the end of the universe and more like a part of

Valdemar. When it was possible to communicate, however infrequently, with those outside the confines of Lord Breon's holdings, people didn't feel forgotten anymore.

Then there was the Fellowship.

Keisha nodded a friendly greeting toward the Fellowship booth, and the soberly clad woman tending it smiled and nodded back, her smile widening as Shandi's footsteps suddenly (and predictably) lagged and her eyes went to the delicate wisps of fabric draped temptingly over a line at the back of the booth. The Fellowship, a loose amalgamation of a dozen families related only in their religious beliefs and a firm commitment to peace and a life with no violence or anger in it, had arrived in Errold's Grove two years ago with their herds, their household goods, and their readiness to work and work hard. Within months, they had built an enclave of a dozen stout houses and barns enough for all their animals; within a year, traders were coming especially to buy what they produced.

For what the Fellowship specialized in was producing remarkable textiles: lengths of tapestry-woven fabric; intricate braids and other trims; and a very few simple garments such as shawls and capes—woven, knitted, knotted, and braided of the beautifully spun and dyed wool from their herds.

The creatures providing the wool were no ordinary animals. The Fellowship had goats with coats so long and silky that it was a pleasure to touch them, sheep with wool the texture of the finest thistledown, and a special variety of *chirra*. They were a little smaller and had a sweeter, more delicate face than those used as winter pack animals, and they possessed a coat of wool that, when woven, was softer than the finest sueded deerskin, light, dense, and so warm that one had to wear a cloak of it to believe it. These animals all needed more tending than their mundane counterparts, so much so that it was likely that few folk would be willing to put that much work into their care. Nevertheless, it was obviously worth it to the folk of the Fellowship, since traders came from as far away as Haven itself to purchase items such as their *chirra*-cloaks and blankets, their intricately patterned fabrics, and their "wedding" shawls, wraps of knitted lace so fine and delicate that they could be drawn through a wedding ring.

Keisha had heard that it had become the fashion for the high-born of Valdemar to present one of these shawls to daughters of their houses to mark a betrothal, or for a suitor to offer one in token that he intended to ask for a woman's hand.

Well, what was desirable for the highborn of Valdemar was also the heart's desire of every girl of marriageable age in Er-rold's Grove—and the folk of the Fellowship were pleased to make it possible for these less-than-highborn suitors and parents to grant those yearnings with special prices for the folk of their home village. Small wonder Shandi's eyes and feet were drawn to the booth; she had three current suitors, all hotly pursuing her (and completely unsuitable in their father's estimation), any one of whom could give her the reason for selecting such a shawl and pointing her choice decorously out to him.

"Shandi—" Keisha called her wandering attention back with a touch of exasperation. "Look, let's see if there's a red dye first, *then* you can go look at shawls while I see if anyone's brought medicines or herbs that I can use."

"All right," Shandi agreed, though with an audible sigh. Satisfied that she had her sister's attention for at least a little while, Keisha and Shandi made the rounds of all three dye-buyers' booths, looking for that so-elusive red.

Keisha deliberately went to Barlen's booth last; he was—in her opinion—the most honest of the three. As they neared his booth, he twinkled at Shandi and crooked a finger at her. They hurried to his counter.

"I think I may have something for you young ladies," the cheerful, weather-tanned man said. "I've only been waiting for our good Healer's expert opinion on it." He nodded at Keisha, who flushed.

He cleared bundles of dried fungus off the counter and reached beneath it, bringing out a cake the size of his hand and as black as dried blood, together with something that looked like a seed pod made of dried leather. He placed hands with nails from beneath which no amount of soap and water would ever remove the traces of dye on the counter. "Here's the dye, and here's the thing it comes from; now you tell *me* if this is going to be as good as I think it is."

Keisha crumbled a bit off the cake, smelled it, very cautiously tasted it, and tried dissolving it in a cup of water he provided. It didn't dissolve, and she raised an eyebrow at the dye-merchant, who only grinned.

"Won't dissolve in water, nor in water and soap," he said in triumph. "Here—" He tossed out the water, and poured a bit of clear liquid into the cup from a stoppered bottle It appeared to be thrice-distilled spirits, by the potent smell, and very nearly made her drunk just to sniff it. She dropped a crumb of dye in and was rewarded by a spreading crimson stain.

"Let me add a bit of salt for mordant, and you see for yourself what this stuff does." He brought out another cup and poured water into that, then obliged her with some scraps and threads to try in the dye.

The samples they dunked in the dye became gratifying shades of scarlet, and no amount of rinsing in the water he'd provided would take the color out. As Shandi sucked in her breath with excitement, Keisha brought the threads up to her nose until she was nearly cross-eyed, examining every crevice and crack to see if the dye was "taking" evenly. Finally, she pronounced judgment.

"I think it will fade *eventually*, but it will take years as long as you keep the color out of the sun," she told both the merchant and her sister. "Dyeing with distilled spirits will be tricky, maybe dangerous, what with the fumes being flammable—worse for someone doing large batches of thread and yarn than for you, Shandi—but this is probably the best red I've ever seen." She turned her attention to the "pod," and picked it up to peer at it. "Just what *is* this thing?"

"A snail," the merchant said gleefully. "And no one would ever have noticed what secret this little creature held if Terthorn hadn't tried to cook them in white wine. I'm the only one he told, and I got him to promise me an exclusive market."

Shandi had to laugh at that. "So Terthorn's famous palate and cooking experiments finally have some use! I suppose we should just be glad he didn't try to cook them in *red* wine!"

The dye-merchant laughed, "Oh, now he'd never have done that! Haven't we heard him say a thousand times that no one with any real taste would cook snails in *red* wine?"

Keisha's thoughts were more practical. "So exactly how

much are you going to part us from for this wonder?" she asked dubiously. She knew it wasn't going to be cheap; not as strong a red as this, nor one as colorfast. She also knew Shandi would take it at any price, and was just fervently glad that it was *this* merchant who had the supply, not one of the other two.

"For you, Shandi, I'll trade it weight-for-weight in silver." Keisha tried not to wince, but the price was fair. If he had any sense, when he got the stuff into civilized lands, he'd trade it weight-for-weight in gold.

Shandi grimaced, but didn't argue when Keisha didn't. "Fair enough," she said bravely, and dug out four silver coins, placing them on one side of his scales. He crumbled dye into the pan on the other side until they leveled off equal, then winked again, and crumbled a bit more into the pan. He pocketed the coins, then tilted the pan of dye into a paper cone, tapping it to get every crumb into the container. With a little bow, he handed the precious packet to Shandi, who twisted the open end of the cone tight and put it carefully into her pouch.

"I'll tell you something else, young ladies," he said, as they were about to move on, "I haven't looked any further than to get the scarlet. If you can tell me how to get a deep, fast *purple* as good as the red out of that, I'll halve the price if you give me an exclusive from here on."

Keisha's eyebrows both went up. "Really," was all she replied, but her mind was already on changing the mordant, adding other possible ingredients, experimenting with double-dyeing with indigo.

Barlen's look told her that he'd all but seen her thoughts written on her forehead. "If anyone can do it," he continued with a wave, "you two can. Oh, and Keisha, you ought to go talk to Steelmind; he came to market by himself, and I think he's got some seeds you might be interested in."

"Really!" she exclaimed, as Shandi headed straight for the Fellowship booth, one hand protectively cupped over her pouch. "Thanks, Barlen!"

"No problem." Another villager approached the booth, and Barlen turned his attention to the potential new customer. Keisha moved along to the shaded arbor next to the new Temple that the Hawkbrothers used as a booth when they came to Errold's Grove.

Normally Hawkbrothers only appeared for the quarterly Faire market days, and when they came, they came in force, with a half-dozen bead-and-feather-bedecked traders and their fierce-looking birds of prey. They took over the arbor and put up a pavilion as well, and traders buzzed around them like bees at a honey pot, for the things they brought, though (aside from a few items) never predictable, were always fantastic. Sometimes it was lengths of silk fabric in impossible colors and patterns, sometimes it was trims and ribbons made of the same silks and silk embroidery thread that girls saved for their wedding dresses. They had been known to bring jewelry, glassware, odd spices and incense, vials of scent and massage oils, rugs sometimes, and, once, simpler variations on their own tunics and robes. Those items that *were* predictable were always welcome: ropes and cording much stronger than anyone else could make and much lighter, too; hammocks made from that same cord; amazing feathers; furs unlike anyone else brought; leather tanned so that it was as supple and soft as their silks; rare woods; and carvings in stone, ivory, and wood.

But sometimes, one called Steelmind came by himself, bringing strange ornamental or useful plants, herbs, and seeds. Keisha liked him, for all that he never said one word more than he absolutely had to; she also liked his bird, a slow and sleepy buzzard who was perfectly happy to accept a head scratch from her.

Sure enough, Steelmind had tucked himself and his bird into the depths of the arbor, with bare-root plants (roots carefully wrapped in damp moss) and an assortment of well-grown seedlings in small plugs of earth arranged beside him. His blue eyes brightened when he saw Keisha, and he waved—a welcome and an invitation to sit, all in the same gesture.

"Barlen says you have some seeds?" she said, giving the bird his scratch before settling on the turf beneath the arbor, her tunic puddling around her. She bent over to look at the plants he'd brought, and recognized the bare-root ones to be young rose vines.

Roses! She tried to imagine what Hawkbrother-bred rose vines would be like, and failed. She resolved to take at least one of them home with her—maybe more. *Mum would love a climbing rose going over a trellis at the front door—and it would be nice to have* one *plant in the herb garden that isn't useful for anything!*

She felt the same avariciousness that Shandi must have felt over the dye—if there was one weakness she had, it was for her garden. . . .

"It is spring, so mostly I have flower seeds and seedlings and these—" he gestured at the rose vines, but she sensed he was teasing her.

"Mostly?" she replied.

"Our Healer suggested a few others before I left," Steelmind said and smiled, an expression that transformed his face and made it obvious that he wasn't much older than she was. He laughed a little. "Actually, it was stronger than merely suggestion." He rummaged in a basket at his side and brought out fat little packets of tough silk, sewn at the top to resemble tiny sacks of grain. Each one had a symbol painted on it in a different color. "This stops pain, this stops cough, this is a balm, this stops itching from insect bites and rashes. There are instructions in each packet on growing and use."

"They work better than what I use now?" she asked skeptically.

He shrugged, and the beads woven into his hair clicked together. "Different, that's all I know. Better? I don't know, I'm not a Healer, and we do not know what you have to work with. No worse, certainly. And I have been given *orders* that if you want them, your price is—nothing. Healer to Healer, is what I was told."

Nothing! They do *trust me to know what I'm doing!* And that these herbs were different from those she had been using—she knew from her own experience that a medication that one person responded well to might not work on another—and might make a third sicker. That was the peril of working with herbs. "I'll take them, and thank your Healer very sincerely for me," she replied. "And how much for the rose vines? It will be nice to have something in my garden that isn't for healing people."

"And who is to say that a rose cannot heal?" He smiled and named his prices, they haggled amiably, and settled on a price that didn't leave either of them feeling cheated.

She gathered up her spoils—two rose vines, which would make everyone happy—and gave the bird a second scratch, which he seemed to expect. Then she left the arbor to go find Shandi and tear her away from the Fellowship booth.

Or try, anyway. If she got to talking embroidery and dye with the attendant, nothing less than a miracle would take her away before the sun went down.

Keisha squinted against the bright sunlight, and peered up the street as a flock of crows flew overhead, yelling cheerful insults at the village below. As she had half-expected, Shandi and the Fellowship woman were deep in conversation. Keisha shrugged her shoulders and sighed, wondering if it was going to be worth the trouble to try to pry Shandi away. If so, she had the choice of looking very rude and bossy and actually getting the job done quickly, or spending far more time than she wanted to and looking polite and courteous. If there had only been Shandi to consider, there would just be a few sharp words and it would be done with . . . but she really didn't want to look boorish in front of a member of the Fellowship.

It was a short internal debate. *There's no point. If she finished her chores, I've got no call to tell her how to spend her free time. And if she hasn't, she can take the consequences herself.* Shandi's one fault was that she tended to "forget" things she had to do when she disliked them. When they were younger, it had been Keisha's task to supervise her and see to it that the "forgotten" chores were done—because if Shandi didn't do them, Keisha would have to pitch in later. *Mum's idea of a proper form of incentive for me to be an ogre. But I don't have time to spare to pitch in now. I'm not her keeper, no matter what Mum thinks, and Shandi's sixteen and old enough to take the consequences by herself.*

She ambled slowly up the street, enjoying the novel sensation of having people around her who were *not* in discomfort or pain—who were, in fact, entirely contented. Lately, it had become uncomfortable for her to be near people in any sort of distress, as if she shared their feelings. . . . She'd fancied once or twice that it was the sort of Empathy power that she heard told of in stories, but dismissed the thought quickly. Things like that didn't happen to ordinary people from little towns like Errold's Grove, and her Gift was an extraordinary enough fluke.

It wouldn't be too long until Spring Equinox Faire, and the booths of those who sold their goods to the far-ranging traders were stuffed full, while the booths of those who depended on those same traders to bring *them* goods from outside were getting mighty empty. The dye-sellers, the folk who bought up a great deal of the Hawkbrother trade goods, and the Fellowship would all send most of their stock with the traders when the Faire was over.

The blacksmith needs metals, the baker needs spices and sugar, the girls are craving glass beads, laces, and ribbons, I need things I can't get here—

Healer Gil Jarad would be just as happy if she didn't have to rely on those medicines, though. That was one subject on which they didn't, and probably would never, agree. *He* couldn't tell her how to use her Gift—more importantly, he had no way to oversee her and tell her what she was doing right or wrong, the way he could with medicines and the knife. How was she supposed to *use* this so-called Gift effectively, or even safely?

I suppose it would be quite useful if I could make head or tail out of those texts, she thought glumly, as she neared the Fellowship booth and Shandi. *It's almost as if they were written in a code that is perfectly understandable to everyone but me!*

And I am feeling far *too sorry for myself!* Determined not to spoil what was a perfectly fine spring day, Keisha decided to stop thinking, and simply enjoy.

A light breeze brought a hint of incense from the Temple, which joined harmoniously with the fresh flowers some of the stallkeepers used as decoration. The sunshine warmed her with the promise of a fine spring to come. The annual village-wide spring cleaning took place only a few days ago in preparation for the Spring Faire, and as a consequence, the entire village was as charming as a highborn child's toy. Streets had been swept of all the winter accumulation of junk and debris, houses and fences were newly whitewashed, market booths all neatly mended. *What a perfect scene this would be for a painter or a tapestry maker to reproduce,* she thought, just as she came even with Shandi. *This is how the highborn think all our villages look, all the time.* Still, she shouldn't be so cynical. *It really is pretty—the red shutters, the pale gold of the thatched roofs, the rainbow colors of the flowers everywhere, the handsome white horse posing right at the end of the street—*

—white horse? There were no white horses in Errold's Grove!

Keisha shook her head and looked again, but the vision didn't go away; instead, it drew nearer. There was a blue-eyed white horse decked out in blue-and-silver riding gear at the end of the street nearest the bridge—and he was coming straight toward the market square. There was purpose in each and every step he took. He had no rider.

And—was he looking at *her?*

You had to have lived in a cave all your life not to know what a blue-eyed white horse was, and meant, in *this* kingdom. This was a Companion, and alone like this, with no urgency in his demeanor, he hadn't *lost* his Herald, nor was his Herald in trouble. No, he had to be on Search.

And that meant he was looking for a new Herald—well, Herald-trainee—the person to whom he would be bonded for the rest of both their lives.

It seemed that the entire market saw the Companion at the same time that Keisha did. Everyone stopped talking, and the silence that fell over the square was broken only by the soft chiming of bridle bells and the matching overtones of the Companion's deliberate steps. He knew very well that all eyes were on him, too—he arched his neck and lifted each hoof so high he might have been on parade.

Keisha froze; out of the corner of her eye, she saw that Shandi had done the same. The Companion was looking neither to the right, nor to the left, and there were only two people of reasonable age for him to Choose from in the direction he was moving. Of course, Companions *had* been known to Choose full adults in the past, but it wasn't usual. No, the only two people likely to be Chosen in *this* village who were present at the moment were Shandi—and Keisha.

For a moment, Keisha was stunned, too shocked to think. This was *not* supposed to be happening! But as the Companion moved closer, she wrenched herself out of her shock with a grimace, as dismay washed over her.

Don't you dare, she thought with annoyance bordering on anger at the Companion. *Don't you* dare *try to Choose me!* Her hands balled into fists as she stared into his eyes, willing him to hear her. *Don't even think about Choosing me! I have responsibilities here, you dolt! People here need me for what I can do, and I can't just ride out of here and leave them! Listen to me, you fool! Don't—*

Maybe staring into his eyes had been a mistake.

She felt the rest of the world vanishing around her as she fell into those twin pools of sapphire. But before she could drown in them, she bit her lip to bring her back to herself and hurled her denial at him.

I. Am. Not. Expendable! she thought, working up real heat at the thought that anyone, even a Companion, could march into her life and proceed to reorder it for her. *I. Am. Not. Going!*

She sensed surprise. *Pick somebody else!*

Now she sensed—amusement? Why amusement?

Her anger evaporated.

The eyes turned away from her, let her go. Had they ever really held her, or had that only been her imagination?

She didn't get a chance to think about it, because movement beside her caught her attention. The Companion stood quietly, and now it was Shandi who walked with slow, entranced steps toward *him.*

She looked like a sleepwalker, and Keisha stifled the impulse to grab her arm and keep her where she was. Still . . . *I'm not her keeper. If this is what she wants, she should try to make it work. She's old enough to make up her own mind, just as I am, and live with whatever comes of it.*

Although, it looked as if consequences were the last thing on Shandi's mind right now.

Shandi stopped, just a step away from the Companion's

nose, and slowly reached her hand forward, as if she feared to touch him. Keisha waited, heart pounding, biting her lower lip. The Companion made short work of Shandi's hesitation, craning his neck forward as his bridle bells chimed, and putting his nose in her hand. Then they just stood there for a long, long time, and Keisha's breathing seemed very loud in the silence.

Then, as Keisha's nerves wound tighter and tighter, like an overtuned harpstring, the spell—or whatever it was—finally broke. They both moved, the Companion tossing his head and sidling around so that his stirrup and saddle were in easy reach. Shandi reached for the cantle, then turned to her sister with eyes brimming with wonder.

That snapped everyone else out of their tense silence, and before Shandi could speak, she was surrounded by friends and neighbors, all of them contributing to a conglomerate of babble that sounded like a shouting match between a flock of hens and a gaggle of geese. As far as Keisha could make out, none of them had anything very intelligent to say, but they were all very intent on saying it.

Through a gap in the crowd, Shandi peered entreatingly back at her sister; Keisha sighed and pushed her way past everyone else to reach her.

Shandi paid attention to no one else, holding out her free hand entreatingly. "Keisha, I didn't mean—I mean, I *want* to go, but I didn't ask—I mean, I didn't intend—" Shandi was doing a good job of babbling herself, and Keisha reached out and gave her shoulders a friendly shake.

"Of course you didn't mean for this to happen, you ninny," she half-scolded, half-cajoled. "Choosings aren't planned, everyone knows that—and it's not as if you'd gone and made an appointment for this hairy beast to show up! I mean, if you could simply *decide* to be a Herald, what would be the point? Herald would be like any other job. You get Chosen because you're the right person to *be* a Herald, you know that."

And I, most certainly, am not!

Was it her imagination, or did the Companion swing his head around and wink at her, just as she thought that?

Oh, there's probably a fly buzzing around his ears.

"But Keisha, I have to *go*, I mean I have to go *now*, and—" Shandi looked at her, pleading with her to understand, tears brimming in her eyes and rolling slowly down one cheek.

"And if you didn't have to go *now*, you know that Mum would find a thousand reasons why you couldn't go, ever. *I* know that; Havens, probably everybody in town knows that." Keisha tried to smile, but it was a great deal more difficult than she had thought it would be. "Shandi, that's why it happens this way—I'll bet that, otherwise, every single mother in Valdemar would have a thousand reasons why her child couldn't go haring off into the sunset just on the say-so of a big white horse!"

"But—but—" Shandi's expression was painfully easy to read. *Fix things for me*, her eyes pleaded. *This is more important than anything in my life, but I can't go if you don't promise to fix things for me!*

Keisha closed her eyes for the briefest of moments, no more than a blink, stifled a sigh, and nodded. Just like always—it looked as if she was going to have to "pitch in" after all, and help clean up the mess. . . .

But that's not being generous, and if it was me—oh, if Shandi could have substituted for me, I'd be at Healer's Collegium now.

"Go," she urged her sister, and meant it. "Go, and go now. I'll take care of everything."

Shandi believed her; Shandi always believed her. With a sigh of relief and a sudden smile like the sun emerging from a thundercloud, she kissed Keisha, hugged her tight, then fumbled loose the strings holding her belt-pouch to her belt. "Here—" she said, pressing it into Keisha's hands. "Take the dye, see what you can do with it, maybe it'll be good for a medicine." Then she turned away and mounted the Companion's saddle with such ease and grace that it looked as if she'd been doing it all her life, never mind that she'd never ridden anything before but their aged pony. The Companion clearly was taking no chances; he gave Shandi no further chances for farewells or regrets. He danced a little, shook his harness, and pivoted in place on his hind feet. That got people to move out of his way, and pretty briskly, too. He moved out at a fast walk, allowing Shandi time enough only to wave good-bye before breaking into a canter at the end of the street. In no time at all, they were over the bridge, then lost to sight as the road was hidden by trees.

Keisha let out the sigh she'd been holding in—and the exasperation. While the rest of the villagers gathered in knots, still babbling with excitement, Keisha felt the weight of yet another burden fall on her shoulders. *Let's see—one hysterical mother, three heartbroken suitors, half a dozen friends left forlorn and a little jealous—I can handle that. I hope.*

Keisha stood with her back to the wall in the warm, soup-scented kitchen, and wished she were anywhere else but there. Sidonie Alder had reacted to the news that her youngest daughter had been Chosen as a Herald precisely as she would have if Shandi had been abducted by barbarians. This made no sense, of course, but Keisha hadn't expected anything else.

She tried not to wince when Sidonie's voice rose to new and shriller heights. "I can't believe you just let her *go* like that! How could you just stand there and let her be carried off?"

This was only about the hundredth time Keisha's mother had repeated that particular accusation, and it didn't look as if she were going to stop thinking Keisha was the villainess of the situation any time soon. Each time Sidonie uttered another outburst, before Keisha had a chance to say anything sensible in reply, she broke down into hysterical sobs and cast herself into the arms of her husband or one of her two oldest sons. This time it was her husband's arms where she sought shelter from her traitorous offspring. He patted her back and said consolingly, "Now, Mother, you know that's how it is. Keisha couldn't have done naught. That's how they always do these Choosing things, I suppose, so they can make a clean break and all."

"But she's only a *baby*! She can't take care of herself all alone!" was the inevitable reply, followed by a fresh spate of tears. Keisha wisely kept silent this time, since anything she'd tried to say until how had only brought on another outburst; her brother Garry was injudicious enough to put in his two bits.

"Aw, Mum, she's not so little as all that!" Garry protested. "She's old enough to take care of herself, and anyway, you know them Companions see to it the kids they Choose are right and tight. You'd have been losing her pretty soon, anyway. She's had three beaus, an' like as not, she'd have been married in a year or two—"

Oh, no. Now he's given Mum something else to weep about, Keisha thought with dismay.

She was right. "Now I'll never see her wed!" came the wail, muffled by her husband's shoulder. Keisha swallowed, as her stomach roiled. This was beginning to make her sick—literally.

But her father had a thoughtful look on his face, and it was pretty clear that he was thinking there was another side to all this, one that had a lot of advantages besides the obvious. Female Heralds, if they wed, generally married other Heralds; on the rare occasions they married outside the Circle, it was with men who asked nothing more of them than their company outside of duty, usually Healers or Bards. So if Shandi married, there would be no dowry to raise. If she wed, it would be with someone who would live far from Errold's Grove—so there would be no need to put up with a son-in-law he disliked (and he disliked all three of Shandi's suitors, each for a different reason).

The obvious reasons for being pleased about the situation were many, and he'd already brought them up to his wife, as had Keisha. Their daughter was going to be a *Herald;* they'd be the parents of a Herald. People would look up to them, they'd have new importance in the village; people would listen to what they said, even ask their opinions on matters of importance. Oh, of course she was going to be doing work that was often dangerous, but not for *years* yet, and it still wasn't all that safe here in Errold's Grove—after all, what if the barbarians came back?

Keisha could tell that her father had clearly come to the opinion that this was no bad thing; his thoughts might just as well have been written on his face for Keisha to read.

"Mum, she's going to be fine," Keisha said, once again, as her mother's sobs quieted. "When have you ever heard of a newly Chosen Trainee coming to grief on the road? She's going to be a very important person now, and people will look up to you because she's your daughter. We might even get invited to Court someday and see the Queen! And *if* she decides to get married, what ever gave you the idea that she wouldn't come here to do it?" This time—*finally*—this attempt at comfort wasn't met with another outburst, and Keisha continued as soothingly as she could. "Mum, she's going to be in the safest place in the world for at least four years—you just don't *get* any safer than Herald's Collegium. I mean, think! It's right inside the Palace grounds! Think about that! Your daughter is going to be living on the Palace grounds, and not as a servant either! She'll be back every long holiday, you know she will. After all, you couldn't keep her away. Which one of us always throws herself into the holidays, hmm? Shandi, of course! Just because she's going to be a Herald, that doesn't mean she doesn't love her family!"

Oh, but I'm getting very close to not loving my dear family right now. . . . All of this excitement had given Keisha a *pounding* headache; she felt as if all her nerves were scraped raw and someone was pouring saltwater on them. Her stomach was so sour she probably wouldn't be able to eat any supper. *But Shandi was the baby—my baby sister, the one I looked after and picked up after—and if I didn't have to help calm Mum down, I'd probably be the one bawling like a bereft calf right now. I can't do that, and make sure Mum gets through this and starts to look on the bright side—*

But right now, given the least sign that her mother was getting over her hysterics—or at least that some of her mother's friends were going to come help console her—Keisha would be only too happy to get out of the house and go somewhere—anywhere—else.

Evidently she had been good enough and patient enough that for once her unspoken prayers were answered. As if the thought had been a summons, relief came bursting through the kitchen door at that very moment.

"Sidonie! Ayver!" Three of the neighbor women came bursting into the kitchen like a force of nature, all three of them managing to squeeze in at the same time, not waiting to be invited inside. "Is it true? A Herald? A Healer and a Herald in the same family, how proud you must be!"

A Healer and a Herald! she thought, startled for a moment by the phrasing. *Oh, my—bless them for noticing!*

Like the people in the market, they were all talking at once, but since there were only three of them, they didn't step all over each other's sentences so much that it all turned into a confused gabble. They surrounded Sidonie and Ayver, faces flushed with excitement at being so close to the great event. "Oh, Sidonie, just think! Our little Shandi is going to be so important!"

Sidonie took her face out of her husband's shoulder, and though it was tear-streaked and red with weeping, it seemed that the arrival of her friends pulled her the last few steps out of hysteria. She wiped her face with her apron, and began to look more like her normal self. Keisha deemed it practical at that point to remove herself.

But she hadn't gotten more than a single step out the door—in fact, she was still standing on the threshold—before she ran into another of the Fellowship women, one whom she knew well. Alys was in charge of the health of all of the herds, and as such, she and Keisha had spent plenty of time together dosing the animals for a variety of illnesses and other problems. This afternoon Alys looked hesitant as she approached the house, and great relief spread over her blunt features when she saw that Keisha was just leaving.

"Oh, Keisha—I'm sure this is a bad time, but that *chirra* I was worried about has definitely got wet-tail—" she began; Keisha didn't give her a chance to say more. She took Alys's elbow and pointed her toward the workshop, just as she spotted four more women bustling in their direction, heading for the Alder house.

"It's always a bad time when a beast gets sick, you ought to know that!" she said, making a joke out of it. "They *never* choose reasonable times to have problems! No worry, I'm going to be the last creature Mum thinks about for a while. Not only will I not be missed, I can make you up what you need in no time; you've caught it early, so you should have a cure by tomorrow."

The more distance she got between herself and the house, the better she felt, and chatting with Alys about the beasts of her herds was such a commonplace matter it could not have been a better antidote for the hysteria she'd just endured. Alys was a calming person to be around anyway; she had to be, as the animals she worked with were quick to sense agitation and become upset themselves. She was older than Sidonie by a year or two, sturdy, brown, and square, with a friendly face and open manner. Like all the women of the Fellowship, her workday clothing was fairly drab, not unlike Keisha's, except that the tunic and breeches were of a better fit and not hand-me-downs.

The two of them entered the workshop, and Keisha began pulling down the boxes of herbs she needed as Alys went on about the most recent births. The sharp and pungent scents of herbs filled the air as Keisha worked, and the cool of the workshop allowed her headache to ease. It occurred to Keisha that Alys' arrival provided not one, but two excellent excuses for staying away from home for a while. After all, it was spring, and that meant insect season; in particular, the fleas and ticks that would infest the Fellowship herds, given half a chance. So as soon as she had finished the wet-tail potion Alys needed, but before the woman could pull out her purse to pay for it, Keisha made her an additional offer.

"Look, this year I'd like to get ahead of the bugs instead of trying to catch up with them after your beasts are scratching themselves raw," she said, trying to be as persuasive as she knew how. "Why don't I make you up some batches of that repellent dip we talked about last year *and* a good supply of the kill dip. You can try the repellent right away, and if you see it isn't working, you'll be able to dip them all again with the kill before it gets to be a problem."

Cautious, and frugal as always, Alys wrinkled her forehead and bit her lip cautiously. "That would be very helpful, but—"

Keisha already knew what she was going to say; at the moment, the Fellowship's coffers were pretty bare. They wouldn't have made any major sales to traders since the Harvest Faire two seasons ago. "We'll just make it a credit against a shawl trade later for one of my brothers—at least one of them is *bound* to settle on a girl by Harvest. Or if you'd rather, when the traders get done with you at Spring Faire, you can pay me then." She grinned and held out her hands. "I'd rather have you on credit than have to deal with an infestation like we had three years ago!"

Alys shuddered and nodded agreement. The Fellowship folk normally didn't much care for credit, but as Keisha had known it would, the mere mention of that horrible flea infestation made the difference. It had taken weeks to clear up, and worse, the poor beasts had yielded inferior fleeces that year. Between the cost of the dips and the loss of quality fleeces, the Fellowship's steward had been beside himself. Alys had already been beside herself; anything that caused her beasts pain caused her anguish, too.

And since the dips are all made from things I can harvest in the woods right now, rather than things I have to pay for, I can afford to extend them the credit.

No sooner agreed than done; making up the batches of sheep dip ate up enough candlemarks that by the time Alys left, both arms laden down with baskets packed with jugs, the Alder home was full of friends and neighbors to the point where another body could not possibly have squeezed inside. Afternoon sun gilded the kitchen wall as Keisha stood out in the yard and listened for a moment; from the general emotional tenor of the cacophony, Sidonie had gone from grief to pride—

As it should be.

—and now the gathering had all the signs of turning into an impromptu celebration.

But Keisha still didn't want to be anywhere near it. And she didn't want to have to deal with the three heartbroken boys either, for all three suitors would be bound to show up on the doorstep of her workshop, looking for consolation. At least, she didn't want to deal with them right now.

But since I'm out of flea-wort, lerch buds, tannim bark and elo root now, I have the perfect reason to go harvest some. And, if they think I am sulking because my sister was Chosen and not me, well then, let them think that. Maybe it will make some of them do something nice to comfort me. That way I can get some reward I can call "appreciation" to make up for the times my generosity was taken advantage of in the past.

With a big basket over one arm and harvesting tools in the pockets of her tunic, she set off to the woods to do just that. She took the long way round, using the path that skirted the edge of the fields rather than cutting straight through. Young plants were just starting to show whether they'd be successful or not; the weak ones were ready to be weeded out, and the strong ready for a bit of manure. She exchanged some sort of greeting with everyone working out there as she passed; it was impossible not to. The good thing was that since she was carrying her gathering basket, it was obvious that she had work to do, and there were only a limited number of candlemarks before dusk fell. No one would delay her when it might be medicine *he* would need that she'd be gathering.

Self-interest isn't that bad a thing, when it comes down to it. We all tend to do things in self-interest, even—maybe especially—when we can couch it in terms of nobility and self-sacrifice. And look, Shandi gets the pretty white horse and a room at the Collegium while I get Errold's Grove's sicknesses and complaints.

The farther she got from the village, the better she felt; she felt her steps growing lighter once she entered the woods proper. Her stomach calmed down, and by the time she reached the lerchbush thicket, she was humming under her breath, and her headache was just about gone.

This probably isn't the last time I am going to feel like there's been some kind of injustice over Shandi being Chosen and not me—even if I don't really want to be Chosen anyway. Besides, I have my own Gift and some appreciation, from some folks anyway. Valdemar wasn't founded on things being fair in life, it was founded on coping with the unfairness of life. The tradition continues, Herald or not!

The lerchbush was a hardy creature and didn't react badly to having a few of its buds pruned away. A woodpecker trilled just over her head, and as she carefully held each branch and pared every third bud off with a tiny knife, the rich, green scent of lerch sap spread on the air and she drank it in with pleasure. Each bud went into the hempen bag she had tied to her belt. She dabbed each "wound" with pitch from an unstoppered jar, to seal it and keep insects and fungi from infesting the branches as Steelmind had taught her. *Taking care today means plenty tomorrow.* That's what he'd said, then smiled, as if at a joke only he understood.

When her bag was full, she tied it off, put it in the basket, and went in search of flea-wort, a kind of shelf-fungus that grew on the fallen bodies of winter-killed trees. For that, she had to seek out trees that were too rotten to use for firewood, whose deaths were due to insects or rot, and not storm.

When she returned to the village, basket full, it was already dusk and the sky had just begun to blossom with stars in the east. The village itself seemed oddly quiet, the houses dark and deserted. Only the faintest threads of smoke came from chimneys that should have been showing evidence of suppers on the hearth. She was puzzled, though not alarmed, by the quiet, until she got into the vicinity of the Alder home. Then it was quite obvious where the people had all gone!

An enormous party—a kind of extemporaneous Spring Faire in advance of the actual date—had invaded the house and the lawns and gardens of all the neighbors around it. She watched in some bemusement as her normally sober neighbors acted like adolescents on holiday. The house itself must have been packed to the cciling, since there were people spilling out the door, and the celebration perforce had spread into the yard.

Evidently all of Errold's Grove rejoiced in the Choosing of one of their own.

Well, she thought, *it's the most important thing to happen around here since the barbarians. That wasn't exactly pleasant! Afterward, well, even though things came out all right in the end, I imagine no one was in any mood to celebrate anything. What was there to be happy about, after all? That only one relative was killed or that only half the house burned? That Lord Breon or the Hawkbrothers were there at the rescue? Well, all right, perhaps that, but the circumstances eclipsed such elation. By the time any survivors could think clearly, their rescuers were long gone. This cause for the whole village to celebrate is well-timed.*

Controlled campfires burned in the pottery bowls prescribed for fires within the village bounds, warming the folk gathered around them against the growing chill in the air.

Some people were toasting sausages and the like on the ends of sticks, just exactly as they would during the Faire. From the wildly varied scents on the breeze and the way everyone seemed to be eating, guzzling, or both, every neighbor had contributed to the impromptu celebration by adding to the provender.

There would be no heartbroken former suitors showing up looking for comfort tonight, at least. A celebration was the last place any of them would want to be. They were probably brooding by the river somewhere, or weeping over one of Shandi's ribbons—

Or they've given her up completely, and they're chatting up one of the other girls at the party right this moment. When it came down to it, that was the likeliest.

Pausing for a moment in the shadows just outside the circles of light cast by the fires, Keisha pondered just exactly what she wanted to do. Did she really *want* to be engulfed by a party tonight? Was she in any kind of mood for a loud, boisterous celebration? Granted, she was happy for Shandi, but it wasn't the type of emotion that drove her to go to a party.

No, she told herself immediately. *No, I do not want any part of this. Mum, though, is in the best of hands, and a celebration is just what she needs. It'll turn her right around.*

Already, her head gave her faint intimations of what would happen if she allowed herself to be drawn into the commotion. A quiet night in her workshop, then a little reading before going to sleep—*that* sounded much more attractive than being plied with wine, babbled at, and staying up until the dawn. As for trying to find a corner of the house where she *might* be able to get some sleep, that looked pretty impossible.

So she reversed her steps and went straight to her workshop, closing the thick door firmly behind her. The heavy stone walls closed her in comfortably, effective blocking out noise. She sighed with content and relief, and felt her headache fading. It didn't take long to get the fire going again, and it was the work of a few moments to get the kettle ready and swing it over the fire to boil.

While she waited for her tea, she bundled the herbs and hung them up from hooks in the ceiling to dry, then spread the buds in a drying tray and hung the tray from brackets over the window. By the time she had finished clearing up, the water was ready for tea, and she washed her hands and set to fixing it with a good appetite.

She kept a stock of food at the workshop in case she missed a meal at home, and there was more than enough for a fine dinner. Dinner was toasted bread and cheese, with roasted chick peas, and a satisfying and hearty tea with honey. She read a little while she ate, enjoying the luxury of being able to do so—but most of all, she cherished the quiet.

After she tidied up, she spent another contented candle-mark or two putting together more of the common remedies she never seemed to have enough of, with special attention to those for headache and queasy stomach—for there were bound to be plenty of *those* after tonight's indulgence.

She changed her mind about reading further, though, after she climbed up into the loft to her cozy feather bed. Instead of reading, she reached over to the shelf beside the bed and picked up her cross-stitch embroidery—at the moment, it was the makings of a fancy blouse. It wasn't that she didn't *enjoy* pretty things, after all, it was just that they were very impractical for someone in her vocation. . . .

On the other hand, she didn't always have to be working, and there were enough celebrations to warrant having pretty clothing. Over the winter, with Shandi's help, she'd picked out a light brown linen for a festival skirt, a lighter beige for a blouse, and had charted out a very pretty pattern in browns and golds for both. The skirt was done; now she was working on the sleeves and neckline of the blouse. It wouldn't be finished for Spring Faire, but it probably would be for Midsummer. Cross-stitch—regular geometric patterns, that is—was very soothing, she had found. It allowed her mind to drift to other subjects, and sometimes as she worked, she was able to come up with answers to problems she needed to solve.

As she worked her needle through the linen tonight, she found herself wondering where Shandi was, right at the moment.

Would she be at an inn, I wonder? Or would that Companion take her to a waystation instead? In either case, Shandi would make herself at home. No one could resist her smile and her open friendliness, so she would be a welcome guest at an inn—doubly so, as newly Chosen. She'd probably be treated like a person of importance, and wouldn't have to lift a finger for herself. If, on the other hand, she was at a way-station, she'd have herself tucked up snugly in no time at all. From all that Keisha understood, waystations were well provided for; Shandi was more of a housekeeper and cook than Keisha was. It was not as if Shandi would have to sleep out-of-doors, supperless.

That might be why the Companion was in such a hurry to leave, Keisha realized. *They probably had a long way to go before they came to either an inn* or *a waystation!* That would be a good thing to remind her mother of tomorrow, if Sidonie felt slighted that Shandi had left without waiting to say good-bye.

By now, I'll bet Shandi's probably wishing she waited long enough to gather up her *work basket!* she thought with a chuckle. *I've never seen her sitting down without something to work on in her hands. Well, there ought to be at least one trader from Haven here at the Faire; I'll box up all her handiwork and send it off to her with him. With luck, I may be able to send her some scarlet thread as well.*

Would she be lonely, all by herself in a little waystation? Probably not; she'd have the Companion, after all, and everyone knew that Companions and Heralds had a special bond that was as close as anything two humans could have. *I won-der if she can Mindspeak to him? I wonder what that would be like?* Marvelous, but maybe a little scary; at least, that's what she thought it might be like for *her.*

Did Shandi miss Keisha? I certainly miss her already. Brothers just aren't the same as sisters. It was hard to think of what things would be like without her. . . .

She found herself nodding over her work, so she folded the blouse pieces carefully, putting them away in her work basket and stowing everything on the shelf beside her bed. She blew out her candle, and curled up—

—and even as she wondered if Shandi was awake or dreaming, she fell asleep.

Steelmind

Two

Morning broke clear and cool, with shreds of fog drifting above the fields and birds singing with all their hearts in the thatch of Keisha's roof. The faint hint of wood smoke mingled with fresh air laden with the perfume of spring flowers and the tang of new leaves—normally she woke to the odor of cooking porridge or pancakes. Keisha's nose, which was all that was peeking out from under the covers, was cold; she preferred to sleep with a window open. The birds woke her, and her cold nose twitched at the unaccustomed aromas; all the rest she saw from the small open window in her loft-bedroom.

She stretched luxuriously and snuggled underneath her down comforter and blankets, enjoying the simple pleasure of lying abed for as long as she cared to. Had she been at home this morning, she'd have been rudely jarred awake before dawn by the noise of five clumsy young men stumbling about the house, getting fed and ready to go to work. They couldn't seem to accomplish this simple task without a great deal of hunting for boots and clothing, accompanied by shouting questions to each other concerning the location of those articles. Once awake, there was no point in even trying to go back to sleep, since Sidonie would come roust Keisha out to help with household chores before she joined her husband and sons on the farm.

Instead of being jolted awake, Keisha had been serenaded awake, and after dawn, not before. Instead of being hauled off to wash dishes—or, dear gods, pick up after last night's enormous party—she had enjoyed absolutely undisturbed sleep.

Of course, the penalty for this is that I have to make my own breakfast and heat my own wash water, but I think that's a fair trade. Given that Shandi was gone, there would have been twice the work to do on a normal morning, and after the celebration last night, well, the amount of cleaning up didn't bear thinking about. And would Sidonie even *consider* taking care of the cleanup gradually, say, by putting off things like floor washing and yard cleanup for a few days? Not a chance.

Sidonie would insist that it all be done at once. Well, with neither Shandi nor Keisha there, maybe she'd finally get the boys to do their own share of the work—after all, each one of them made more mess than Shandi and Keisha put together.

It certainly wouldn't hurt them to start taking care of themselves. Maybe they'd start being more careful if they had to take care of the consequences of their own laziness.

That was a satisfying thought.

Well, what have I got left here to wear? How long ago did I bring things over? She took a quick mental inventory; since the last time she'd brought in cleaned smocks and breeches, she hadn't had any major injuries to deal with, so all three outfits were still here. *Good.*

She always kept at least one spare outfit here in case she got particularly bloodied; Sidonie had an aversion to seeing her daughter come in with bloodstains on her clothing, though she had no such problem with the same stains on her sons. Why was that? Sidonie had no fear of blood; she'd been born and raised on a farm. She was a farmer's wife, and the spillage of blood was part of farm life. Besides, women weren't exactly strangers to blood themselves.

She sat up a little more and wrapped one of her blankets around her shoulders. As she propped her knees up, one possibility came to her.

You know, it occurs to me that Mum's problem is less with bloodstains and more with the notion that it isn't lady-like for a girl to do things that would get her hands bloodied on a regular basis. I mean, even at slaughtering time, Mum doesn't get into the butchering until the carcasses have been bled out and gutted.

That brought up some new things to think about; with

Shandi gone, Sidonie would only have *one* female child to concentrate on rather than two. Now, that meant more than simply having the number of domestic helpers halved. Shandi had been as dainty and ladylike as her mother could have wished, relieving Keisha of the need to be either of those things. Now, though—

Now she's going to be at me to get a suitor, to act like a proper lady, to start having children. Besides all the chores, she'll want me to spend my free time doing needlework and making pretty clothes, putting together a dower-chest, not studying my books or making medicines.

She groaned softly. It seemed that Shandi had saved her from more than she ever realized. Just by being there and being what she was, Shandi had kept their mother's attention fixed on *her*, leaving Keisha freer than she would be now.

I'd thought my life was complicated before!

It was so *hard* to balance all the demands that were made on her. If they had *their* way, her parents wanted her to help with the domestic chores, the farm work, get married, have children. As far as the people of Errold's Grove were concerned, the villagefolk wanted her to concentrate on nothing but their injuries and ailments, or the hurts and illnesses of their animals.

Not that I don't prefer the animals, when it comes to that. They don't spend most of their time complaining! But that was unkind; of course people complained, it kept them from feeling quite so afraid. When they were sick or hurt, they lost control over their very selves, as they perceived them, and had to rely on the skills and tools of someone else—so it was only natural that they would complain. Up to a point, the more they complained, the more frightened they were known to be.

Past that point, they're too paralyzed with fear to do anything. I guess I should be grateful that they're still complaining. Handling the dead is worse than listening to the living.

Healer Gil, on the other hand, never lost the opportunity to let her know that he *still* felt she should be at the Collegium; that he had no real confidence in her ability to get beyond herb- and knife-Healing if she didn't go.

Well, he's got a good point there. I am making no headway

with those books. How I wish that old Wizard Justyn was still around! Surely he could have helped me make sense of those pages!

Perhaps she *would* have to go, but who would take over for her? Could she train someone like Alys?

Oh, no one would take this on who wasn't a volunteer, and if anyone had been willing to volunteer before, they wouldn't have needed me. As for Alys, she'd made it quite clear that she was in no way willing to extend her services beyond the animals in her charge.

Not that I blame her. She is far more reticent and shy than I am.

Now how was she to reconcile all these differing plans for her future? Obviously, *someone* was going to be angry with her, no matter what she did.

Something else occurred to her as she worried at her thoughts like a puppy with a bit of rag. This was the first morning in months when she hadn't woken up with the claustrophobic feeling that her entire family was closing in on her. *It always seems as if they're right beside me, breathing over my shoulder, even when they're in the next room.* Now that *might* have been because the cubby she had shared with Shandi was scarcely bigger than a closet. . . .

But it might not. People are all beginning to irritate me lately. How many times have I gotten away from someone feeling as if they've been rubbing my nerves raw? How many times have I wanted to shove them away? For that matter, how many times have I been feeling as sick as the person I was treating until I got away from them?

Not that she was all that comfortable around people; that had always been Shandi's gift. Shandi could make a friend out of a stranger in the space of a few words; unless Keisha was giving explicit instructions to someone or bargaining with a merchant, she always felt tongue-tied and awkward with strangers and friends alike. She actually preferred to be around the sick and injured, in a way, because then she had complete control over the situation.

For that matter, you couldn't really say that I actually have friends, not like Shandi's. For me, a friend is someone I

*can get along with, like Alys of the Fellowship—but you
don't see her inviting me to dinner or sharing confidences.*

She had to chuckle a little at that, despite the morose turn
of her thoughts. Sharing confidences, indeed! And what sort
of confidences would Alys be likely to share? Stories about
the love lives of the *chirras?*

Still and all, maybe that was why she got along better with
Alys than her neighbors or her family. *Neither of us is very
good with people. Animals are simpler, I suppose. Animals
certainly have less complicated emotions, and are never upset when you say the wrong thing.*

In the thin, clear light of dawn, she saw yet another whole
new side of Shandi that she hadn't really expected; Shandi as
her guardian. In retrospect, Shandi *had* spent a lot of time
protecting her from having to deal with other people in day-
to-day matters.

A thousand memories came flooding back, of Shandi re-
sponding to silent summons or unspoken entreaties as if she
heard them, and taking the attention of others off Keisha
with a word or a laugh.

*And Shandi spent a lot of time keeping Mum and Da from
worrying at me.*

How had she *not* noticed, all this time? And now what was
she going to do without that protection?

She frowned at herself for being such a coward. *Cope, that's
what I'll do. I'm a big girl.*

She would just have to steel herself and *learn* how to inter-
act socially with other people. She wasn't stupid, after all, she
could learn.

For a moment, though, it almost seemed as if her best option *would* be to travel to Haven in Shandi's wake and enroll
in Healer's Collegium!

*Oh, yes, and just how am I to do that? I've nowhere near
enough money to travel that far, and there's no magic Companion to carry me off and see that I don't get into trouble
along the way—*

No, that was a specious argument, and she knew it. Lord
Breon would not only *give* her the money to travel on, he'd
probably assign one of his guards and two horses to take

her there. And if he wouldn't—she had only to get as far as the nearest House of Healing, and the Healers *there* would see to it.

That was the trouble with arguing with herself—she had to be honest. She chuckled sourly and adjusted her blanket. *I'm so bad with people I can't even win an argument with myself.*

All right, the obvious problem of leaving her people without someone at least marginally qualified to help them, was an excuse. She had to face it; the real reason she didn't want to go was—

I don't want to leave, to go off somewhere among total strangers for at least two years, to some huge city where I would be totally lost.

The very idea made her skin crawl. All those strangers, and nowhere she would know to go where she could escape them! *All those strangers . . . oh, gods. No, and it's no good to say that at least Shandi would be there, because she's going to be at Herald's Collegium. She'll be so busy becoming a Herald that she'd be just as far from me there as she is now.*

She just was not like her sister; she didn't make friends easily, and she never would. She'd get so tongue-tied with the people at Healer's Collegium that they'd probably think she was feeble-minded! *It could be months before I managed to say anything sensible to strangers. And I'd be so lonely. . . .*

The larger the crowd around her, especially of strangers, the more she withdrew and wanted to hide. The only time she didn't feel that way was when she was on ground familiar to her—actually, or metaphorically. She was able to make desultory conversation with people she knew, with strangers in her own home, or if the topic had to do with things she already knew. At the Faires she invariably hung around the outskirts; at celebrations—well, generally she did exactly what she'd done last night, go to bed early. *I'm just no good at social chitchat, I suppose.*

She was absolutely certain her own nature would condemn her among the expert teachers at Healer's Collegium. *Until they actually gave me something that I already knew how to do—I'd look like a right idiot, I know it. And worse, I'd sound like one, too.* She could just imagine being called on in a class to recite something from a lesson—it would be worse than when she'd had her lessons with the other village children! The old woman who'd taught them had soon learned not to call on Keisha for any recitations; any time she'd wanted to know what Keisha had learned, she'd have Keisha write it out.

But that was here—they wouldn't give me that kind of special consideration at the Collegium. How could they? I'd be nothing special there, just another student, not someone they were going to rely on to tend their ills.

Shandi, on the other hand, would be fine in Haven even without the Companion. *That's what Mum doesn't understand about Shandi; everyone likes Shandi at first sight and goes out of their way to help her. They always have, and probably always will. That's why she has so many suitors; they all think they're in love with her just because she smiles at them and they're enchanted. They don't realize that they feel that way because she's just that way and can't help being so nice to them that it makes them feel as if she's nice only to them. Shandi has always assumed the best of everything, everyone, and every situation, and more often than not, they live up to it.*

Keisha shook her head, and reckoned that *she* must have been born somber, or at least, without humor. *Without humor, I suppose; I never can see what most jokes are about. Havens, I generally can't tell when someone is telling a joke! And no one seems able to figure me out, that I don't really enjoy noise and carrying on like everyone else seems to.*

Even her mother complained constantly that Keisha was far too inscrutable, and that she could never tell what Keisha was thinking or feeling, not that Keisha always wanted her to be able to do so. *If Mum knew what I was thinking—oh, would I ever get in trouble.*

But she also complained that Keisha was always taking everything too seriously. So did her brothers. And so, for that matter, did her father, even though he seldom complained about or even commented on anything.

Am I putting people off? I suppose I must be.

Well, just look at the difference between the number of suitors Shandi had and the number—none—that Keisha had. *There's no other reason why. Shandi and I look an awful lot alike—we share similar features, the same hair and eye color, and her figure is no better than mine.* Oh, granted, she does *generally dress better than I do, but I've worn pretty things without getting the attention she gets. It has to be that I'm putting people off.*

Now she had to ask herself as she often did—*Am I jealous of Shandi?*

She thought back over the selection of young men available in Errold's Grove and shook her head, thought about the sort of things that Shandi and her friends did for amusement and knew she'd be utterly bored. *No, I'm absolutely not jealous! There's only so much discussion of bodices and embroidery patterns that I can stand. And as for coquetting and flirting about—why bother?*

No, it was just another sign that she just didn't fit in with other people. Without Shandi's vivacity, animation, and sunny smiles, Keisha attracted about as much attention as a piece of furniture. *Which is, after all, the way I prefer things. How would I get anything done if I had young men mooning around after me the way they follow Shandi about? What a nuisance!*

So she wasn't entirely unhappy with the situation. Not entirely. It would have been nice to have *one* friend, or *one* suitor. Someone sensible, someone she could actually have a conversation with, somcone who had an interesting life of his own.

Well, this is wasting time. I've been slothful long enough. She threw off the blankets and flung open the lid of the chest that shared the loft with her bed. Quickly she got out clean clothing, and just as quickly scrambled into another oversized tunic and worn pair of breeches, shivering in the chilly air.

She half-climbed, half-slid down the ladder to the main room, ducked her head under the pump at the sink and performed a shivery wash-up, then stirred up the fire. In a reasonable length of time the room was warm, and a decent breakfast of bread and butter and tea was inside her. She put three eggs on to boil, picked out a withered apple to finish her breakfast, and with a grimace of determination, opened the book still on the bench to the last place she'd gotten stuck.

It was time to go to work.

She was interrupted four times before she gave up, still baffled by references to "shields" and "grounds." Once it was because she had to take the eggs off to cool, three times because children came knocking on her door with injuries. By then she was hungry again, and threw together a salad of young greens from her garden to eat with her eggs.

When she'd washed up afterward, she tidied up the workshop, then looked around and sighed. She couldn't put it off any longer; she had to go back to the house.

Bother.

Knowing that with all the work last night's celebration had generated, Sidonie would still be at home, her conscience goaded her into going back to pick up some of the work. *I can't say "my fair share," since I wasn't generating any of the mess, but it's not fair to leave Mum with all of it, I suppose.*

With reluctant steps, she made her way back through the village, to be greeted at the door with the expected, "Where have you been?" from her mother at the sink, up to her elbows in soap and water.

"Working, Mum, and studying." She didn't feel *any* guilt over that—after all, that was her job!—and although she didn't put on a defiant air, she did face her mother's eyes squarely.

Sidonie sighed. "Well, next time the entire village decides to celebrate something, I hope they choose someone else's house. I've been here all day, and I'm beginning to think we ought to move back to the farm."

"Well, I'd have to stay here—" Keisha began, and her mother interrupted her.

"I know, and that's why I haven't said anything to your father." Sidonie rinsed a plate and stacked it with the rest to dry. "Go clean up the yard, would you? I've been that busy in the house, I haven't had time to get to it."

Since that was a better job than washing dishes by Keisha's way of thinking, she was perfectly happy to go back outside and take care of the tidying up.

It was rather amazing, the amount of trash people could generate. Portable fireplaces had just been tipped over and the cold coals and ashes dumped before their owners carried the fireplace home, for instance. Sticks used to toast sausages were just littered about, and bits of kindling, the odd kerchief or scarf, and a wooden cup. The village dogs had already taken care of discarded food, and what they hadn't gobbled up, the crows had—good enough reason to put off clean-up! Keisha worked her way methodically across the yard; coals and kindling went into the Alder's own kindling stack, ashes were scooped thriftily onto the flower border, and other folks' belongings placed on a window ledge where the owners would presumably find them. She swept gravel back onto the path, put ornamental stones back along the border, and put the tiny plot of herb garden back to rights. Where markers had been inadvertently knocked over or flattened, she replaced them, where sticky stuff—of unknown origin—had been spilled, she dusted a little ash over it so it wouldn't attract insects.

She'd just finished when her mother emerged, bearing a basket full of wet clothing. Sidonie thrust it into her hands and bustled back into the house without a word.

Oh, dear. I suppose she's pretty irritated with me.

Better say nothing, then, and stay out of further trouble. She took the heavy load of clothes and set it down next to the rosemary hedge.

Sidonie had her own order of things, one that was not to be deviated from. Keisha followed that order as faithfully as any medicinal recipe. She spread shirts and underthings on the top of the hedge where the sun would bleach them; since today there was little or no breeze, there was no need to pin each garment to a branch to keep it from flying away. Stockings and breeches she pinned to the clothesline with wooden pegs her brothers carved during long winter nights—but they *had* to go on the section of line that would be in the sun. Anything embroidered or made with colored cloth went on the line in the shade to preserve those precious colors.

When she did her own laundry, everything went on the line, regardless, but Sidonie felt that the shirts and other white things got more sun if they were laid flat on the hedge.

Not that it would matter all that much with my clothing!

Sidonie came out twice more with baskets full of wet clothing; by the time Keisha was done, there wasn't a single bud or stem visible on the hedge and clothing on the line had been double-pinned, two garments sharing the same space. When Keisha brought back the third basket empty, Sidonie met her at the door with the Alder's lone bit of carpet and a brush.

No need to ask what that was for either. Keisha took it downwind of the drying laundry, out to the railings of the neighbor's fence, and laid it over the top rail. She brushed and beat the bit of rug until no more dirt or mud would come out of it and her arms were tired.

She brought both back, and this time her mother accepted them with a smile. She smiled back, relieved. Evidently she'd performed enough penance.

"Here—go sweep up," Sidonie told her, handing her the broom. "I seem to have all our dishes and most of our neighbors' as well—"

And Sidonie would never return so much as a cup if it was still soiled. Keisha ventured an opinion.

"Mum, why aren't the boys helping you?" she asked, digging the broom into the cracks of the wooden floor to dislodge crumbs that would attract mice. "They make more than their share of mess, and it wouldn't hurt them to help." At Sidonie's quizzical look, she added slyly, "And they're stronger; they could really do a *good* job of scrubbing."

"Oh, they're such clumsy louts," Sidonie began, but she sounded doubtful this time, and Keisha took advantage of that doubt to press her point home.

"I wouldn't trust them to do dishes, or to wash *good* clothes, but they can't hurt anything scrubbing floors and walls or washing sheets and their own clothing. Maybe if they had to scrub their own clothes, they wouldn't be so quick to get stains all over them."

Her mother laughed. "Isn't that the pot saying the kettle's black?" she asked gently.

Keisha snorted. "At least my stains come from work, not drinking wine and beer with my friends—and what's more, I *do* scrub my own, I've never asked you to do it, not since I started this Healing business." She warmed to her subject. "What's more, *I* never get stains on my good clothes!"

"You never wear your good clothes," Sidonie pointed out.

"Because I'd get stains on them," she countered. "And I *do* wear them, just not every other day to impress some girl! I just think they'd be more careful if they knew they'd be the ones doing the work."

This time, instead of dismissing the idea, her mother actually looked as if she was thinking about it—and thinking about the fact that half her work force was gone, and the other half—as she'd discovered this morning—was not always reliably available. "You might have a point, dear," was all she said, but Keisha was encouraged. "Would you go pack up Shandi's things for me? Ruven of the Fellowship says that there will be a trader for their shawls and trims coming straight from Haven and going straight back after the Faire, and he'll take Shandi some packages, probably in exchange for her embroidery threads."

"Then I'll give him a little more incentive," Keisha told her. "Shandi and I had gotten some scarlet dye; I'll go ahead and make up some thread, you know how hard it is to get scarlet, and that should seal the bargain."

"Oh, now that would be a help," Sidonie replied, brightening, since as Keisha knew, the trader would probably ask for a coin or two as well, and this would save the Alder household from having to part with those hard-earned coins. "Just—try not to get your hands all red this time, dear."

Keisha pretended she hadn't heard that last as she went to the back of the house to the little cubby-bedroom she shared with Shandi. After all, it had been ages since the incident when she dyed her hands with red ocher, and how was she supposed to know the stuff had to wear off? It had been her first experiment with dye for Shandi!

Shandi was so neat that it didn't take long to make her things up into a few tightly packed packages. Keisha left her a generous supply of embroidery threads for her own use but kept out the rest to use to bargain with the trader. Shandi's friends would just have to find another source for their threads from now on—

Or they can spin their own and pay me to dye them.
She also kept all of the undyed spun thread; not only was she going to dye as much of it scarlet as she could tonight, but she intended to make that experiment with overdying in indigo and see if that didn't make a purple.

I'll have to dry it in the workshop, though—and without a fire. In fact, I'd better dye it before dark so I don't have to use a candle. The fumes could be dangerous.

She was just as glad that she was the one doing this batch of dye and not Shandi. She wasn't certain she could have impressed on Shandi just how dangerous those fumes could be in close quarters. None of the dyes Shandi had used until now needed anything but water and a solvent followed by a fixative, and none was poisonous unless you were stupid enough to drink it.

But my medicines can be very poisonous. The bruise potion, for instance, or the joint-ache rub; they could both kill you if you weren't careful.

She paused for a moment to admire Shandi's undyed threads, the wool, the linen, and the special baby *chirra*-wool that she got from the Fellowship. No one in the village could spin a tighter, smoother thread than Shandi, and no one made thread better suited to embroidery. Shandi's threads were not inclined to knot, break, or catch; that was why everyone liked them.

But Andi is almost as good—and this will just give her incentive to do better.

When Keisha had finished, there was just enough daylight left to do the dyeing that she'd decided on. She took the hanks of undyed thread, left the packages on Shandi's bed, and headed out the door at a fast walk before Sidonie could recruit her to help with dinner. "I've got something I have to do, Mum!" she called as she went out the door. "I'll be back for dinner!"

She got herself out of shouting distance by breaking into a run as soon as she let the door slam behind her—thus making it possible to claim that she hadn't heard Sidonie, if a reproach was to come over dinner.

She closed the door of her workshop behind her and leaned

against it for a moment, conscious of a profound feeling that she had reached a sanctuary, and guilty for having that feeling.

Then she dismissed both emotions, caught up in the excitement of having something new to experiment with. The pouch with the dye in it waited in a patch of sunlight on the workbench, and she had the rest of the afternoon before her.

She quit only when it was getting darkish and the fumes from the dying thread made her feel as if she'd drunk three glasses of wine and then hit herself in the head with the bottle. By then, the last couple of hanks came out noticeably lighter than the others, which meant that the dye was losing strength.

That's all right, she thought as she hung them to dry with the rest, along the line where she usually hung bunches of herbs to dry. *They'll either be a nice rose-pink, or I can use them for that overdying experiment.* She had more than enough thread to make the trader willing to seal the bargain, and she'd used up three-quarters of the dye to do it. If Shandi's friends complained, she had enough dye left to dye *their* spinning, which wasn't good enough to tempt a trader. *That's a reasonable compromise, I think.*

She'd been careful to dye equal amounts of all three kinds of thread, too—linen for embroidering on light fabrics, sheep's wool for tapestry work on canvas, such as highborn ladies indulged in, or for embroidering woolen clothing and leather, and *chirra*-wool for work on heavier fabrics than linen.

She made sure all the windows of the workshop were open before she left; by morning the fumes should be gone and the threads dry. Her work was probably not quite as perfect as Shandi's—for her sister would make certain that every skein in a dye lot matched, and discard the dying solution as soon as the color showed any sign of weakening—but as rare as a good scarlet was, she doubted that would matter. As she left the workshop, she was gratified to see that she had managed *not* to get any of that scarlet dye on herself.

She'd thought about discarding the dregs, then thought better of it, sealing the bowl with another placed upside-down atop it. If those last skeins came out pink, it might be worth the trouble to keep dying, letting the color grow fainter and fainter, as long as it stayed colorfast. Shandi did that with indigo, and the girls loved being able to do subtle shadings with the results, producing flowers that looked real enough to pick.

Dinner was already on the table when Keisha arrived, and there were no reproaches for her from Sidonie when she pulled up her stool and helped herself to bread and soup.

Her father picked up what was obviously a conversation in progress before she arrived. "Na, then," he said, looking pointedly at Tell, the middlemost of the five boys. "It's about time you started helping out your Mum, like. You're of an age, and you think she's been put in the world to be your servant? Not likely, then."

Keisha kept her head and eyes down and ate quickly. The expressions on her brothers' faces had ranged from astonished to offended, sullen to rebellious. This did *not* bode well for her.

"What about Keisha?" asked Rondey, the oldest, whose expression had been the offended one. "She's a girl, and it's *her* place—"

My place? *Oh, really?* Keisha thought, anger rising.

"Keisha was here doing her share *and* yours today, for *you* were lazing about with your friends this afternoon," Sidonie snapped. "Trish saw you, so you needn't deny it and say you were working."

"And as for talk about *place*, I'd like to know where you got ideas like that," Ayver said, with some heat of his own. "There's no *places* in this family unless I put you in it, and I won't hear any more nonsense like that, talking about your sister that way! It wasn't you that was Chosen, was it, and maybe now your mouth has just given us the reason why!"

Keisha risked a glance out of the corner of her eye and saw Rondey redden to the same glorious scarlet hue that she'd dyed into the threads.

"As to *places*, you might take thought, you boys, as to who's going to be doing your cooking and cleaning when your Mum is gone and your reputations keep any girl from wanting to take you as a husband, hmm?" Ayver chuckled, and Sidonie continued that line of thought.

"Oh, indeed, let me tell you that there isn't a girl in this village who'd wed a man who's likely to treat her as his private servant!" she snapped. "And as for me—I may well stop keeping house *before* I die—I won't be spry forever, you know! Your good Da knows how to care for himself, but you lazy louts can count on it that *he* won't be waiting hand and foot on you!"

"So there you have it, lads. No choice for you." Ayver chuckled again, quite heartlessly, and Keisha almost choked on her soup, suppressing a chuckle of her own. "You'll be doing your own wash and picking up from now on, and each of you will take a turn at the dishes and cooking supper. If you don't want to cook, you can buy a meat pie or pasties from the baker, or pay a neighbor to make us soup. If you don't like having to share the chores, you're free to find some other household that will take you in, or live in the woods."

The groans that arose from his words were heartrending, but Ayver's word was law, and the boys knew it. Keisha finished her portion quickly and took her bowl to the sink; much as she disliked doing dishes, she decided it would be politic to volunteer tonight, and began on the soup pot and cooking utensils already waiting there.

Evidently the boys hadn't figured out that *she* was the source of their new chores—or else they were hoping for an ally—because they were decent to her when they brought her their bowls. That was certainly a relief! And Sidonie's quick hug when she brought the rest of the dishes was a welcome surprise.

"I know you've been worked hard, lovey, and you haven't complained about it till now," her mother said in her ear. "And it *isn't* fair, not when the town depends so much on you. You're a bit young to have that on your shoulders, and I keep forgetting that you're more than just my little girl. And I know you kept getting lost in Shandi's shadow—that wasn't fair either."

Keisha had often wished she could go off into the woods to live as a hermit, but not at that moment. She flushed, and smiled at her mother. "It's all right—now that the boys are going to pitch in to help," she said. Then an awful thought occurred to her. "You aren't *really* going to make them cook, are you?"

Sidonie laughed. "If they give up one night in the tavern, they'll have enough to buy us all supper for that night," she pointed out. "And if they really *want* to cook, I'll be overseeing everything to make certain what comes out in the end isn't going to poison us."

"Oh, good." Keisha heaved a sigh of relief and rinsed the last spoon. "Oh—I got you a rose vine from Steelmind yesterday; I'll plant it tomorrow. Where do you want it?"

Sidonie beamed and gave her another hug. "And I just this afternoon thought about putting up a trellis by the bedroom window, and I was wondering what to train on it! There, please, lovey. Going to study before you go to sleep?"

"Of course," she replied with wry resignation. "What else?"

"Then you might as well take the kitchen candle with you," her mother replied, and kissed her on the cheek. "Good night, sweet."

She took the proffered candle and went to her little cubby, now strangely empty without Shandi, but scented with her favorite herbs. She studied until her eyes grew too heavy to keep open, then blew out the candle and pulled the blankets over her head to block out the snores and grunts of her brothers. Tonight as she fell asleep, her thoughts were not of Shandi, but about the old wizard, Justyn. She'd never seen him; they were too far out in the country for a child to come into town and she'd never been sick enough to need his attentions. She wished that she *had* known him.

For all that her parents loved her, they still didn't really understand her. *It's the feeling—the feeling I have that's so strong, that I have to help people. Like seeing two ends of rope and wanting to tie them, just because they are there, as if they are somehow incomplete until I join them. It's as strong as needing to breathe or eat, and they just don't grasp that. I can't help myself, I never could; when someone is hurt or sick, I have to help them no matter what.* She had the feeling that *he* would have understood her, though, or else why would he have stayed and stayed during all the years when he was disregarded?

He had that feeling, too, he must have. Oh, how I wish he were here now, to teach me all the things I don't know!

Darian and Kuari

Three

Hooves made very little sound on leaf-littered forest floor, which was a welcome change to everyone from the steady *clicking* of *dyheli* hooves on roads packed rock-hard from generations of use. And after four years of so-called "normal" forests and entirely domesticated Valdemaran fields, Darian Firkin was glad to see a forest that looked normal to *him.*

It's so good to be on home territory again! Trees so tall you can't see the tops from the ground, with trunks so big it takes three men to circle them. This is more like it! He didn't crane his neck and gawk upward the way a "foreigner" would, but all the same he was very aware of how high the trees above him reached, simply by virtue of the fact that he had to look *up* before he saw any branches springing from the huge trunks standing all around him. Darian had grown up on the edge of the Pelagirs, and what the Valdemarans seemed to think of as proper-sized trees looked like saplings to him. Most of his life had been spent in the forests with his trapper-parents, rather than in his home village of Errold's Grove, and he felt as comfortable among trees as did his adopted Hawkbrother-kin.

Oh, it's very, very good to be home. Now I don't feel as if the sky is going to swallow me up. Despite the pleasure he took in his surroundings, he remained alert. The rest of the team rode ahead of Darian; he usually rode tail-guard, and took his responsibility seriously.

They were all on their way home now—not to Errold's Grove, at least not immediately, but to k'Vala Vale. This little group of Tayledras—one of many, be it added—had taken on the task of spending four years away from their Vale for the purpose of cleansing some of the northernmost Valdemaran territories of pockets of "trouble" left over from the mage-storms that had swept the entire world a few years ago. Darian had personal experience of the Storms and of their results, most of which were anything but beneficial, and he could see why the Valdemarans needed help with it. "Trouble" could take many forms: bizarre creatures warped and twisted from ordinary animals; dangerous animals "imported" from some other far lands within the area of Change-Circles; even pools of magical energy with the potential to affect anything that fell into it. And while they were at it, they were establishing new ley-lines and nodes, or reestablishing old ones, so that magical energies, just like rainwater, could again flow into and through convenient channels.

He smiled to himself, shrugging the quiver on his back into a more comfortable position; it tended to ride down a little. *Not that they wouldn't establish their own, eventually, but I rather fear my adoptive kin have a passion for neatness in magic.* It was no accident that the ley-lines and nodes established in or near Tayledras territory all fed into Tayledras Heartstones, for instance, instead of messily running this way and that without any consideration for the convenience of the would-be users.

For, as all mages knew to their sorrow, the mage-storms had disrupted everything, spreading magic, much like a fall of freezing rain, evenly across the face of the world. For the most part, magic collected in nodes or stored in objects had been dispersed as effectively as all the rest—some few reservoirs had been shielded and saved (most notably, the Heartstones of Tayledras Vales), but when the Storms were over, those reservoirs no longer had sources to replenish them. By reestablishing the ley-lines, mages of the level of Master and above would eventually have reliable and powerful sources of energy to tap into.

"Eventually" though—that was the key. It would take time for enough magical energy to trickle into those channels and collect again. For now, as Darian's very first teacher had told him, the powerful magics that Adepts and even Masters had been able to perform were things of the past—there just wasn't enough readily available, amassed energy available to perform them. He had heard it spoken of as "fog" by Starfall— sure, there might be enough water in a barn-sized mass of fog, but it did you no good if you wanted a drink of water.

Well—that's almost true. If three or four mages got together and pooled their personal power, you could do one fairly impressive piece of work. But you couldn't hold it for long, and the mages would be useless for a week after. Or worse, they'd be dead, which is certainly a scandalously wasteful use of mages and one which the mages would probably object to. The faint sound of a twig snapping behind them made him swivel to peer back along their trail, only to see a deer in the far distance stare back at him, then bound away out of sight.

By Adept Starfall's way of thinking, even leaving mages exhausted and drained was just a little too expensive a price for a temporary achievement. Darian tended to agree, at least in principle, though he could think of a few occasions when it might be worth it. On the whole, he preferred Starfall's precept that it was better and more effective to use small magics cleverly than big ones clumsily.

:Kuari?: he Mindcalled to his bondbird. *:Anything back there but deer?:*

:Fox. Tree-hare. Was squirrel. Tasty, too.: Kuari's mindvoice was overlaid with sated pleasure, but it wasn't as intense as it would have been if he'd stuffed himself.

:Do me a favor and circle a bit, then come back to the line.: Something had caused that deer to come out of cover—it might have been the animal's own curiosity, but if it wasn't, Darian wanted to know the cause.

Kuari gave willing assent, and Darian's thoughts returned to their original track.

After helping to defeat a barbarian army that had decimated the countryside and occupied Errold's Grove, Darian had been formally adopted by Mage-Scout Snowfire as his younger brother, and had left the area he'd known all his life to follow his new kindred. The Tayledras as a whole had made a treaty-agreement with Valdemar to cleanse their land in return for payment; each Clan and Vale that sent one or more teams out would decide just what form the payment for their team would take. In the case of k'Vala, it would be in the form of raw materials, such as wool, linen, metals, and the like—especially metals. Tayledras disliked mining, and without the magical means to bring metals to the surface, mining was the only way to get them. As to *why* it was the Tayledras and not the Valdemarans themselves that were cleansing the land—well, as Darian had learned, the Valdemarans were unaccustomed to magic use in the first place, and in the second place, the Tayledras were uniquely suited to the task. In the *first* set of mage-storms, in the wake of the Mage-Wars of Urtho and Ma'ar, the Tayledras had taken on the task of cleansing the lands at the behest of their Goddess, and had been given unique traits, skills, and knowledge to enable them to do so. *Interesting that they managed to come up with a tradition of running off strangers at knifepoint all by themselves, though, and not at the Goddess' orders,* he thought, casting an amused glance at his adoptive brother's back. *Well, some people take their jobs more seriously than others. I wonder if the Shin'a'in are just as bloodthirsty?*

The other reason lay in Valdemar itself. In the time of Herald Vanyel, a spell had been set that prevented knowledge of "true" magic from taking hold in the minds of Valdemarans—along with another, guaranteed to send any "true" mage mad if he worked his powers within the borders of Valdemar. Those spells were gone now, of course (they would never have survived the mage-storms, even if they hadn't been taken down deliberately), but centuries of living without real magic had left the Valdemarans without many mages of their own.

Darian understood that mages *were* being trained at the capital of Haven, under the auspices of Adept Darkwind and Herald-Mage Elspeth, among others—and like Darian, not all of those were Heralds—or even human. They were taking things slowly, however. There were many pitfalls to avoid, not the least of which was to make very certain that no ally got the impression that Valdemar was trying to build itself an army of mages!

There was talk of establishing a fourth Circle, a Mage Circle, just like the Bardic Circle, Heraldic Circle, and Healer Circle, and a proper and separate Mage's Collegium. I don't know how far they'll get with that one, though. Some of the teachers are bound to be mages from established schools; will they be willing to give over students into something like that? Then again, the point was to instill ethics into young mages from the beginning, and what sane mage would argue with that?

Well, that was all complicated political matters, and not of much interest to *him* at the moment. Right now he was just glad to be riding beneath the shadow of his much-loved trees, with the familiar pine- and fallen-leaf-scent of home all around him. One of the Heralds they had worked with during their task had once been on the circuit that included Errold's Grove, and had told Darian that the huge trees of the Pelagirs always reminded him of the huge columns of the Great Temple of Vkandis in Karse. It struck Darian, then and now, that this was a particularly apt description; the hush beneath the trees, with the calls of birds so high above, and shafts of golden sunlight piercing the occasional breaks in the foliage always filled him with peace, pleasure, and a touch of awe or wonder. He couldn't imagine a temple or cathedral of any kind that deserved the name that wouldn't evoke a similar set of feelings.

The group followed a faint but discernible path in the shadows of those trees, riding not the horses of the Valdemarans, nor the Companions of their Heralds, but *dyheli*, strong and slender deerlike creatures with twin, curving horns and a formidable intelligence. They were, in fact, not beasts of burden, but allies of the Tayledras and their equals in intelligence. Though they did not bond with a particular person in the way that a Companion would bond with a Herald, they did express preferences in riders, and Darian's mount was, oddly enough, the king-stag of the herd, Tyrsell.

One would think that the king-stag would be carrying one of the two leaders of the group, either Adept Starfall or Snowfire. . . .

:Now why should I do that,: Tyrsell asked ironically, *:when you are so very much lighter than they?:*

The *dyheli* turned his head a little on his long neck, so that one wickedly amused golden eye looked back at Darian. He wasn't at all surprised that Tyrsell had been following his thoughts; *dyheli* in general were the strongest Mindspeakers of any creature alive, and the king-stags were the strongest of the strong. *Dyheli* had no concept of the privacy of thoughts either; so they had no scruples about "eavesdropping."

Not that Darian cared; in their way, *dyheli* were so alien in their thinking that having Tyrsell privy to his thoughts was no more embarrassing than sharing them with his eagle-owl, Kuari. Certainly he had linked minds so often with Tyrsell that he never really bothered to shield against him. By this time he was so used to sharing his thoughts with *dyheli* that it came as second nature, as natural as breathing.

:Because it wouldn't be true?: he suggested. *:I've been growing, you know. I'm not the skinny little brat you used to carry around like a leaf. I'm almost a match for Snowfire now.:*

Tyrsell tossed his head with amusement—down, not up, or he'd have impaled Darian on a horn. *:Almost, indeed! You may be his match in height, but not in muscle, youngster, and you by no means weigh as much as he does. But you are right, it would not be the entire truth. What is the duty of the king-stag?:*

:To drive the herd from danger, to take the rear and guard, to stand and fight enemies off,: Darian replied promptly.

:You are one of the stronger Mindspeakers, you are light, and you are a fighter. You and I have linked minds many times in battle. If danger comes on us, you are the most comfortable with me, and are the best combination of skills to pair with mine to keep your herd and mine safe.: Tyrsell's logic was, as usual, impeccable. Darian could combine his mental strength with Tyrsell's to overcome panic in the herd, he *was* a match for any bowman in the group but Snowfire, so playing rearguard was a logical choice for him, and he and Tyrsell had proved more than once in close combat that their skills added together made them formidable foes. Darian was still flattered and pleased, because the same could have been said of some of the others, too.

:Your Mindtouch is unobtrusive, and when you are thinking, your Mind-voice is pleasant to listen to,: Tyrsell added. *:The others sometimes babble most annoyingly, or obsess over trifles. You only obsess over things of importance.:*

That pleased him, too. He took a certain pride in being able to *think* well; it was a skill Justyn had tried to teach him, and he wanted his abilities to reflect well on his old teacher.

In spite of the fact that I didn't value him while I had him. But that was a thought and a shame he kept to himself, under shield. It was his grief, and his alone to expiate.

By now Kuari must have circled on both sides of our backtrail— He sent a wordless, soft touch back to his bond-bird, who responded immediately.

:Anything?: he asked.

:Deer, quiet, go from grass to water,: was the reply.

Darian was glad to hear that; anything on the backtrail would have spooked the entire herd, so evidently his group had crossed the deer's game trail at the time when they were moving purely by coincidence.

But there was someone else who'd like to know about a herd of deer behind them. *:Stay with the herd, Kuari. You'll have company in a bit.:* He cast his thoughts upward, changing the "feel" of his Mindsending to that of another friend.

:Kel! Kuari's got deer in sight, on our backtrail.:

He got an instant response; the young gryphon was in a growth spurt, and *always* hungry.

:Deer!: Kelvren exulted. *:Oh, yes!:*

That was all he got, as Kelvren sent his thoughts winging after the owl's. Kelvren was up ahead of them, and higher in the tree canopy than Kuari. If there was any skill that Kelvren had gained above and beyond any other gryphon, it was the ability to move through the high branches of the great trees with barely a wingbeat. In a moment, though, he would be winging back *above* the canopy until he came up with Kuari. Then, using the owl's information, he'd dive blind through the screen of foliage just like a goshawk going for a rabbit in the brush, and with any luck, he'd get a deer before the deer knew he was there. Otherwise, he'd be in for a tail-chase.

Kel could catch a deer in a tail-chase, it just wasn't his favorite form of pursuit—though the injuries that often resulted from tail-chases gave him plenty of extra attention. He'd much rather make a clean kill, and a quick one; chases were a waste of energy.

Faintly, from behind him, came the noise of something large crashing through the branches, and Kuari's excited hoots. Kuari loved watching Kel hunt; all bondbirds were far more social than their raptor ancestors, and took pleasure in each others' company and successes. Breeding that trait into them had been imperative, since without it, Kuari would have happily made a meal off of any of the other birds in the company. Kuari's talons could easily pierce a cow's skull; he'd make short work of another bird.

:Two! Two!: Kuari projected excitedly into Darian's mind. *:He got two!:*

:Two?: Tyrsell chimed in, impressed. *:By the horns of the Moon-Doe, that's amazing!:*

If Kelvren had managed to kill two deer at once, there was no point in letting them go to waste. "Snowfire!" he called ahead. "I sent Kel on the backtrail after a deer, and it seems he's gotten two instead of one."

Snowfire turned, stared at him to see if he was serious, then broke into astonished laughter. "I had no idea he was *that* hungry!" He called ahead to the rest of the team. "Wintersky! Raindance! Peel off and go back until you find Kel, he's made a kill too big for him to carry."

A short time later, two of the team rode past Darian with a wave, their mounts at a brisk trot, two riderless does from the herd trotting beside them. While Kelvren stood guard, and their own birds circled above as extra protection, they'd field-dress the two deer, strap each to a rough travois, then rejoin the rest. To make it easier for them to catch up, Snowfire slowed the team to an amble. This wasn't the first time that Kel had made kills too large to eat at once or carry, but it was the first time he'd made a double-kill.

Nightwind is going to be very proud of him, Darian thought warmly. *He's going to be just as proud of himself!* Gryphons, after all, were praise-driven, and what they didn't receive from others they often enough filled in for themselves.

Roughly a candlemark later Raindance and Wintersky came trotting back, the riderless *dyheli* now each dragging a travois with the somewhat-mangled carcass of a fine young buck strapped on it. That would slow them all down, of course, but it wasn't that long until they were going to make camp, so the prospect of fresh meat would more than make up for it. Kel would dine tonight on one deer, the team would have part of the other, then Kel would get the remains for his breakfast. It took a lot of meat to feed a gryphon, though fortunately he usually managed to supply it himself. In lean times, breads were used to supplement the meat, mostly to provide mass, and luckily for everyone who would have had to hear his complaining, Kelvren had acquired a taste for sweetbreads anyway. Hungry gryphons were grouchy gryphons.

There were no more breaks in the routine of travel until the light beneath the trees had begun to redden and grow dimmer, a sure sign that the sun was about to set. By then, the advance scouts had found a suitable camping spot and those with lighter burdens and the unburdened *dyheli* had gone on ahead to prepare the camp, leaving the rest to come in at their own pace.

That, or so Darian thought, was one of the advantages of being the rearguard. By the time he reached camp, it *was* a camp; the tents were all set up, a latrine pit had been dug, water fetched, and Ayshen, the chief *hertasi*, had everything ready to make dinner for the entire team. Since the job of rearguard was to make a circuit of the camp before coming in himself, the rearguard never had to do any of the camp chores.

Some nights, in the winter, for instance, when he was frozen from his nose to his toes, or in the pouring rain, that was a hardship. Being the one who had to make certain that all the territory within their perimeter was clear under those circumstances, with dinner scents on the breeze, was assuredly a hardship. Not tonight, though.

He dismounted and let Tyrsell go on into camp, to put himself into the capable hands of the *hertasi* to have his minimal tack removed. No *dyheli* would ever subject himself to the indignity of a bit and bridle; however, they did allow a modified hackamore, similar to that worn by Companions, and a saddle-pad to cover their protruding backbones. As Darian knew from painful personal experience, riding a *dyheli* without that saddle-pad was much like sliding naked down a cliff, but not nearly as comfortable.

He and Kuari made the circuit of the camp without incident,

marking good places for sentries with something unobtrusive, natural, but unmistakable to any of the Tayledras—feathers, usually wedged into the bark of a tree.

When he got back into camp, the first set of sentries had eaten a light snack and were ready to go out. They'd get a second meal when they came back in, but, no Tayledras would stand sentry with a full stomach; it was too easy to doze off.

Ayshen had his dinner ready and waiting for him: a savory butterflied venison steak and journey-bread, with some mixed, unidentified shoots and greens. Ayshen and the other *hertasi* knew the forest and what it could provide as well as they knew the patterns of their own scales; they foraged as the team traveled every day, and Darian never knew what they would come up with. They always had something green and growing in addition to meat and bread, even in the dead of winter, for Ayshen took great care with the diet and health of his "charges."

Darian knew better than to leave so much as a scrap of that green stuff on his plate, too. Ayshen would show no mercy to anyone who didn't eat what was given him.

Darian sat down to eat in the blue dusk beneath the trees; he polished off the last scrap in full dark. He was the last to eat, and brought Ayshen his empty plate just as the *hertasi* cleaned the last of the pans.

"We are not far from the Vale now," Ayshen told him with a toothy grin. "One day, two at the most. Then you will see! Nothing we passed through in Valdemar compares!"

"Nothing we passed through in Valdemar was bigger than two or three villages put together," Darian reminded him. "We were not exactly traversing through the height of Valdemaran civilization, you know."

"Oh, indeed." Ayshen chuckled. "You will see."

Darian laughed, and slapped the little lizard-creature on the back. "I'm certain that I will," he agreed. "But for tonight, all I want to see is my bed."

He wouldn't have thought, back when he was Justyn's apprentice, that simply riding all day long would be tiring. After all, it was your mount that did most of the work, right?

Well, that turned out to be only partially true; riding was more work than Darian would have imagined four years ago.

Riding literally from dawn until dusk was enough to tire anyone out—riding as tail-guard was exhausting mentally as well
as physically.

So he wasn't joking when he told Ayshen that all he
wanted to see was his bed. He continued to share a tent with
young Wintersky; it was a tent made for three, but only the
two of them used it now. Snowfire had long since made his
union with Nightwind a formal one, which just gave Wintersky and Darian more room.

Wintersky sat beside a small campfire in front of their tent,
contentedly toasting a stick. Darian sat down beside his
friend and took another dry twig, breaking it into tiny bits
and casting each bit into the heart of the fire. "Ayshen says
we'll be at the Vale in the next day or two," he said, and
Wintersky nodded.

"Probably late tomorrow," he replied. "Everybody's pretty
anxious to get home. My guess is that they'll roust us out before dawn and tell us to eat in the saddle."

"Which is why you're roasting a stick to calm down so
you can get to sleep quickly," Darian finished for him, and
yawned. "Believe me, I don't need that to get *me* to sleep."
Then he snickered. "Poor Snowfire—he and Nightwind won't
get much chance to cuddle tonight!"

Wintersky snorted and elbowed him; Darian elbowed right
back, and both made moon-calf faces at each other so that
they both broke into peals of laughter.

As the two youngest members of the team, they spent a
great deal of time together, got into a certain amount of mischief together, and despite coming from such different cul-
tures, had far more in common that Darian had found with
the boys his age in Errold's Grove. Darian really felt by now
that he *was* part of a family, with Wintersky the brother he
had always wanted.

They chortled themselves breathless, paying no attention
to the quizzical looks of some of the other Hawkbrothers;
Wintersky tossed his stick into the fire, Darian followed
it with the remains of his, and they both went straight to
bed. Wintersky's bird was already asleep on his perch inside
the tent, Kuari dozed in the branches of the tree above them.
Although most owls were nocturnal, the eagle-owls were

comfortable in darkness *or* daylight; their size gave them a hunting advantage in the daytime, and their night-sight and silent flight the advantage after dark. Kuari could adapt his sleep schedule to suit his bondmate.

As Wintersky had predicted, *hertasi* rousted them out while it was still as dark as the inside of a cold-drake's belly in an ice cave. They weren't given a lot of time to ready themselves, either. *Hertasi* were efficient under any conditions, but Darian had never seen them work quite so quickly before. The camp was down and packed up by the time he had Tyrsell saddled, and Ayshen must have known last night that this was going to happen, because one of his helpers came by with pastry-wrapped venison that Ayshen must have put to baking in the embers of the cook fire the night before. Darian actually got to eat his without being in the saddle; no one had told him he had a new assignment, so he was tail-guard again this morning. Tail-guard's morning duty was to make sure the camp was clear, that all the fires were out, that nothing had been left behind. So he ate his meat-roll and drank his bittersweet, hot *kava* while everyone else bustled about, getting their riding order straight, then started the day's trek—still in the dark. Darian was entirely unsurprised to see that Snowfire had lead-duty; with not one, but *two* owls as bondbirds, he was the only logical choice for a ride in total darkness.

As soon as the last *dyheli* cleared the camp, Darian summoned up a mage-light and made a thorough inspection of the site. This time he uncovered evidence of the hasty departure in the form of a couple of misplaced small articles of clothing and adornment, a bit of trash that needed burial, and one fire that had not been thoroughly extinguished and still smoked. These small tasks attended to, he mounted Tyrsell, and with Kuari following in the trees, he caught up with the rest.

He banished the light as soon as he drew up with the rearmost rider—Sunleaf, whose forestgyre dozed on a perch incorporated into the saddle-bow in front of him. Riding in the darkness like this, the team now depended on the eyes and ears of only three birds and Kelvren to protect them. Even Daystorm's flock of crows rode—two on the saddle-bow perch, two on the horns of her *dyheli* Pyreen, and the rest on the horns of any other *dyheli* that would let them.

With nothing to look at but the vaguest of shadows, Darian was acutely aware of every calling insect, every time a bird chirped or squawked its sleepy protest at being disturbed, every crackle of dead leaf or rustle of undergrowth. None of this made him at all wary or nervous; he'd grown up in forest like this, and these were all normal night sounds. He'd be alerted only if they stopped, or if a sudden burst of noise betrayed that something had disturbed the sylvan sleepers.

Kuari was perfectly composed—and perfectly full; he'd eaten well last night, and would not need to eat again until tonight. He wasn't tempted to hunt, not even by the flocks of drowsy birds he passed beneath. What Kuari saw danced like a ghost-image in front of Darian's eyes, a double-vision that did not disconcert him in the least now, though it had taken him months to get used to it.

The air was very still, not a breath of breeze; it was cold, and smelled of damp, old leaves, and fog. It *felt* heavy, somehow; morning before dawn almost always felt like that, as if it was just possible that the sun might not rise, after all.

It was difficult to judge the passing of time; Kuari would rise above the treetops once in a while, to take the measure of the dawn, and for what seemed to be the longest time he saw nothing but darkness and stars.

Finally, though, the strange sense of heaviness lifted, ever so slightly. Kuari lofted through the leaves to catch the first brightening in the east, and the first tentative notes of the birds' dawn chorus drifted down to the travelers below.

Sunleaf's forestgyre roused all his feathers with a quick shake—still more heard than seen—as those first notes brought him out of his doze. Gradually, faint light filtered down through the trees; at first the light was so very faint that everything seemed painted in shades of black and gray, but as the sun rose, the light brightened to a thin, dusty rose, and color came back into the world.

Up and down the line of riders, birds were shaking out their feathers, stretching their wings, preening and yawning. Then, one by one, they hopped onto their bondmates' gauntleted arms to be tossed into the air.

The crows were the first, and taunted the others as lazy loafers with their derisive caws as they rowed up into the canopy. Stung by the good-natured insult, the younger birds followed immediately. The older birds were too seasoned to be tempted into flight by a pack of delinquents before they'd warmed up their muscles; there was plenty of stretching and flapping before the rest took to the air.

Two enormous shapes lofted silently toward the line beneath the lowest branches, one from ahead and to the right, one from the left. These were Hweel and Huur, Snowfire's bondbirds; that meant that Snowfire had dropped back and someone else with a fresher bird had taken over the forward position. There were three *dyheli* in the herd with peculiar saddles—more of a perch, than a saddle—and no reins. These were for Hweel and Huur, and sometimes Kuari, who were all far too large to sit a perch in front of anyone. It was all Darian could do to carry Kuari on his shoulder or give him a short and temporary ride on his gauntleted arm; the eagle-owls were *big*, and awfully heavy. On Snowfire's advice, Darian had built up his arms and shoulders with a great deal of lifting and carrying and wood-chopping in order to be able to support the weight of his friend.

It's just a good thing that nobody with us has real eagles as a bondbird, Darian thought, as he watched the eagle-owls disappear somewhere up ahead, presumably making a landing on their mounts. Snowfire had once told him that the only person in k'Vala to have a true eagle and not a hawk-eagle as a bondbird was the blacksmith! All bondbirds were easily twice, even three times, the mass of their wild counterparts. Darian could hardly imagine how large a true bondbird eagle must be. . . .

The morning passed uneventfully, and so did the afternoon, except that the break for lunch was hardly more than a pause while more pastry-rolls were passed out to the riders and nosebags of grain to the *dyheli*. They all ate on the move, something that until now had been done only during wretchedly cold weather, to enable the team to get to shelter faster.

It was late in the afternoon that the biggest bird Darian had ever seen in his life swooped down out of the trees and screamed a greeting as it passed over the heads of everyone in the team. The wingspan alone was so wide not even Huur could match it; more than the height of a mounted man, easily.

All the bondbirds set up a deafening chorus of replies, converging on the riders from every direction, and taking to their perches to go into full, wing-spread display. The huge raptor that had triggered the cacophony made another pass over the heads of the team, this time flying from the rear to the frontmost rider, then disappearing into the branches again.

:Darian, you can stand down.: The mind-voice was Snowfire's; no point in trying to shout, he wouldn't be heard. *:Remember the eagle I told you about, that's bonded to a blacksmith? That's her; we're under k'Vala guard now. You can relax.:*

Darian took a deep breath and let it out in a low whistle; the birds were finally quieting down and settling. *So that's a bondbird eagle? If I were dyheli, I think I'd make her walk!.*

As dusk fell, there was a distant glow through the trees ahead of them, and just as the last light of day faded from beneath the trees, the next lot of escorts met them.

This was a veritable stampede of *dyheli*, first an avalanche of young stags and does, then followed by the older does and their fawns, with five king-stags bringing up the rear. They poured around the line of riders, the youngsters frolicking, the older *dyheli* trotting up to rub noses with friends, and the king-stags making straight for Tyrsell. Judging by all the vigorous head-nodding going on, the king-stags went into an immediate six-way conference, one which would probably last for several days. After all, Tyrsell was an ambassasor to Valdemar in his own right, one looking for new grazing lands for *dyheli*, and he had negotiated his own set of treaties with various Valdemaran populations through the medium of different Heralds.

Unburdened *dyheli* separated from the group and joined the massed herds, who all cleared off, heading back to the Vale. That left room for the next lot of greeters, a flood of *hertasi*. They seemed to appear out of nowhere—as *hertasi* were wont to do. There were probably a few hundred of them, but it seemed as if there were a couple of thousand at the least. When they had finished swarming the team and disappeared back into the darkness, there was not a single scrap of baggage left anywhere in the line, for they had stripped it from every burdened *dyheli*, leaving *them* free to run ahead as well.

Then came the first of the wonders that would leave Darian breathless for most of the evening.

Lights approached the line of riders, lights bounding along just below the level of the first branches. As the many-colored lights neared, Darian identified them as mage-lights, but they were carried—or rather, pulled along—by bondbirds. Mage-lights weighed nothing, of course, but how wonderful to see the bondbirds, each trailing a different colored sphere in its wake!

The birds with the team again set up their greeting display, and the birds from the Vale remained with the team, lighting their way home, perched overhead in the lowest branches. As Darian passed the birds at the rear, they flew ahead to the front of the team and took up new perches.

Then, as the light ahead grew stronger and stronger, they came to the entrance to the Vale itself, and the crowd of friends and relations waiting there for them. A cheer went up as the long-absent team broke through the cover of the forest.

Now, for the first time, Darian saw Hawkbrothers in all their festal glory, and he was, to put it mildly, dazzled. No one on the team had brought any sort of "fancy" garments with them—though Hawkbrother clothing had been exotic enough to Darian's eyes—so he'd had no idea what he was going to see. No wonder Ayshen had warned him that he'd be surprised!

Men and women alike dressed in spectacular costumes— what one wore seemed to be more a reflection of his or her personality than gender. Long pale hair was beaded, braided, feathered, dyed, and cut in the most amazing styles. They didn't look *real*, somehow, yet they surged forward like any group of folk meeting with people they'd been parted from for too long.

But, of course, no one came forward to greet him. . . .

Now, for the first time in years, Darian felt very much the outsider, and painfully alone. A young *hertasi* skittered up and took his bridle, looking up at him expectantly. Tyrsell lifted his head up, and the small *hertasi* was lifted off the ground for a moment, squawking at first, then emitting a long burble of laughter as he was lowered back down. Older *hertasi* appeared on each side, sharing the laughter. He dismounted from Tyrsell's saddle and let the *hertasi* strip his friend of tack and carry it off. Then Tyrsell himself stepped away, leaving him even more alone with all of the meetings and greetings swirling around him.

"Dar'ian!" Snowfire pushed his way through the crowd, with an older man and woman in tow, his face alight. "Here— Mother, Father, this is Dar'ian Firkin, k'Valdemar; Dar'ian, this lady is my mother, Dawnmist, and this is my father, Heartwood." He grinned. "*Yours*, also."

The two Tayledras smiled warmly and each held out a hand. Darian took them, tentatively at first, then with the dizzying sensation that he was settling into something real and solid and welcoming. His loneliness evaporated, and with a wonder-filled grin he entered k'Vala Vale with the rest of the Tayledras.

From the moment that Darian passed through the impressive vine-covered entrance to k'Vala Vale to the moment that he fell asleep, he was half afraid to blink lest he miss some new wonder. Now he knew why Ayshen had been so smug!

Just past the faintly visible barrier that protected the Vale from outside weather, he stepped into an entirely new realm.

The barrier distorted some of what lay beyond it, and cloaked the rest, so that from the outside it appeared that there was nothing beyond it except more ordinary forest. But when he passed through it, feeling a faint tingle as he did so, he saw what it had concealed.

Before him lay a softly curving path that wound deep into an exotic garden within only a few paces from the entrance— but it was not at all dark, for light glimmered and gleamed through the foliage. He followed the path to its first turning; mage-lights were supplemented by fantastic lanterns in glowing colors—round, square, oblong, in the shapes of flowers and leaves, stars and the phases of the moon. The lanterns hung from decorated poles crafted of carved wood on either side of the pathway. Some of these poles were carved with vines twining about them, some in the shapes of fantastic animals and birds, some decorated with geometric shapes or abstract curved lines. The path itself, "paved" in tiny pebbles of river gravel, was bordered in larger, water-smoothed rocks and was intersected at frequent intervals by a tiny sparkling stream that danced and laughed over similar stones. Where the path crossed these streams, it led over charmingly carved bridges, no two alike. The stream wasn't so wide that the bridges were needed, they were simply there because they were attractive.

Unlike the forest outside, where undergrowth was sparse, here plants, bushes, and even smaller trees throve to the point of luxury. Blossoming vines formed screens and curtains, flowering bushes poured scent onto the breeze. More flowers, closed now in the fragrant half-light along the path, gave promise that day would bring even more beauty. It was noticeably warmer here, the same gentle warmth of a summer night rather than the cool of a spring evening. Frogs and crickets sang in little pockets of shadow, and overhead, nightingales poured out melody into the darkness above the lanterns.

But that was only the beginning of the wonders. As Darian followed Snowfire and his parents deeper into the Vale, other sounds overhead made him look into the branches of the huge trees. It was at that point that he realized that the trees were even bigger than the ones outside the Vale—and that they held *dwellings* cradled in their huge boughs! The *branches* were as big as the trunks of the trees that he was used to. So high up were these living places that at first he had taken them for more elaborate lanterns.

So these were the famous *ekele* of the Hawkbrothers! Darian marveled at the highly individual "nests" resting above. Once again, so far as he could tell, no two were alike; some showed lights and movement, some were dark—and lights twinkling further up the trunks suggested that there were still more of these *ekele* higher up. The mere thought of *how* high they must be made him dizzy. Staircases spiraled up the trunks, showing how the Hawkbrothers gained access to their homes, and the staircases were just as ornamental as anything else Darian had seen so far.

No wonder everyone is in such good shape—they have to be, just to go to and from their homes!

"We've been in this Vale for a very long time, Darian," Snowfire said over his shoulder. "Longer, I think, than any other Clan has been in one place. Three, four generations at least, I think, and our people are very long-lived; it's more than enough time to really make this Vale into a work of art—a place none of us wants to leave."

"I can certainly see why," Darian replied, dazed. That was when they passed the last screening of vine and came out into the open.

This was clearly the center of the Vale. There stood the Heartstone, right in the middle—

It was a tall, smooth spire of natural rock, something like an enormous stalagmite, and of the same creamy alabaster color and texture. It glowed warmly, welcomingly, as if it, too, was a kind of lantern. Stepped, fitted stones partially encircled it, and kept it clean of debris.

It also glowed and pulsed to his Mage-Sight, so brightly that he had to block that part of his abilities.

"About three years ago we finally got enough power coming into the Heartstone to put up the Veil again," Snowfire's father said with satisfaction, as they all paused for a moment at the edge of the clearing. "There's still not enough to power nearly as much as we used to do, but we're the first Clan to get their Veil up."

Not nearly as much—I almost hate to think what they used to do! was all Darian could think, as the Heartstone seemed to pulse in time with his heart with all the power it held. It was magnificent, awe-full in the strictest sense of the term. He had never in all of his life Seen that kind of power before, and he rather doubted that he would ever See its like again. Certainly not in his own little Vale. It would probably take generations before his own Heartstone ever accumulated this level of power.

Snowfire sighed, lifting his face to the Heartstone as one starved of light would raise his face to the sun. "Oh, it is *so* good to be back within the reach of a Heartstone again!"

For a very long time Darian simply couldn't look away

from the wonder, though he did not make the mistake of using his Mage-Sight again; when he finally did look away, it was with the realization that *this* was what his team had been trying to reproduce in a crude form in every long-term camp they'd made.

Here was the source of the little stream they'd followed, and now it was clear that many more little streams took their water from here to run through other parts of the Vale. To his right lay a spring-fed series of cascades that in turn led into a cool, clear pond with colorful fish drifting just beneath the surface. A multitude of waterlilies and other water plants throve there, and a series of steps cut into the side showed that more than just the fish were wont to swim there.

Next to this was an herb garden, as ordered and mathematical in its layout as the rest of the Vale was not, though there wasn't a straight line to be seen there. It lay in the quarter of this clear area directly in front of Darian, as the pond was in the quarter to his left. He had overlooked it at first in gazing at the Heartstone directly beyond it, perhaps because it was so—ordinary. It looked exactly like every other large herb garden he'd seen over the course of their travels, in the courtyards of all of the larger temples and Healers' enclaves. Neatly laid out in a curving maze, every herb had its own little patch, each patch's growth trimmed off in edges as straight as a rule. Nothing grew taller than his waist; most growth lay between his ankle and knee.

To his right was a cluster of low buildings, beautifully integrated with the landscape to the point that they even had hanging plants and flowers growing on their flat roofs. At first glance he had taken them for an unusually regular stone formation, in fact.

"The hot spring and the main soaking and bathing pools are on the other side of the Heartstone," Snowfire told him, "And I don't know about you, but after today's ride, that's the first place I want to go."

The mere thought of relaxing in a hot pool made his aching limbs all declare in favor of the idea, so he just nodded and followed Snowfire and his parents around the fascinating Heartstone and past a screening of tall, jointed plants with stalks as thick as his calf and graceful leaves that formed a solid wall hiding all beyond them.

Once past that screen, a complex of interconnected pools on multiple levels stretched out in front of them, some so small they could only hold two or three people at once, some big enough to hold the entire team, *hertasi* included. It looked, from the amount of steam rising from the water, that the hottest pools were on the highest level, the coolest on the bottom. It also appeared that everyone in the team had the same idea as Snowfire, for they were all up to their chins in hot water—this time actual, instead of metaphorical.

Nightwind waved at them from a middle level, her hair piled high on her head and held there with wooden skewers, her face flushed and damp from the heat. Snowfire waved back at her and climbed the rocks to join her—but Darian had already picked out which of the pools was hottest and headed straight for it, forgetting everything but how good that water would feel.

Of course, after being with Tayledras for four years, he shed his clothing at the edge of the pool as a matter of course and eased himself down into it, knowing that *hertasi* would gather up the clothing and that towels and replacements would materialize when he needed them. The water was just as hot as he'd hoped it was; too hot to stay in for long, which was probably why he had this small pool to himself, but it was just what his aching muscles wanted.

The polished, sculptured sides of the pool formed seats of varying heights. He shifted around until he found one that allowed him to lean back with just his head above the water and relaxed into the smooth stone, eyes closed, until even he could no longer take the heat.

He didn't want to leave just yet, though; there were still aches that hadn't been soaked out. So instead of abandoning the pools altogether, he moved down to another, not so warm. In fact, in contrast to the one he'd just left, this one felt positively tepid. He remained there until it, too, felt too warm, then moved again, joining Nightwind and Snowfire and several more of the team and some strangers in a community soak.

The others were involved in a rambling conversation that seemed to consist of trading stories of what had gone on in the Vale in the team's absence for stories of what the team had done. Darian simply slid into an unoccupied seat and listened, adding a word or two if he was spoken to directly, but otherwise just listening.

But finally, one of the strangers turned to him. "What think you of all this, new Wingbrother?" the young woman asked him, her eyes sparkling impishly.

He shrugged, at a loss for words. "Amazing. Just—amazing."

"Well," another girl drawled lazily, "there are things in other lands that equal or surpass a Vale, but on the whole, this is a fine place to live."

"So says a former dweller in White Gryphon!" laughed the first. "High praise indeed!"

So this was another of Nightwind's people, a Kaled'a'in! Darian wanted to ask a hundred questions, but felt too shy and tongue-tied to voice any of them. The first girl saved him from having to make any conversation.

"If you are hungry, Dar'ian, and I think you must be, since the rest of your team ate like famished wolves when *hertasi* brought them food, there will be more provender over yonder, in the building nearest us." She pointed with her chin at the group of buildings. "There always is; we often must keep irregular hours, so the *hertasi* keep foods out that do not readily spoil or suffer growing cold or warm."

"Thank you," he said shyly, relieved that he would not have to ask what he should do about the hunger-beast awakening in his belly—but she was not quite finished.

"You will also find sleeping places there for those who are not used to *ekele* or who have not built one of their own," she continued. "Those are our guest houses. Simply look until you find one that no one has taken, and make it yours. The *heritasi* will bring your things there."

Grateful that he would not have to interrupt Snowfire and act like a very little brother indeed, he blushed, and thanked her again.

She giggled, as did the other girl. It was the Kaled'a'in who spoke next, poking her friend with her elbow.

"Snowfire's messages home about the barbarians and his

new Wingbrother were so fulsome and interesting that Summerdance here wanted to meet you as soon as you all returned," said the Kaled'a'in wickedly. "So she thought she could manage to *casually* be your guide to the Vale!"

That was too much for Summerdance, who whirled, seized her friend's head in both hands, and shoved her under the water. Her friend came up spluttering, but mostly with laughter.

Summerdance turned to Darian with a flushed face, and he thought quickly, hoping to find a way to salvage the situation. Simple gratitude and politeness seemed the most effective and direct approach.

"That was very kind of you, to think of how a stranger might be so confused here, Summerdance," he told her. "Especially as I am certain you have many tasks of your own to tend to, and it could be irritating to find yourself saddled with an idiot!"

"Oh, but I already am," Summerdance replied sweetly, staring pointedly at her friend, "And in contrast to poor, defective Nightbird here, why, even the most *imbecilic* stra—"

She didn't get to finish the statement, for Nightbird returned the favor by dunking her.

As Summerdance came up gasping for air, the situation might have escalated, had not a silver-haired elder called out lazily, "Enough, my children. You know the rules—take your romping to the swimming pools and the waterfall. If you wish to remain here, save your revenge for later."

That quelled both of them for the moment, though their merry eyes boded mischief to come. Summerdance managed to conquer her blushes, and Darian politely pretended that she had never been embarrassed. "So those buildings there are for guests?" he asked. "I had the impression that Tayledras didn't particularly encourage 'guests,' yet you have many of those buildings."

"Well, we've kept to ourselves, but times do change, you know, and we are not going to lag behind them," Summerdance replied as she pulled her soaked hair out of her eyes and began braiding it back, with Nightbird's help.

"The truth of it is that we Kaled'a'in descended on them six years ago, and they *had* to build us guest houses," Nightbird added. "Since then, most of us have either made our own dwellings or moved in with congenial Tayledras, so the guest quarters are open again." She tied the braid she was working on with a bit of cord. "There! Reasonably tidy."

"And the rest of the truth is that now we have no need to discourage visitors, so when there are those brave enough to dare the fearsome Hawkbrothers in their lair—" Summerdance bared her teeth in a mock-snarl and crooked both hands into claws, "—we reward them by giving them a decent bed."

"It's only fair," Nightbird finished, getting in the last word.

Darian looked from one girl to the other and back again. "Are you *sure* you aren't sisters?" he finally said. "You certainly sound like it."

Both girls dissolved in laughter, which spread to the half of the occupants of the pool who'd chanced to overhear the remark.

"So we have been telling them since Nightbird arrived, youngling," the elder said, still chuckling. "I'd be wary of them if I were you. Where these two tread, trouble follows."

"Us?" Nightbird cried indignantly.

"Never," Summerdance declared. "We're harmless."

"Innocent."

"Absolutely."

The elder rolled his eyes, but said only, in the driest voice imaginable, "Indeed."

Summerdance looked stricken. "But, Father—!"

"Save it for one who did not see you born, when you came into the world with mischief grasped in both hands," the elder interrupted, closing his eyes and leaning back into the embrace of the hot water. "Now let a poor old man soak his bones in peace."

Nightbird snatched at a towel, and stood up. "Come on, friends, no one appreciates us here. Let's just get dressed and show Dar'ian around a little!"

Summerdance was not at all reluctant, so Darian found himself shortly clothed in the loose-fitting, cool garments that the Hawkbrothers favored for lounging, with each arm being held by an extremely attractive young lady as he was steered toward the guest houses.

"Have you actually got weather in the Vale?" he asked curiously, seeing that the strangely built houses had proper roofs under all their foliage.

"Controlled weather," Summerdance said proudly. "Though before we had enough power back to put the Veil back up, we had regular weather in here for a while. All we really do is keep things warm; if it rains out there, it rains in here—if it *snows* out there, it rains in here."

"Why keep rain out?" Nightbird continued from the other side. "The plants still need it, and besides, most of us like rain, as long as it's warm."

"And in the summer, we never let it get *too* warm in here," Summerdance added. "No droughts either. Though we try not to let any droughts happen outside—with trees the size of the ones in the Pelagirs, an uncontrolled forest fire would not bear thinking about. We arrange for controlled fires of course, to keep the forest healthy, but the forest has to be well-watered before we dare do that. That's why, when we were doing without, we gave up the Veil so that we could keep doing weather-magic."

Darian nodded, with a shiver. He and the team had helped to fight a forest fire, the first he'd ever seen, and Summerdance was right. A forest fire loose among the great trees of the Pelagirs would be nothing short of a holocaust.

There were no doors on these buildings, only a living screen of leafy vine, which Summerdance parted so they could all walk inside the first building of the group. The walls were half-structure, half artwork; windows of colored glass gave way to carved panels of wood which in turn gave place to living walls of braided tree trunks and vines, all of it lit by lanterns rather than mage-lights. There, as promised, was a table spread with simple foodstuffs: breads, fruit, cheeses. They all helped themselves, and poured drinks from covered pitchers of cool juices, then took their loot to a grouping of several fat cushions on the floor. There were proper chairs and tables, more groupings of cushions, and even a couch or two, but the girls clearly preferred to sprawl on cushions.

In between mouthfuls they told him about the Vale, saving him from having to make any conversation at all. He made interested sounds from time to time, but otherwise kept his mouth full and closed. He heard more than he could store away in his memory about the Vale itself, who was partnering with whom, who was quarreling with whom, who had designs on whom, what projects were going, stalled, stupid, or planned—in short, it sounded exactly like a village, with all the village gossip. Only with much better scenery and clothing!

Even the strangest people have familiar habits, he thought wryly, and let them chatter on until he was comfortably full.

Then he sat up a little straighter and began to insert some questions of his own.

"Where did the *dyheli* go?" he asked first, for he hadn't seen a single one since they'd all disappeared with the massed herds. "The all vanished together when we got here."

"They have their own big meadow at the far end of the Vale, farthest from the entrance," Summerdance told him. "I've got my *ekele* in a tree on the edge of the meadow."

"And Kelvren? Where's he?"

"With the rest of the gryphons, in the cliffs above the Vale; that's where *I* live." That was Nightbird, of course—and suddenly something clicked in Darian's mind.

"You're Nightwind's sister!" he exclaimed. "The *trondi'irn* apprentice—*that's* why you got letters from Snowfire!"

For some reason that revelation seemed excruciatingly funny to both girls, as they burst into laughter again. "I *told* you he'd figure it out all by himself!" Nightbird chortled.

"Well, I never said I doubted you—" Summerdance retorted.

Darian turned to her, and stared at her in thought for a moment. "You can't be Snowfire's sister, because he's an only child. Are you a cousin?"

She mimed shooting an arrow. "Dead in the black! Oh, it is so *nice* to know that Snowfire wasn't exaggerating how smart you were! Not bad, not bad at deduction at all!"

"Not that most people in the Vale aren't related in some way or other," Nightbird pointed out. "But they're *very* near cousins; Dawnmist's brother and Heartwood's sister are her mother and father, so she's what we call a double-cousin. I hope that's not too confusing."

"Not at all, remember, I come from a little village, and

practically everyone there is related to everyone else in some way," Darian smiled. "I think I can keep it all straight."

Now it was *their* turn to ask about Errold's Grove, and his tiny, prosaic little village was at least moderately interesting for them—but what they really enjoyed was hearing about Valdemar in general. Some things he had to answer truthfully with the preface of "I've never seen this myself, but I've been told that—" They seemed utterly amazed that people could live without any magic at all for hundreds of years, and were just as fascinated to hear what had taken the place of that magic.

"I feel sorry for people who have to live without weather control," Summerdance sighed, as he described a four-day blizzard he and the team had endured. "Even though we had it, for a while we had to save the energy for things that were really important, and it was horrible. It was worse being in the Vale without weather protection! I don't *ever* want to see snow on my *ekele* steps again!"

"I know how you feel," Nightbird agreed. "I thought I would never get warm, the whole winter."

"People are used to it," he pointed out. "Not having seasons would seem strange to them. And there's some enjoyment in it—Errold's Grove used to have a Winter Faire with all sorts of special snow and ice games and sports, and I met some people who really love the snow. They'd be horrified if they had to do without it."

"There's something to be said for a good, rousing thunderstorm," Nightbird agreed. "Especially when you're snug inside."

"Maybe—" Summerdance sounded doubtful. "I still draw the line at snow, though."

Darian yawned, covering his mouth hastily with his hand, but Summerdance was instantly all contrition.

"Oh, bother, here we've kept you up nattering at you, and you're probably perishing to get some sleep!" she exclaimed. "Look, just what kind of quarters do you like anyway?"

"Dark," he said promptly. "No hammocks. I still haven't gotten used to sleeping in anything that moves. But mostly as dark as possible; one thing I *don't* suffer from is fear of being shut in."

Summerdance glanced at Nightbird, who nodded. "I think I know just the place," she said, "And no one's taken it since the Kaled'a'in *hertasi* all dug their own burrows. Follow me."

He did; she led him through the building complex—they were all linked together, apparently—to a long, low-ceilinged structure made up entirely of cozy, rounded sets of rooms. There wasn't a straight line to be seen, and as Nightbird had promised, none of them showed any signs of occupation.

"These give most Hawkbrothers the shivers," Nightbird told him, as Summerdance lingered just outside the complex. "Doesn't bother me. White Gryphon is full of lairs and dens like this, and the *hertasi* and *kyree* prefer them. This place is actually dug right under the hill, so it'll be quiet enough."

"It's not what I'd choose to live in permanently, but right now . . . this is perfect," Darian told her with satisfaction. "I could sleep for a week in here." Again, a huge yawn caught him quite off-guard. "Excuse me! And from the way I feel, I probably *will* sleep for a week! Do you know, they got us up and in the saddle way before dawn, and we didn't stop even to eat. I've done harder riding on this trip, but nothing that was longer."

"Better not sleep for a week, though, or you'll miss the celebration," Nightbird warned him, and then waved her hand in a shooing motion at him. "Go pick out a set of rooms, then, and I'll tell the *hertasi* where you are. Rest well, Dar'ian."

"And to you, and thanks." He raised his voice a little so it would carry to the doorway. "Thank you, Summerdance! I hope I'll see you both tomorrow!"

She laughed, and so did Nightbird. It seemed to be a common response for them. "Just try to avoid us!" Summerdance replied, and the two of them sauntered away, leaving him alone in the building.

He picked a single room at the back of the complex; it was simply furnished. There was a low bed with clean, folded bedding waiting on it, a single lantern on the floor beside the bed, and nothing else. However, the room did have a heavy curtain he could drop down across the entrance to shut out the light. There wasn't much to shut out, just the two lanterns illuminating the "corridor" connecting all the rooms.

He took one of the dry splinters beside the lantern and got a flame from the lantern nearest "his" room, then lit his own lantern so that he could see to make up his bed. By the time he'd smoothed down the last of the covers, his baggage had appeared on the floor behind him. *Hertasi*, of course; by now he was used to the way they would make things "appear" and "disappear" in complete silence, including themselves. Those abilities had proved useful in more dangerous contexts, too; *hertasi* made wicked strike-and-run fighters, for all their small size. The packs looked shrunken; he had no doubt that they'd extracted his dirty laundry, and that by the time he woke up tomorrow, his clothing would be waiting just outside the curtain, cleaned and mended.

Havens, they'll probably have put together an entire new wardrobe for me by then, he thought, climbing into bed and stifling another yawn. *Ayshen made more than a few remarks about that during our mission. What incredible creatures they are!*

Then he blew out the lantern, closed his eyes, and never felt his head touch the pillow.

He woke slowly, and at his own pace—which was a bit more leisurely than he'd been able to manage when he was with the team. He heard a second creature breathing in the room with him, and by the faint scent of raptor-musk knew that Kuari had found him after his bondbird's own homecoming. Mindtouch told him that Kuari was deeply asleep and probably would not wake for another few candlemarks.

Which is hardly surprising, considering how hard he worked yesterday. It wasn't the first time that Kuari had figured out where he was by Mindtouch, then made his way to his bond-mate, walking if he had to.

Kuari definitely deserved his rest, and Darian had no intention of disturbing it.

What was it that the girls said about not sleeping a week? That I'd miss the celebration? He chuckled softly, as he had a pretty good notion just what that celebration was going to be about. Not the homecoming; any "celebrations" for that reason would be between and among families and friends. Although Tayledras enjoyed a good festival as much as anyone, successful completion of what was essentially a fairly simple job by Hawkbrother standards would not warrant a Vale-wide party.

But he certainly knew what *did*.

Starfall warned them, but they wouldn't believe him.

Nightwind and Snowfire had given in to the inevitable two years ago and become formally mated, much to Kelvren's delight—deciding that they would much rather have a small, intimate ceremony with the closely bonded team. Starfall, however, had warned them both that neither Snowfire's parents nor Nightwind's Kaled'a'in kin were going to be cheated of "their" celebration. He had told them that it would probably signal an excuse to turn out the entire Vale and they had scoffed at the very idea, but it sounded as if Starfall was right.

I bet the Elders even make the two of them pledge all over again! Well, maybe this time Snowfire wouldn't be so nervous about the whole thing. He'd kept fretting that Nightwind would change her mind at the last moment. After being pledged for two years, by *now* he ought to be sure of her!

Darian stretched, and consulted his stomach, which informed him that getting breakfast wasn't going to be an emergency. And for once, he wasn't waking up with a kink in his neck or a rock imprint in the middle of his back. *I think I am really going to enjoy living in a Vale for a while!*

He got up quietly, pulling back the curtain just enough so that he could see to dress. And there, next to the curtain, were two evenly stacked piles of clothing; one of his old things, neatly mended, and another of entirely new garments, such as he would never have dared wear in Errold's Grove. These were genuine Tayledras garments, not the scout clothing in relatively drab colors that they'd all worn in Vademar so as not to startle the natives or betray themselves to the monsters they were hunting.

Darian loved bright colors, and always had. Given a choice, he'd have dressed as gaudily as any mountebank, so he was absolutely delighted to see the second pile of clothing waiting for him. Without hesitation he chose a pair of loose breeches in a dark blue silk, a shirt in a lighter blue, a sash woven in blue and silver-gray, and a knee-length suede vest in a shade between that of the breeches and that of the shirt. Soft, low boots of black deerskin took the place of his riding boots, and he stepped out of the guest rooms and into what he now thought of as the Great Room feeling quite the Hawkbrother dandy.

There was no one there at the moment, so he took a little food with him and went in search of Starfall or Snowfire, munching as he walked. He soon realized, however, that his dress was quite conservative compared with *some* of his Tayledras kin. For one thing, he didn't have a single bit of jewelry or so much as one feather braided into his hair—and for another, there wasn't even a thin edging of embroidery to his shirt and vest, much less the overall patterns of embroideries some of them sported.

On the other hand, maybe he wasn't quite ready for all that finery—

Well, maybe just one or two feathers and a bit of trim.

There were two kinds of *hertasi* living in the Vale, as he well knew; the Tayledras, who were mostly shy and invisible, and the Kaled'a'in, who were mostly very visible and quite outgoing. When he finally spotted one of the latter—one not in the middle of some other task, for interrupting it would have been very rude—he asked it where Starfall and Snowfire might be found. In that amazing communication all *hertasi* shared, as if they didn't merely have Mindspeech but actually shared a single mind, it told him after a moment of contemplation that Snowfire was engaged in private business, but Starfall was available, and where to find him.

"Many thanks," he told it, as it looked up its long snout at him, its big eyes much graver than Ayshen's ever were. "And please thank the others for their care of my baggage and wardrobe last night. I really didn't have anything suitable for the Vale."

Now the little lizard-creature's eyes took on a sparkle of merriment. "The things we brought will do for *now*," it said, deprecatingly, "but when we come to know you, we will have something truly suitable for you later."

Then it trotted off; Darian knew better than to try to tell it that there was no need to go to any more trouble, because it wouldn't listen. *Hertasi* were like adolescent girls when it came to clothing, but with largely better taste and much better execution. Nothing made them happier than to dress humans up, as if their charges were so many oversized dolls. Their nimble fingers fairly flew through embroidery, and what was most remarkable of all, they never had to trace a pattern on the cloth beforehand. They replicated their designs or the patterns that others gave them as perfectly as the original.

Perhaps giant dolls are what we are to them in a way, he thought with amusement. *And dressing us up is their hobby. I have the feeling that I'm going to be turned into a Tayledras peacock whether I'm ready for it or not, especially if there's a celebration coming.*

He followed the *hertasi's* instructions with care, though it was all too easy to be distracted here. Every turn in the path brought something new: a huge tree trunk with a spiraling stair; boughs loaded with *ekele*; a tiny, private pool; a miniature water-garden complete with waterfall, lilies, and a colorful fish or two; a sculpture in stone or wood; a living sculpture in plants and flowers. It was all wonderful, and every new sight brought with it the wish that Justyn could have been there to share it with him.

At last he reached his goal—Starfall's *ekele*, which was not in one of the huge trees that supported several in its branches, but was situated in a tree of more modest proportions and had only Starfall's dwelling in it. The base of the tree sheltered a garden planted entirely in flowers of the most subtle and delicate shades of white and the palest of pastels, with a stream and a cascade trickling through it. Starfall himself sat on a low stone bench, enjoying what was either a late breakfast or an early lunch, his falcon in the air above him, playing a game of "tag" with a smaller bird.

This was a game that Darian had seen before, especially between two very agile, swift flyers. Each bird had a streamer of paper attached to one bracelet; the object was to keep your opponent from snatching pieces of it. The bird that lost every bit of its streamer first was the one who lost the game.

Starfall waved Darian over as soon as he emerged from the cover around the path. Darian walked across a lawn of grass as plush as a carpet and as thick, and joined him as Starfall's bird ripped off a bit of his opponent's streamer with an outstretched talon.

"I won't ask you what you think of our home; your eyes said it all last night," Starfall said, offering Darian a plate of small, savory meat pies. Darian politely took one, but only nibbled at it. "I have got a question for you, though; do you want a few days to settle in, or do you want to get to work right away? You have a great deal to learn in the way of magic, and now that we are in the Vale, it will be much easier to teach you."

"I'd like a few days first, sir," Darian replied. "Though if I'm going to have more teachers than just you, I'd like to meet them informally and talk with them a little before we start. I wouldn't—" he hesitated, choosing his words with care. "I wouldn't want to have anyone teaching me who didn't approve of my being here."

"Nor any conflicts with personality; that can be disastrous in the teaching of magic." Starfall nodded. "I think that can be arranged without too much difficulty. I will not be your primary teacher; I have taught you all that I can. You'll have three temporary teachers, and I can certainly arrange for you to meet with them first. Eventually, though, you are going to need a whole new *kind* of teacher to match your talents, and I am afraid that you are not going to have much choice on that score. You need to learn from a Healing Adept, and there are not very many of those available to teach you. Healing Adepts, when teaching in their own path, never take on more than one student at a time, and we will have to find one who has not got a student at the moment."

Darian's heart sank a little at that, but he resolved that he *would* manage to get along with whomever Starfall found for him, for it would be poor repayment for all that the Tayledras had done for him to quarrel with the teacher they assigned him.

"I actually have someone in mind," Starfall went on, watching Darian closely. "And I think this might be the best possible combination of student and teacher if he's free—but I won't hear from him for a while."

"In that case," Darian said bravely, "I hope that he is free. I trust your judgment."

In the meantime, his mind buzzed with questions. Just what was a Healing Adept? Was *he* going to be an Adept when he was finished with his learning? How hard was it to learn? Who was this person that Starfall spoke of with such caution? Wasn't he in k'Vala Vale?

"In the meantime," Starfall went on, "we will continue your lessons as best we can. One thing that *you* can do, even while you are settling in, is simply to observe. One day soon—certainly before the year is out—you will be returning to *your* new Vale near your old village; what you do with it in the beginning will set the character of the place for all time. You should begin thinking now and planning now, even though many of your plans will not come to fruition in your lifetime."

Darian nodded, for he had already had some thoughts along those lines. "Yes, sir," he answered. "Is there anything else I should do?"

"Only that you should get to know the folk about you— and if you see a way to make yourself useful—" Starfall stopped, and smiled. "Well, I know you, and I know that I needn't tell you *that*. Enjoy a bit of a holiday; I think we will resume your studies after the celebration, for if you are going to take a break before you begin, there is going to be no point in starting anything before then."

Since those words were clearly a dismissal, Darian thanked him, and left him alone again.

But from the twinkle in Starfall's eyes when he mentioned the "celebration," it was obvious that Darian's guess was right.

And just wait until Nightwind and Snowfire find out!

k'Vala Vale

Four

How can a ceremony be so solemn and so unrestrained at the same time? Darian wondered, though he made very certain that his thought was tightly under shield. It wouldn't do for anyone to "hear" him; especially not now.

He'd been standing here for what seemed like half the day, though it couldn't have been even half a candlemark. As Snowfire's nearest junior male relative, he had found himself drafted for what he could only think of as a High Temple Ceremony, with every bit of ornamentation and trimming a notoriously ornamental people could fabricate for the occasion. He was right up in the center of the circular raised platform that had been erected yesterday in the *dyheli* meadow, that being the only cleared place big enough to hold everyone. He wasn't alone, of course; he was one of the "wedding party" along with Snowfire and Nightwind, three k'Vala Elders, Nightbird, and six independent witnesses unrelated to either of the two being joined.

Now, given the length and seriousness of the ceremony, and the importance everyone attached to it, the logical assumption would be that both the participants and the assembled Clans watching it would be as sober as presiding judges and solemn as a Herald in full formal array.

Wrong.

Even though the audience was quiet, so quiet Darian heard the occasional cough or shuffling of feet, they were all grinning from ear to ear, and it was obvious that they were barely repressing their exuberance long enough for the ceremony to conclude. Everyone seemed to consider the whole thing to be a grand joke at the expense of the long-suffering mated pair, and the best reason ever created for a no-effort-spared, Vale-wide festival.

The long-suffering aforementioned pair were not told what was in the offing until well after the preparations were complete, and it was obvious that the thing *would* take place even if the two main participants had to be carried to the Pledging Circle, bound hand and foot and gagged. There had, in fact, been a suggestion that holding the ceremony under such conditions would be rather amusing, though Snowfire leveled a glare at the person who'd made that suggestion that was so intense he was probably still putting balm on his burns.

One way or another, it was clear that Snowfire and Night-wind were not going to escape k'Vala's plans for them. So they agreed to go through with it all, with acute embarrassment, but what Darian considered to be astounding good grace.

The wedding garments alone must have taken months to complete; if the *hertasi* enjoyed dressing up their human charges as if they were big dolls, this time they had dressed their subjects up as if they were a pair of sacred images!

Take Nightwind; part of her hair had been piled up on the top of her head and secured with beaded and bejeweled combs and skewers, while the rest was in braids entwined with more beads, tiny crystals, silver charms and silver chains. At the moment there was only a single feather in her hair—one of Kel's, set in a silver-and-crystal clasp. Her robes, sky-blue and embroidered with silver gryphons (both realistic and representations of her badge), had a train so long it needed its own attendant to manage it, and sleeves that trailed along the ground nearly as far as the train. She probably wouldn't have been able to move if Nightbird hadn't been there to help carry and arrange the train. Around her neck were two necklaces. The first, a slender silver chain that encircled her neck so that its pendant lay in the hollow of her throat, was a simple one and the twin to one that Darian wore. The pendant was a hawk-talon, mounted in silver and accented with a blue moonstone. The second was a huge silver pectoral collar of thin flat strands twisted and twined about each other in a way that had made Darian dizzy when he'd tried to trace their routes earlier; her badge as a Silver Gryphon nestled into the front as if the collar had been made to accept it— which, obviously, it had. Her final ornament was a belt that fitted about her hips and hung to the ground in front, made of more flat silver strands which matched the pectoral collar.

Nor did she outshine Snowfire. *His* robes, though lacking the overlong train, were otherwise similar. Also in sky-blue and silver, his featured owls embroidered on them, and a silver-ornamented sleeve-glove that extended to his shoulder. He wore a pectoral and belt no less magnificent than Nightwind's, but differing from hers in that his featured enormous blue moonstones cut to resemble the moon in her several phases instead of Silver Gryphon badges. Both of them wore blue-dyed deerskin boots with silver trimmings—not that anyone could actually *see* them under all that finery.

To Nightwind's left stood her sister Nightbird and Kelvren; to Snowfire's right stood Darian and, on a single enormous stand, Hweel, Huur, and Kuari, side by side. Had their bond-birds been smaller, both Darian and Snowfire would have been carrying them, but the weight of the eagle-owls rendered that impractical.

Nightbird wore a scaled-down version of her sister's robes; with no train, sleeves that reached only down to the ground instead of trailing out behind her, embroidery only on the hems of the skirt and sleeves, and an embroidered belt instead of a silver one. Her jewelry was limited to her Silver Gryphon badge at her throat and a couple of silver hair sticks with pendants of blue moonstones. Darian, however, wore something entirely different from Snowfire's outfit, although it was in the wedding colors of silver and blue.

Instead of a long, floor-length robe with hanging sleeves, he had on a blue silk shirt with a silver-embroidered placket, long sleeves gathered into silver-embroidered cuffs, and a band of silver embroidery at the hem of the shirt. Like Snowfire's robes, the embroidery on his shirt was of owls. The long shirt was held in at the waist, like a gathered tunic, with a silver belt worked with more owls. Beneath the shirt he wore absolutely plain blue silk breeches and boots similar to Snow-fire's, and over the entire outfit, he wore a blue, floor-length silk-velvet vest.

It was the vest that had touched and pleased him and brought a lump to his throat when he first saw it, for the *her-tasi* had duplicated in silver the embroidery that his mother had done on that cherished but long-outgrown leather vest she had made for him.

Darian carried Snowfire's weapons, his bow and quiver, climbing stick, and short sword and daggers. Nightbird carried Nightwind's. This was supposed to show that both were warriors in their own right, and expected to defend each other on an equal basis. A rather nice touch, Darian thought, especially since there were no other weapons anywhere in sight—other than the occasional belt-dagger. Warrior to warrior, man to woman, mage to Healer, it was a good pairing.

The six witnesses were arranged behind all of them in a half-circle; consciously or unconsciously, they had each dressed in a different rainbow color and had arranged themselves in rainbow order—purple, red, orange, yellow, green, blue. The three Elders, one woman and two men, all with silver-white hair, all wore green with gold embroidery—one with a motif of suntail hawks, one with cooperihawks, and the third with peregrine falcons. None of the Elders or witnesses was closely related to either Snowfire or Nightwind; this was according to custom of long standing.

The audience—as much as Darian had been able to see of it—had turned out as splendidly arrayed as the witnesses and the Elders. It wasn't all humans either, for there were plenty of *hertasi* in embroidered vests and sashes or curiously cut robes, *dyheli* bedecked with flower wreaths and ribbons, and gryphons in jeweled harnesses. There were *kyree* in attendance as well, but they flatly refused to bedeck themselves in anything, and amid the riot of color their gray fur left them blending with the shadows.

The ceremony began with the leftmost of the three Elders speaking first.

"Here stands before us this day, Nightwind k'Leshya, warrior, *trondi'irn* of the Silver Gryphons, Healer among the Kaled'a'in," Elder Leafspear declaimed. "Here stands before us Snowfire k'Vala, warrior and mage, coleader of the first expedition into Valdemar, well known to all of us. These two wish to join together in sight of our clans, to be as a living bridge between k'Leshya and k'Vala. If there be any here who object to this joining, give tongue that we may hear and consider what you have to say."

He waited a moment, but of course there was no objection—though Kel looked around so fiercely that anyone who *might* have considered doing so would instantly have reconsidered the idea as a very bad one. Perhaps that was the idea behind having such firm friends stand on the platform with you. . . .

"For this joining, Nightwind k'Leshya pledges to remain here, far from her birth-home, to bring her skills to k'Vala. For this joining, Snowfire k'Vala pledges to give her home, hearth, and hand, that she never feel the loss of her birth-home and all she has left behind. For this joining, the Elders of k'Vala and k'Leshya have sworn to honor these pledges in their stead, should ill luck befall either."

He paused again for effect, then continued when virtually everyone nodded in agreement.

"The Vale is more than this place and its Heartstone; if the Heartstone were no more, if we sought another home, where *we* were would still be k'Vala. There is no k'Vala without the people; there is no Clan without all of us. Our strength is in our bonds to one another, and to make another bond strengthens us all. To make a bond between two so near in heart, yet so different in origin, makes both our clans stronger."

When he was done, the rightmost Elder, Rainlance, picked up as smoothly as if they were one person and not three.

"This bond, this joining, is not meant to be a fetter. A joining is a partnership, not two people becoming one," the second Elder said, though not as sternly as Starfall had said it the first time they took their vows. "Two minds cannot fuse, two souls cannot merge, two hearts cannot keep to the same time. If two are foolish enough to try this, one must overwhelm the other, and that is no love, nor is it compassion, nor responsibility. You are two who choose to walk the same path, to bridge the differences between you with love. You must remember and respect those differences and learn to understand them, for they are part of what made you come to love in the first place. Love is patient, love is willing to compromise—love is willing to admit it is wrong. There will be hard times; you must face them as bound warriors do, side by side, not using the weapon of your knowledge to tear at each other. There will be sadness as well as joy, and you must support one another through the grief and sorrow. There will be pain—but pain shared is pain halved, as joy shared is joy doubled, and you each must sacrifice your own comfort to share the pain of the other. And yet, you must do all this and manage to keep each other from wrong actions, for a joining means that you also pledge to help one another at all times. You must lead each other by example. Guide and be willing to be guided. Being joined does not mean that you accept what is truly wrong; being joined means that you must strive that you both remain in the light and the right. You must not pledge yourselves thinking that you can change each other. That is rankest folly, and disrespectful, for no one has the right to change another. You must not pledge yourselves thinking that there will be no strife between you. That is fantasy, for you are two and not one, and there will inevitably come conflict, that it will be up to you to resolve. You must not pledge yourselves thinking that all will be well from this moment on. That is a dream, and dreamers must eventually wake. You must come to this joining fully ready, fully committed, and fully respectful of each other."

Now the third Elder, Silverswan, took up the thread of ceremony—and a silken cord of silver and blue. Nightwind extended her right hand, and Snowfire his left, and the Elder bound them together with the cord.

"Now you will no longer fear the storm," the Elder said, in ringing tones, "for you find shelter in each other. Now the winter cannot harm you, for you warm each other with love. Now when strength fails, you will be the wind to each other's wings. Now the darkness holds no danger, for you will be the light to each other's path. Now you will defy despair, for you will bring hope to each other's heart. Now there will be no more loneliness, for there will always be a hand reaching out to aid you when all seems darkest. Where there were two paths, there is now one. May your days together be long upon the earth, and each day blessed with joy in each other."

With their hands still bound together, Snowfire carefully took a silver hair clasp he had been holding in his right hand, one with two feathers hanging from it—one of Hweel's and one of Huur's—and clasped it onto the elaborate construction that was Nightwind's hair. At the same time, she fastened a similar clasp with one of Kel's smaller feathers into his hair with her left hand. *That* had been a rather clever touch; Nightwind had no bondbird, of course, but everyone agreed that her bond with Kel certainly was of the same order.

Then, the ceremony finally over, they turned to face the crowd and as the witnesses parted so that the audience could see them clearly, raised their bound hands above their heads.

The cheer that erupted literally shook leaves and blossoms out of the trees, showering them both with fragrant petals. More flowers flew at them from the audience and dropped onto their heads from the talons of bondbirds, who seemed to take a great deal of pleasure out of picking a target and hitting it. Flowers were everywhere, the air so thick with them that it looked like a blizzard. Nightwind and Snowfire were exempt from the pelting, but Darian had to put up a hand to fend off all the blossoms intended for his head. Beneath the storm of flowers, the pair paused long enough for a rather heated kiss—a sure sign that though they'd been bonded for two years, they hadn't become bored with each other!

No one could have possibly enjoyed a party in those cumbersome ceremonial outfits; however, the Tayledras had long since solved that problem. The six witnesses stepped forward and removed the cord holding the pair's hands together, cutting it into six pieces and each taking one as a physical token that the marriage had been made. Should they ever decide to dissolve the joining, the six pieces would have to be retrieved and burned in another ceremony. Once the ceremonial cord was taken off their hands, Nightwind and Snowfire simply touched hidden clasps and stepped out of their outer ceremonial robes, leaving them in the hands of the witnesses, who had been waiting to take them. They didn't have to hold the garments for long; in a moment, previously invisible *hertasi* whisked them away—to be shortly displayed on stands during the celebration for the admiration of anyone who wanted to examine them. From this moment on, the robes became the heirloom works of art they truly were, and would be displayed on the walls of Snowfire's *ekele*. Now looking far more comfortable wearing shirts and breeches just like Darian's, they joined the throng of wellwishers. Meanwhile, more *hertasi* materialized among the crowd with trays of every kind of finger food and drink imaginable. Ayshen appeared at Darian's elbow to take Snowfire's weapons, the three owls flew up into the boughs so that the perch could be removed, and a group of musicians took over the ceremonial platform. Darian was amazed to see that one of the musicians was a creature that could only be a member of the *tervardi*, the bird-people. He'd never seen one until now, for although the *tervardi* were traditional allies of the Tayledras, there was no colony of them near k'Vala Vale.

Darian tried to stare without staring; he could not tell if the *tervardi* was male or female, but if coloration followed the same pattern as in birds, and if the feathers weren't painted as some of the gryphons' were, then it was probably male. Its head, covered with scarlet-and-black feathers with a hint of a crest, had a definite beak rather than lips. The arms were feathered as well—wings, but nonfunctional ones, too abbreviated to be of any use even in gliding. There was a broad, feathered tail, and it wore a type of wrapped garment that left the tail free.

The musical group consisted of the *tervardi*, two *hertasi* playing drums, and four Tayledras who played harp, gittern, flute, and some sort of horn, respectively. It was soon evident, once they struck up a melody, that the *tervardi* was their vocalist.

It was also evident why; no human voice could duplicate the haunting sounds that emerged from the *tervardi*'s fluttering throat as it broke into song.

Havens! Darian thought, listening with his mouth agape. *No wonder they never sing for anyone but Hawkbrothers! They'd be carried off before you could say "soprano"!*

"There was a thriving trade in *tervardi* entertainment-slaves in the distant past, until the survivors managed to gather under the protection of the Vales," a voice said softly behind him. He turned, to find himself gazing into the eyes of a second *tervardi*, this one drably plumaged in black and red-brown. Well, "drab" compared with the first one's black and scarlet; her markings were quite lovely, and if he hadn't already seen the male, he'd have thought her quite striking.

The enormous eyes, so dark a brown as to seem black, gazed back at him with no expression that he could read. "It was easy for the slavers to get what they wished from us," the female (the singer's mate?) continued, her voice a softer version of the singer's though no less melodious. "After all, what male would not sing, when his captors threatened to torture his mate and female chicks if he refused?"

She saw that I'm not born Tayledras, and she's testing me—but what should I say? "What song could sound sweet under those conditions?" he countered, after a moment of blankness. "Whoever would order such an atrocity had no heart. The only songs worth hearing are those sung in happiness and freedom."

He had only *thought* that he could not read the *tervardi*; now he realized that she had the same feather-language as the bondbirds. When she first spoke, her feathers had been slicked down with tension; now she relaxed, the feathers around her beak puffed up, and her face looked rounder and softer than it had a moment ago.

"You speak wisely for one so young," she replied, with trilling chuckle—or a chuckling trill. "What bird fly you?"

"Kuari, fledged of Huur and Hweel," he replied promptly, and held out his arm, with a quick Mindtouch to Kuari himself. He braced himself for the weight as Kuari came in, and ducked his head a little to avoid the impact of those huge, silently powerful wings. The only warning that Kuari was near came when the wind his wingstrokes created made a second storm of all the flower petals scattered about.

His arm strained as Kuari settled gently on the guard, and the great talons closed carefully about the leather. The *tervardi* trilled something at Kuari, who cocked his head to listen, then replied in a series of soft hoots like those made to nestlings. Then he closed his eyes and reached out with his beak to preen a strand of Darian's hair.

The *tervardi* chuckled again and relaxed further, her facial feathers puffed up so that her beak nearly disappeared. She held out a four-taloned hand—three long claws and one short and opposed, exactly like a thumb. Darian took it without fear.

"Rrrillia k'Treva," she said.

"Darian Firkin k'Valdemar k'Vala," he replied.

"A long name," she observed. "You have not changed it in Tayledras fashion?"

He shrugged. "I thought about it, but—Tayledras take new use-names when they change, and I haven't changed, not really. I'm still Darian, with more knowledge and more memories, and a bit more common sense, I hope. I have more skills now, and I've got more friends. But when you come down to it, I'm still myself. I've grown, but I haven't changed."

"Then wear the name you are, Darian Firkin k'Valdemar k'Vala," she told him firmly. Suddenly, with the lightning change of topic he was to come to associate with *tervardi*, asked, "And what think you of Sarrrsee's singing?"

He waved his hands helplessly at that. "Unbelievable!" he finally managed, "Indescribable! I could listen to him all night!"

"Well, with pauses for refreshment, that opportunity you will have, passager," she said, clearly very pleased with his reaction. "Indeed, on so romantic an occasion, we are to sing courting ballads, we two. And that, for outsiders to hear, is rare."

He bowed, hoping that also would please her. "Then I hope you will allow me to thank you in place of my brother Snowfire and his mate, who will be enchanted—and overwhelmed—by the honor you do them."

Now she laughed aloud, a silvery gurgle of sound, and spread her arm pinions. "Oh, you are wasted among the mages, passager," she crowed. "Such delicate speeches mark you as an Elder afore the time!"

She didn't give him a chance to reply to that, turning away instead and taking the platform with the other musicians.

Somehow, the group of musicians managed to go from the first song straight into the next without pause to consult one another—although it was entirely possible they were using

Mindtouch instead. The second melody must have been one of the "courting songs," for first the male sang, then the female, trading melodies and replies until the two strains joined in unexpected harmonies. Darian gathered Kuari to his chest and absently scratched the owl's back and neck—much to Kuari's pleasure—while he listened with his eyes closed to be able to better concentrate on the music.

This song came to a definite end with a moment of silence followed by applause and cheers. Darian opened his eyes again to see the two *tervardi* bowing slightly in acknowledgment—and the female looked directly at him and deliberately winked before turning her attention back to the rest.

The musicians launched into a piece that was purely instrumental, and Darian gave Kuari a boost back into the air so that he could rejoin the other bondbirds in the canopy. Then he wandered off, intending to find something a little more substantial than the tiny savories being handed around by the *hertasi*. He hadn't eaten since he woke up; Ayshen had kicked him out of bed far too early, and he'd been running errands since. He'd really felt too keyed up to eat anyway, but now that everything was safely *over*, and nothing disastrous had occurred, he was *starving*.

And a couple of tiny bites of sausage-stuffed pastry wasn't going to take the edge off his hunger either.

The most logical place to look first was the guest lodge—and going there had the added advantage that he could take off his wedding finery and put on something he wouldn't have to worry about ruining. Once he made his way to the point where the crowd thinned out a little, he made decent progress to the far side of the Vale—although the temptations to stop were many. Besides the group of musicians from k'Treva Vale that included the two *tervardi*, there were other musicians from k'Vala scattered here and there, carefully positioned so that no group's music interfered with the music from another individual or group. Darian passed three individual musicians and two groups on his way to the guest lodges; the groups had set up in spaces big enough to allow for dancing. One group was playing a slow-paced, couples dance, and the second a faster, heavily syncopated group dance.

As he had suspected, the hot pools were in use, though as it was early in the day, they were not heavily crowded. It was a bit of a surprise to see the number of people swimming, though.

That isn't my idea of what you do at a wedding—well, maybe I'm just being provincial.

Wonderful aromas met his nose before he even reached the door of the guest lodges, and the tempting array of food spread out there made him waver in his resolution to change before he ate. Only the fact that his favorite foods were always the messiest to eat made him stick to it, even though the scents seemed to follow him down the corridors and into his room to taunt him.

He changed quickly, retaining only the new silver belt from his wedding costume, and sprinted back down the corridors, tracking the scents with his nose in the air like a hungry hound.

A short time later, blissfully nibbling on a square of pastry wrapped around a filling of finely chopped nuts and honey, he felt ready to join the rest of the Vale. He strolled out into the open and started back toward the *dyheli* meadow.

Darian stopped long enough to listen to one of the solo musicians, then obtained something to drink from a passing *hertasi* and went on to his destination. Arriving just in time for the *tervardi* to begin singing again, he sat himself down near the platform on the soft grass and proceeded to lose himself for some undefined length of time while the music created fantasies in his mind.

When he emerged from the spell that the music cast on him, he found that he had company. Beside him, with her blue eyes still filled with the dreams that *tervardi* singing sent into her mind, was Summerdance.

He had not seen her for the last few days, but that was no great surprise, as they had both been working on the wedding preparations and their errands hadn't overlapped. In addition, she was apprenticed to Steelmind, the specialist in plants who was the caretaker (among other things) of most of the garden spots in the Vale, including the herb garden. As a consequence, she hadn't had any free time over the past three or four days.

He was happy to see her at last, and glad that he had changed into what had been his "best" outfit until he got the one for the wedding. She certainly looked spectacular, gowned in something silken, that flowed over her, a waterfall of luminous fabric in several shades of green. She wore as ornaments a collar of braided gold, silver, and copper wire, with strands of crystal beads and feathers braided into her black hair.

She smiled at him, and nodded her head at the platform. "What do you think?" she asked. "This is the fourth time I've heard this group; they travel among the Vales, and we try to get them to come once every year or so, but this is the first time they've come for a pledging."

He tried to come up with enough superlatives and failed. "It's the kind of singing you hear in dreams and know you can't reproduce when you wake up," he said finally. "There's nothing like it."

"And nothing more beautiful, except when a *tervardi* flock sings in chorus, and I've only heard that once," she agreed. "I had to go to k'Treva for that, but it was worth the journey. I got to see them dance, besides singing. Do you dance, at all, in Valdemar?"

"Every chance we get," he laughed. "But if you're asking if I, personally, dance—I do, and I learned a couple of dances from the team while I was with them, too. Is this an invitation?"

"Well, the group is taking a break, so there isn't anything going on here for a while," she pointed out. "And it's a lot more fun to dance when you have a partner. Round dances are all right for children, but couple dances and group dances are livelier and more interesting."

"That's the truth," he agreed as he stood up, then extended a hand to her to help her to her feet. He took the lead, since he knew where the dancing circles had been set up, and as luck would have it, the first one they came to was just starting a new set as they arrived.

He soon saw how she had gotten her use-name; she was quick, graceful, light on her feet, and evidently untiring. He had no intention of quitting before she was ready, and found himself panting and with a raging thirst by the time the musicians paused for a break themselves. He was half afraid that she'd suggest finding one of the other dancing circles, but she took pity on him. Laughing, she led him to the side of the circle and left him for a moment, only to return with cool drinks for both of them.

He didn't know any of the people they'd been dancing with, but they all knew who he was—not so difficult since he was the *only* outsider in the Clan! With his brown hair and eyes he couldn't be mistaken for anyone else, not when the only variation on blue eyes, golden skin, and black hair among Tayledras or Kaled'a'in was the blue eyes, golden skin, and *white* hair of mages who'd worked with Heartstone and node magic.

Oh, not quite true—some scouts, if they had white hair, dyed it in patterns spring through autumn to camouflage themselves. But none of them had *plain* brown hair.

For the most part, his erstwhile dancing partners were just as winded as he was, and the *hertasi* circulating among them with more of the refreshing mint-flavored drink soon found themselves emptyhanded. Summerdance was the only one who still had breath to talk; she introduced him to the other dancers, but he promptly forgot most of their names. He had just about caught his breath and cooled down when the musicians began again and she drew him back into the circle for another round.

It wasn't until after the third round was complete that she professed herself tired, and by that time his legs were getting wobbly. When she suggested a hot soak, he was only too happy to agree.

But when she led him, not in the direction of the communal pools, but down a tiny, vine-shadowed path that threaded between trees away from the sounds of celebration, he started to wonder if she had something more than a soak in mind.

Steady on, he told himself. *She just might want some privacy rather than the mob.*

But things were certainly promising to be interesting. . . .

She stopped at a place where the path appeared to end, and parted a curtain of flowering vines. On the other side of the vines lay a bubbling pool, one fed, obviously, by the same hot springs that fed the communal pools. Beside the pool on a small stone bench was a thick pile of towels—well, why not?

It wasn't as if they were going to get rained on in the middle of a Vale!

"Here, isn't this better than jostling for a space with everyone else?" she asked, as she slipped unself-consciously out of her dress and into the pool without making so much as a splash. He lost no time in following her example; the water was deliciously hot, and all of his tired muscles melted under its influence.

Ah, there is no comparison with Errold's Grove! he thought blissfully, as he closed his eyes and slumped until his chin touched the surface of the pool. *Here I am, entirely alone with Summerdance, no one will care what we do or don't do—she's of age, I'm of age, that's all there is to it. Back home, if anybody found me with a girl like this, her father would be hunting me down with a pack of male relatives and her mother would be making wedding arrangements.*

He took a peek out of one eye at Summerdance; apparently she wasn't as inexhaustible as she'd been at pains to appear, for she was relaxing in the water with the same expression he'd been wearing. Beads of moisture collected on her forehead, and the hair around her face started to curl in the heat and damp.

"Where are we, exactly?" he asked, having only a vague notion of how far they had gone.

"At the furthest end of the Vale. My *ekele's* up there." She pointed straight up, and he followed her pointing finger with his eyes. Squinting upward through the rising steam, past vines and foliage obscuring everything, he made out a bit of staircase against a trunk, and what might have been a piece of floor. "I got tired of having to tramp forever to get a hot soak—or to have to tramp forever *after* I got a hot soak. When we got a reasonable amount of magic back, and I got to pick something I wanted, I picked this."

"Good choice," he said, closing his eyes and leaning back again.

But not before he'd managed to find a fresh blossom growing within reach.

Now came the moment for internal debate. *So, do I offer her a flower?* In Tayledras terms, especially in a situation like this one, offering Summerdance a flower would express without words not just his admiration for her, but that he wanted to share decidedly more than just her platonic company. *Chased, rather than chaste,* as the saying went. It wasn't that he was debating whether he *wanted* to offer her a flower, he was debating the etiquette of it. This was her pool, beneath her *ekele;* her territory, so to speak. So, did he make the first overture, or would it be polite to wait and see if she did? But what if she was waiting for him to express an interest? What if she would be disappointed and hurt if he didn't make the offer?

Of course, all this might be innocent, simply companionable. But among the Tayledras, being offered a flower didn't imply acceptance, and she could always turn him down.

I'm thinking too much. He reached out and picked the flower without opening his eyes, held it for a moment, then turned toward her. "Ah, Summerdance?"

He opened his eyes as he spoke.

Only to stare at her, seeing that she had just turned and was offering *him* a flower at the same moment.

They stared at each other for a long breath, then broke into helpless laughter, leaning into each other's arms for support.

Then, when their laughter faded, they found other things to share.

Sunset, normally all but imperceptible beneath the huge trees, was spectacular from Summerdance's *ekele* high in the boughs of a tree on the edge of the clearing—and they were both in a position to appreciate and pay attention to the sight by then. Still, neither Darian nor Summerdance was prepared to end the celebration quite so early, so they collected themselves and their belongings and rejoined the dancing just as dusk fell. Special illuminations had been planned for after dark, effects that required magic, and Darian was happy to see that they appeared on schedule. Even though he wasn't in charge of the entertainment, he had something of a proprietary interest in it.

The main event was a display of underwater lighting, with constantly changing colors, beneath the cascades of one of the more elaborate waterfall-arrangements. It had three levels of falling water, with each of the three levels subdivided into additional cascades, all plunging into a small, but deep, pool, frequently used for acrobatic play and roughhousing. No one swam there tonight. Mage-lights glowed behind the falling water from within recesses in the rocks, and one in the bottom of the pool turned the foaming water into a froth of light. The clever mage who'd planned this was at hand to control the changing colors, so that no sequence was ever repeated.

"You know," Summerdance remarked, as they spotted Nightwind and Snowfire among those admiring the cascades, "I think it's just as well that they already got their real pledging over with while all of you were out there—" she waved her hand vaguely in the direction of Valdemar. "If *this* had been their real pledging instead of an excuse for an enormous party, they'd have been missing all of this, or else they'd feel as if they *had* to pretend to enjoy it when all the while they really just wanted to be alone together. As it is now, this is just a celebration that happened to involve them, but it's more like an anniversary party. So they can relax and enjoy it along with everyone else."

He realized at once that she was probably right; once Nightwind and Snowfire had given in to popular demand, they'd really managed to be quite relaxed about the entire occasion, far more relaxed than anyone else was, in fact. "Very perceptive!" he exclaimed. "I wouldn't have thought of that, but I think you're right!"

Summerdance shrugged. "I know my cousin," she pointed out. "Look how utterly calm he's been since they got out of their robes, and how he's relaxed and gone along with the fun! They know their pairing is solid and is going to last. They don't feel as if they have to prove how happy they are together to an audience of well-wishers, and now that the ceremony is over, they know they don't have to be the center of everything anymore."

"If I didn't know better, I'd say it was you who was the *trondi'irn* in training and not Nightbird," he teased, as the lights beneath the waterfall cascades changed slowly from blue to purple, *en masse.* "How did you figure all that out?"

She elbowed him. "Just because I'm apprenticed to Steelmind, that doesn't mean I think like a plant," she chided.

"How do you think he got the use-name of *Steelmind*, hmm? He watches everything and everyone, and doesn't say much, but when he does, it's worth listening to. He's quite good at figuring people out, after all that observation. I'd like to think I've been learning that from him, too."

"I think you can bet on it," he told her seriously, and was rewarded with a sparkling smile. "I also think you've got to be getting hungry by now."

"And you're observant as well, or else you heard my stomach growling; let's see what new goodies have been put out. There's bound to be supper dishes by now."

She dashed off, casting a glance behind to see if he was following, and he responded to the challenge. They raced each other down overgrown, little-used paths to the guest lodges. Summerdance had a distinct advantage because she knew the Vale so well, but he had longer legs, so they burst out of the undergrowth neck-and-neck, and found themselves part of a goodly crowd of equally hungry folk crowding into the entrance to the main hall.

By now Darian's appetite had returned with a vengeance, and the wonderful aromas nearly drove him to distraction. A real meal had been spread out this time, with hot and cold dishes to choose from, instead of just snacks. Darian motioned Summerdance to go in ahead of him, feeling as if he would make a poor showing if he let hunger overcome manners. They took plates made of flat bread from a stack waiting at the side of the table, and heaped them with their choices; at Summerdance's urging, Darian took portions of things he didn't recognize. They stood together for a moment, looking around to see if there was anyone here that they knew, then spotted Nightbird. She sat in the middle of a congenial group of young men and women, most of whom were strangers to him. A few of Nightbird's companions were younger than Darian was, but most were about the same age.

As soon as they'd spotted her, she noticed them, and waved them over. They found a couple of unused cushions and sat down with the rest of the group.

"Everyone, this is Dar'ian," Nightbird said, giving his name the Tayledras pronunciation. "Darian, pay attention," she continued. with a giggle. "I'm only going to introduce people once!"

He paid quite careful attention to their names as Nightbird introduced her friends, and fixed names properly with the faces in his memory.

Meanwhile, he ate, enjoying all the new flavors. It was all quite different, except the thick slices of meat—and even that was spiced in a way he'd never tasted before. Round puffs of pastry proved to be breaded and fried slices of vegetable, a green paste that Summerdance had greeted with enthusiasm was probably from another vegetable of some kind and made a fantastic garnish on just about everything, little red squares were not sweet, as he'd expected, but crisp and peppery. He wished he'd taken more of the flat round bread; it was wonderful when wrapped around the meat.

He spent more time listening than talking; for one thing, it was the first time he'd seen so many of his age in one place. For another, he was interested in what they did, since no one was ever idle in a Vale to his knowledge.

This was where he got some surprises. He had somehow gotten the vague idea that most Hawkbrothers were mages— that Snowfire and the other scouts were the exception. In a few moments, he learned that his perception was backward.

"So what's your next assignment?" Nightbird asked a group of three sitting close together in a way that suggested close friendship rather than an amatory grouping.

"You'll laugh," said one of the two girls. "Mushroom hunting. The morels are coming up now, and the cooks want plenty."

Nightbird didn't laugh, she shrugged. "You can't always be the ones patrolling the border," she pointed out with inescapable logic. "Especially not with seven scout groups in training at the same time. You were just lucky on your first assignment, and got the exciting one. Besides, the cooks aren't the only ones who want morels!"

"Exactly so," agreed an older boy. "As I can tell you from *my* training last year. We spend more time hunting game and finding fungi than we do in patrols—and much, much more time in boring, uneventful patrols than in actually fighting anything dangerous." He laughed. "As Whitehawk says, 'Six weeks of boredom punctuated by half a candlemark of sheer terror.' I think I'll volunteer for the next Valdemar expedition; at least *they* saw some action."

"Wouldn't mushroom hunting be more in the line of *hertasi*?" Darian asked.

"Not really," the boy replied. "The *hertasi* have plenty of work here in the Vale, and we can hunt mushrooms and check up on the territory inside our border at the same time. Despite what they might tell you, they can't do everything!"

Darian discovered from the subsequent conversation that a little less than half of them, male and female both, were scouts or scouts-in-training—a generic job that included hunting and gathering foodstuffs found growing wild in the woods outside the Vale as well as patrolling the boundaries of k'Vala territory. Two were mages—farther along in their studies than *he* was, but since they had begun earlier, and had certainly applied themselves better, that was only to be expected. One was a weaver and worker with textiles, which rather surprised him, as he'd gotten the impression that the *hertasi* did most of the crafting work.

But when he ventured to ask, he found out that the "trades," so to speak, were practiced by as many Tayledras as *hertasi*. "Isn't that dull compared with being a scout?" he asked tentatively.

The weaver laughed. "You heard the others. Now that we've got most of the nasties cleared out, and it's easy enough to discourage poachers, it's scouting that's boring! I love what I do, and my teacher is Silverbird, the weaver who made the wedding robes. How could anybody be bored, learning to weave works of art like that? I even get to spend as much time in the woods outside the Vale as any scout, because I'm also working with Azurehart, the dyer, and we're always looking for new colors."

"It's just as good doing metal work," added another. "The *hertasi* haven't got the strength to make anything large, or anything out of iron or steel. If you want a sword with a proper blade of twelve-folded steel, it has to be one of us who makes it—and who could get tired of that sort of work?"

"The *hertasi* can't blow glass either. It's too dangerous for

them to get that close to the furnaces," said a girl with a profusion of scarlet-and-gold glass beads strung on the hair of
one side of her head. "The glass work *has* to be done by
humans."

The others chimed in with similar praise for their profes-
sions, and he now learned that most of the Hawkbrothers of
k'Vala were actually craftspeople, with only minor abilities at
magic. In this little group alone, there were the weaver and
smith, both in training, as well as Nightbird who trained to
care for the gryphons, Summerdance who was going to be a
plant worker, and the girl glassblower and a young man who
was already a practicing fletcher. A Vale was truly a largely
self-sufficient organism; certainly as self-sufficient as Errold's
Grove had ever been.

After they'd all finished eating, the group somehow stayed
together, and went off to virtually take over one of the dancing circles. At that point, Summerdance found a partner with
as much energy as she, and relinquished Darian's company to
Nightbird. Since Nightbird had not yet heard the *tervardi*
sing, and Darian's lessons had not included the complicated
couple dances the others were performing, he went with her
back to the platform and happily sat through two more ses-
sions of their music.

Finally, though, the long day began to catch up with him,
and he caught himself yawning.

"I'm ready for more dancing," Nightbird declared, when
the music group took another break. She glanced over at him,
caught him in mid-yawn, and giggled. "You look more like
you'd rather be asleep."

Since she'd carefully said "asleep" and not "in bed," he
took the comment at face value and not as another invitation. He rubbed his eyes with the back of his hand and
grinned sheepishly. "Well," he temporized, "I was up at the
break of day, and running from the time my feet hit the
ground."

She laughed. "I'll tell you what; partner me for one dance
set, and then we'll see how you feel."

He nodded agreement and helped her to her feet; they
wound their way across the Vale until, quite by accident,
they came across a third dance circle and joined it. This one,

populated by people of Snowfire's generation, wasn't quite as rowdy as the one that Summerdance had gravitated to, but it was lively enough for Darian.

Once again, these were dances that Darian had not learned, but they were easy enough to follow. This was a cross between a couple dance and a round dance, with each couple performing the moves of the set in turn while the others kept time, clapping. The dancers put Nightbird and Darian at the end of the line, which gave him seven chances to learn the next move before he had to do it. The dances moved briskly, with some pretty acrobatic moves as the dances grew more complicated with each new tune. There was quite a lot of twirling, turning, and lifting one's partner, and Darian found himself running out of energy after a while. So did Nightbird, too, evidently; after that one set of dances, she retired from the field, declaring herself defeated by her own lagging energy. "I'm for a swim," she decided after a moment. "What about you?"

A swim seemed like a good idea; a fine way to cool off after all that dancing. Conveniently enough, the large swimming pond turned out to be just on the other side of the trees and bushes screening the dance circle; Nightbird just led him around the corner, and there it was. There were other people at the swimming area who'd had the same idea, but the place was quiet and only dimly lit with flickering lanterns with colored paper shades, and no one seemed bothered by two more joining them. Single swimmers drifted across the still surface with leisurely, slow strokes, barely making a splash, or floated on their backs, feathering the water with gentle movements of only their hands.

Nightbird slipped out of her gown while he was still letting his eyes adjust to the relative darkness, and she plunged into the water without a backward look. He peeled off his clothing and followed, taking sensuous enjoyment in the silken feeling of the cool water on his hot skin. He concentrated only on making as little sound and turbulence as possible, to preserve the tranquil atmosphere.

Darian crossed the pond a few times, then the last of his energy ran out completely. Spotting a pile of towels and robes at the side of the pond, he climbed out, dried off, and helped himself to a loose, comfortable robe from the piles beside the pool.

Most of the other swimmers were gone, leaving the quiet pond, the soft light, and the sound of music drifting over from the dancing circle. Darian yawned. *I don't want to go to bed yet—but I'd like to find a place to lie down and rest for a little bit without getting in anyone's way.*

It occurred to him that there should be several lounging places here, tents made of insect netting draped over frames with flat cushions inside, just large enough for one or two to rest in after swimming, or for child watchers to sit in while keeping an eye on little ones playing in the pond. After a moment, he found several, tucked into a curve of foliage. They were all empty, and he parted the netting and settled himself down inside one, feeling luxuriously indolent but no longer sleepy—or so he thought.

The next thing he knew, it was quite light outside his shelter, and there were *hertasi* moving about, picking up the odd plate, cup, or pair of breeches left beside the water. He felt entirely rested, so he must have slept soundly and well—so soundly that, whatever had gone on around him, it hadn't disturbed him in the least.

And, as he had expected, Kuari had found him. Apparently baffled by the enshrouding folds of the insect netting, the eagle-owl perched on the frame of the shelter, vaguely visible through the fog of netting.

He found the opening in the net and fought clear of it, shaking the frame just enough to wake Kuari. The bondbird opened one eye halfway, then roused all his feathers with a pleased expression when he saw that it was Darian and he was awake.

:Hunt?: Kuari asked eagerly, his huge golden eyes staring unblinking at Darian. *:Real hunt, not stupid coop birds?:*

:Poor Kuari. It has been a while since we went hunting, hasn't it?: he said with sympathy that was in no small part induced by the fact that he himself felt very good. *:Come on, I'll get changed. You go see if you can get Kel to go along, and we'll go for a real hunt.:*

Kuari hooted with enthusiasm, and shoved off from the frame, which threatened to topple over as he left it. Darian saved it from imminent collapse, then gathered his robe around him, picked up his clothing from where he'd left it, and trotted for his quarters.

When he emerged from the door of the guest lodges, clean and dressed in one of his old sets of scout clothing, with a bow and quiver in his hand and a light pack on his back, Kelvren and Kuari were waiting for him. Kuari was fluffed up and standing on a branch with one foot tucked under his feathers, and Kelvren posed in a beam of sunlight.

The young gryphon had actually grown a bit since Darian had first met him four years ago, adding muscle to his chest and legs. His head had matured as well; definitely aquiline, it no longer had that faintly "unfinished" look that young eagles and adolescent gryphons shared.

Every gleaming, golden-brown feather was neatly in place, from his ear-tufts to the tip of his tail; his talons were freshly honed, and his bright eyes gleamed with sheer delight in living. Obviously, though others might be suffering from a little too much self-indulgence last night, Kel wasn't one of their number.

"Wind to thy wingsss!" Kelvren saluted him genially, his eyes flashing with good humor and eagerness. "And I hope yourrr courrting wass asss ssssuccesssful asss mine!"

Darian laughed; Kelvren was as much a hedonist at heart as any other gryphon, and as frankly uninhibited. "And if it was?" he asked.

"Then neitherrr of usss will have complaintss about ourrr homecoming," Kel replied with a wink. "Kuarri sssaid we hunt; that iss a good thought. Nothing much getss done the day afterrr a celebrrrration, even the *herrrtassi* do not do much but pick up a bit. No one cookss, mealss will be what wassn't consssumed yessterday. Sssince I will make my own kill, I will make my own choice, and it would be good to get sssome frrresssh *wild* meat."

"That's essentially what Kuari said, and I'm all for it." Darian hefted his bow and quiver of arrows by way of confirmation. "Where should we head for?"

"Norrth of the Vale entrance," Kel replied promptly. "I hearrd good rrreporrtss of the hunting in that dirrrection."

"I packed up some of the leftovers from the feast for myself, so we don't have to come back until dark—how do we post word of where we're going?" When he and Kel had gone out hunting together back in Valdemar, that had been the inflexible rule—post where you are going, and be back no later than a candlemark after dark. That way, if something happened to you, people would know that you were overdue, and what direction you'd been heading when you ran into trouble.

"I alrrready did," Kel assured him. "With Firrrelance the chief *trrrrondi'irrrn*, with Peluverrr, the seniorrr grrryphon, and with both theirrr *herrrtasi*. Ssso sssince you have prrrovissionsss, we can go!"

He was obviously itching to be on the wing, because as soon as he had finished speaking, he launched himself up into the sky, sending clouds of dust and debris in all directions. Darian was used to his impatience by now, so he sent Kuari up after him with a nudge of his thoughts, then followed both of them afoot, a little eager and impatient himself.

"Ahhhhhh—" Kelvren spread his wings and legs out in the sun, flattening himself against the soft meadow grass, and started to get the glazed, half-conscious look he always wore when he was *seriously* sunbathing. He looked drunk, or drugged, or stunned, or—

"You look like a gryphon-rug," Darian observed, layering meat, cheese, watercress, and sliced peppers between two rounds of the flatbread he'd first tasted last night. He set out more of the honey-and-nut pastries on a broad leaf, and propped his flask of cool spring water beside them. Kelvren turned his head just enough to give him a disgusted look.

"What a vile notion," the gryphon replied. "Wherrre do you get thossse perrrverrrted ideasss?"

Darian took a hearty mouthful of his meal, and made a point of chewing it thoughtfully before he swallowed it and responded. "Mostly from the fact that you've flattened yourself out until that *is* exactly what you look like. The only other comparisons I could make would be a lot less flattering than that one. The only thing round about you right now is your crop."

Since an entire young wild pig now resided in that crop, it might well bulge. Kelvren had not only been successful, he'd had just enough of a chase to give him some excitement, followed by a fine, clean kill.

Kuari had been just as successful, snaring an unwary tree-hare, and he drowsed on top of a stump in the shade of a small tree on the edge of this clearing.

The meadow itself, formed when one of the enormous Pelagirs trees toppled over and took several of its brethren with it, made a fine place for everyone to rest. Darian was going to come home just as much of a mighty hunter as the others, though he had no wish to eat *his* catch raw. He had four fine young brush-grouse, a delicacy that everyone enjoyed; he intended to present Starfall with one, Snowfire with two, and keep the fourth for himself. There was no reason at all why he couldn't roast it on a spit for dinner tonight; he knew how to cook, and maybe Summerdance might be interested in sharing his meal. She'd probably want some of the handsome feathers, too, so he'd remember to save them.

He'd hung them to bleed them out; he'd field-dress them before he put them in his now-empty pack. Kel and Kuari would probably clean up after him when he did.

That would be later in the afternoon; for now, they would sunbathe and enjoy their holiday, because tomorrow, Darian's education in magic would begin in earnest, and he expected to have few holidays for some time to come.

He finished his meal and washed it down with spring water. Off in the distance, birds sang and a couple of crows yelled at each other; in the meadow, crickets and spring-frogs vied to see who could chirp the better mating calls. Darian lay back in the soft grass and shaded his face with a fallen, leaf-covered branch he'd stuck in the earth at his head.

"So you had a lady-friend last night, did you?" he asked lazily. "Do I know her?"

Kel revived from his trance, pulled in wings and legs, and brought his head up. "Do I know yourrrss?" he replied.

"Probably. Summerdance?"

Kel chuckled. "And yourrr courrting wass ssuccessful." It wasn't a question. He sounded knowing, and Darian raised his own head to look at his friend with suspicion.

"And just what do you know?" he demanded.

Kel examined his right front foot and daintily preened a talon with the tip of his beak. "Oh, jusst that Nightbirrd and Sssummerrdance arrre besst frriendsss and often nearrrr my lairrr. The otherrr day they werre therre, and both sspeaking— hmm—*ssspeculatively* about you. Gryphonsss," he added wickedly, as an afterthought, "have verrry keen hearrring."

"And what did they say?" His own ears burned, but he couldn't help but be interested. *Kel wouldn't be teasing me if it wasn't good.*

Kel's eyelids drooped lazily. "Who am I to rrreveal a lady'sss sssecretsss?" he demanded. "That would be ungentlemanly." As Darian rose, outrage at being led on and impatience warring for supremacy on his face, Kel made haste to add, "I can sssay that they werrre flatterrring, and that Nightbirrd *generrrousssly* sssuggesssted that, sssince herrr sssissssterr might be a little *too* interrresssted in the matching of herrrsssself and you—given that Snowfirrre issss yourrr elderrr brrrotherrrr— well, ssshe conceded the field to Sssummerrrdance, who hasss no such complicationsss with relationsss."

Darian subsided, his ears and neck now so hot that he really didn't want to hear anything more. "We had a good time," he replied lamely. "What about you?"

Kel chuckled again; if there was a way to embarrass a gryphon on the subject of "courting," Darian had yet to find it. "Ah, *my* parrrtnerrr wasss the lovely and lissssome Arrrkeyla. Trrruly a magical crrreaturrre! Ssshe isss of my yearrr in the Sssilverrrs, and told me afterrr that ssshe wissshed to make my homecoming trrruly memorrrable." He sighed, and stretched out his talons, digging them into the grass in blissful happiness. "Sssuch a lady! Bright of eye, ssswift of wing, and sssso ssskilled! We matched each otherrr in the airrr, ssstrrroke for ssstrrroke, rrracing againsst the moon in courrrting flight. Once we werrre alone, out of sssight of the otherrsss, ssshe—"

"Kel, I don't *really* need the details!" Darian interrupted, his embarrassment redoubled, if that was possible. "I'm just glad you had a good time together."

Kel cast an annoyed glance at Darian, and now finally noticed how fierce his friend's blushes were; Kel's annoyance melted away under his amusement. "You could sssay that. You could alssso ssssay that the sssummerrr sssun cassstssss reasssonable light, and be asss accurrrate. I tell you—"

"*Kel!*" he said forcefully. "I *believe* you. You don't have to say anything more!"

Kelvren's gurgling laugh did nothing to ease his embarrassment, but at least the gryphon was appeased enough to drop the subject.

"I hearrd that you arrre expected to take yourrr Vale sssome time afterrr Midsssummerrr," he offered, after Darian's blushes finally cooled a bit.

Darian seized the change of subject gladly. "That's what they've told me," he confirmed. "Of course, it won't really be *my* Vale until I'm a lot older, but everyone seems to take it as written that I'll eventually be the one in charge there. They want a permanent presence in residence before the first snow falls, so I expect they'll be sending a group out there as soon as they think I'm ready." He paused for a moment, then added, "Want to come along? We'll need a good team, but one that's committed to permanent residence."

"I would be affrrrronted if you hadn't asssked me, and I would have been forrrced to find a way to enssurrre you did!" Kel exclaimed. "I am all but cerrrtain that Nightwind and Sssnowfirrre intend to be parrrt of the grrroup. They ssshould have one grrrryphon, at leassst."

"Well, I was wondering if you'd want to leave here so soon," he teased, "After all, when your courting is going so well—"

"And I am harrrrdly rrready to sssettle and nesst build!" Kelvren shot back. "I have no intention of choossssing a mate until asss many ladiesss asss posssssible arrre contending forrr the honorrr. Besssidesss, the new Vale at Errrold'ssss Grrrove is not ssso farrr frrrom herrrre that a lady could not fly in forrr a visit—orrr a gentleman rrrreturrrn the favorrr!"

"Point taken," Darian conceded. He rubbed at an insect bite and wished that the time for departure had actually been set; then he'd know how much time he had here and could make some plans of his own. "I wonder if this new teacher that Starfall wants for me is expected to come with us? For that matter, I wonder if Starfall's been able to get him to agree to *be* my teacher! I haven't heard a word, so far."

"Hmm. I have." There was no mistaking that tone in Kelvren's voice; he was quite ready to tease Darian all over again. He would have to be coaxed for every revelation.

"So what have you heard?" Darian decided to play along; Kel loved to tease and be teased in return.

"I have hearrrd—that the teacherrr in quessstion wasss reluctant at firrrsst, but agrrreed." Kel considered a talon with a thoughtful expression that was entirely feigned.

"Why was he reluctant?" Darian *did* want to know that much; was it because he was essentially an outsider to the Tayledras?

"Becaussse he wissshed a holiday frrrom ssstudentsss. Ssso I hearrrd. Ssstill, Ssstarrfall convinced him." Kel stretched his neck out and laid his head down in the grass. "I gatherrr that Ssstarrfall hasss sssome connection with him. Rrrelativesss, perrrhapsss. Enough to be of influence."

"Have you heard anything else about this teacher?" *Like his name?* Darian added silently. *It would be nice to know his name and clan.*

"That he isss held in high rrregarrrd. I think hisss clan isss k'Trrrreva." Kel rumbled something indecipherable in pure contentment.

"How about his name, O gryphon whose hearing is so keen?" Darian countered. "Surely you managed to overhear that!"

"Rrrr." Kel lifted his head and looked at Darian sheepishly. "I *did*—but musssst confesss I cannot rrrrememberrr it!"

"You forgot his name? On, come on, featherhead, you can do better than that!" Darian cried. "You can't be that forgetful!"

"Well, it wassss in the middle of the celebrrration, and I had otherrr interresssstsss," Kel protested weakly, flattening his ear-tufts in chagrin.

"Oh, so you let a pair of bright eyes and a flirty tail drive everything important to your best friend right out of your memory!" Darian countered, in mock-disgust. "What kind of friend are you anyway?"

"Absssolutely and without apology! I do have my prrriorrritiesss! But I did not forrrget *everrrrything* imporrrtant!"

Kel protested, flattening his ear-tufts down so far they became invisible.

"Only the most important part!" Darian threw up his hands. "Remind me never to ask you to tell a joke, you'll probably forget the point of it."

"You would not underrrssstand ssssophisssticated humorrr," Kel grumbled back.

Darian sighed. That was certainly just his luck—and it wasn't Kel's fault, after all. It wouldn't be all that long before Starfall would tell him the all-important name of his new teacher, and Kel *did* remember that the reason the teacher had been reluctant had nothing to do with Darian.

"Hey, it's all right," he said, his tone softening. "You can't remember everything, not when there're a hundred people talking in your ear and a full-blown party going on. At least now I know that this teacher is going to be here, and that Starfall isn't going to have to find a second choice. That's the really important part."

Kel's head rose, and so did his ear-tufts. "Well, now that thissss teacherrr comesss, what do you plan to do? It isss clearrr that the Elderrrsss of k'Vala intend *you* to be theirrr ssspokesssman to Valdemarrr herrrreaboutsss orrr they would not be trrraining you to be Elderrr to a Vale. Ssso it rrreally *will* be yourrr Vale and you would be wissse to make long-terrrm plansssss forrr it, and yourrrsssself."

"I know; Starfall has made that pretty clear." He laughed. "And I've been thinking about it off and on for a while—not to mention cvcry night before I go to sleep. If you don't mind listening, I can tell you what I've figured out so far."

Kel's ear tufts were jauntily high again, and he nodded. Darian took a deep breath, and began.

"First of all, we should have enough people that we can defend the place until help comes if we have to—but not so many that it's anywhere near the size of k'Vala." He brushed a beetle away and continued. "This isn't going to be so much a Vale as an embassy, as I see it. So I don't think we should have many more people than our original team—except, of course, if you *do* decide to nest with some charming thing, and she's agreeable to joining us."

Already he spoke of "us" as if he had his little outpost built and settled! He'd have laughed at himself, except that after all his thinking and planning, it really seemed as if it existed.

"Anyway," he continued, "we don't want to have so many people that Lord Breon thinks of us as a possible threat, or that we Tayledras have designs on *his* holding and estate." He'd spent a lot of time thinking this over, and felt that Kel would understand why that was so important. Breon could become a real stumbling block if he wasn't treated correctly, and with respect. "There's another thing—we don't want to make ourselves into Lord Breon's *social* rival either."

"Do you mean, sssetting up a kind of Courrrt of ourrr own?" Kel asked, cocking his head to the side. "I can ssssee wherrre that could put his nossse out of joint, ssso to ssspeak."

"Exactly. We want to keep him on our side, completely, because he's the nearest highborn." He was glad that Kel saw what he was getting at so quickly.

"I know about touchy highborrrrnsss," Kel chuckled. "With the Black Kingsss our nearrr neighborrrsss and alliesss, we have ample opporrrtunity to ssstumble unwittingly into offense!"

"I'd also like to establish a real Healer's enclave at our Vale," he continued. "That would take some pressure off Lord Breon's Healer and earn the gratitude of the local Valdemarans without doing anything to compete with Lord Breon. The presence of Healers—well, that basically shows people we're peaceful and intend to stay that way."

"Had you any thought to trrraining magesss therrre?" Kel asked curiously.

"Other than our own people?" He shook his head. "I don't think that's a good idea. Herald Elspeth and Adept Darkwind have built a Mage Collegium at Haven where they can keep a careful eye on those with Mage-Gift who aren't also Heralds. They did that for a reason, Kel. I'm not sure that Valdemar trusts mages even now, and to have someone teaching mages *in* Valdemar without the sanction and the oversight of the Heralds could be trouble."

"Urrrr. Bessst we not offend therrre eitherrr. I sssee what you mean." The gryphon roused all his feathers and shook. "Sssso, asssside frrrom not offending anyone, what plansss have you?"

"I want to make our Vale into the place where people come to resolve their differences," he said, his eyes alight and his voice alive with enthusiasm. "All kinds of people. I want it to become a place where everyone knows they'll be safe to work things out without any outside influences. I want it to be the place where Hawkbrothers come when they need to work things out with Valdemarans, or where Lord Breon brings people who aren't comfortable being in *his* manor. We could do really good things, Kel!"

"I agrrree!" Kel's enthusiasm rose right along with his. "Urrr, would I be the only grrryphon in this Vale? Unless I should find a lady, of course."

"Well, you'd certainly be the one with the most experience and seniority," Darian temporized. "I wouldn't bring in anyone who wasn't junior to you."

"That would incrrreassse my ssstatusss consssiderrrably!" Kel's beak gaped with delight; Darian had suspected he'd get that sort of reaction.

"I'd like *you* to be the chief gryphon of the Silvers there," Darian told him fondly. "Frankly, I don't see why it shouldn't happen that way. I suspect that the others may not realize what kind of an opportunity we will have until it is too late."

"Asss it ssshould be." Kel chuckled. "Afterrr all, they have had theirrr chancesss, and they ssshould let otherrrsss take risssskss of theirrr own."

"In other words—if they're so fond of the comfort of the Vale that they can't see opportunity hiding behind a little temporary hardship, then they don't deserve that opportunity." Darian laughed, and Kel burbled with delight. "Let's talk about this on the way home," he added, getting to his feet. "It won't take me a moment to clean these birds."

"Anotherrr good plan," Kel agreed. "We mussst sssee jussst how many morrre we can make!"

Ayshen

Five

Keisha kept her eyes down and bit her lip to keep from giggling as she passed her two youngest brothers. Of all the things that she thought she'd ever see in her lifetime, this was certainly the least likely of them! Here they were, up to their elbows in soap and water, doing their own laundry in the yard in full sight of everyone!

I have to admit they're going about it the right way, too, she thought as she opened the gate and hurried off to her workshop. *Theirs is a better system than Mum ever had.*

Her mother had always washed the clothing *in* the house, then brought the baskets of wet clothing out to hang on their lines in the sun to dry. The boys, however, had a different system. Instead of using the sinks in the house, they'd had the cooper make them two half-barrels on legs, with stopcocks as in a wine barrel in the bottoms for drain holes. One half-barrel was for washwater, the other for rinsing. They had a fire going in the fire pit with a tripod and a kettle over it, burning trash as well as heating the water for washing. The barrels held easily twice as much as the sink, maybe more, which meant that stubborn stains could soak while they scrubbed other garments. One boy scrubbed, the other rinsed, wrung, and hung, and they traded jobs each time they drained the tubs and refilled them with clean water or water and soap.

From the determined way in which they were scrubbing, they were doing a good job of it, too. *I think they're going to get the clothes done in half the time it takes Mum,* Keisha thought with admiration. *They're faster than she is, and*

*stronger; they'll surely get half a day on the farm if they
want to. Of course, the fact that their brothers are* paying
them to do their *clothes isn't hurting their feelings at all!
Who knows—maybe they'll start getting business from people outside the family and have a trade of their own!*

Keisha assiduously did her *own* laundry; it wasn't that difficult to manage with only the clothing for one person. Just like keeping the workshop clean, it wasn't a lot of work as long as you kept up with it.

She had underthings that she'd left soaking in the sink overnight as a matter of fact, and she intended to do a batch of tunics as soon as she rinsed out the underthings. That was why she was in a hurry; she wanted to have her laundry out of the way before anyone came to her with a complaint.

She reached the workshop without being intercepted, and shortly had a neat line of white things drying in the garden. The tunics went in to soak in the same bleaching solution that she'd had the underwear soaking in—she'd decided that it wasn't going to hurt to try to bleach out the old stains, even if it removed all of the old color as well. Now that she was doing a little of the dyework that Shandi used to, she was getting more and more interested in doing something with the same substances that had caused those stains in the first place.

One of them had been a very quiet gray-green; not the same, rather attractive new-mint color that the trainee Healer-tunics had been, but if she could bleach all the stains out and redye the tunics that color—

It wouldn't be a bad thing to get people used to seeing me in green. I could ease into it. Besides, sooner or later I'll have to wear the trainee uniforms, and the moment I do, I just know I'll get them stained, too.

Maybe she could get herself used to being in green at the same time.

Meanwhile, while the tunics soaked and her experiment in bleaching worked—or didn't—there was the garden to tend.

She left all the windows open as well as the door, even though it was a little nippy, for the bleaching solution gave off fumes she was suspicious of. In her oldest and shabbiest tunic with a canvas smock over it, she went into the herb garden and knelt down beside the rows of seedlings, a bucket beside her.

Immediately, she felt good: calm, happy, and productive. The garden had that effect on her nearly every time she worked in it. These sprouting shapes under cones of cheesecloth loose enough to allow them sun but heavy enough to protect from frost and heavy rain were from the new seeds she'd gotten from Steelmind. Since she hadn't known what they were going to look like when they came up, she had very carefully dyed handfuls of splinters and stuck one into the ground right next to each seed before she covered it with earth. Now as she worked beside each row, she pulled out anything sprouting that didn't have a colorful little splinter beside it. Of course, this was *far* more work than anyone would want to do normally, but it was only for these new plants. Her perennials, of course, were already well-grown, and it was no work to pick out the annuals she knew from the weed sprouts.

I'm just glad these new ones are all perennials, she thought, as she pulled out sprouting weeds that were barely visible and dusted them into her bucket, replacing the cones over her precious new seedlings as she worked. *There will only be one season of this kind of care.*

She pulled weeds until her back ached, and her hands had grime ground under all the nails. Then she judged that she'd done enough, and called it a done task. She dumped the bucket of weeds onto her compost heap and took the empty bucket into her workshop.

The fumes weren't as bad as she'd expected, and the experiment in bleaching was a qualified success. Once she'd rinsed out the tunics and wrung them dry enough to dye, she looked them over carefully and judged that the dye she'd prepared would probably cover the faint stains that were left. Even if it didn't, she wasn't any worse off than she'd been before.

The dye itself simmered in a big pot over the fireplace; she'd left it there all night to strengthen. Now she built up the fire a bit and dumped the first tunic in, stirring it with a peeled stick until it reached the color she wanted. Shortly after that, a line of gray-green tunics flapped beside the line of white underthings, and Keisha had replaced the pot of dye with one of soup fixings.

That was when she got her first patient of the day.

A knock on the doorframe made her look up, as Ferla Dawkin came in with her five-year-old in her arms, blood splattered liberally all over both of them.

By now, Keisha was a shrewd and instant judge of situations. Ferla wasn't hysterical, wasn't running, wasn't even out of breath. Therefore, the situation wasn't anywhere near as bad as it looked.

Ferla's words confirmed that. "If you're not busy, Keisha, Dib's gotten into a fight—"

"Bring him over to the fire and lay him down on the rug," she said, and his mother put the boy down while Keisha got clean rags and a fresh bucket of water. The boy had been quiet right up until the moment that Keisha sat down on the floor beside him; then he set up a howl like a Pelagir monster before she'd so much as touched him. He was a sorry sight, face red, blood in his hair and oozing from his nose and mouth, angry tears running down his fat cheeks. Keisha ignored the tears and the howling, she was used to them; she went straight to work, gently washing off the blood until she could make an accurate assessment of the damages.

"Well, Ferla, he's lost a tooth, he's got a nosebleed, and he'll have a fine black eye in a bit, so I'd say he was the loser in this battle," she finally told the anxious mama. "Here, Dib—" She made him lie down on the floor and pinched a rag over his nose. "You lie there and we'll see if we can't get your nose to stop bleeding. Who'd you take on?"

"Maffie Olan," came the muffled reply. "He called me a dumbhead."

"Well, that'll teach you to ignore people who are bigger than you are when they call you names, won't it?" she asked matter-of-factly as one big brown eye gazed at her around the rag held to his nose. "Do you know what I used to say when my brothers called *me* a dumbhead?"

"Huh-uh," the child replied.

"I'd say, 'It takes one to know one, so what are you, then?'

Try that instead of tearing into a bigger boy next time." She winked at him. "Maffie's not so dim that he can't work that one out for himself, and it'll make *him* madder than you. Remember, if *he* comes after you and hits you first, then he's a bully picking on you littles, and you can tattle to his mum, for she won't put up with Maffie turning into a bully. And you know his mum will tan his hide for him."

"Keisha!" the mother said, half laughing and half aghast. "Is that anything to tell him?"

She cocked an eye at Ferla. "All I know is it worked for me. My brothers stopped calling me names because they got tired of getting a licking from Mum that was worse than anything they dealt out to me. They couldn't complain either, because they'd started it by name calling."

Her bit of advice had certainly silenced the child anyway; he seemed to be pondering it as they waited for his nose to stop bleeding. When Keisha judged that it had been long enough, she had him sit up and cautiously took the rag away from his nose. There was no further leakage, so she got up and mixed him a quick potion; chamomile for the ache in his eye and nose, marsh-mallow and mint to counter any tummy upset from swallowing blood, and honey and allspice to make it into a treat.

"Now," she said, handing him the mug. "Here's a sweetie for being brave and doing what I told you." His face lit up, for every child in the village knew that when Keisha told them something was a "sweetie," it was worth eating or drinking. She never lied to them about the taste of a medicine; if it was bad, she told them, and advised them to get it down fast so they could have a sweet to take away the bad taste.

He seized the mug and happily drank down the contents. She made up a poultice of cress and plantain, and gave it to his mother.

"Have him lie down a bit more with this on his eye, and when he can't keep still any longer, let him go play. It's a pity about the tooth, but at least it's a baby one." She looked down at Dib, who stared solemnly up at her. "And mind what I said about fighting."

"Yes, Keisha," the boy said, with a look as if he was already contemplating mischief, as his mother helped him to his feet. The two left with Dib trotting sturdily along beside his mother, battered but unrepentant.

Keisha went out to check her drying laundry and found it ready to bring in; a distant growl from above made her glance quickly up at the sky to the west, and she frowned when she saw how quickly clouds were building in that direction. Thunder-towers, for certain sure. No telling how long it would last, either; a spring rain could be over before sunset, or linger for days.

She gathered in her clothing without folding it as she usually did; she just unpinned it from the line and dumped everything in the basket, anxious to beat the rain and get her things inside the workshop. She made it inside before anything came down, but the first drops started plopping into the dust just as she closed the door. It was as she was doing the folding inside the workshop that she heard thunder rumble again, much nearer, then heard the rain suddenly strengthen, rattling the thatch and pelting the path outside.

A moment more, and it wasn't just a few drops, it was a downpour—a downpour without much thunder, just more growling now and again. There wasn't much wind, which didn't augur well for the storm blowing past in a hurry. She shut all the windows as some rain splashed inside, then lit her lanterns to ward off growing darkness; when she cracked the door open and peeked out, what she saw confirmed that this was not going to be a simple cloudburst, over quickly.

Not with the amount coming down, the slate-gray of the clouds overhead, and the relative lack of lightning and thunder.

I'm glad the seedlings are up and they're in drained beds, she thought with a sigh. *And I'm glad I put those gauze cones over them to protect them. This is likely to last for the next three days.* If she hadn't put the cones over them, her precious new plants would be flattened before sunset.

With that in mind, she considered going out now and collecting some foodstuffs; she might be spending a lot of time in the workshop or tending flus and colds. *I'd better; I can't just live on vegetable soup.*

Getting out her waterproof rain cape, she put the hood up,

slipped on a pair of wooden clogs, bowed her head to the storm and plodded out into it. Beneath the hood of the cape, she watched her footing; already the rain had pooled into some deepish puddles—deep enough that her clogs wouldn't keep her feet dry if she blundered into one. As she came to the hedge around her house, she looked up, wondering if her brothers had the sense to bring the clothing in. The line at her house was empty, so her brothers had saved their laundry from a drenching, but the righthand neighbor hadn't been so lucky. Tansy Gelcress struggled with wet clothing, flapping rain cape, and a basket she didn't want to put down—Keisha couldn't simply go into the house with that going on next door. She stopped long enough to help Tansy gather in her things, then went on up the path to her own house.

Everybody will be coming home—they can't work in the wet. I'll get the fire going, so they have a warm house to come back to. She built up the fire in the kitchen, then surveyed the kitchen stocks, deciding what her mother wouldn't mind her taking. *Ham, cheese, eggs, butter, a jug of cider—that'll do. I have beans, flour, basic staples at the shop. I have a quarter of a loaf of bread, and I'll be out enough that I can get more bread from the baker. We've plenty more of what I'm taking at the farm; she can send Da after more if she needs to. People will start bringing barter stuff like eggs and milk around here as soon as I start handing out cough potions.* That was part of the arrangement with the village, after all; since Keisha wasn't a single male who needed to be cooked for and looked after, the family got foodstuffs on an irregular basis. Things usually started appearing when Keisha had done a lot of work in a short period of time.

Gathering her spoils up into a basket and covering it with a fold of her cape, she went out into the storm again, only to see the neighbor waving frantically at her from the door of her house.

She splashed across the yard, fearing that someone had already gotten sick.

But Tansy handed her a bundle wrapped in a clean dishcloth. "I made seedcakes, and I thought since you'll probably be busy in this nasty weather that you might like to take some to your workshop to nibble on in between emergencies," she said as she patted Keisha's hand. "There, just a little thanks for being a good neighbor."

"Thank *you*," Keisha replied, touched and pleased, and a little dumbfounded. "Thank you very much. They'll be appreciated—"

"Now don't let me keep you standing here, go!" the woman told her, making a shooing motion. "I don't want to be the one responsible for drowning you!"

Keisha left, making her way through the growing runnels of water, protecting both sets of provisions under her rain cape. *People are noticing! They're really noticing what I do!* It wasn't just a reward for helping with the laundry; the neighbor had specifically said "I thought you'd probably be busy in this nasty weather."

Somehow, she felt immensely better than she had a few moments ago and quite ready to meet whatever the weather brought with a steady spirit.

The wind picked up, sending the edges of her cape flapping, and there was a definite edge to it that there hadn't been before. It was getting colder, and that wasn't good.

Cold-teas, sore-throat syrups, cough syrups, fever-teas, herb-and-garlic packets for chicken soup— she started cataloging all the things she was going to need as soon as she got through the door. Her workshop seemed doubly cozy after the bitter weather outside; she shook out her cape and hung it up, then slipped her clogs off and padded around in her stockings, knowing that she'd have to put the clogs back on as soon as someone called on her. Quickly stowing her provisions in her food cupboard, she put beans to soak for soup tomorrow; if the rain lasted, tomorrow would be the day when the first colds made their appearance, and she'd be busy all day.

She took long enough to eat her vegetable soup with sliced bread and butter; if things got bad, it might be bedtime before she had another chance to eat. Then she set about inventorying her cold medicines, and putting together batches of whatever she thought she'd need more of.

Her hands flew as her mind worked; was it likely that anyone would get caught by flooding? With the way this rain was coming down, it was a possibility, though people tended to be pretty sensible about rising water this time of year. It was only in the summer that people got lazy, were too busy, or were having too good a time to pay attention to the possibility of flash floods.

Last year had brought a fine honey harvest and she had plenty stocked away for making soothing syrups. With a surplus of extra jugs, she'd gone ahead and made more decoctions of comfrey, lobelia, hyssop, and horehound than she usually did. Now her preparations paid off; it didn't take long for her to mix those four ingredients, chamomile, and lemon-balm tinctures, plus the honey, for cough syrup. Work didn't stop just because people got colds; it was up to her to make certain they could do their work even with one.

Late afternoon brought the first of the emergencies; people might be sensible about flooding, but unfortunately, cows were as stubborn and stupid as rocks. Some of the water-meadows started getting knee-deep and several folk had to wade in to lead their cattle out—the floods were too deep for the herd dogs to work in, so each fool cow had to be caught and led to safety by hand. So a handful of people came home chilled to the bone and blue around the lips—and Keisha was there with hot medicinal teas and packets of preventative herbs to go into the evening soup or stew. No harm if the rest of the family got the medicines either; all that would happen was that everyone would get sleepy earlier, and go off to bed. A warm bed was the best place anyone could be on a night like this one.

The cattle had to be treated, too, for the results of their boneheadedness, so out she went to three different farms, making sure each silly cow got her drench.

Keisha had her villagers well-trained; at the first sign of a sniffle, mothers came to the door for syrups and teas for their littles. There was a steady parade of them just after supper-time, as children who'd gone out healthy came home sneezing, because they *would* play in the puddles and not come in until they were as soaked and blue as the men who'd rescued the cattle.

These weren't the things she charged for; she'd early come to the conclusion that if she took her "pay" for run-of-the-mill Healing in the things the villagers were already supplying her, it was more likely that they'd come to her early rather than waiting until the illness was truly serious. Doses with enough sleepy-making potential to make people stay abed a candlemark or two longer when they were mildly sick would keep them from getting sicker—keeping a cold at the level of sniffles and coughs in a child kept it from turning into something that could kill. She'd charge the farmers for the cattle-drenches, but only after the rains were over, and only because they had asked her to give the doses herself.

Then again, she thought wearily, after she'd trudged back to the shop from what she hoped would be the last call of the night, *I can get the stuff down their throats without them fighting me; when they do it, more of it goes* on *the cow than in it, poor things.*

Absolutely, positively, no point in going home to sleep; everyone knew that in weather like this, she'd be at the shop where everything she might need was at hand. *I'm just glad I got the laundry done,* she told herself, as she closed the door behind her, and surveyed the wreck of her workshop. *I hope they give me some time to get this cleaned up in the morning before they haul me out again.*

She followed her own prescription and added a packet of her herbs to the last of the soup before she ate it—as she'd anticipated, she hadn't had a chance for a meal after that first bowl. The she put the beans, seasoning, and some ham into another pot and put that over the fire to cook all night. She managed to wash up the dishes and the first soup pot, but ran out of energy, and took two seedcakes and a mug of cider up to the loft where she snuggled into her bed, leaving them on the little table beside the bed for a quick bite if someone pulled her out in the middle of the night.

But that night, at least, her sleep was unbroken, and the cakes and cider made a perfectly good breakfast. It was an unexpected luxury to eat breakfast in bed, with the rain drumming down on the roof outside and the savory aroma of bean soup filling the workshop.

She didn't linger long, though; she was up and washed and clothed quickly, dressing for the weather. No telling when she'd be called out again.

I could do myself a big favor by getting baskets ready to

snatch up, she decided, and lined up four on the workbench. Into one went standard remedies for minor human ailments, and into the second the same sorts of things for animals. Into the other two went medicines for more serious complications. She didn't think she'd have to use the one for people—but the Fellowship beasts were so sensitive—

She'd no sooner finished the fourth basket when someone knocked on the door, then came in without waiting for a reply.

It was Alys, from the Fellowship.

Keisha grabbed the fourth basket without waiting to hear what brought her. "It's the sheep, right?"

Alys nodded. "Cough," she said anxiously. "It's odd, a dry, hacking sort of cough."

"Hah!" Alys didn't recognize it, that was clear, but Keisha did. Her own family flock had gotten the illness in a rainy spring like this one. She turned to get a different jar of heavy concentrate down off the top shelf and put it in her basket as well. "No worries, I've got what we'll need; they'll be fine as long as we get them warm and dry and get my stuff into them. Come on."

She swung on her rain cape and slipped her feet into her clogs, heading straight out the door. Alys followed, her brow creased anxiously.

"How are we going to get them dry and warm?" she asked. "They're soaked to the skin!"

Keisha stopped in the doorway and made a mental inventory of the Fellowship buildings, and realized Alys was right, there was no way to get the sheep under cover on Fellowship property. But there *was* the village threshing barn, empty and unused at this time of year, and with the favors the Fellowship had done the village, *they* were certainly owed a favor from the village in return.

"Get your dogs and herders and bring all the sheep up to the threshing barn," she ordered. "We'll use that until the rain is over. Don't worry, I'll make sure it's right. I'll meet you there."

Alys took her word as good, and trotted off through the puddles toward the Fellowship holding. Keisha stopped just long enough at the Mayor's house to confirm the right of the

Fellowship to use the octagonal barn until the rains were done—so long as they supplied fodder for the sheep and cleaned up after them.

Keisha hurried to the barn and let down the oiled canvas interior sides that shut out the wind and rain when need be. The canvas hadn't come cheap, but in the rush of prosperity following the sale of the barbarians' looted goods, it had been a sound investment. Now the barn could be used for many purposes in all weathers, even in the dead of winter—it became a tight, weatherproof and windproof tent with a fine shingled roof and seven external supporting walls of wood. It was a tight squeeze, but you could even hold a Faire in there.

The eighth wall, the one opposite the door, was of stone, and did not have a canvas cover, but that was the very last thing it needed.

By the time she'd done lacing all the canvas panels together, the poor, sodden sheep showed up, bleating and coughing pathetically. No doubt about that cough; Keisha had heard it before, and the illness "felt" the same as soon as she touched her hands to one of the sheep.

"Bring them in, then start squeezing the water out of their fleeces," she ordered, as Alys and four more Fellowship shepherds hustled their charges into the barn. "When you've got them all as dry as you can, bring clean straw in here for them to bed down in. I know it'll seem like a waste, but trust me, I want it belly-deep for the sheep in here. They have to get warm and stay warm, or you might start losing lambs."

Nods all around, neither questions, nor arguments. Keisha went outside to start a fire in the big oven built into the eighth—stone—side of the barn.

The door of the oven faced the outside; inconvenient to say the least, but entirely necessary when you realized that the floor of the barn would be covered in flammable things like straw whenever the barn was in use. There was always a huge pile of wood under a cover next to the oven; it would be a while before the stone wall heated up enough for the warmth to build up in the barn, but that was all right. This would solve the problem of getting the delicate sheep warmed clear through.

And if any other animals start looking seedy, they can be

brought here, too. She reminded herself to tell the Mayor that on her way back to her workshop. Once the fire was going well, Keisha stacked logs all around it, and went back into the barn.

With the only light coming from a couple of storm lanterns the shepherds had thoughtfully brought with them, it was pretty dim, but Keisha knew the contents of her basket well. Before very long, she had the water skins she generally used to dose animals full, and had the concentrated cough potion mixing with the water inside. As each poor sheep was squeezed relatively dry, she took it from the hands of its helper over to the stone wall where one of the lanterns hung.

There, she looked deeply into its confused, frightened, eyes, and told it without words that it was *safe*, that she would be helping it, and that if it drank what she gave it, the nasty cough would stop. Then she promised that there would be warmth, dry straw to lie in, and peace for as long as the rain fell. She filled her mind with those images of warmth and safety, until she felt the sheep relax under her hands and saw the eyes lose their fear.

Then she eased the sheep's mouth open, and slipped the neck of the water skin past the back of the tongue. *How* she could tell that she'd gotten enough of a dose into each sheep, she couldn't have said in words; she only knew that something told her when she'd poured exactly the right amount down its throat.

That was when she let the sheep go; it would wander off and join the rest of the dosed flock making beds in the straw that more of the Fellowship folk were spreading on the floor.

This was tedious work—not hard, except for those drying off the sheep, but tedious. "Talking" to the sheep without words was tiring, too—Keisha wasn't sure why, but it took something out of her. The good part was that about the time she was half through, the stone wall began radiating warmth, so the second half of her task was accomplished in relative comfort.

When she turned the last of the sheep loose—and now none of them was coughing—she stood up with a little groan and put the now-flat water skins back in her basket. Alys waited patiently to hear what other orders she had.

"You'll have to keep the oven stoked, and if anyone wants to bake something in it, or put in a casserole or something, let them, that's part of the bargain," Keisha told her. "Mayor said you'll have to supply your own fodder." She already knew she didn't have to tell them to clean up after themselves; when the sheep left this barn, you'd be able to eat off the floor. "Now, what your little beauties have got isn't exactly a sickness, not yet, anyway."

"It's not?" Alys said, puzzled.

Keisha shook her head. "It's some Pelagir-fungus, like ergot, but it grows on sheep-sorrel instead of wheat, down near the roots. Heat and freezing kill it, that's why you won't see it in summer or winter, and it needs a warm spring with a lot of rain to start. Which we've had."

Alys nodded. "But we've had warm springs with lots of rain before."

"You're still all right so long as the ground stays dry, not soaked like it's been. Then what it needs to *spread* is a cold rain in the middle of the warm spring." She shrugged. "Here's where I don't know why, it just does. Otherwise, it just sits down at the roots of the sheep-sorrel and your sheep will crop right over the top of it and never come to harm. Since this is a lung sickness, maybe they have to breathe something in. All I know for certain is that if you don't have the fungus in your fields, your sheep will be all right, and if you don't have a cold, steady rain, your sheep will be all right—and if you bring your sheep *off* the fields where the fungus is until after it's been raining for a day or so, you'll be all right. Our sheep got it a time or two, and it knocked them down hard; I'm afraid yours would be in trouble if I hadn't got the stuff into them that kills the rot that they breathe in. Now, though, with heat and good food and the medicine, they'll be strong enough to fight it off and come out fine."

Alys looked relieved, and nodded. "The *chirras* all went into their barn and wouldn't come out as soon as the rain started, and the goats are in their shelter—and none of them are coughing. It was just the sheep that kept grazing in the rain."

"Then the *chirras* and goats won't have any trouble from

this, but mind what I told you from now on; either get rid of the sheep-sorrel or the fungus, or keep animals out of those fields as soon as it starts to rain in the spring." Keisha stretched, easing cramped arm and back muscles.

Alys looked around the barn at her contentedly drowsing charges, and sighed. "I suppose if there's anybody else that needs the space here, we're to make room for them?"

"I won't allow an animal in that has something yours can catch," Keisha assured her. "It might happen that we need the room, but this place is big enough that you won't have to vacate."

Alys and the other shepherds looked satisfied with that. Alys had something of her own to offer. "If someone gets flooded out, remember we have extra beds at the Fellowship, all right? It's only fair, with us getting to use the barn and all."

"I'll tell the Mayor, and thanks in advance," Keisha replied. "You won't need me anymore, so I'd better get back to where people can find me."

She waved good-bye to the other shepherds, as they settled themselves in for as long as the rain lasted, the dogs making nests in the straw around the flock of sheep. *It could be worse for them,* Keisha thought, as she faced the storm, bowing her head under the frigid deluge. *They could have to watch the sheep out in this mess. At least they'll be warm and dry, even if they do have to feed the oven and haul over fodder and straw.*

And in the long run, it was a good thing that the sheep were here and not in the field; only about a quarter of the ewes had lambs at their side, the rest were still all heavily pregnant. Sheep always picked the worst time to lamb, and it was even odds that they'd decide to drop in the middle of the storm. If there were any problems, there wouldn't be any hunting about on storm-drenched hillsides to find the missing ewe!

They might not lose any this year, if they all decide to drop while they're in the barn; that would be a blessing.

When she got back to her workshop, there was a patient waiting for her, huddled in the chair by the fire. And it was

Piel, one of Shandi's most romantic and least-sensible suitors, who was, if possible, the very last person she wanted to see. She tried not to let her resignation show.

No need to ask what brought him; his red nose and swollen eyes, steady sneezing and rasping cough told the whole story. "Oh, Piel," she sighed, putting her hands on her hips and shaking her head. "You *are* a right mess, aren't you?"

"I subbose id's by own fault," he wheezed miserably, blowing his nose on his handkerchief. "I wad oud on *our* hill, and when id starded do rain, I wad thinging so hard aboud *her* thad I didn' nodise—"

"I promise you that it's all your own fault," she said severely. "You are more than old enough to know better than to play a fool's trick like that, and Shandi wouldn't thank you for catching pneumonia and dying! Only idiots in ballads get sick and pine gracefully and painlessly away for love, Piel. I can guarantee that pneumonia takes longer and hurts a *lot*."

"Bud—somedimes I thig id wouldn' be a bad thig—" he said forlornly, his voice trailing off, as she turned away and got some of her stronger medicines.

"Oh, you don't, do you?" She was *not* going to let him wallow in self-indulgent misery, not in *her* workshop. "And just how would your parents feel about that? How would Shandi, may I ask? Just how do you think I'd explain *that* to her, that I let you die of a stupid chill? Idiot! It isn't as if she left you for another suitor! And it isn't as if she flew off to the moon!"

"Bud she mid as well *be* on da moon!" he cried plaintively. "Why wadn id *you* thad wad Chosen instead ob *her*? Why couldn id hab been *you*? Nobody's in lob wid *you*!"

"I will have none of *that* nonsense here!" she told him briskly, turning around with a particularly nasty-tasting potion in her hand. She was in no mood for any of this, and he had, by the Havens, earned a good scold. "First off, if *I* had been Chosen, who would be taking care of you this minute? Second, it's none of your business, and nobody asked you who should and should not be Chosen; you leave that to the Companions. Third, if you're so desperately in love with Shandi, you'd do *far* better by spending your time thinking of a way to make a good livelihood in Haven where she is, than sitting around on hills moping! Showing up in Haven in a good suit of clothing with the money in your pocket to take her to a fine inn for supper would charm her and finally impress my father. Dying stupidly would *not*, and moon-calfing about on hills in the rain when other folk are working *does* not!"

Not that I expect him to exert himself that much, she thought scornfully, for she shared her father's opinion of Piel. The fellow was in love with the idea of being in love, and with Bardic notions of romance, not really in love with Shandi. *It's easy to lie around on hills and weep. And it impresses other fools with how deep your feelings are. One month from now, he'll be desperately in love with one of Shandi's friends, or one of Lord Breon's maids at the keep.*

"Here," she said abruptly, thrusting the mug at him. "Drink this. All of it. Now."

He looked from the mug to her face, saw no hope of reprieve, and gagged it down. It *was* truly awful, and she'd made no effort to sweeten it.

"Now go home, get into bed, and sleep," she ordered. "When your mother gives you soup and tea, don't play with them, drink them—I know she's already got the medicine she needs for you, she came to get it last night."

Piel gave a long-suffering sigh, and draped himself with his rain cape as if it were his shroud. She saw him to the door, and nobly refrained from slamming it behind him.

The rest of the day was spent in dosing similar illnesses—and in listening to the complaints of the sufferers. Most of the complaints were actually more fretful and pathetic than anything else; neighbor Tansy pretty well summed them up when she came for cough syrup.

"I wish young Darian would get back here and set himself up like he's supposed to," she grumbled. "Even if he couldn't have sent this storm elsewhere, he'd at least have been able to warn us about it, and he'd be able to tell us how long it's likely to last!"

When darkness fell, she finally made a dinner for herself—a good one, not just the soup but a nice slice of fried ham and some scrambled eggs and toast. The only thing she'd had all day was those seedcakes and a couple of bites of soup in between patients, and she was so hungry she was close to being nauseated.

She didn't let her irritation with Piel spoil her meal either, though she'd been damned annoyed with his self-indulgent bleating. *The sheep didn't make that much of a complaint,* she told herself, as she took careful sips of the hot soup. *And as for that business of "why weren't you Chosen, nobody is in love with you—"* Ooh, *I could have strangled him if I weren't so tolerant, and* he *weren't a patient!*

The rain still hadn't let up, though it had lessened a bit. *A storm this big will probably get Haven, too. I wonder how Shandi is doing?* It was too soon for a letter, but Keisha couldn't help wishing one would come.

I wish I had someone else I could talk to. She sighed and took her dishes to the sink to wash. *If I'd been Chosen, I'd have my Companion—*

Fantasy, foolishness. There was never a chance that she'd have been Chosen; any hesitation on the part of the Companion had been her imagination. *Why would any Companion Choose me?* she thought sourly. *Not only is nobody in love with me, nobody even likes me. There wasn't a chance that Companion would have Chosen me; Mum and Da named me right. "Keisha," that's me, the tree all over thorns and no fruit worth anybody's effort. If people didn't need me so badly, they'd never come near me.*

Uncomfortable thoughts, uncomfortable feelings, and she knew if she didn't get her mind off them she'd sink into a well of self-pity as deep as Piel's.

So she picked up one of her Healing texts and put her mind into study, until she was so tired and sore of eye that she practically crawled up the ladder to her bed.

After four days, the rain finally stopped; the sun put in a brilliant appearance in cloudless skies, and a dry, warm breeze made colds—or at least, complaints of colds—disappear. It never failed to amaze and amuse Keisha that a couple of sunny, warm days in spring or fall could make everyone forget about feeling ill. Unless, of course, they were very ill indeed.

Piel did not put in a second appearance, nor was he anywhere in the village when Keisha was about, which either meant he had taken Keisha's lecture to heart and was actively seeking a way to make his living in the greater world (not likely) or that he so feared another tongue-lashing that he wasn't going to come anywhere near her (far more likely). The sheep got over their illness, and there were many more to herd out of the barn than went in, for many of the pregnant ewes took the opportunity to drop lambs. The folk from the Fellowship took such good care of the threshing barn that the Mayor declared they could make free of it whenever they had another such emergency.

In short, everything was back to normal.

Everything but Keisha herself, that is.

Since the onset of the storm, she'd felt edgy most of the time. Whenever she treated a patient, she'd start to reflect the emotional state of that patient herself, and it wasn't pleasant. The only reason she'd even known that she was being influenced in that way was because she'd been perfectly calm and contented on the third morning of the storm, and had her mood utterly reversed by the first patient to enter the door. Once someone left, she was fine, but while they were in the same area she had to keep a steady head and remind herself that *she* was not the one feeling rotten. It was worse if she had to touch the patient; that opened her up to all manner of things she didn't understand and did not in the least like.

This was making things unexpectedly uncomfortable at home. Rain made the trip to and from the farm pure misery, made chores at the farm a burden, and kept all the boys in the house when they weren't at the farm. Cooped up like that, for lack of any other amusement, they picked fights with each other. When the boys argued, she found herself getting angry for no reason at all; when her mother got upset, *her* eyes threatened to overflow. She discovered that beneath her father's calm exterior, *he* often suffered from a tensely knotted, aching gut, by experiencing these things herself. That, at least, was useful; she took him aside and convinced him he needed her help unless he wanted to start spitting up blood one day. At least he stopped suffering and felt immensely calmer after following her prescriptions, even if she didn't.

Four days after the storm ended, Lord Breon's Healer Gil arrived for his monthly visit. He was late by a day, but she'd expected that; he'd probably had the same sorts of patients that she'd had—maybe more serious, since Lord Breon's men were duty-bound to be outside no matter the weather, and to rescue any of Lord Breon's folk who'd gotten themselves into difficulties.

She was replacing her depleted stocks of preprepared medicines when he tapped on the doorframe and walked on in. She knew both the tap and the step, and even if she hadn't, she'd have known it was him by the feeling of steadiness and patience that he always brought with him. He might be a cranky curmudgeon on the outside, but inside he was the steady rock on which all hysteria drove itself in vain.

At that moment, however, she needed both hands and her eyes to get her comfrey and lobelia concentrate into its jug. "Welcome, Gil," she greeted him without turning. "Give me a moment, will you? I have both hands full."

Gil helped himself to one of the two chairs and she heard him sit down. "Am I?" he asked. "Am I welcome, that is?"

Hmm. Is he expecting a fight out of me? If so, why? She put the jug up, then measured her herbs and put the finished mixture into a steeping bag, tying the drawstrings tight. No point in starting a new batch now, but she'd have it ready to go when Gil left. "I haven't killed anyone this month, directly or indirectly, and I don't have any plans to do so today, so of course you're welcome," she retorted, turning to greet him properly. "Mind you, I was tempted once or twice during the rain, but I managed to contain my feelings."

Gil was a withered little raisin of a man, whose normal movements were so deliberate that it shocked people when, in an emergency, he moved with the speed of a hummingbird. His hair was an iron-gray, his legs bowed, his eyes small and black and seemingly able to see whatever it was you most wanted to keep secret. He didn't look like a Healer; he looked like a weatherbeaten old horse tamer, and, in fact, he did tame horses using a Shin'a'in method he'd learned on Lord Ashkevron's estate of Forst Reach where he'd grown up (where horse tamers were honored and very, truly needed). Children and animals trusted him immediately, and he had the no-nonsense aura of competence and authority to make even Lord Breon's most battle-hardened fighters listen to and obey him. There couldn't have been a better Healer for that particular position in the entire Kingdom, even if his Gift was so weak it was negligible.

"I see you're wearing Greens now—so to speak," he continued, raising his eyebrows. "Not exactly orthodox color, though."

She brushed her hand down the front of her tunic self-consciously. "I thought I'd use some old clothing of my own for a dye experiment before I ruined those nice uniforms the Collegium sent." She shrugged. "Why use those new uniforms for work when I have plenty of old things that can take a beating?"

"You know, a uniform isn't there to make *you* conform, it's to reassure your patients as a symbol. Heralds know that; that's why they wear Whites; people wouldn't take them half so seriously if they didn't show up in uniforms. I take it that with the rains you had the usual crop?" he asked, looking her up and down, still with that penetrating expression on his face.

"And one young idiot," she replied with a laugh, and sat down and told him about Piel. He grunted with disgust when she described how Piel had gotten sick and soaked in the first place, and broke into a cackle of unexpected laughter when she told him the lecture she'd read the romantic fool.

"Bright Havens, I wish I'd been here!" he chortled, slapping the arm of the chair with his hand. "Sounds to me as if you're getting your proper attitude, young lady. If people won't *give* you the authority and respect you need to make them listen, then by the gods, *take* it! You can apologize after they're better. What good's a Healer that no one listens to? That was where poor old Justyn got into trouble; he was too soft on people."

"Well, all I can say is I'm grateful that Piel hasn't decided he's lifebonded to Shandi. He's quite enough of a wet mess as it is, and I swear to you, even if he was shaved bald he'd have more hair than wits. Why Shandi ever encouraged him in the first place, I'll never know." She sighed, and ran both hands through the hair at her temples in exasperation. "Maybe it's just that she was too kind, and afraid to break his heart.

Other than young Piel's crisis, the Fellowship's sheep got that dry cough I told you about, and the preparation you recommended cleared it up in them as fast as it did my folk's flock."

"Just watch that particular medicine in the early stages of pregnancy, it tends to make cattle miscarry, and it might do the same in sheep," he cautioned. "Late stages, no problem, but the first month—"

"If it's a choice between possibly losing the sheep or losing the lamb, I think most people would prefer the latter, but I'll be sure and give them that option if the situation comes up," she promised. "But that might be the reason why so many of the pregnant ones decided to drop lambs in the barn—which was a fine thing as far as their keepers were concerned."

"Heard anything from your sister yet?" he asked, changing the subject so quickly that she immediately suspected an ulterior motive.

She shook her head. "It's a little too soon, I'd think," she replied, watching him with care. "I should think they'd have her so busy at first that she'd be going from the moment she got up to the moment her head hit the pillow."

I wonder why he's asking? Is it curiosity or something more?

"And *I* should think she'd want her sister with her so much that she'd be sending you letters three times a day," he began. She held up her hand, stopping him at that point.

"Don't start." she said shortly. "I won't listen, and we've been through this a hundred times. How would you cope with me gone? You couldn't, and you know it."

"But *you* have the Gift, and *I* can't teach you to use it," he countered stubbornly. "We've tried, and I can't tell you what you need to know, and so far you haven't made any progress with the texts either."

"Then we'll *wait* until someone with the Gift can come here to teach me for a couple of months," she retorted, just as stubbornly. "Right now I'm doing as well or better than Justyn did for all of *his* training at the Collegium, and right now, that's what this village needs and can't afford to do without. Whatever happens here, I can at least buy time for a fully trained, fully Gifted Healer to get here. And you have to admit that in some cases that's all *you* could do!"

Gil shook his head, but he gave up the argument as a lost

cause yet again. He was silent for a space, then scratched his head uneasily. "I'm just afraid that if you keep on like this, your Gift is going to get you into trouble," he said at last, sounding far more worried than she was used to hearing from him.

"How—how could I get into trouble?" she asked, uncomfortably certain that she already knew the answer.

"I'm not sure—since my own Gift is so trifling, they never went into details," he said, frowning with concentration, probably as he tried to recall his long-ago training at the Collegium. "I just remember that they told me an untrained Gift has the potential to cause the owner problems."

She wondered guiltily if she ought to tell him about her strange new sensitivity, and how her nerves always seemed to be raw and open to other people. *But if I do, he'll probably find a way to pack me off to Haven and then what would happen? No, I can get through this. It can't be too long now before someone is sent here to show me what to do. Half the Healers in Valdemar aren't trained at the Collegium, and they do all right! I can manage. I have to.*

To keep him from somehow getting the information out of her, she took him around to see those few of her patients that were still abed, and the now-healthy flock of Fellowship sheep. The Fellowship had put them in a pasture along the edge of the river, an easy walk from the village, and quite an enjoyable stroll in the warm spring sunshine. A feeling of laziness crept over her as they came up to the fence and propped their arms up on the top rail, the wood rough and warm under her hand. He leaned over the fence looking as relaxed as she had ever seen him, watching the silly beasts graze and wearing a small but contented smile.

"I have to admit something to you, young Keisha," he said at last, after they'd both listened to a woodlark sing until it flew off. "I envy you this part of your practice, and I am *very* glad that you aren't one of those who thinks herself too valuable to waste time tending animals."

"If one of those ever gets around me, they'll get an earful," she chuckled, totally relaxed now that the only human anywhere around was her mentor. "If our job is to see to our people's well-being, how can we ignore the well-being of their animals? If their beasties fail, they'll starve, and how've we done our duty then?"

"Good point, and one I'll remember the next time I need it." One of the sheep looked up at them, and for some reason known only to it, decided to come over to the fence to see what they were doing there. Gil reached over the fence to the animal, let it sniff his fingers, then buried his hand in its woolly head, scratching around its ears. The sheep went cross-eyed with bliss, and Keisha giggled at its expression.

"The shepherds tell me they've always been marvelously tame, but it's been really pronounced since the rain," she told the Healer. "I think they were reminded that many of them grew up in boxes next to warm stoves, so now they're almost like pets—which makes *me* glad they're wool-sheep and not mutton-sheep."

"There is something to that," he agreed. "Seems like a betrayal to raise a creature as a pet, then eat it. Most chickens being an exception, of course."

Keisha laughed; she'd been pecked by too many hens and chased by too many mean roosters to disagree with him. "Most chickens can't *be* pets; they've got less brain than Piel, if that's possible," she pointed out. "Since you've got your fingers in it, what do you think of the wool in its natural state?"

"Why do you think I'm scratching her? It's as much for my pleasure as hers; I don't think I've ever felt anything so soft." He finally stopped his ministrations with a gentle pat on the top of the sheep's head; just as well, for the ewe looked ready to fall over at any moment. He looked her over with a measuring gaze as she shook her head until her ears flapped, then went back to grazing. "Just about shearing time, isn't it?"

"Just about. The Fellowship always waits until they're sure the cold weather is over before they take that protection away. I've told you how delicate this lot is."

"Yes, but obviously worth it. The shawls wouldn't be half so desirable made out of ordinary fleece. That reminds me; Lord Breon's son Val plans to pick out a shawl this Midsummer Faire, or so Lord Breon tells me," Gil offered. He caught Keisha's interest immediately. If the son and heir of their liege lord was getting married, the whole village would want to know all about it, and as soon as might be.

"For whom?" she asked. "Anyone we know?"

"Some sweet young thing at the keep where he fostered until this spring." Gil chuckled. "I've got the notion that Lord Breon had that in mind when he fostered Val there in the first place. With eight daughters to choose from, there was bound to be something that would take."

"I'll tell the Fellowship about the shawl first," Keisha replied, already deciding who she'd tell first, and in what order, so as not to upset the delicate ranking order in the village. "They'll probably want to do something special for Val, and they'll want every moment of time to plan it."

"Yes, do that—but I won't tell him they're making a special shawl for him. He's got it set in his mind that he has to pick the thing out—as if there's a special magic to what he'd pick only he and she would appreciate properly or some other romantic nonsense." Gil shook his head. "He's been listening to a lot of love ballads lately—he and that lovelorn lad of yours have that much in common. Sometimes I think Bards do more harm than good."

"Well, they give us all something to dream about, I suppose," she said doubtfully, then returned to the practical aspects of the courtship. "Meanwhile, I think we can all arrange that he gets his special shawl without knowing it's his special shawl, if that makes any sense."

"Complete sense." He looked up at the sun, and pushed away from the fence. "And if I'm to get back before sundown, I'd best collect my horse and be on my way."

They parted amiably enough at the pasture, and Keisha returned to the haven of her workshop. She still had plenty more to do while there was a relative lack of illness and injury, and just now nothing would tempt her back into the proximity of people. She felt relaxed, and she wanted to hold onto the feeling as long as she could.

She truly dreaded having to go back home; lately at least one of the boys would have some sort of unpleasant dream each night, and although the dreamer never woke up and never remembered the dream, *she* did and it woke *her* up.

The workshop was far enough away from the rest of the houses that nothing ever reached her here, and it would be so good to go to sleep knowing that the only thing disturbing her would be her *own* nightmares, if any.

It would be so nice to have a good night's sleep again, the way I did during the rains, she thought fretfully. *I wish I could just live here and be done with it.*

Then— *I wonder why I couldn't just* do *that?*

She abruptly sat down in the chair Gil had used. *All right, I'll be methodical. The reasons why it would be difficult are— Mum would object, firstly.*

True enough, but she could point out that now no one else would get roused in the middle of the night just because someone needed *her*. Besides, it wasn't as if she were going to be living out at the farm, or somewhere else out of sight and alone. She'd still be near at hand, quite near enough to keep an eye on.

I'd have to start doing my own meals.

Yes, but she did that sometimes anyway. The memory of the Fellowship's communal meals popped into her head, and she realized that she could easily trade some of the routine health care of their flocks for the right to eat with *them*. Other than that—she could start taking a little more of her fees in food-barter. It could all be worked out.

I'd be by myself. Mum will say that people might talk.

Now, if it had been *Shandi* who'd wanted to live in the workshop, that would have caused a scandal. Shandi was pretty and had suitors, and people would certainly start to gossip. For this purpose, Keisha's prickly personality gave her all the protection she needed, for there wasn't a young man in the entire village who had ever showed any interest in courting her, and they surely wouldn't start just because she was living alone.

And what's more, Rafe can move into the cubby Shandi and I shared, and that will break up the quarreling with Torey. For that reason alone, Papa will back me up on this.

But it was easiest to get something done if you didn't stop to ask permission first—so before anyone came home from the farm, she decided to get all her things and move them over to the workshop. *Move now, and argue about it later.*

She went straight home, and working quickly, had everything she could truly call *hers* piled on both beds. Clothing, of course, that was the largest pile; the carved wooden box Papa had made to hold her jewelry was on top of the pile of underthings. She ran her fingers over the smooth wood of the top, following the familiar course of the curls and whorls he'd incised there.

Beside that were her two dolls; all the rest of her toys had been handed down to her brothers as she outgrew them. One was a faceless, battered, and much beloved rag-doll; worn out with loving and much play, but too much adored to be discarded. Beth had been the subject of many an adventure, many a peril, and so much hugging that the stuffing was permanently squeezed out of her middle. She had been rescued by Heralds and Hawkbrothers from every hazard imaginable, from forest fires to slavers—then, as Keisha's interest in Healing strengthened and grew, had not only been rescued, but had been cured of every illness and injury possible, and some that would have been the death of any lesser creature. Her embroidered mouth was stained with all the potions that had been pressed to it; her goat-hair braids a little matted from the compresses tied to her head, and every limb had been stitched and restitched with sutures for imagined wounds. Keisha gave her a self-conscious little kiss, and put her down again.

The other doll, an immaculate and beautiful porcelain-headed lady-doll that she and Shandi used to practice on when they were first learning sewing skills, was in near-new condition, for Anestesi had been a gift to a much older Keisha than Beth. In fact, Shandi and Keisha still used this doll to work out a new cut for a gown or the like.

She picked it up and smoothed down the folds of the last gown they'd sewn for it, a dainty creation for Shandi on the occasion of her being chosen Harvest Queen last fall. Of course, the doll's gown was a patchwork of scraps with a network of chalk lines and other marks on it, which gave the gown a rather odd look—but Shandi had looked like real royalty. . . .

Yes, both dolls would definitely have to come. They could share the loft with her bed; that way no one would see them and tease her about them, and Beth could reassure hurt little ones.

Next, basketful of toiletries. Scent, lotions, the cosmetics she and Shandi had created that Mum would have had a fit over, had she known about them—no doubt there; these had better come too. At least now she'd have some privacy to experiment with those cosmetics without anybody finding out. *And if Mum discovered them, I hate to think what a scene it would cause.*

All of the extra sheets and blankets came next, but there was really no need to take them.

I'll leave the bedding, I've enough at the workshop, and if I need more, I can barter for it. She stowed it all under the bed where it had been kept before.

Embroidery basket, knitting basket, plain-sewing basket— all of her handicrafts stored in baskets, making them portable enough to take along anywhere. Shandi had come up with that idea, and now Shandi's baskets were somewhere between here and Haven in a peddler's wagon.

Yes, yes, and yes. I'm still going to need my baskets. I've got all that wool to knit up if I want a new sweater this winter.

A pile of fabric—which had mostly been Shandi's choices, but which Shandi was hardly going to need now, seeing as how she would spend the next several years wearing Trainee Grays exclusively. Keisha had kept the pile of fabric when she'd sent on Shandi's clothing and handiwork baskets. *Will I have time to do any sewing for myself?* Well, probably. And colors that suited Shandi would also suit Keisha. True, the fabrics would do for new shirts for the boys, but when was Mum going to have time to sew them? She hesitated, then added the pile of fabric to the growing list of things she was taking. *I have plenty of things that I can wear to work in, but not much else. It might be nice to have a pretty gown or so.*

Rag bag—

Definitely. No one can have too many rags.

The big box of odds-and-ends she was always meaning to do something with—brilliant feathers, a cured snakeskin, seeds that looked as if they might make good beads, half-finished bits of carving and crafting—

Maybe I'll get some of that done.

Eventually she had it all sorted through, and decided that three trips would do to get it all to the workshop. On the second, neighbor Tansy came outside with a basket of wet clothing and looked at her with a surprised expression.

"Keisha!" she called, before Keisha could escape out of earshot. "Have you fought with your parents over something? Is something wrong? Why are you moving?"

Keisha paused and peered around her burden, licked her lips nervously, and said, "We haven't quarreled, but—Tansy, with Shandi gone, the house is just too *small* to hold all those boys and just me. Besides, I'm in the shop more than I'm here."

Tansy looked relieved, and nodded. "That's the truth, and I've been saying to my Olek that you must feel like a kick-ball, in there with all those rowdy boys and no Shandi to make them behave like gentlemen. Well, good, as long as you haven't gone and had a fight with your Mum or Da. I'll remember you're on your own, and bring you over a bite to eat now and again."

Keisha flushed, and smiled. "Thank you, Tansy. That's more than I'd expect."

"Oh, it's no more than we did—or should have done for Wizard Justyn, bless his brave soul." She waved her hand vaguely in the direction of the statue in the square. "I won't keep you, dear—and I hope you enjoy a night without having to listen to your brothers for a change!"

"Oh, Tansy—" Keisha laughed, "—they snore so loudly I'll probably *still* hear them!"

When she returned for the third load, Tansy was back inside her house, and she brought over the last of her things with a feeling of profound relief.

The relief deepened into pure content as she stowed her belongings away—clothing into the clothes-chest in the loft and the wardrobe-cupboard downstairs, fabric up on a shelf where it wouldn't get dirty, one workbasket in the window seat, one in the loft, and one beside the fire. The dolls sat side-by-side in state on her bed, and all the rest of her possessions fitted into nooks and corners as if they'd belonged there all along.

Now it looked like a home. Her samplers and embroidered tapestries were on the wall, a lap rug lay over the back of the fireplace chair, embroidered cushions softened seats, and her blue glass vase sat on the tiny table where she ate her meals.

And it was hers, all hers, with the stamp of no other hands on it.

Wizard Justyn would never recognize the place, she thought happily. Not that she had ever seen it when Justyn was in residence, but some of the village women had given very succinct and pungent descriptions. They all boiled down to one word—one which made a world of sense to women, though it baffled men.

Bachelors.

Justyn had been a bachelor, and an old one at that. Bachelors didn't clean up after themselves, for some unknown reason—nor did they really allow anyone else to clean up after them. The place would have been a right mess when Justyn lived here, with shelves crammed full of dusty oddments, clothing lying about on the floor or draped over a chair where the wizard had left it, and dirty crockery filling the sink.

Now, every perfectly straight and level shelf held its proper contents arrayed sensibly. The big table that had taken up most of the space was gone, replaced by her tiny table, a short stool, and a couple of comfortable chairs. A tall stool stood beside her clean, orderly workbenches, the floor was swept, the hearth clean, and enough firewood to take care of the fire for the entire evening stacked in a log holder beside it. Kindling was in a bucket beside that, not scattered across the hearth. The biggest of the two windows had been deepened, and a window seat built into it. Her embroidered Windrider hung over the hearth, her first and second samplers on either side of it, and her Moonlady up in the loft over the window. Braided rag rugs softened and warmed the floor. All the food was stored out of sight in a closed and mouse-proof cupboard. There wasn't a crumb to tempt mouse or insect anywhere to be seen.

On the "domestic" side of the cottage, shelves were laden with her personal books, handiwork, linens, and other purely personal belongings. Here, the wardrobe and cupboard resided. On the "Healer" side, shelves were burdened with more books, prepared medicines, raw materials, bandages, the knives and probes, needles and Tayledras silk and catgut of her trade. This was where the workbenches were, and the sink with its pump. The fireplace divided the two "sides," and beside it was a rolled-up pallet, where she could treat anyone who couldn't stand, or needed sewing up. That way the victim couldn't thrash around and fall off a table or bed— and what was more important to her, if he was delirious or uncooperative, she could sit on him to hold him still if she had to.

Acres and acres, and it's mine, all mine! She giggled, remembering the punchline to a salacious joke she wasn't supposed to have overheard.

Everything was as neat and clean as soap and water could get it, including the loft where her bed was.

And that, of course, would be another change. I remember when we cleaned this place up. Dirt had actually packed into the corners!

Still, that was a little uncharitable, for Justyn *had* kept his own treatment areas clean. It was just that—

Well, bachelors don't seem to realize that dirt gets under things and into corners where you can't see it. Bachelors think that as long as it's not gritty underfoot, the floor's clean.

It was time to think about making supper—

Or going to talk to the Fellowship. I think I'll be lazy.

As she closed the door behind her, she realized that there was something gone from her—*resentment.* And another thing—a feeling of being desperately crowded.

It's because now I don't have to share anything, that's what it is. Not the washbasin, not the chores, not a room. Bright Havens! I can choose to share, I don't have to! I'm going to have privacy! *Real, and total, privacy!* She couldn't remember having had complete privacy in her entire life. It was such an astonishing thought that she couldn't think of anything else right up until the moment that she knocked on the door of the Fellowship's Hall, their main building.

She recognized the old man who answered the door as the "Eldest"—not really a leader, but the oldest man of the founding family, the grandfather of Alys. As such, he had the authority to make simple bargains for the Fellowship such as the one she had in mind without putting it to a vote.

"Eldest Safir," she said, with a half-bow. "I have a proposition I would like to put to you."

"Then please enter, Healer," he told her, his expression carefully neutral. She entered and followed him into the communal hall where they all took their meals. At his invitation she sat down on a bench; he sat on one opposite her.

"May I hear your proposition, Healer?" he asked politely. "I cannot say yet if I may consider it alone, or the Fellowship as a whole must debate it."

"I understand that, Eldest," she replied, just as soberly. "It is a minor proposal—and simple. The Fellowship currently owes me for certain medicines and treatment for the sheep during the rains—I should like to barter that credit for a certain number of meals taken with you."

The old man's brows had furrowed during the first part of her statement, but rose to his hairline in surprise as she finished. "Don't you have your own family?" he blurted.

"I have irregular hours, and it came to me today that we have far too many people stuffed into a single small house," she said with a smile. "We all agree that I am fully adult, so I moved into my workshop, to free some space for my brothers. Since I will no longer be contributing to the family income, it seems wrong to take bread from their table."

"I can see that." He pondered the proposal while she waited patiently. "And I am certain that you already know of our custom of the hearth kettle."

"Actually, Eldest," she smiled, "I was counting on it."

The "hearth kettle" was a kettle of soup or stew always kept on the kitchen hearth, so that anyone who was hungry could be fed. One of the Fellowship's customs was that anyone who begged charity was granted three meals and a place to sleep with nothing in return asked of him—and the kettle also served a useful purpose for people whose lives were built around their animals, and who thus, at certain seasons, would also have "irregular hours." Keisha could *always* count on getting a bite from the hearth kettle, day or night.

"Well, then—" Now the old man smiled broadly, and Keisha knew she'd won him over. "What if I say that we will barter unlimited meals in return for all routine care? Not emergencies or unexpected illnesses, like the sheep just had, but all the routine health checks and medicines and tonics and so forth."

She saw no point in bargaining further; this was exactly what she wanted. "Then I would say that the bargain is set." She held out her hand.

He took it, and shook it three times to seal the bargain. "Will you stay for tonight's dinner? We've egg-pie." He raised his eyebrows again. "My wife Alse's egg-pie."

She sighed happily at the mere suggestion, and smiled at him. "Eldest," she said with complete truth, "For your wife's egg-pie I would arm wrestle a bear."

She returned to her cottage— her cottage, not her workshop anymore, and the mere thought filled her with proprietary pride—carrying a basket of warm rolls for breakfast and with the satisfied content of having had a truly fine meal. Alse had a way with spicing and adding chopped bacon and greens to egg-pie that raised the humble dish to something suitable for the table of the Queen herself. There could not have been a better omen for the start of her bargain with the Fellowship than that first meal.

She put the rolls away and lit two of her lamps, then went out into the garden to cut a few blooms for her vase. With lamps shining brightly and flowers on the table, she felt happier than she had for months.

And instead of studying, tonight she gave herself a holiday of sorts. With a small fire to warm the room, she picked up her knitting; with luck, she'd finish the back of the tunic tonight. That would leave the front and both sleeves to do before winter, which was hardly an insurmountable task.

She listened to the songs of crickets and tree-frogs, the murmur of voices in the houses nearest hers, and the distant rushing of the river. There were no shouting boys, no clumping boots—nothing but peaceful quiet.

Why didn't I do this sooner? I'd have had far fewer headaches!

Perhaps because Shandi had kept peace in the house—or as much peace as anyone could. But surely at some point even Shandi had gotten tired of playing peacekeeper. . . .

Maybe that's one reason why she was so ready to ride off to Haven. That, and Mum. Mum didn't really want her to grow up, I think. Poor Mum; like it or not, children do, and there's nothing to be done about it.

So, it could be that Shandi had done both of them a favor, by making the break clean and quick. *Yes, and me, too. If Shandi's grown up, I'm more than grown.*

Was this how Shandi felt now, on her own, making her own decisions, having a place she could truly say was hers and no one else's? If so, Keisha was glad for her; it was a fine feeling, and one she would be glad to share.

I hope she has a room of her own at that Collegium place. She certainly deserves one at this point.

She'd always been an early riser—more from necessity than virtue, it was true, but a Healer didn't have much choice in the matter—and it had been a long day. She found herself yawning over her work just as she bound off the knitting, and realized that there were no noisy boys to keep her awake if she tried to go to sleep "early." She lit a lantern in the loft, blew out the two downstairs, and banked the fire for the morning. As she went back up to the loft to change for bed, she sent a silent prayer of thanks to whatever deity had put this notion of moving into her mind. *And if it's the spirit of Wizard Justyn, who didn't want his cottage to stand empty most of the time, thank you, too!*

Once the hurdle of breaking the news to her mother was over and done with, the move was going to make life easier. Much, much easier.

Now if the mysterious Darian would just return to care for the magical needs of Errold's Grove, life here would be just about perfect.

Starfall

Six

Once, back when he was enduring his lessons with Justyn, Darian would have been conscious of nothing except how uncomfortable he was at this moment—either too hot or too cold, sitting on a rock or on a sharp branch. He could always find something to distract him from his hated lessons in magic, lessons he considered useless. That was a long time ago, far distant in time and maturity, or so he hoped. Now, none of those possible discomforts mattered, and if you asked him about the temperature or his surroundings, he'd tell you honestly that he hadn't noticed.

Especially at this moment, a moment of epiphanal break through, when intense new experience overwhelmed every other consideration.

"There!" said Healer-Mage Firefrost in triumph. "Now you see it, you feel it, don't you?"

Darian "stared" at the slow, smooth flow of energy that was literally all around him; it had taken days of coaching, but now, at last, he was able to do what Starfall had not been able to teach him—was in the overworld of energy, a world overlying the "real" world and a part of it, yet with its own separate life and rules. He used Mage-Sight at a deep enough level to actually watch the passage of life-energy from living creatures to the tiny feeder lines, and from there to the ley-lines, and on to the nodes. Every mage knew that energy flowed in that way; it was one of the first lessons in energy control—but only certain types of mages could actually *see* it happen at the level of individual blades of grass and insects no bigger than pinheads. Most mages couldn't actually detect mage-energy until it had collected in the threadlike initial runnels, leaving them with the impression that the energy took the form of a web, rather than an all-pervasive flow. More than that, as Firefrost said, he *felt* it, a sensation entirely new to him and yet as familiar to him as his own heartbeat—exactly like the faint pressure of sunlight on his skin. Healers saw and felt the same thing according to Starfall; so did minor mages like earth-witches and hedge-wizards—these were the energies that they used, for they were unable to handle anything with more power than a small runnel. This energy was tedious to accumulate and granted them a relatively low level of power, but it was omnipresent. An earth-witch never had to search for a ley-line, and for a while after the mage-storms, hedge-wizards could accomplish more than Adepts, who had never been forced to learn all of the minor magics that needed only the merest whisper of power.

Experimentally, he moved to one of the little runnels collecting the flow—nowhere near large enough to be called a ley-line—and sensed the pressure increase when he interposed himself in the flow.

"It feels good, doesn't it?" Firefrost said with satisfaction. "I always think it feels like bathing in sun-warmed silk."

He nodded absently; it both felt and looked good, a warm amber glow the exact color of the light near sunset on a cloudless summer evening, and a sensation of being slowly revitalized.

"If you go somewhere that the energies are distorted or marred, you'll feel that as well," Firefrost told him. "It will make you sick, and you'll learn to tell what's wrong by how it affects you. Right now you need most to learn to snap in and out of Mage-Sight and Mage-Sense accurately and infallibly, so that if you ever do come across such a place, it won't entrap you. Now that you have the trick of Seeing this level, your assignment will be to practice exactly that until I think you're ready for the next step."

"Can the good magic entrap you, too, with not wanting to leave that feeling?" he asked.

"Not if you're mentally healthy—no more than you're entrapped at the feast table," she replied. "Once you're 'full,' you'll feel willing to leave."

The mage did—something. Darian couldn't quite tell what it was, but it felt a little like a static spark arcing from the mage to himself, more of a shock than pain, but enough to bring him back to the ordinary world with a startled gasp.

"This is why you need a Healing Adept to teach you properly," Firefrost said, still sitting serenely where she'd been all along, cross-legged in the shade at the edge of the meadow where he and Kel had picnicked. "Starfall is a fine mage, experienced and full of wisdom, but he cannot see and sense the earth-energies in the way a Healer-Mage can, he cannot move about in the realm of pure energy the way we can, so he could not teach you how to access them. I am a Healer-Mage, but I can only take you so far—*you* have the potential to become a Healing Adept, and your teacher should also be at that level, if you are going to reach that potential."

Darian nodded; he also sat where he had been all along; his "movement" in the overworld of energies had all been with something other than his physical body. "I think I know why you brought me here, too," he said shrewdly. "Even though most of the mages have been teaching me in the safety of the Vale, if I'd made the breakthrough there, I'd probably have been blinded."

Firefrost beamed at him, her young-old face suddenly wreathed in the wrinkles of her proper age—well over seventy. Smile-lines, mostly; Firefrost was a very cheerful person. "Very good! Yes, and I advise you to practice and learn to control this type of Sight in a safe place outside the Vale until you've gotten it well in hand. So many ley-lines come into the Heartstone in the Vale that you *would* be blinded if you can't dim things down for yourself. And you'd have a headache for a week that would make you wish you were dead!"

Darian was still conscious of that faint pressure of energy; he realized that he always *had* been, he just hadn't known what to call it. "So this is why some places in Valdemar made me sick until we cleaned them up!" he said wonderingly. "That's why Snowfire and Starfall would watch *me* so closely—they couldn't feel where things had gone wrong, and they used me to find the places for them!"

Firefrost nodded, and her approval warmed him clear

through. "And you understand why they had to do that, don't you? Or now are you feeling misused?"

That was the last thing on his mind. He shrugged. "They didn't have much choice, did they? I mean, they *did* have a kind of choice, they could have used dowsing or some other way to find the bad places, but it was so much quicker to use me—and besides that, it didn't cost them anything in magical energies of their own. They wouldn't have risked me if they didn't think that we could all do what we did without any harm to me."

He couldn't resent being "used;" not after the way he'd been vehemently angry with them over using up energies they could ill afford in order to accomplish things that *he* had been able to do at far less expense. He'd essentially offered himself for whatever need they had at that point, so there was no reason to resent the fact that they'd taken him up on the offer!

"This—this form of the Gift that you have—is very similar to the Earth-Sense of some monarchs," Firefrost went on in her low, age-roughened voice. "*They* can't actually see the energies most of the time—not unless they are also mages—but they feel them. They can also feel what is wrong with the energies of their land at a distance, which can be very useful. The monarchs of Rethwellan have it, the highest of the Priests of Vkandis have it, the Son of the Sun Solaris has it, and the new King of Hardorn has it. In the King of Hardorn's case, though, it was—imposed on him. With his consent—though I sometimes think he didn't know what he was consenting to." She raised an ironic eyebrow. "There is an ancient earth-religion sect of that land that still retains the full knowledge of the Earth-Taking ceremony, and has managed to give Earth-Sense to every monarch of Hardorn except the late and unlamented Ancar."

"Will I be able— Scratch that. I *will* be able to do what Starfall did about cleaning places up, but faster and more easily, won't I." He made it a statement, but was pleased to see Firefrost nod. "It'll be like Healing for a Healer; instead of having to figure out what's gone wrong, I'll already know by how it affects me, and because of that I'll know how to fix what's wrong and get it right the first time, instead of fumbling around using trial and error."

"It will be quite natural to you—as will some other things, such as moving and acting in the overworld of mage-energies, once you've gotten the proper instructor. And you will be able to accomplish things I can only watch and admire, if you ever have access to enough energy." Firefrost sighed. "Still, we all have our abilities, and—"

"And anyone who can reverse the effects of frostbite has no reason to feel self-conscious," he replied, daring to interrupt her. "Any Healer can save what there is left of the damaged tissue, and so could most mages—but anyone who can restore and rebuild all the damage that has already occurred has nothing to be ashamed of!"

That was how Firefrost had gotten her use name at the age of fourteen, when she was newly come into her abilities. While she was scouting the boundaries of k'Vala, a blizzard too huge to be steered away had swept across the forest and everyone who could was out scouting for those who might have been caught in it. She had been the only person anything like a Healer to come upon a family of *tervardi* taken by surprise by the storm. She had not only saved them from freezing, but had almost completely reversed the effects of the profoundly crippling frostbite (or "firefrost" in the Hawkbrother tongue) that they had suffered. By the time the help she had called for arrived, most of the damage was Healed, and no one suffered anything worse than a little superficial scarring at the extremities.

"I sometimes suspect that the only reason I could was that I didn't know I couldn't," his teacher said, only half in jest. "Still . . ."

"Still, a little magic used with precision and at precisely the right time is better than a great deal of magic used sloppily and clumsily, too late or too early," he said firmly. "I can't tell you how many times I've seen that!"

"Very well! The student rightly rebukes the teacher!" Firefrost laughed, throwing up her hands as if to fend off a blow. "Now, I would like to see if the student can evoke his Mage-Sight in the realm of the overworld without the coaching of his teacher!"

"I hear and obey," he said, bowing a little at the waist, and sent his mind down that peculiar "twist" that Firefrost had shown him.

Once again, the world around him was overlaid with the overworld of energies. This time he had a kind of double vision, with the real world showing through the flowing energy-fields, and he decided to see if he could narrow his focus—

Even as he thought that, in a dizzying rush that "felt" exactly as if he were diving off a cliff into the river, he found himself contemplating the life-forces of a single blade of grass. Except that he was far, far "smaller" in perception than that blade of grass!

Oh. My. The slender stem loomed "over" him like one of the great trees of the Vale. As he gazed "upward," his mouth falling open, he tried to take in the immense complexity of this seemingly insignificant bit of flora, and failed.

I think my brain is overflowing! He tried to break free of the fascination and couldn't—tried again and still couldn't—and gave a wordless cry for help to his teacher.

With another of those startling shocks, he found himself looking only at the real world again, from his proper perspective, and sighed with relief.

"Next time, *ask* before you do something like that," Firefrost told him sternly, crossing her arms over her chest, and giving him a harsh glare. "That was not what I asked you to do, was it?"

"I didn't know I was doing it until I'd done it," he admitted shakily.

She shook her head, the fine silver hair escaping from its braids with the movement and floating in fly-away strands about her face. "Now you see why you need a Healing *Adept* to teach you. It's entirely possible that you could get yourself into something that I *can't* get you out of! In the future, tell me what you think you want to do before you're in the overworld, all right? With someone of your potential, a wish often becomes fact before you have the least idea what's going on."

He felt very tired, all at once, and certainly he and Firefrost had put in more than enough work for one day. It had taken all afternoon before he'd learned that twist that brought him into the overworld. "Can we stop now?" he asked meekly. "I'm getting worn out."

Firefrost lost her stern glare and smiled ruefully. "And so you should be—and it's my fault for letting you go back in when I knew you would be getting tired. Just run through those primary exercises I showed you, and we'll go back to the Vale."

Now that he knew what they were for, the "primary exercises" in energy manipulation were far easier than they'd been earlier this afternoon, and he ran through them accurately, if not quickly. For the last one, he guided energy from the tree he sat beneath to a particular runnel rather than allowing it to flow into several as it would normally have done, and this time nothing escaped his "herding."

"Clean," Firefrost approved. "Very clean. I couldn't have done it better. Let's get ourselves back home, shall we?"

He got to his feet and aided Firefrost to hers. She was as much Starfall's senior as Starfall was Darien's and, until Darian arrived, the only Healing-Mage that k'Vala had. She had greeted his arrival with relief—and pleasure, when she learned his potential.

She was the kindest and most patient of his three teachers, although Starfall ran a very near second. If his unknown Healing-Adept teacher was half as easy to get along with as Firefrost, Darian thought that he would count himself lucky.

The other teacher, Adept Darkstone, was much more difficult to like. He gave Darian his full attention, true, and was absolutely punctilious in giving Darian the most precise and accurate instructions, but it was all done without any feeling whatsoever. Darian still didn't know a thing about Darkstone's background, not even something so minor as which tree his *ekele* was in, and he'd been getting lessons from the Adept for a week.

The one thing that he did know was the single thing Darkstone made clear at the very beginning; the Adept was entirely against the idea of working with Valdemarans in any way. He did not want outsiders in the Vale, around the Vale, or even aware that the Vale existed. He wanted Hawkbrothers to be a frightening presence in the forest, a glimpse of eyes in a shadow, the warning arrow out of nowhere.

Darkstone wasn't the only Tayledras who felt that way, though all the ones that Darian had met so far had treated him with distant courtesy at least. There was, after all, a tradition of Tayledras accepting the *occasional* outsider into their ranks and Clans. The thing that this particular faction opposed was the wholesale "adoption" of Valdemar on the same basis as the Kaled'a'in.

Hard as it was to believe, there was even a faction that didn't want the Kaled'a'in in k'Vala Vale! Their reasoning was a bit obtuse, along the line that "if the Goddess had wanted k'Leshya back with the Tayledras, the Goddess would have led them to us after the Sundering."

Useless to argue that this was precisely what had happened— if a bit later than they would have preferred. This lot no more wanted *trondi'irn* and gryphons in Tayledras Vales than they wanted Shin'a'in and their fighting mares in Tayledras Vales.

Fortunately, Firefrost was as amused by them as they were outraged by her—and *she* had power and seniority in the Council over most of them.

Even if she didn't, she could probably reduce them to gibbering just by chuckling at them, tickling them under the chin, and telling them to "run along and learn to play nicely with the new children." He began to see that there were a lot of advantages to age, some of them enough to provide compensation for losing some of the advantages of youth!

In deference to Firefrost's age, they'd ridden here on a pair of *dyheli* rather than hiking on foot. The two does had wandered off somewhere, but Kuari had kept track of one, while Firefrost's snow-white peregrine had followed the other. Now, without prompting, the birds came winging back, flying under the level of the branches, while the *dyheli* does sauntered along behind at a brisk walk. Darian offered his linked hands to Firefrost; with a half-bow of her own, she stepped into them, and he boosted her into the well-padded saddle, then hopped onto the other waiting doe. Firefrost avoided the elaborate robes some of the mages—Darkstone for one—liked to wear, and the intricate hairstyles as well. Long, easy-fitting tunics and loose trews of silks in simple colors were what she preferred, and she kept her hair in two braids or a coiled braid at the nape of her neck. Today she wore green, with a necklet of rainbow-moonstones, a single white primary from her bird fastened into her braids.

"The other day someone asked me why I hadn't changed my name for a use-name," he told her, as they rode side by side. "I told them it was because I *felt* like the same person. Does that make sense to you?"

"Perfectly sound, good sense," she replied with a laugh. "Really, Dar'ian, the reason we change our use-names in the first place is because the ones we're given as children don't fit us when we become adults. Think about the use-names for the children you've heard—Bluefeather, Littleflower, Honeyfawn, Jumpfrog—who'd want to be saddled with something like that as an adult?"

"Huh—or as an adolescent!" he countered, from the lofty vantage of eighteen. "So how do people get their adult use-names? Yours was given to you, right?"

"Yes, and if you manage to do something notable at about the time you're ready for an 'adult' use-name, that's usually what you get. Sometimes you get tagged with something notable that *happens* when you're ready for a new name." Her eyes crinkled at the corners with amusement. "That's how Starfall got his—it was at a Midsummer celebration, and he'd climbed to the top of a cliff overshadowing the main swimming pool at the Vale we had back then. This was on a dare, you see—the usual male foolishness over a girl—and he jumped from the cliff into the pool at *precisely* the same time as an extremely bright shooting star flashed overhead, mirroring his fall, even to the same angle. So—'Starfall' he became and has remained." Her eyes crinkled up even more. "And the funniest thing about it is that because he was diving at the time and had all of his attention on the dive so that he wouldn't break his silly neck, *he* never saw the falling star that gave him his name!"

"Steelmind?"

"He never forgets anything, and proved it by reciting to one of the Elders a speech he had made that was precisely contradictory to the position he supported at that moment." She laughed. "Potentially embarrassing, but he didn't do it in public. Nevertheless, the Elder in question told everyone that the boy had a mind like a steel cage—nothing that got locked into it ever escaped."

Darian grinned. "What about Darkstone?"

"His personality," she responded promptly. "Pessimistic, unchanging, and cold as a stone. And believe it or not, he chose it himself. It was an affectation when he was young; he liked that particular aloof image. Now he couldn't change it without more effort than he's willing to put in."

"Wintersky? Raindance? Summerdance?"

"All juvenile names; they haven't gotten use-names yet, and their childhood names weren't so silly they were in a hurry to lose them."

"Hmm. Would anyone label me with a use-name that I don't like, but am stuck with?" He could think of a number of unpleasant possibilities.

"People can try, but if you refuse to respond to their name for you, it's considered good manners not to persist. You know the proverb—'It isn't what you call me, it's what I answer to that counts.' " She nodded with understanding at his obvious relief. "As long as you feel you are Dar'ian and continue to respond to that name, no one will force you to accept another."

At this point he certainly couldn't foresee ever wanting to take a use-name. *Not even if I were to do something really impressive.*

"Do remember if you do take a use-name that after you've had it for many years, it becomes a great effort to change it again," she cautioned. "Usually something very dramatic has to happen before the change sticks in peoples' minds. I can't think of more than two or three people who've successfully gone to a new use-name later in life."

By then, they'd reached the entrance to k'Vala, and they discussed when and where they would meet for his next lesson. Once inside the Veil they dismounted and thanked the *dyheli* for their help; Darian escorted his teacher to her *ekele,* one that was quite low to the ground, by Tayledras standards. There he left her in the hands of her *hertasi* helpers, and decided to see if Nightbird or Snowfire and Nightwind had eaten dinner yet, as he was in the mood for some company.

I'll try Kel's sunning rock, he decided. That always seemed to be the place one or more of them ended up.

Since he was in a very good mood, it came as an abrupt shock to him to walk straight into the middle of a fight between Snowfire and his beloved. He simply rounded a curve in the path, walked out into the open near the group of boulders that several gryphons liked to use for sunbathing, and there they were—

Oh-oh.

"—and no one is going to dictate whom I talk to!" Nightwind said, clearly and precisely, just as Darian stopped in his tracks. Her eyes, dark with anger, were the color of a thundercloud and looked just about ready to produce lightning. Her hands were clenched, her knuckles white, and her posture as stiff as an iron rod. For his part, Snowfire was actually white with rage, *his* eyes had gone to a pale gray, and his jaw was set so hard that Darian expected to hear his teeth splintering at any moment.

It was even more of a shock to Darian since they were arguing in a place so very public. They'd argued before, even in his presence, but never where anyone could just walk into the middle of the spat.

They were both using those sharp-edged, oh-so-civilized tones that meant they were really, really angry. They were both so caught up in their fight that neither of them paid the least attention to what was going on around them; he could have been a leaf, for all the attention they paid to him. Kel, wise young gryphon that he was, must have fled the moment the fight began.

Darian was taken so much by surprise that he froze where he was—and it looked as though he wasn't the only one who'd been caught off-guard and trapped by the altercation. Nightbird stood with her back to the trunk of a tree, looking very much as if she were bound there and not much caring for it, on the other side of the line-of-battle from Darian.

"Look, I *told* you what he said—and to my face!" Snowfire said between clenched teeth, his face set, his eyes blazing with white fire. "He's lucky I didn't call him out in front of the Elders for it! That's reason enough for you to avoid him."

"No, it isn't. And who are you to choose my friends for

me?" Nightwind shot back, matching him glare for glare. "I am not going to give up friends I've had all my life, just because you can't get along with them! He was my scouting partner all the way from White Gryphon, and I'm not going to act as if he's come down with spots just because *you* got your precious masculine pride a little bruised! You don't *own* me, and the last time I looked, the Tayledras didn't keep slaves!"

That was more than enough for Darian; he managed to catch Nightbird's eye and made a little motion with his head in the direction of the path. She nodded violently and edged around her sister until she got clear of the pair, then made a dash for safety. He grabbed her hand as she reached him, and they both beat a quick retreat up the path.

"What was all *that* about?" he asked as soon as they were out of earshot and felt as if they could slow down to a walk. "And how did you get caught in the middle?"

"Lessons with my sister, with Kel serving as the willing client," she said, a little out of breath. "Snowfire came charging into the middle of it without so much as an 'excuse me' and began ranting about a friend of hers." She paused, then said carefully, "And if you don't mind, I'd rather not name names."

He waved a hand at her. "Don't worry, I'd rather not know!"

"Well, the fellow in question is pretty well known among the Kaled'a'in for saying stupid things without thinking and regretting it later," she replied. "I guess that's probably what he did this time. That, and I think there's some jealousy there, too, since he used to be Nightwind's partner, like she said, and the fact that she'd chosen to take someone else as her mate came as a nasty surprise." Nightbird looked very, very worried, though she didn't say anything more, and Darian had a fair idea why. She hadn't seen her sister for four years, and probably thought this represented a truly serious rift between Nightwind and her mate.

"So he's been brooding about it and maybe today he was out-of-sorts and he said something rude to Snowfire." Darian nodded. "And I bet Snowfire was out of sorts, too, so Snowfire was in no mood to be forgiving." He sighed, then smiled reassuringly at her. "Don't let this worry you. I've seen them fight before, you know. They don't do it often, it's always when both of them are on edge or feeling sensitive about something, and they always make it up afterward. Truly. Couples do this sort of thing; Nightwind says it's because you can't live life so much a part of each other without eventually doing or saying something that's too irritating to ignore."

"Really?" Nightbird lost some of that anxious look.

"Truly," he told her firmly. "I've been caught in the middle of explosions just like that one. They'll make it up. *Especially* if you can get whoever it was to come apologize. To both of them, if you can manage it."

"Me?" she squeaked. "Why me?"

"Because you carefully didn't tell me his name." Darian was amused to see the expression on her face when she realized she was caught in a trap of her own making. "Besides, I'm not a Kaled'a'in, and I *am* Snowfire's little brother. I'm expected to be on his side. You, on the other hand, can go tell this fellow that he's a blithering idiot and deserves to have Kel drop him into the lake from treetop height, and get away with it." He put a little coaxing into his voice. "Look, you all but admitted that the fellow deserves it, and you are *awfully* good at dressing fools down in a way that rubs their noses in it. You're also awfully good at making them admit that they were idiots."

"I am, aren't I. I wonder if that's an undiscovered power, the Gift of Insult." She looked thoughtful for a moment, then smirked. "You're right this time. I'm the logical choice, and what's more, I can make him feel so guilty about causing a fight at the same time I'm dressing him down that he'll be begging me to help him make an apology." She grinned suddenly. "I have every right to be the one to make him feel guilty, too—since I'm the one who got caught in the middle! You know, Sister always says I know how to work people around so well I ought to become a *kestra'chern* instead of a *trondi'irn*. I just tell her that it would be no fun if I had to do it professionally."

"There you go!" he encouraged her. "Tell you what, I'll arrange some dinner for both of us, you go give him what he's got coming, and then come meet me at the far end of the lake and tell me what happened. I promise to heap admiration upon you."

"It's a bargain." She strode off, determination making her spine stiff, energy giving spring to her step, without looking back—probably because she was already rehearsing in her mind exactly what she was going to say. He chuckled a little, and went in search of food that would put her in a very good mood.

She liked finger-foods—because what she liked was variety without getting filled up—so he hunted in a couple of the places where *hertasi* put out dishes for those who preferred to "graze" for dinner. When one of the *hertasi* learned what he was doing, things became a little easier, and he waited at the appointed spot with a special basket with a warm stone in the bottom of it to keep the steamed dumplings, sausages, and spiced fish-cakes hot, and a second basket with a *chilled* stone for the sliced vegetables, dipping sauce, and special rolls Nightbird particularly liked, made of boiled grain, thinly sliced fish, vegetables, and spices all rolled in seeds. Sweet spring water in a glass bottle chilled in the same basket, and hot tea in a pottery jug stayed warm in the first basket. And when Nightbird arrived, looking just a little smug, he rewarded her efforts by opening both baskets, handing her a huge leaf to use as a plate, and giving her first choice. Wonderful aromas rose from the first basket, and the contents of the second had been so artfully arranged by the *hertasi* that she actually paused to admire the creation.

She went straight for the chilled grain-rolls, which was what he had thought might happen. That was perfectly all right with him, for he had no idea how anyone could eat the things; he helped himself to vegetables and steamed dumplings, and did *not* press her for details until after she'd had her first roll.

"Well?" he asked archly.

"He should be groveling in front of both of them now," she said with supreme satisfaction. "And since they were already at the kiss-and-apologize stage when I left him with them, it should be even more gratifying for Snowfire. My sister will probably be exasperated with him, but she'll forgive him, so all will be well."

"I told you they'd get over it pretty quickly," he reminded her. "Havens, with any luck, Snowfire and this mysterious fellow will actually become friends out of this."

She nodded because her mouth was full, swallowed, and said, "That's what I'm hoping, though it may actually take both of them trying to pound each other to powder before that happens. Why do some men have to be such idiots?"

"Ask Tyrsell," he suggested. "Seems to me there's a lot of king-stag stuff going on there."

She snorted, and tried a dumpling for variety. "Well, I hope I never get caught in the middle of one of their fights again. It was so *civilized*, but so angry, it gave me chills! How can anyone fight like that?"

"I don't know; I think it must be something they've worked out. It's pretty astonishing to watch, actually; not *pleasant*, but astonishing. *I've* never seen anyone argue that way before."

"Where do they get the self-control?" she asked, her brow wrinkling. "What have you seen them do?"

"It's what they don't do. They don't call names or make personal accusations. They get what's making them angry out first thing, and you'd swear that they're a short step away from killing each other! But then, they get into *why* it made them angry, they actually take turns and try not to interrupt, and then—and I think this must be the important part—go into exactly how bad this made them feel. And at that point, the fire just goes out of the fight! They get things sorted out, then apologize, get things more sorted out—then things are actually better than they were before the fight, I think, because they've made another compromise with each other."

Nightbird's eyes widened at that. "My! I think maybe I'd better not get joined to anyone, after all. I don't think I could manage that! It sounds like an awful lot of work to go through just to stay with someone."

He licked his fingers clean of juice from a dumpling. "Maybe they couldn't either, at first. I'm sure they had fights before the one I got caught in. I guess . . . if you're going to get mad about something, it's better to get it out than let it sit in-side and steam." He laughed wryly. "I tend to steam, and it got me in a lot of trouble, because things would build up and then let go without warning and I would *really* get it!"

She bit her lower lip. "Uh-huh," she agreed. "That's my problem, too. Maybe we'd better make a vow just to stay friends. I have the feeling that we could really do damage to each other, if we started getting really intimate then got an-gry with each other over something important."

Oh, hellfires. But she's right. If we started getting very, very close, that's exactly what would happen. "Don't make vows about the future," he warned. "But you're right, and we could make a pledge that we'll *try* to just stay friends for that reason. Bargain?"

"Bargain," she replied solemnly. "Besides, we're practically related, and that feels too much like incest! Want to head over to Summerdance's *ekele* and see what she's doing? Maybe we can get a game-group together—or maybe you can get Firefrost to tell us some juicy old gossip!"

"Good idea," he agreed, and in a short time they had pol-ished off the last crumb and packed up the baskets to take back to the *hertasi* at Summerdance's *ekele*.

When he returned to his rooms later that evening, it was with some surprise that he found Snowfire waiting there for him, sitting on Darian's bed and sharpening one of his knives. Snowfire rose as soon as Darian entered and stopped short at seeing him there.

"I hope you'll forgive my invading your rooms, but I wanted to apologize for making things unpleasant for you this afternoon," Snowfire began.

"Accepted," Darian said instantly. "It sounded as if you had plenty of provocation. But—"

He stopped, not sure he had the right to make the observa-tion that had just occurred to him.

"But?" Snowfire asked.

Darian sat down, feeling awkward. "Is it just me, or are people getting into a lot more quarrels here than we did out in Valdemar?"

"Hmm. Yes, and no." Snowfire rubbed the side of his nose. "The thing is, the team we had put together—the team you joined—was made up of people who all knew each other well, well enough to make a lot of effort at getting along, but purposefully not so close that personal problems could arise. And we had a great deal to do, so we were often too busy to pick quarrels. Here," he gestured, palms up. "Here there are a great many more people, and when there are that many people, not all of them get along, not all of them have the same opinions on important matters, and for that matter, not all of them agree about what an important matter *is*! So there are conflicts, which are going to cause factions and quarreling." Now he smiled. "*And,* to my mind the most important factor, we all have a fair amount of free time! That's time we can use to brood about wrongs, to decide we've been insulted—and to pick quarrels for no particular reason. I'm no less prone to that than anyone else."

Darian had to laugh at that. "I guess that's something all peoples have in common, then," he agreed. "When there isn't a crisis going on, there are going to be some people who want to make one; when things aren't dramatic enough, they feel impelled to create drama. And the more stress you're under, the fewer stresses you notice."

"We're no different from the people of your village in that way, little brother," Snowfire admitted. "At least not that much different. At any rate, I am sorry you walked in on our argument, and so is Nightwind. We both owe you and Nightbird apologies and thanks for your *constructive* plotting. I'm glad you're picking up the *hertasi* habit of benevolent conspiracy. So again I apologize, and thank you for deciding to stay involved."

"I'll accept both only if you promise to try to remember that whoever it was is an insensitive moron—or at least he is according to Nightbird—and try to keep your temper next time." Darian tried to look stern and Very Adult, but had a hard time keeping a straight face over this blatant role reversal.

Snowfire saw the joke and managed to act meek. "I will," he whispered, bowing his head. Then he lost control and started laughing. Darian joined him.

"I will make that promise, but I have an ulterior motive," Snowfire admitted. "Nightwind swears that if he does something like that again and I'll just report it to her calmly, *she'll* give him the tongue-lashing of a lifetime and I'll get to watch."

Darian made his eyes widen. "Oooh, I *am* impressed. Promise to tell me all about it, if she does! Or better yet, get her to invite *me*, too!"

"*Now* who has too much spare time?" Snowfire asked, slapping him on the back as he stood up. "Maybe I ought to ask Starfall to find you a fifth teacher!"

Darian tried to think of a good retort, but his mind went blank, and Snowfire took the opportunity to bid him good night and walk out the door.

The next morning, Darian steeled himself for his usual lesson with Darkstone, but when he arrived at the shielded area where he usually met his teacher, Darkstone was nowhere to be seen. Instead, Starfall, Snowfire, and Firefrost were all waiting for him there.

"What is it?" he asked, searching their faces and finding worrisome traces of concern there.

Firefrost seemed to be spokesperson by mutual consent. "How upset would you be to have to leave the Vale?" she asked, "You've made some friends here, perhaps close ones. . . ."

"Not so close that I'd have a broken heart over leaving," he replied, wondering what was going on. "Have I offended anyone? Darkstone, maybe? Am I being asked to leave?" If that was the case— A chill gripped him, and his stomach clenched.

"No, absolutely not, nothing like that!" Firefrost actually laughed, destroying his fear before it got started. Then she sobered, and gestured to Snowfire. "I think you'd best explain what is going on."

"We've had gryphons on long patrols to the north since that clash with the barbarians," Snowfire explained. "We— by that, I mean k'Vala—assumed that if *one* group has found a way through the mountains, others might well, too. That's what seems to have happened; there's a barbarian group coming slowly south; very slowly, not much like an army, though. They have women and children, and large wagons— they've even got some herd-beasts as well."

Firefrost chuckled. "I wish you'd had a chance to hear the gryphons go on about those herd-beasts, the greedy things! Apparently these creatures are to ordinary deer what war-horses are to ponies, and there isn't a one of the scouts but wants a chance to sink his beak into one!"

"The gryphons are more certain that these people are not dangerous than I am, or the other Elders, for that matter," Starfall amended, with a worried frown. "Yes, they might settle down; yes, they might never reach either Valdemar or k'Vala lands. Nevertheless, they *are* heavily armed, and they are taking the same general route as that first lot. So the Elders of k'Vala want *your* Vale in place, fortified, and manned as soon as possible."

"In fact, we have gyrphons flying *hertasi* in to get buildings up for us before we even get there," Snowfire interjected.

Huh! This was moving awfully fast for him. *Well, now I'm glad I gave Snowfire that map of ideas for the Vale!* "You could do this without me," he offered tentatively.

"We could; we'd rather not. You are Valdemaran, and you have a perfect right to establish a holding in unclaimed Valdemaran lands, but *we* don't," Firefrost said briskly. "If we're challenged, *you* are our answer."

"You're also known to the village and to the local Lord," Snowfire pointed out. "You're fluent in both our tongues. We *are* going to alter our plans and have an armed force living in this Vale; you can at least help Starfall explain why we're bringing in fighters without either causing a panic or arousing suspicion of our motives."

"You're not bad with your tongue, boy," added Firefrost wryly. "I've heard you. And you've got the benefit of an honest Valdemaran face."

Darian laughed a little at that. "Well, I suppose that's *some* sort of qualification!"

"You're also a good fighter, if it comes to that, and a scout and trapper," Starfall said soberly. "If we assume that these barbarians *are* coming south. On the whole, we would rather find that it's possible to negotiate with them. Your local Lord may have other ideas. He may want to drive them back. In either case, we can't do anything without having a strong base to work from."

Darian nodded, now just as sober as his teacher. "I'd be a poor student if I hadn't learned that by now. Yes, I *want* to go now, the sooner the better. It sounds as if we need all the time we can get. I'd be really disappointed if you didn't take me, danger and all! But I'm going to go hoping that this turns out to be a false alarm."

Firefrost ruffled his hair in the way only a very elderly woman can get away with. "I thank the Star-Eyed that you have the good sense to know this isn't an adventure."

Darian licked his lips, as memories of four years ago flashed through his mind. "Experience, Elder," he said honestly. "Not necessarily good sense."

"Experience will do, and don't misjudge your very real good sense," Starfall corrected. He looked satisfied, and a bit more relaxed than he had been. "Snowfire, Firefrost, and I will put together the settlers for the new Vale. I'd like you to sit down and see if you can come up with anything you think we would want from a *Valdemaran* point of view. As you said, the sooner we're in place, the better. If we can, we'll be leaving with a pack train within a few days, and your new teacher will just have to catch up with us."

They sent Darian off to go make his list, and it wasn't until he was sitting down with pen and paper that he realized he *still* didn't know the name of the new teacher, who now would "have to catch up!"

King Stag Tyrsell

Seven

An entire week went by before anyone in her family even noticed that Keisha wasn't sleeping in her room at all anymore, a week during which she enjoyed the best stretch of sound sleep she had ever experienced in her life. There weren't even any midnight emergencies to disturb her, and gradually people who came for treatment figured out that she had made the move a permanent one. In fact, she began to wonder if everyone in the village knew *except* her family!

Predictably enough, it was her youngest brother, Trey, who first poked his nose into the vacant room and discovered that not only had the bed not been slept in, but that Keisha's things were all gone. Trey had been the one who had to be threatened with a near-death experience to keep him out of his sisters' room; he had the curse of insatiable curiosity combined with incredible mischief and the apparent desire to make the lives of his sisters difficult. Such a combination doomed him to a never-ending round of conflict within the family, conflicts from which he always emerged beaten, but uncowed. Keisha suspected he would have played similar tricks on his brothers, except that they'd have boxed his ears for his efforts. At least, when he teased his sisters, he could count on the fact that his worst punishment would come from his mother or father, and probably would only involve physical labor in the form of punitive chores.

This was normal behavior for a boy between the age when he was no longer willing to play with girls and the time when he discovered that girls were fascinating and desirable creatures. Keisha knew that, though it didn't stop her from chasing him out with a brandished broom more than once. Shandi had been known to mutter from time to time that if *she* had her way, Trey wouldn't live to grow out of his pranks.

Somehow, though, Trey did survive, and when he invaded his sisters' domain, he was careful not to let them find out about it.

At this point in his life, Trey was far more interested in the girls his sisters could get to dance or spend time with him, and he had mostly grown out of his bad habits, but some things, like curiosity, are not the sort of traits that a boy grows out of. Neither is opportunism; instead of going to his parents with his fascinating discovery, Trey came straight to Keisha.

He walked right in through the open door of her cottage with a hint of a swagger; fortunately for him, Keisha had no patients at the time, or he'd have gone right out again on his ear, just on the basis of his smug expression. *I know something*, his face said, as plainly as if he'd spoken it. *And I bet it's something I can get advantage out of.*

As it was, she was amused, rather than annoyed; he thought she wouldn't want Mum and Da told, and he had no notion that she didn't give a pin whether he told or not. Still, as first to discover the vacancy, he *would* benefit, and that would probably satisfy him.

He had taken particular pains with his appearance; his light brown hair was slicked back with water, his shirt neatly tucked into his trews, his face so clean that it was shiny. Evidently he intended to impress her—which meant that he had actually thought things through, for a change.

So Trey is the first to notice. That's not bad. And he's been planning to see if I want to buy his silence. You know, if he's actually started to think before he acts, he may actually survive to adulthood!

"Say, Keisha, all your things are gone from your room," he said without preamble.

"I know," she replied calmly, continuing to roll strips of laundered and bleached cloth into bandages, the task she'd been doing when he barged in. "I've moved in here; I'm tired of waking Da or Mum up when I get called out in the middle of the night, and I'm *very* tired of all the noise. You barbarians are bad when you clomp around in the morning, but the worst is the snoring. One of these nights, the house is going to vibrate apart, and the roof will fall down on you all."

Trey ignored the insult, concentrating on the only important piece of information she had granted him: that the move really was a move, permanent, and not just for the summer. "Does that mean you aren't coming back?"

"Not only that," she confirmed, "but I've packed everything up that I didn't take with me and gotten it out of the way, up in the attic. I take it that you want to take possession of the room? Be my guest. I don't need it, and neither does Shandi. When Shandi comes back for visits, she can sleep over here; I've space enough."

He grinned. "That's what I was hoping you'd say! You're sure, now?"

"Very sure." She kept her expression as placid as a grazing sheep. "It's about time I set up on my own, anyway. People will give me more respect if I have my own household."

"And I can have the room?"

"Absolutely."

He didn't jump for joy, but he might just as well have, given the expression on his face. "Thanks, Keisha! You're a good 'un!"

"You're welcome," she responded, but he hadn't waited to hear her; he'd pelted out of the cottage and up the path as fast as his feet would carry him, with the obvious intention of having himself in full possession of the precious cubbyhole before any of his brothers knew it was vacant. Possession being nine-tenths of the law, it would be very difficult for them to evict him, and if he worked fast enough, he could even get one of the two beds disassembled and out before anyone came home, thus giving himself a room without anyone sharing it.

The longer he remained in undisputed possession of the room, the less likely it would be that he could be ousted from it, so it was also in his best interest to keep any of his brothers from finding out that Keisha wasn't going to use it anymore. Eventually, of course, they'd notice the change in occupants, probably within two or three days, but in the meantime, Keisha's absence would not be mentioned by Trey. By that time, both of them would be too well entrenched in their respective places to move.

That gave her another three days of peace and quiet before Sidonie appeared at the door, time that she used to her advantage. Keisha had already made certain that *her* reason for setting up in the cottage had been firmly planted in the minds of every gossip in Errold's Grove. She'd made it clear how much more convenient this arrangement was for everyone, and she had the cottage so clean that not even the most fanatical housekeeper could have found fault with it.

Sidonie walked straight in, just as Trey had, in the early morning just after Keisha had cleaned up after breakfast. This time Keisha sat in her favorite chair with both hands full of a sock, a wooden darning egg, a blunt needle, and wool yarn. She was in the middle of mending, which gave her an excuse to stay where she was as her mother strolled around the cottage, not speaking at all, but examining the place minutely, as if she had never seen it before. Sidonie's expression was closed, arms crossed over her chest, but Keisha knew that her mother could not hold in her feelings for long. "Well," she said, finally, "you've certainly made yourself at home here."

But her daughter had gotten a week's grace in which to decide exactly how she was going to handle the inevitable confrontation, and even though her stomach knotted and her head began to throb with tension, she kept her face calm and her manner casual. "I started thinking after Shandi left, thinking that the house could do with a few less people in it. Bright Havens, Mum, the boys would crowd Kelmskeep, much less our place! Then I thought of other things. There was no need to keep disturbing you and Da with my night calls, since I have this place," she explained, keeping her voice warm and slightly amused. "I haven't been much help around the house in the last six months, what with all the patients I've had, and with Shandi gone, it seemed as if it would be easier on you if I were to take care of myself. Now that the boys are doing their share of the work around the house, you really don't need *my* help at all, anymore. This arrangement should be more convenient for everyone."

"Convenient?" Sidonie's voice got a bit shrill, and her control over her expression slipped. Strangely enough, she looked a little frightened as well as upset. "Convenient for what? You aren't old enough to be living by yourself, and right at the edge of the village, too, out where who knows what could happen to you! What will everyone think? Here you are, all alone, no one to chaperone you—people are going to talk! They're going to say we drove you out, or that you ran away, that we're wretched parents to let you be on your own in the first place!"

Keisha laughed, startling her mother into silence. The laughter was strained, but Sidonie was too full of her own emotions to notice. "Talk? Good gracious, Mum, what are they going to talk about? No one is going to think that you are bad parents, and if there *had* been a fight, you know that the neighbors would have overheard it! They didn't, so obviously there wasn't one."

"You can't be living alone!" Sidonie insisted. "There's no one to protect you here."

Keisha shook her head, and wished that she hadn't. "I doubt that will ever be a problem. No one ever comes here that isn't sick or hurt. No one would dare hurt me. The rest of the village would have his head on a plate. As for this cottage being on the edge of the village, well, that hardly qualifies as isolation! If I even whispered for help, the neighbors would hear me."

"Maybe you don't think that living out here alone is going to cause people to gossip," Sidonie said darkly, "But—"

"Mum, there're no 'buts' about it," Keisha interrupted, wanting to get the unpleasant scene over with. "Not when anyone in the village can come here at any time of day or night, knock on the door, walk straight in, and see that I'm *quite* alone. You forget what I am—people have every right to come here whenever they need help. I have less privacy here than I did at home! If I were carrying on an illicit love affair, moving here would be the *worst* thing I could do!"

"Keisha!" Sidonie cried, shocked.

"Well, it *would*!" she insisted. "If I'm *not* here, it's going to be noticed right away, and people are going to want to

know where I am and look until they find me! There is
no way that I could go off for a romp in the hayfields, Mum;
sure as I did, someone would get sick or hurt, and the whole
secret would be all over the village. And I can't have a young
man *here* without someone eventually walking in on it! So
there you are. Not only am I chaperoned, I have the entire village as my chaperone!" She shrugged. "Besides, as you well
know, I haven't any suitors. I doubt that there's a boy in the
entire village who thinks of me as a *girl*. I'm the Healer, and
for them, I'm about as likely a source of romance as a tree
stump."

"Maybe, but you still aren't old enough to be on your own
like this," Sidonie replied stubbornly.

"I'm old enough to be married, with a family, and you've
said as much yourself," Keisha countered, as her stomach
soured and her neck muscles knotted. "So I'm old enough. I
have all the proper domestic skills, and I can take care of myself quite neatly. Well, look around you. If you see anything
amiss, I'd like to know."

"But what are people going to say about us, about your father, about me?" Sidonie's voice was no louder, but there was
a definite edge to it. *This*, then, was probably the source of
her anxiety. "They're going to say that we drove you out, that
we were such wretched parents that we fought, that—"

Again, Keisha interrupted. "They're going to say what
they've *been* saying for the past week, that I am a very considerate daughter to see that not only were night calls disturbing *you*, but that I was afraid that some folk hesitated
to call me out because they didn't want to wake the rest of
the household just to get me. I've made a point of telling
everyone who noticed that I was actually living here that this
was the reason why I moved. They'll say that only someone who was raised right would be polite enough to want to
save her parents from such disturbance, *and* at the same time
make herself more available to the village than she was before." She chuckled, shocking her mother out of incipient
hysteria. "And if you don't believe me, ask Mandy Lutter;
she's all but taken credit for the idea herself. She's got half
the village convinced that it was a chance remark from *her*

that made me see it would be easier for people if I moved to the cottage."

"Oh," Sidonie said weakly, all of her arguments overcome.

Keisha's own symptoms of stress began to ease, and she felt that she was winning the confrontation.

"Mother, love, I'm hardly living away from you when the house is all but next door," she pointed out, a little more gently. "How big is the village, after all? If it will make you feel better, I'll make sure and come home for dinner as often as I can. If you need me to help, you've only to ask, and you know that. If I really *wanted* to leave you all, I'd let Gil arrange for me to go to Healer's Collegium. I'm here, aren't I? And haven't I said all along that I'm *not* going to the Collegium? I promise you, I haven't changed my mind."

She would have said more, pressing home the point, but just then two young men came in, supporting a third, whose arm bent at an entirely unnatural angle at the shoulder joint. Keisha dropped her mending and forgot everything she was about to say, forgot even her mother's presence, until it was all over and the dislocated shoulder was back in place again. By then, of course, Sidonie was gone.

But she had simply slipped out, so Keisha *had* won; or at least, her mother had gone off to think about what she had said. Sidonie was perfectly capable of thinking clearly when her emotions didn't get in the way.

So when she's thinking dispassionately about what I told her, I will win. Keisha sighed, the last of her tension ebbing. It hadn't been nearly as bad as she'd thought it would be.

A dislocated shoulder didn't create nearly the mess of the average wound, and there was very little to clean up after the young man had gone. Keisha put the room to rights again, returned to her chair, and picked up her mending, but her mind was still on her mother.

It would probably be a good thing if I showed up at supper—or before, actually, with some fresh herbs or salad greens. That way I'll just show that I meant what I said, that I'm not actually leaving the family, I've just put a little distance between us.

She finished the mending, took care of several children

with insect stings and some ugly thorn scratches, then spent the afternoon dosing some horses for worms. As suppertime neared, she finished that task, returned home, and went into her garden to gather a peace offering.

She entered the kitchen with her basket of clean salad makings, expecting to find her mother there. But Sidonie wasn't at the house, she'd gone out to the farm, according to Trey, who was in charge of the evening dinner. He welcomed Keisha, her offerings, and her help with pleasure, and the two of them put together a good warm-weather meal of soup, bread, and salad in short order.

Sidonie came back arm-in-arm with her husband, sun-browned and smiling under the rim of her work hat, and greeted Keisha with calm pleasure. That told Keisha something important: that her mother *had* checked with Mandy Lutter, that most notorious of village gossips, and what she had heard had pleased and reassured her. Mandy was not likely to withhold anything juicy about *anyone*, not even to the subject's mother.

So everyone is saying what a good girl I am to be thinking of my family and of the village's welfare, she thought with conscious irony. *Mandy and the rest are all seeing how convenient the arrangement is for them, no doubt. Well, it is convenient for them—and I don't mind if I get a few more midnight calls than I would if I was still living here. They can say whatever they like about me. As long as it makes Mum and Da feel better about this situation, that's all that matters to me.*

She sat down with the rest to dinner, Sidonie having greeted her bonus of salad with a smile of thanks, and discovered that as of this afternoon, there was another topic entirely to interest everyone in the village. *She* had taken second place to a much more entertaining subject.

"I saw Mandy Lutter today, while I was on my way out to the farm. For once, there was a good reason to get Mandy's mouth going," Sidonie said, once the soup had been ladled out and everyone had started on the meal. "I won't tease you and make you guess what her news was, though. It's too exciting for that. Young Darian Firkin is coming back at long last! He's going to come back, just as he promised Lord

Breon, and there's going to be a mage here again! Can you believe it?"

For a moment, Keisha drew an absolute blank as to who "Darian Firkin" was, but only for a moment. She blinked in surprise; the young boy who had been Wizard Justyn's apprentice had been gone for at least four years, and she honestly hadn't expected him ever to return, no matter what he'd promised. Why should he? He'd been adopted by Hawkbrothers, he'd gone out to see the world, what could possibly tempt him to come back here except that old promise? "Back where? Here? Is he going to set up in Errold's Grove?"

And for one, panicked, admittedly selfish instant, she thought, *Am I going to have to give the cottage back? Oh, Havens, no. That can't be the reason Mum is so pleased!*

"No, no, not *here*, not the village," Sidonie corrected, waving a chunk of bread vaguely at the window. "He's going to have a place outside the village, he's going to have a lot of those Hawkbrothers there, and of course they wouldn't feel comfortable living right in the village. But he *will* be within easy fetching distance of Errold's Grove. If we need his skills, we'll be able to get him."

Thank goodness. . . . My refuge is still mine, was Keisha's relieved thought.

"Most people wouldn't feel comfortable with those bloody great birds about, staring at their hens," Ayver pointed out with a laugh. "So it's just as well he isn't planning on moving back into Errold's Grove. Don't forget, *he's* got one of those huge birds himself, so even if his friends didn't want to stay here, if *he* did, that bird would be here, too. Poor hens and ducks would likely never lay again for sheer nerves."

"Where, outside the village?" one of the boys wanted to know. "How far from here?" They glanced at each other, and Keisha thought she knew the notions dancing in *their* heads. Hawkbrothers—there were all sorts of things the Hawkbrothers knew or could do, and anyone who got friendly with them stood a good chance of picking up some interesting information and skills. If this place they were settling was close by, a fellow had a chance of slipping over there now and again without being missed from his work.

Sidonie shrugged. "Mandy had no idea—just somewhere

outside the village, but on this side of the river. Far enough away that it won't bother us, near enough that he'll be able to work magic for us when we need it." Her eyes widened, and she smiled broadly. "Think of that! We'll have a real mage again! The Hawkbrothers will be mages, too, of course, but they'll have their own concerns to deal with; Darian will be *our* mage."

"A Weather-Watcher," Ayver said in satisfaction. "Damn, it'll be good to know when there's a monster storm on the way! Be even better if he's gotten to be a Weather-Worker. We won't have to fret about a lot of things, I reckon."

Sidonie sighed happily. "I'll feel safer, that's for certain sure. Oh—and Mandy says he's going to have at least one gryphon with him, to come live at this place he's building! Think of *that!*"

A gryphon? Keisha felt her own eyes widening. For as long as she could remember, she had wanted to see a real gryphon, and now it appeared she was not only going to see one, she'd probably get to see one on a weekly basis! If this gryphon was going to patrol for danger from the sky, his flights would have to take him over the village at least that often.

Those were all the facts that Sidonie had gotten; the rest was all speculation, and Keisha could do that on her own. While the others chattered, she ate the rest of her meal without tasting it, and after helping with the dishes, went out looking for more solid information.

She didn't have to go far; she simply followed her ears, A gaggle of folk had gathered in the village square just in front of the inn, and the murmur of their voices drew her to the gathering. The lantern over the inn door was lit, and underneath it, on the wall where anyone could read it, was an announcement with Lord Breon's seal at the top.

So this has come from Kelmskeep! That makes it official. How wonderful! Whatever Lord Breon has sent over will be solid truth, and no guessing.

Keisha couldn't get anywhere near the posted message herself, but that hardly mattered, since the priest, Father Benjan, was reading it out loud for the benefit of those whose reading skill was limited to the ability to keep an inventory. He'd evidently gone through it at least once already, for some of those who had gathered here were going off to their own houses, while newcomers pressed closer. Keisha had arrived just in time to hear it all from the beginning.

"This is all under Lord Breon's seal, see, there it is on the top, and it came over by messenger just this afternoon," he was saying as Keisha got within earshot. His voice was a little hoarse now, from all the repeating. "What it says, with all the fancy language pared off, is that Mage Darian Firkin and some of the Hawkbrothers from Clan k'Vala are fulfilling the promise they made back when Darian left with them. They're coming to settle outside the village, about halfway between us and Kelmskeep. They're planning to stay permanently, and there's going to be more mages than just young Darian living at this settlement, but they'll probably all be Hawkbrothers except him. There's going to be one gryphon at first, maybe more later on. There's no date for when they'll be settling in, just that it'll happen by Harvest. What they're doing is building a kind of Hawkbrother village, they call it a 'Vale,' and it's going to be a place where people besides Hawkbrothers are welcome. They plan to keep an eye on all of us as part of their treaty with Valdemar, and the gryphon is going to be here to give us warning of anything nasty coming from a distance. This is going to be what Lord Breon calls a 'formal presence inside Valdemar.' What he means is that these people will be Hawkbrother envoys here, and that's going to give us a lot more attention from the Queen."

"Well, that'll be grand!" the blacksmith called out. "You think maybe they'll be giving us our Guards back?"

"There's nothing about that here, but then Lord Breon wouldn't know what they've decided in Haven," Father Benjan replied. "At a guess, I'd say it's likelier than not. Attention from the Crown is probably going to mean at least that much. Who knows? Maybe they'll give us our own regional Herald in permanent residence. Maybe some mercenary guards because of the added trade."

There were little murmurs of relief all through the crowd, and no need to guess why. Those who had been here for the barbarian invasion—which was universally called "The Great War," for it had certainly seemed like a war to this isolated place—had never quite gotten over it. Folk coming in from the Pelagirs were always closely questioned for any signs that the barbarians might be coming back, as were traders and travelers out of the north. No one *quite* had the courage to question the Hawkbrothers, but it was generally assumed after their initial intervention they would certainly give warning to Errold's Grove, if warning were warranted. Still, having someone *here* to give that sort of warning sooner would allow everyone to sleep easier at night.

Keisha walked back through the soft, warm dusk to her cottage, half listening to the crickets singing and trying to think out all the possible things this could mean to Errold's Grove—and by extension, herself.

One thing's certain, she thought, as she settled next to the fire with the rest of her mending. *People are going to suffer less from nervous complaints.* Between the gryphon and the mages keeping watch for trouble, the folk of Errold's Grove would no longer have to be quite so vigilant. *I bet I get a lot fewer requests for nerve tonics and sleeping possets.*

By her reckoning, they would almost certainly get those Guards back—mind, they might well be men that were one step short of retirement, but they would be *Guards* all the same. If there was going to be a Hawkbrother embassy, for certainly that was what this "Vale" thing was, the Queen would want an armed presence in the trading-village nearest it.

And a lot more traders will start coming, I bet. If they're certain to contact Hawkbrothers every time they come to our market, they'll come more often and start requesting specific things of them in the way of trade goods. More traders would mean more prosperity; that, too was a fine thing for the village as a whole.

More prosperity means more people coming here to settle, though, and that means more injury and illness. Surely, surely someone would see that Errold's Grove needed a fully trained Healer! *I'd even share the cottage, if I could just become the Trainee instead of the primary Healer. . . .* That could solve all of her problems at once—but only if someone in the Healers' Circle decided that Keisha wasn't capable of handling the increased work.

But what if they think I am? Then things aren't going to change at all. . . .

She sternly told herself not to panic ahead of time. No getting upset. She wasn't going to think about it. No use in creating trouble where there wasn't any. She'd be like the silly girl in the story, crying over lost sheep she didn't have, bought with the money from hens she hadn't yet hatched, from eggs her two little half-grown chicks hadn't yet laid!

When she finished the last of the mending, she went out into her garden and took a seat on the bench there, looking up at the stars. A warm breath of a breeze carried the scent of honeysuckle past her, as crickets sang nearby and a nightingale in the Forest declared his love for his mate. The moon was a slender nail-paring of a crescent, and Keisha shook her hair back, letting the breeze cool the nape of her neck.

Her thoughts circled around to the returning prodigal. *I wonder what Darian Firkin is like. "Firkin" isn't a name from around here.* She'd have a general idea of what he looked like if she knew his family, but it seemed to her that she remembered he was an orphan. *That's right, that's why he was apprenticed to the wizard in the first place. Whenever people talk about him, they talk about a boy, but he's at least my age by now. Eighteen at the least. That's a young man, not a boy.*

He'd be old enough to do all the things people expected of him, she would think.

So by now he's a mage, and he's got a Hawkbrother bird. He'll have traveled more than everyone in the village combined! He'll certainly have seen more of Valdemar than anyone here, except maybe Lord Breon and his family and liegemen. They hardly count, though; we never see them except at Midsummer and Harvest Faire. He should make quite an impression when he gets here, especially when people realize he isn't a young boy anymore.

She smiled wryly. There was one thing that was as predictable as the sun rising; every unattached young woman in Errold's Grove would be setting her cap for him. How could they not? He wasn't so homely as a boy that anyone made note of it, so he could hardly have grown into an ugly young man—and he would not only have the cachet of being a new, unknown male, but an exotic and a traveler!

The older folks might be thinking of him as a boy still, but the girls are going to add up years and figure he's of courting age. There's going to be a lot of sewing and embroidery going on for the next few months, she decided. *I wish Shandi were here! She'd be right in the middle of it all, and tell me all the tales!*

Personally, she was just anticipating finally seeing a gryphon, maybe hearing it speak. It would bring a touch of excitement to the skies over the village if she could look up from time to time to see the enormous wings passing overhead, or see a momentary gryphon-shadow against the moon! *That* was all the magic that she needed in her world!

The gryphon was a certainty; she considered other possibilities that the Hawkbrothers might bring. *So the other thing this means is that if Hawkbrothers are coming to settle, they'll be bringing more of* their *medicines and treatments. Would they bring a Healer?*

Now *that* was worth getting excited about. The Hawkbrothers were mages, everyone knew that, so any Healer they brought with them would—must!—have the secret to unlock those puzzling texts of hers!

Steelmind's from k'Vala; their chief Healer sent seeds through him to help me. So they already know that I'm here. Healers always work with other Healers, that's part of the Oath. So if they bring a Healer with them, it's bound to be someone who knows all about using Healer's Gift and it's bound to be someone who'll at least give me enough help to get me on my feet!

This could be the solution to all of her problems; never mind Darien Firkin, and even the gryphon. *Now* she could hardly wait to meet the Hawkbrothers and learn if they *did* have a Healer among them!

Whatever it takes, I'll find the way to get him to teach me!

She laughed out loud in relief, as a burden she had carried so long she hardly noticed it anymore lifted from her shoulders. No more mysteries, no more making excuses to Gil! It would only be a few short moons, and she would be learning the last skill she needed to consider *herself* a real Healer!

With the lifting of the burden, after the initial feeling of giddy pleasure, came a sense of relaxation. A few moons? She could wait that long.

And meanwhile, there were babies coming, childish illnesses to dose, broken bones to set, gashes to stitch. She would have her hands full enough to avoid fretting between then and now.

She went to bed and slept the soundest sleep she'd had in years, waking with the birds, feeling as if *she* had been Healed.

That day, after a round of children who'd gotten bellyaches from eating too many half-ripe berries, she went out into the garden for some fresh mint. As she stooped to pick the pungent leaves, a strange shadow crossing the ground in front of her made her glance up.

It was a gryphon. It couldn't be anything else.

It wasn't alone either, there were more of them, carrying baskets suspended between pairs of them. She couldn't make out what was in the baskets, they were too high, but there was no doubt of what they were.

She stared at them until they vanished over the trees, tending vaguely upriver, where the Vale was alleged to be, all but forgetting the mint in her hands until they were gone, and she realized she had crushed it.

Snowfire

 Eight

The news that a new invasion of barbarians had been sighted changed everything, turning what had been leisurely planning into a spate of frenzied activity. Gryphons carried basketloads of *hertasi* to the new Vale to get it ready in advance, as the rest of those who had volunteered or been specifically requested to populate the place packed up their belongings and prepared to make the move to their new home. By the time everyone arrived, there would be quarters waiting for them; somewhat more primitive quarters than they were used to, to be sure, but living spaces that could be improved upon and enlarged until they met the standards of those accustomed to living in a long-established Vale. After all, it wasn't even Midsummer yet; there were three more moons of warm and sunny summer weather to go, and another couple of moons before things got uncomfortably cold. A Vale full of *hertasi* and humans working together would have fine living quarters put together long before then, and the only improvements after that would be cosmetic.

Darian alone of all of them didn't have much to pack, so he was ready to go long before anyone else was. He tried to lend a hand to some of the others, but his help was always politely declined. That gave him time that he tried to fill as best he could, studying hard with Firefrost, working on further plans for his Vale, and (for a while, at least) spending as much time as he could spare from both those tasks with Summerdance.

He paid very close attention to his feelings about her and tried his best to decipher hers for him; he didn't want to leave without her *if* what tied them together was closer than mere friendship. Their dalliance on the night of the wedding had been an entirely new set of experiences for him, and like a child with a new tooth, he felt as if he *had* to probe his feelings constantly to see what they were.

He might even have convinced himself that he and Summerdance were meant for each other as permanent partners, if it hadn't been for the fact that she didn't act any differently toward him than she did toward any other young man whose company she enjoyed. In fact, when it came to the company of young men, she was a great deal like the tiny blue butterflies that shared her use-name of Summerdance, going from flower to flower (or boy to boy) without spending very long with any of them. So, after careful consideration, he came to the somewhat reluctant conclusion that if a romance between himself and Snowfire's cousin were ever to happen, it probably wouldn't occur until after she got a new use-name—if then.

He consoled himself with their friendship and her very clear enjoyment of his company. If he was not to be her great love, at least he was still *a* love! No sooner had he come to that conclusion than he found that was just as glad that she didn't have any special feelings for him because she kept introducing him to friends, who apparently wanted to give the "Valdemar Hawkbrother" a memorable send-off! Life was very interesting during that time, and he simply enjoyed his new-found popularity, knowing that when his special teacher arrived, he would have little, if any, time for a personal life.

For a time, it seemed as if the Hawkbrothers were never going to get themselves organized enough to make the move. Then, suddenly, everything *was* organized, packed up, and ready to go. The announcement came late one afternoon, taking him by complete surprise.

He had returned from a lesson with Firefrost, followed by dinner, and was about to change for a hot soak followed by bed, when his room was invaded by a swarm of *hertasi*. Before he knew what was happening, the *hertasi* were carrying off his belongings and double-checking to make certain nothing would be left behind. Then they vanished, leaving him alone with the single set of clothes he pried out of their eager, stubby talons. He got his soak, all right, but only because he had changed into one of the communal lounge robes—he didn't *have* any other clothing left but what he needed for the next day! He soaked until he thought he was relaxed enough to sleep, returned to his room, laid out the set of his old scout gear that the *hertasi* had left him and fell into his bed for his last night in k'Vala as anything but a visitor.

The next day, he was awake before the *hertasi* came to fetch him, too excited to sleep anymore. He'd had dreams all night long about the new Vale and the journey to get there— and more ominous ones about his new teacher, who seemed to be a combination of Darkstone and everyone in Errold's Grove who'd ever disapproved of him. He took his time over breakfast, once he realized that the sun wasn't in the sky yet; it might be a while before he enjoyed the kinds of food available in k'Vala. Ayshen was going to be in charge of the *hertasi* there, though, so even if it wouldn't be possible to replicate the feast-day delicacies of the wedding celebration, it would still be good food.

Finally a *hertasi* came to tell him that everyone was gathering to leave, and he mounted Tyrsell's saddle for the first steps of the journey with the unsettled feeling that he wasn't ready for all this.

What am I doing? I'm not a leader. How am I going to take charge of a new Vale? Maybe I should change my mind— maybe I ought to be staying here—

But he shook off that momentary panic with self-derision; that was specious. He wasn't going to be in charge for many years to come, not until Starfall, Nightwind, and Snowfire, the new Vale's Elders, judged him ready to take his place with them. He had a lot to learn between then and now. They'd consult him, of course, especially on matters involving Errold's Grove, Lord Breon, and Valdemar, and they'd involve him in discussions, but he wouldn't be a leader for a long while.

Eventually I'll go back to Errold's Grove; I wonder how they're going to react to me? He wasn't a boy anymore. In fact, if his memory served him correctly, he'd be a match for most of the men in the village. He was a *better* fighter; he'd been taught to fight in every style from bare-handed to bow, and with the men who'd been trained to be the village Militia all dead, there was probably no one left in the village who had been *taught* to fight. Not of the original villagers, at least. According to the Tayledras who went there to trade, the village had grown considerably since he'd left.

Nevertheless, he was a warrior, and that ought to give him a certain cachet and respect.

You know, to a certain extent, I'm actually Lord Breon's equal—or his son Val's, anyway. Now that was certainly an intoxicating notion, but in the hierarchy of Valdemar, it was true. The new Vale would qualify as a lord's holding, and he was the heir-apparent to the leadership position.

:I hate to interrupt your introspection,: Tyrsell said dryly in his mind, *:But just about everyone has left. I'd wait until you were done with your mental soliloquy, but then I'd have to gallop to catch up, and I don't believe you'd enjoy that.:*

He came to himself with a start. Tyrsell was right, the last of the laden *dyheli* herd had lined up to pass through the entrance of the Vale, and it was time for the rear-guard—himself and Tyrsell—to get on their way.

:Uh—thanks,: he said with embarrassment, as Tyrsell took his place at the end of the line. *:I promise, I won't do any more woolgathering.:*

:I should hope not,: the *dyheli* stag replied with dignity.

As he and Tyrsell passed through the Veil, Kuari dropped off the branch on which he had chosen to perch and winged silently past them, into the uncontrolled, mist-wreathed forest outside. At this time of the year, the first couple of candlemarks before and after dawn brought floating streamers of mist up out of the ground to circle among the trunks until the heat of the day drove them off. There were no such mists inside the Vale of course, except on the rare occasions when the Elders decided that mist would make a pleasant "effect." It was cooler out here, too, understandably damper, and the first thing he noticed when he came out through the Veil and took his place at the end of the group was the absence of flower scent. Flowers bloomed constantly in the Vale, day *and* night, regardless of season, but not out here. It was too late for spring flowers, which were all that bloomed in a heavy forest; spring was the only time that enough light reached the ground for blossoms, except in places where there were clearings. So the perfumes he had become accustomed to were replaced with the metallic tang of fog, the earthy taste of decaying leaves and needles, and the faint musk of the *dyheli*.

Tyrsell led a new herd, much bigger than the previous one, composed of his original core and most of the adolescent and young adult *dyheli* from the other herds of k'Vala. This gave some much-needed population relief to the k'Vala home-herds, and a much-needed outlet for the youngsters. It also greatly increased Tyrsell's status—both that his herd was three times the size it had been, and that he was considered capable by the other king-stags of controlling so large a herd. Darian had been suitably impressed when he'd been told; this new herd established Tyrsell at the very top of herd hierarchy, a kind of *dyheli* Great Lord of State.

Because of the size of this herd, and because gryphons had been ferrying baggage and would continue to do so as long as there was baggage to ferry, there had been no need for anyone to have to leave anything behind. All in all, this would be a relatively easy resettlement, as orderly as any migration from an old Vale to a new one.

Except that we can't just step across a Gate to get there, more's the pity. It would take a week, roughly, of dawn-to-dark riding to get there, and he had no doubt that Snowfire meant that quite literally. They would rise before the dawn and not make camp until after dusk.

Still, it wasn't anything he hadn't done before, and he fell back into his habits of rear-guard, habits that fit him as comfortably as a well-worn and supple hawking glove.

:*We're about to be relieved of duty,*: Tyrsell said suddenly, on the last afternoon of the journey, as they passed beneath trees that had changed very little with the passing of a mere four or five years. The *dyheli* pricked his ears forward, and Darian turned to see a figure riding back along the line of baggage-laden *dyheli*, coming toward them. A moment later, he recognized Nightwind, and waved at her. She waved back, and when she got into conversational distance, told him, "Kel and I are going to take rearguard; we're just about at the new Vale, and Snowfire and Starfall thought you two might like to enter at the head of the line instead of the tail."

:*Well! That's a courteous thought!:* Tyrsell said with approval. :*Thank you; I know I would prefer it.:*

"Me, too," Darian agreed self-consciously. He sent a brief thought to Kuari, then relinquished his duty to Nightwind.

By going into a hard canter, he and Tyrsell came up to the front of the line well in time to go through the titular entrance side-by-side with Starfall and Snowfire. He felt a swell of pride so powerful that he flushed as they gravely made space for Tyrsell to fit between them.

There was no entrance as such, no Veil, for there was as yet no real Heartstone, only a kind of superior node anchored in a physical rock formation. But the *hertasi* and the few Tayledras who had preceded them had set up two rough pillars of stone on either side of the pass that let them into their valley, to mark where the Veil would one day be.

And they had done some subtle defensive improvements as well, although you would have to know what you were looking for to find them. They had made the sides of the hills far steeper, making it very difficult for an armed force to get into the new Vale by climbing the hillsides. There were well-camouflaged guard points on those hillsides, and anyone who tried to invade that way would shortly be full of arrows. But to look at them, there was nothing more unusual here than exceptionally steep rock formations, formations that had probably been this way since the beginning of the world.

No swarm of *dyheli* and *hertasi* met them this time; the *hertasi* were probably working hard on the building. But Ayshen, who had gone on ahead, *did* meet them, standing in the center of the path, actually bedecked in his formal costume, bowing ceremoniously to all three of them.

"The *hertasi* of k'Valdemar Vale welcome you to your new home, friends and brothers," he said ceremoniously. "May there always be as much pleasure here as you bring with you."

Starfall smiled, and bowed in return. "Your welcome doubles our pleasure, my brother," he replied. "It is good to be home."

Starfall dismounted, which seemed to be the signal for everyone else to do the same. "Allow me to guide you to your new *ekele*," Ayshen said, and without waiting for a reply, led the way up the path that looked increasingly *un*familiar with every step. It wasn't one of the paths in k'Vala—but it also wasn't the path that Darian remembered.

Someone had been hard at work on the plantings, someone like Steelmind, who could coax plants into amazing growth spurts in a very short period of time. Although by no means as lush as k'Vala, there were the vine screens, plantings of exotics, and tree sculptures that Darian had come to think of as "proper." The path twisted and turned, crossing over the little stream he remembered, with rustic bridges and artistically placed stepping stones providing dry-footed crossings. From time to time, Ayshen stopped, and pointed out a dwelling of one sort or another—most of them proper tree-built *ekele*, though the trees never supported more than one, and access was by means of a rope ladder more often than a staircase. When he stopped, those who found the place attractive would pause long enough for a discussion of who was the most taken with the situation. The discussions never lasted too long; one person (or two, if it was a couple) would remain, the *dyheli* with the appropriate baggage would remain, and everyone else would go on. Starfall quickly took possession of an *ekele* built in the tree where his old camping place had been, and no one disputed him. Then Ayshen stopped in front of what appeared to be a vine-covered mound.

"This was your original camping place, Snowfire," he said. "And I wondered if either you and Nightwind or Darian would have a preference for it."

"Have you made an *ekele* in the cliff where Nightwind and Kel originally camped?" Snowfire asked.

Ayshen nodded. "Actually," he said with evident pride, "I designed that one, and it's built both *on* the cliff and *in* the cliff—rather like an *ekele* without a tree, with a balcony outside. But I thought I'd offer you this first."

Snowfire laughed. "You needn't have bothered; it sounds

like a White Gryphon home, and I already know what Nightwind will want. How about you, Darian? Do you want this site?"

Although he wondered a little just what was underneath that mound of leaves—which certainly seemed bigger than the primitive hut that he remembered—Darian knew one thing for certain. *This* place was on the ground, and there were going to be storms in *this* Vale for some years yet. It would take a long time to power up the new Heartstone to the equivalent of the k'Vala Stone. And until k'Valdemar—whose idea had that name been?—was sealed against the weather and the seasons, he did *not* want to live in a tree that would sway in a storm!

"I'll take this," he said instantly. "If no one else likes it better than I do."

Snowfire laughed again, as did several others. "Little brother, I doubt that anyone here but a *kyree* or a *hertasi* would care for a dwelling on the ground the way you do," Ayshen said genially. The *dyheli* carrying Darian's baggage separated from the rest, and the group went on, leaving Darian in solitary possession of his new home.

The first thing he did was to take the baggage off the patient *dyheli* so that they could go off to graze or rest. As they paced off with the click of carefully-placed hooves, he turned his attention to the *ekele*.

It took him a moment to find the door, and it *was* a door, now, a good, solid, wooden door with a handle, not a mere screen of vines. When he opened it, he stared in open-mouthed disbelief at what lay behind it.

This place could not be more unlike the hut that had once stood here. Beneath the vines were solid walls, as thick as his forearm was long, at least. Outside, they were the same color as the vines; inside they had been whitewashed. The floor had been covered in flat paving stones, cunningly fitted together so that a sheet of paper could not fit between them, and sealed with grout. There was a stone fireplace in one wall, real windows with glass in them in the others. The windows were fairly well covered by the leaves and didn't let in much light, but there were skylights in the remarkably thick roof that took care of that deficiency. Like most Tayledras dwellings, there wasn't a straight line to be seen, for all the walls and even the doors and window frames curved. Instead of furniture, there were window seats, low tables, thick rugs of fur and fleece, and cushions everywhere.

A door in the same wall that held the fireplace led to a second room, but Darian waited to bring his baggage inside before he explored further. When he did, he discovered that the fireplace was shared with this room, which was a sleeping chamber, quite windowless and without a skylight, with a bed built into the wall and chests woven of willow branches for clothing. There was yet another door leading out of this room, and his curiosity took him onward.

Much to his delight, it was a bathing chamber, as he had found in the guest houses in k'Vala, with a pipe leading into a spacious tub, another into a washbasin, and a water-flushing "necessary" that would be *far* more comfortable to use than a privy! One of the first things he had learned from Snowfire was how to use magic to heat his bath water, so even the cold water coming from the stream in midwinter would be no problem. Light came from another skylight, and someone in a fit of whimsy had built containers to hold plants all around the edge of the skylight and planted flowering vines in them. Now as long as he could remember to *water* them, he'd have a touch of k'Vala here all year long!

The thick walls would keep this place warm in the winter and cool in the summer, the vines screening the skylight would keep out direct sun in the summer, but when they lost their leaves, would allow warm sunlight to penetrate in the winter. There was no direct light in the bedroom, exactly as Darian preferred. If he had designed the place himself, it could not have suited him more—and all of this, hidden under an innocuous mound of leaves!

He unpacked his baggage quickly, stowing it away wherever things seemed best to fit. What little furniture there was matched the *ekele* perfectly, being formed of bent, polished branches with the bark removed, or woven of willow withes. And as he put the last of his belongings away, the thought hit him with the suddenness of a lightning strike that this was *his own* home! He shared it with no one, it wasn't a guest house, this was *his*, entirely his to decorate as he chose, to clutter as he chose (or rather, as much as the *hertasi* would let him), to change as he chose.

My own place. . . . Bigger than the cottage he had shared with Justyn, and far, far superior to that dark little hovel.

Dear gods, I think I feel grown up!

That was certainly the measure by which people judged in Errold's Grove. You weren't an adult until you had a house of your own, however tiny and poorly built. Until then, you were a child, and subject to the orders and whims of the adults in whose house you lived.

He sat down in one of the window seats and took a deep breath, savoring the moment.

Then he went out to find Snowfire and see this peculiar cliff house of his.

He knew where Nightwind and Kel had set up housekeeping, of course, so he headed for the lake at the end of the valley and the cliffs overlooking it. Kel was already in residence, stretched out on a ledge near the top of the cliff in the sun, overseeing a line of *hertasi* carrying baggage up a stair that had been carved out of the living rock. At the top of the stair was a balcony with a low stone railing. A dark recess behind it probably represented the door into the new dwelling. The ledge Kel had draped himself over had a similar dark recess behind it, and belatedly Darian realized that this must be *his* home as well.

He followed the last *hertasi* up the stair, and tried not to think about how far down it was as he climbed, nor how much he wished that there was a railing on the staircase. Though the railing about the balcony ledge was no more than knee-high, he was very grateful for its presence.

There *was* a door cut into the rock, and windows, too; that was all he had a chance to see for the moment, as Kel greeted his arrival by leaping to his feet and bounding over to the balcony from his own ledge.

"Isss thisss not a marrrvel?" the gryphon chortled. "Ayssshen isss a geniusss! Except that it isss a lake beneath us and not an ocean, and the rrrock isss grrray, thisss could be White Gryphon! I feel entirrrely at home!"

"And so do I," Nightwind echoed, as she came out onto the

balcony. She was smiling broadly and held out her hand to Darien. "Even Snowfire is happy—"

"Snowfire is more than happy," the Hawkbrother interrupted her. He stepped right up to the edge of the balcony and peered down. "Not only is this as high up as any good scout-*ekele*, but I think I can dive into the lake from here."

"Don't you dare!" cried Kel, Nightwind, and Darian all together.

"Why not?" he asked, turning away from the ledge, wearing a grin that was the equal in mischief to his cousin Summerdance's.

"You'll break your silly neck, that's why not," Nightwind said tartly. "It's not deep enough, and the cliff slants *out*, not in. There is at least one thing you don't have to do to keep up with Starfall."

"Yet," added Ayshen from the doorway, "there's plenty of time to dig it deeper at this spot."

Nightwind threw up her hands in exasperation, as all three males, Darien, Kel, and Snowfire, now went to the edge to look down at the sparkling waters of the spring-fed lake with speculation.

"I don't think so," Darien finally said. "You'd have to dive out too far. Nightwind is right, there's too much stuff you could hit on the way down."

"That, too, could be changed in time," Ayshen said agreeably. "But we *do* have many other tasks that will take precedence."

"*Far* too many tasks," Snowfire confirmed, with a sigh. "And by the time we have the resources, I'll probably be telling my offspring why *they* shouldn't dive off from here. Nightwind will never forgive me if I remove the obstacles in their path."

"You can count on it," his mate said darkly, a hint that a laugh would be out of place at this moment, so Darian choked it down.

Instead, when everyone but Kel went back inside, he followed. Kel took up his place on his ledge again, stretching out in the sun with a huge sigh of contentment.

Inside, the walls had been whitewashed just as the walls of

Darian's home had been, and for the same reason, to make the rooms brighter. The windows were larger than Darian had expected, but instead of glass, had that odd transparent substance, tougher by far than glass, that served as windows in tree-*ekele*. It occurred to Darian that his skylights must be made of the same substance, in case of a hailstorm.

The furnishings were similar to his own, though there were more pieces of furniture and fewer piles of cushions. Someone had managed to carve a fireplace out of the rock, though Snowfire was perfectly capable of warming the whole home with magic if he had to.

"The bedroom is as dark as a pit," Snowfire said, as Darian glanced at a further doorway. "Not that this is bad, mind you. I'll just have to get used to it. I *do* admire the bathing room, though, Ayshen, and I do *not* want to think of the amount of work it took to get piped water up here."

"The water comes down, from a cistern of rainwater, until you exhaust it. Then the amount of work will come from your muscles on the pump, my friend," Ayshen grinned. "No free-flowing water without a full Heartstone, you know."

"It's worth it, and by the time I'm too old to pump water, we'll either *have* a full Heartstone or I'll be able to delegate the task to the children." He laughed. "I *also* appreciate the thick walls of solid stone between the master bedroom and the others. That is one advantage one does *not* have in an *ekele*, being able to shut out the shrieks of sibling rivalry or playtime!"

Darian grinned. Well, it looked like Snowfire really *was* settling down, if he was making plans and statements that included future children!

"Why do you think the cliff houses at White Gryphon are such desirable property?" Nightwind responded. "Ayshen, is the rock at the back sound enough to continue to cut new rooms?"

"Quite sound," Ayshen replied. "You'll be able to get a nursery and at least three bedrooms back there before you run into flawed material."

"Hmm." Nightwind's eyes lit up, and Snowfire looked positively gleeful. Darian blushed a little, decided that he'd seen enough, and went back outside.

"Come overrr and ssssee my lair!" Kel called from the ledge. There was a narrow walkway connecting the balcony to the ledge, about as wide as the stair had been, but Kel clearly preferred to leap from one to the other, showing off his agility.

Well, a slip doesn't have the same consequences for a creature with wings.

Darian practiced discretion, and used the walk as Kel rose to his feet. Darian was a bit surprised to see that Kel's lair had a door and windows very like Snowfire's. For some reason, he had gotten the impression that a gryphon would live in something very like a cave. When Kel opened the door to the eyrie, using a latch made for a gryphon's talons, he was soon disabused of that notion.

This place was only a single room. "Forrr now I need only thissss rrroom," Kel said. "When I find the apprrroprrriate mate, I will enlarrrge my eyrrrie with a nurrrssserrry asss well." There was no furniture, only enormous cushions covered in furs, leathers, or extremely tough and colorful fabrics. There was also no fireplace, and it was quite clear that the place would be illuminated by mage-lights, not lanterns,

"Why mage-lights?" Darian asked. "I thought we were keeping magic use to a minimum."

"Grrryphon feathersss are flammable," Kel pointed out, "Ssso I will get to make ussse of magic to heat and light my lairrr. *Kyrrree*, having no handsss, will have theirrr firrressss tended by *herrrlasssi*, but the rrrisssk to a grrryphon isss too grrrcat to have an open flame about."

"This could be very cozy," Darian observed, trying out one of the cushions, and finding it yielded just enough to make it a good seat. "The view from here during a storm should be fantastic!"

"I expect ssso," Kel agreed with contentment. "It isss ssso at White Grrryphon. I have enjoyed many sssshowsss of lightning frrrom the balcony therrre."

Darian resolved to get up here some time when a storm was due; if there was one thing he loved, it was storm watching. Ayshen entered at just that moment, having left the happy couple to arrange their own belongings in peace, and Darian lost no time in telling him what a wonderful job he had done in designing the cliff home and the eyrie. Ayshen couldn't blush, but he enjoyed the praise, switching his stubby tail a little and stretching his mouth in a grin.

"Well, I do not design costumes, nor artwork, nor furnishings," he said modestly. "My talent is only equal to partitioning space, as it were."

Kel snorted. "Parrrtitioning ssspace, indeed! Well, I have told you alrrready that you arrre a geniusss, and I ssshall not botherrr with anotherrr attempt." He turned to Darian. "You ssshould sssee what thisss fellow callsss 'parrrtitioning sssspace'! He had no chance to ssshow hisss talent in k'Vala, but he isss the chief desssignerrr herrre."

"Did you design my place, too?" Darian asked, seeing a similarity in the proportions of his home and Snowfire's. "It's wonderful, perfect! I couldn't have anything better! How did you know what to do?"

"I did design it," Ayshen confirmed. "And, I admit, it was with you in mind. I am glad you like it, I tried to remember what it was that you liked and disliked about various *ekele* in k'Vala."

"I'm just curious about one thing," Darian continued. "How is it made? It's not rock, but—"

Ayshen laughed. "You may not believe it, but I will show you later. Willow withes and earth, little brother! Willow withes and earth! It is the easiest way to build that I know of; it holds in cool or heat, and is altogether an ideal way to make a shelter, so long as you seal the walls well."

"Earth?" Darian *did* find it hard to believe. "But wouldn't it just turn to mud in the first rain?"

Ayshen shook his head. "No, I promise you, we build that way in White Gryphon and learned it from the Haighlei, and it is much wetter in their kingdoms than here. We weave the walls, inner and outer, and support them with timber, then pack the space between with earth rammed hard. Then we make a mix of powdered lime and sand and other things into a thick paste, and apply it upon inner and outer walls to make them waterproof. The roof is similar; the drawback is that we cannot alter a dwelling so made, we can only add to it. Windows, doors, and recesses must be built in from the beginning."

Darian knew better than to doubt the *hertasi*, but the idea of a house as sturdily made as his being constructed of such flimsy materials as willow withes and plain earth seemed fantastical to him.

And yet, what could be more practical?

"You will get a chance to watch and help in such a construction," Ayshen promised. "There are many things that we must still build here, and most buildings on the ground will be made this way."

"I'm looking forward to it," he replied.

Ayshen laughed again. "You may regret saying that when you are in charge of a ram!" he cautioned. "But now I must go see to food preparation."

"And *I* mussst go to hunt my food," Kel chimed in.

"Then I guess I'll go see if I can be useful to Starfall," Darian said, and he followed Ayshen down the narrow stair, while Kel took the more direct route out by leaping from his sunning ledge into the wind.

Darian did find himself on the business end of an earth ram the very next day, for the first of the large buildings that *everyone* wanted put up was the one that would contain the "seed" of a new Vale. The walls had to be reinforced with rock as well as timber, for such a large building, and even with every free hand in k'Valdemar working, the walls rose with painful slowness. It was literally painful, in fact; most everyone went to bed each night with an aching back, neck, and arms, for the earth between the inner and outer walls had to be pounded until it was nearly as hard as rock, itself. Now Darian could readily believe that his house would last far past his own lifetime.

But with so many people at work, the walls were actually finished in a mere week, enclosing quite a large space of land near the lake. Water was brought up from the lake and fed into a channel at the top of the building, to flow into a series of pools and waterfalls exactly like the hot pools at k'Vala. It flowed out again through a channel at the base of the building, and from there to a purifying sand-and-charcoal pit.

Once the water began flowing, the Hawkbrothers scoured the forest for fallen trees, seasoned, but not rotten, and brought back huge beams and support pillars for the roof. Once these were in place, large squares of the skylight material were seated between the beams, and sealed against leaks. Now the communal pools were ready for their living occupants.

Tayledras with the gift of accelerating the growth of plants, including Steelmind, went to work with the seeds and seedlings the gryphons ferried over from k'Vala. When they were done, although the growth was a bit sparse, the building contained a miniature Vale, quite large enough to hold all of k'Valdemar's current inhabitants at once. The colorful little chattering messenger-birds of the Kaled'a'in flew freely in here, as did the hummingbirds that the Tayledras used for the same purpose. A little magic would be used to heat the waters; a luxury, but one that everyone agreed was the sort of thing that made life much easier than it would have been otherwise.

The waiting Heartstone, now fully awakened, had been fed passively by the newly formed ley-lines for the past four years, and Starfall was pleased with the amount of power that had managed to accumulate in that time. There was certainly enough to set up the soaking pools, magical sentries and protections, and basic shields. Darian helped with that as well, feeling rather proud of his ability to contribute to the *magical* well-being of his new Vale.

Next up were communal kitchens, buildings for the sick, for mass laundry, and facilities for those whose *ekele*—most of them, as it turned out—did not have bathing rooms like Darian's. Putting such facilities in treehouses was a great deal more difficult without magic—so until there *was* magic, those who preferred tree dwellings would have to do without. If they had not had Ayshen's expertise, Darian suspected that neither he nor Snowfire and Nightwind would have had their own private bathing rooms either, but he kept his suspicions to himself.

The *hertasi* and *kyree* already had their dens and lairs dug into the hillsides, and lined with ceramic tiles for cleanliness and comfort so nothing more needed to be done for them, but the *dyheli* needed a winter shelter, so that was the next building to go up, also made of rammed earth. *They* didn't mind an earthen floor, however, so their building was finished quickly.

Then, with all of the immediate needs taken care of, it was time to make a call on the neighbors.

The initial greeting committee wasn't to be a large one. It consisted of the three Elders, Starfall, Snowfire, and Nightwind, of course. To that group were added Ayshen, for the *hertasi*, a handsome neuter called Hashi (his real name sounded like a sneeze) for the *kyree*, Tyrsell for the *dyheli*, and, last of all, Darian. It was Darian who had pointed out that they would make a much more favorable impression on Lord Breon if *they* came to *him*, rather than the other way around, so instead of waiting for Breon to come calling, the first thing they did, once the initial settling in was over, was to put that in motion.

A messenger went to Kelmskeep to ask if they might come to present their respects; he returned the same day with a message of welcome, and an invitation to visit in three days. The reply was phrased formally enough to show that Breon took them seriously, but informally enough to show that he was ready to be friends. So their first impression was a favorable one.

"It's good that he said three days," Darian told the others, with confidence. "More than a week would mean that he didn't think we were important enough to postpone other business, and two days or less would mean he didn't think we were important enough to have business that *we* have to clear away." Then he laughed. "Looks as if all that business about Manners that got hammered into my head is going to turn out useful! I certainly never thought it would!"

"Why not?" Snowfire asked. "Courtesy is always appreciated."

"Because it was all taught out of this musty old book meant for people like Lord Breon's heir, Val. Highborn people who have to know all the etiquette of official visits and all that. *Why* would a wizard's apprentice from a backward town like Errold's Grove need that stuff?" He shook his head.

So now, after rising before dawn and riding at a swift pace, possible only because they didn't need scouts to secure the way, they were at the gates of Kelmskeep before noon. This was Darian's first actual sight of Lord Breon's manor, and in spite of seeing plenty of wonders in the Vales, he was impressed.

It was a fortified manor only in the sense that Lord Breon's ancestors had put up some high and formidable stone walls around the manor and its grounds, walls three stories tall with room for men to walk around on top of them, and observation towers at each corner. Inside the walls, the crenelated walls of the manor sat within manicured gardens. They were rather too confined and geometric for Darian's taste, but as well-tended as any he'd seen in Valdemar, though no match for the gardens of k'Vala.

Lord Breon, his wife, the Lady Ismay, and his son Val were all waiting for them, with a token guard of two bored-looking fellows in Breon's livery. The Tayledras had taken pains with their costumes, and now Darian was very glad that they had all put out the effort, for it was obvious that the Lord and Lady had dressed as for an important occasion. Lord Breon, whose hair had gone to salt-and-pepper gray, wore a fine saffron linen tunic with bands of embroidery at the cuffs and hem, and his crest embroidered on the breast, with matching breeches. His wife, gowned in the same saffron linen, with a matching headdress, also wore amber-and-silver jewelry; rings on both hands, bracelets, necklace, belt. Val was dressed a bit more casually in a plain brown linen shirt, open at the neck, with a sleeveless leather tunic and trews, but it was clear from his scrubbed face and wet hair that he'd interrupted whatever he'd been doing at the time for a wash-up and change of clothing.

The group rode up to their hosts, and at Snowfire's nod, dismounted as one. Darian stepped forward to make the introductions.

"My lord," he said, with a little bow. "May I make you known to the Elders of k'Valdemar Vale—Starfall k'Vala, Snowfire k'Vala, both of whom you met before when we were at Errold's Grove, and Snowfire's lady, Nightwind k'Leshya."

Lord Breon bowed and waited for Darian to finish the introductions.

"Here also is Ayshen k'Leshya, who represents the *hertasi*, Tyrsell k'Vala, who speaks for the *dyheli*, and Hashi k'Vala, who speaks for the *kyree*."

The next three members of the greeting party stepped forward and bowed as Darian introduced them, so that Lord Breon would have name and species linked with the appropriate creature. He did not appear to be surprised that these were "animals," so he must have been forewarned. He bowed to them as well; Tyrsell and Hashi nodded their heads gravely, and Ayshen executed a graceful court bow.

"Kelvren k'Leshya, the Silver Gryphon chief, is out in the north scouting, and you will meet him later. And lastly, I will relate what Tyrsell and Hashi say, if you wish, for they are Mindspeakers. They *can* speak into your mind, if you would rather—" Darian paused, and Lord Breon coughed.

"Ah, if you don't mind, I would prefer for you to translate, young sir," the older man said. "I've had one experience with that, and—well, I'm a plain man, with plain ways, and that was just a bit too uncanny for my taste, personal preference, no offense intended." He coughed again, giving Darian a penetrating look. "And you are—?"

"Darian Firkin k'Vala k'Valdemar, my lord," he replied steadily, keeping his gaze even as well.

"Darian? *Darian!* Lord and Lady, youngster—I wouldn't have thought it!" Lord Breon laughed with surprise. "Look at you! We send off a skinny waif that a good wind would knock over, and he comes back the equal of Val! Well met, young man! And welcome home!" To Darian's surprise, Lord Breon grabbed his hand and pumped it vigorously. "Damme, but it's good to have you back! We've all felt the lack of a mage sorely since you've been gone!"

"Ah—thank you, sir," Darian replied, rather at a loss as to what else to say. Starfall saved him, stepping smoothly to the fore as Lord Breon let go of Darian's hand.

"Lord Breon, we are keeping everyone standing here in the sun, and there is much we would like to discuss with you this afternoon. Have we somewhere that we could all adjourn to?"

Starfall placed a slight emphasis on the word "all," and Lord Breon's eyes flickered to Hashi and Tyrsell.

"As it's a fine day, the inner court would be very pleasant and private," he replied, so quickly that if Darian hadn't seen his eyes flicker, he'd have thought Lord Breon planned that venue all along. "Val and my Lady will be joining us, of course."

"Absolutely," Starfall replied. "The more minds, the better the decisions."

Val looked startled at that, and Lady Ismay appreciative. Evidently Val was not used to being included in his father's counsels, and Lady Ismay was all *too* used to being dismissed as insignificant by menfolk. "If you gentlefolk will come with me, then," Lord Breon continued, "We'll settle ourselves in the court, and Ismay can rejoin us after she informs the servants what is toward." He turned toward the two bored guards. "And you fellows can be about your business. Mind that you tell the Weaponsmaster that I dismissed you on seeing that the wicked Hawkbrothers were not about to fall on us and murder us."

Both men laughed, as if hearing the tagline of a joke, and sauntered off, leaving the k'Valdemar party to follow Lord Breon.

He guided them along the paths of the precisely manicured garden, around the side of the manor, until they came to a small archway leading deep under the second floor. At the other end of the tunnel, sun and greenery looked very enticing, though Darian noted the series of strong portcullis gates and drop doors, and the murder holes in the ceiling above. Anyone who thought this would be a weak point in the manor's defenses would have a rude surprise, shortly before coming down with a serious case of death.

They emerged from the dark tunnel, blinking in the sunlight, surrounded by flowers.

Here in the "inner court" was what was often called "the lady's bower" at other Valdemaran manors. The more delicate and frost-sensitive plants and trees were here, and in addition to these, there was a profusion of roses and lavender, lilies and hyacinth. A little less manicured than the gardens outside, flowering vines trained on trellises overhung nooks with inviting cushions in them, rose trees, quince trees, cherry and apple trees showered the grass with petals. Trees were espaliered against the warm stone walls. All of this surrounded a pool full of waterlilies and slow, lazy golden fish. Here and there a bit of forgotten handiwork showed that this was a favored retreat for Lady Ismay and whatever young women attended her.

It made a fine place for a conference, too. Soon after everyone settled down, the Lady herself appeared, with servants bearing the components of a picnic lunch. Nor were Tyrsell and Hashi forgotten; for Hashi there was a bowl of neatly cubed raw meat (probably so that no one had to watch him tear his food from the bone), and for Tyrsell, a large basin of sweet-feed. The bowl and the basin were both of ceramic, clearly from the kitchen and not the stable, serving bowls with Lord Breon's crest glazed onto them. Both Hashi and Tyrsell expressed their pleasure through Darian.

Once food was handed 'round, Lord Breon dismissed the servants with a gesture and got down to business.

"I've been kept abreast of the situation," he said. "Though since the message came by bird, there wasn't as much detail as I'd have liked. So there *are* more barbarians coming this way?"

Starfall nodded. "We have little more in the way of detail than you, but there is one difference from the last time. These people include women and children as well as the warriors, and herds of various cattle as well as war mounts."

"Sounds as if they're planning to stay wherever it is that they're going." Lord Breon frowned. "We have a bit of a quandary here. It's the official Royal policy that *peaceful* groups be allowed to settle on unoccupied lands, and there is plenty of that hereabouts. At the same time, though, the last lot of these folk to come down out of the north were anything but peaceful. Do we defend ourselves with a quick preemptive strike, or do we wait and see what they do?"

Darian kept his mouth shut although his own feelings were quite clear. He would much prefer an attack, enough to send these people back where they came from. He could tell by the look on Val's face that he felt the same.

It was gratifying that Lord Breon treated them all as allies and equals right from the beginning, though. Darian hoped that his advice had something to do with that.

"We should take our time in considering, my Lord," Snow-fire said smoothly. "They aren't within the distance that a gryphon can fly in half a day, and they are traveling slowly, so we will have that time."

"Huh. What we really need is more information," Lord Breon agreed. "I don't like walking into any situation blind." He laughed suddenly. "As you said, we have the time, and there are other things to discuss. For example, what sorts of building materials are you short of, and what are you prepared to trade for them?"

The discussion moved into less martial matters, from trading for building supplies to *dyheli* grazing grounds, and the need to keep hunters out of them unless escorted by Tayledras. Darian spoke for Tyrsell and Hashi, and occasionally for himself, and when the meeting was concluded and Lord Breon expressed his intention of making a return visit, Darian, at least, came away with a feeling of accomplishment.

"I need your help for an *ekele*," Ayshen told Darian, a few mornings after the visit to Lord Breon. Breon's people had brought a train of wagons with some of the building materials that Starfall had negotiated for, and Darian thought Ayshen might have been waiting for these for a particular project. "I already have Wintersky and Whitethorn, and that will be enough for the things that *hertasi* have trouble with."

"Gladly," Darian replied, bolting the remains of his breakfast. "Whose is it?"

"Your teacher's and his entourage," was the surprising reply. "He will be here shortly, or so Starfall says, so there is some need for swift work."

"Did Starfall tell you *who* my teacher is?" Darian asked eagerly, for Starfall had been singularly closed-mouthed about the identity of this mysterious being. No matter how often Darian asked—or how often he tried to catch Starfall off his guard with the question—the mage would only answer, "You'll see soon enough."

"No," Ayshen replied, indifferently. "He only told me what sort of quarters your teacher would need to feel comfortable. Does it matter?"

Darian sighed. "I suppose not. Well, what have you got in mind for me?"

"Pounding earth, for the moment," was the predictable reply.

So Darian found himself on the top of yet another embryonic wall, ram in both hands, pounding away for all he was worth.

But although this dwelling was for one or two occupants, it had a great deal in common with the great common hall with its multiple pools. This place, too, was evidently to have multiple, cascading pools, judging by the work the *hertasi* were doing on the interior.

But there was more building going on in the tree above—and that was curious. Why would there be *two* dwellings here?

Gradually, as the walls in the ground-level portion rose, Darian saw the skeleton of the dwelling coming together. This was to be a very special place, half tree-dwelling, half on the ground.

By the second day, Darian began to wonder about this teacher of his—for what they were building, by k'Valdemar standards, was a veritable palace. On the ground was a tiny version of the communal hall, with the same transparent roof, exotic plantings, and a collection of three small pools. The floors were all tiled, and the pools as well. There was a bathing room, and two other chambers that did not share the transparent roof, chambers that looked a great deal like his own bedroom, though what purpose these chambers were to serve was unclear to him.

In the tree above, was a standard *ekele*—to the k'Valdemar standards, that is, with thick insulation against winter's cold. And yet—not *quite* standard, for where others were making do with walls of rough plank until they had time to carve and polish the interiors of their *ekele* to their liking, *this* place boasted fine walnut paneling, with moldings of carved oak. Everywhere were touches of care that had not been given to the dwellings of other folk. Even more telling—once the *ekele* was finished, *hertasi* began moving in furnishings that looked newly made, yet did *not* move any personal belongings.

All of this preparation did nothing to ease Darian's anxiety, for the newcomer must surely be important if so much time and effort was going into his dwelling!

When the place was finished, it was a tiny jewel of comfort and luxury, with the *ekele* above joined to the chambers below by an enclosed stair. And no one in the entire Vale showed any envy of the unknown who was to occupy it.

Darian did not have to endure the suspense for long. That very afternoon, his mysterious teacher arrived.

"You're to come to the Vale entrance at once," was all the *hertasi* would say. "Please. And dress well. Starfall wishes this."

Then it ran off, as if it had been sent on more than one errand. Probably it had, so Darian made certain that he was reasonably well-groomed and hurried to the entrance marked by the twin pillars of rock. Starfall was already there—and so were Snowfire, Nightwind, Ayshen, Kel, Tyrsell, Hashi—virtually everyone of any importance in fledgling k'Valdemar.

Suddenly Darian wished he had taken the time to change his tunic. Not that it was dirty, or even shabby—but he wished he'd put on the armor of fine clothing before he came to this meeting.

It was too late now, for in the distance, tiny beneath the huge trees, dwarfed by the enormous trunks, were two figures mounted on *dyheli.*

A snow-white bird flew over the head of one, a bird that simply could not be a raptor. Its tail was too long, and even at a distance it didn't look or fly like anything Darian had ever seen before.

It flew aerobatically, as if it flew purely for the joy of flight. Yet there was a palpable tie between it and the rider it hovered over, as if the bond between it and the rider was visible and tangible.

There was something odd about the rider's head—

A moment more, and Darian knew what it was. No human face was that flat—or that colorful. The rider wore a mask.

Another moment, another furlong nearer, and Darian saw more details. Long silver hair, hair that probably fell to the rider's waist when unbound, had been made up into a single long braid for travel, now tossed over his right shoulder. The mask, of painted leather, covered the entire face—and it represented the face of the bird flying above him.

Darian only prevented his mouth from dropping open by force of will. *Oh, no—it can't be—*

The rider's costume was as fantastic as his mask, yet completely practical for a long ride, the ride from k'Vala to k'Valdemar, for instance. The garments were cut and pieced together to imitate the plumage of his white bird; it was truly an uncanny imitation.

The other rider, in his way, was just as striking as the first. His long hair, also braided, was a shining black with a single silver streak running from the temple. The cut of his riding gear was unmistakably Kaled'a'in. After several months in k'Vala, Darian knew the difference between Tayledras and Kaled'a'in styles at once. He was amazingly handsome, but there was nothing about him that suggested that he was either a warrior or a mage—or vain. Whatever his craft, it seemed likely that his only reason for being there was as company for the mage. Was this the so-called entourage?

Darian's thoughts had come to a complete standstill, and he could only stay where he was, staring. The two riders completed their leisurely approach, and the first dismounted directly in front of Starfall.

"Well, Father, here I am," the rider said, in a voice rich with amusement. "You have managed to drag me here entirely against my own better judgment, and if I did not know you as well as I do, I might be asking you what made you think this youngster was worth the effort of hauling me up from the south." He cast a sidelong glance at Darian, and behind the mask, one silver eye winked broadly. "However, since I know you, I shan't ask that particular question. This, I take it, is young Dar'ian?"

"It is, indeed," Starfall replied, in a voice so like the rider's that it was obvious they were related. "Dar'ian, this is your new teacher, Adept Firesong k'Treva, and his mate, *kestra'chern* Silverfox k'Leshya." Only then did he step forward, and he and his son embraced with much hugging and back pounding.

Darian managed to scramble enough wits together to step

forward and make a deeply formal bow. "This is—beyond an honor—sir—" he began, searching frantically for appropriate words, feeling heat rising in his face and ears. *I must be blushing as red as a scarlet jay,* he thought, increasing his embarrassment.

"You won't say that when you come to know me, youngster," Firesong said, with a voice so solemn that Darian would have been tempted to believe him, had he not seen the wicked amusement in the eyes behind the mask. "I am a notorious taskmaster, and I have every intention of working you until you drop, then reviving you and putting you through the mill all over again."

"Yes, sir, whatever you wish, sir," Darian replied automatically, and quickly stepped back, hoping that the other folk would forget about him for a while. He suddenly felt as awkward as an elk-calf, and only thirteen years old again.

Dear gods! How did this happen? How could I be the student of one of the greatest Adepts in a dozen countries?

He slowly regained a little composure as people *did* appear to forget him; father and son embraced again, Starfall introduced Firesong and Silverfox to everyone else present, and the entire group drifted toward the interior of the Vale. Darian followed quietly behind, listening, but not saying anything.

"Oh, I didn't bring all *that* much up with me," Firesong was saying, in answer to a gentle jibe by his father. "We've got some wardrobe, and the more portable of Silverfox's kit. The rest is relatively light, but bulky, and the k'Vala gryphons will be bringing it along at some point. After all your emphasis on speed, I didn't want to slow things down bringing baggage by *dyheli.*"

"We have prepared your *ekele* as you requested, Firesong," Ayshen put in, showing deference, but not servility. "I hope that you and Silverfox are both pleased."

Silverfox, who until that moment, had not said a word, laughed softly and clapped Ayshen on the back. "I remember your talent at design and construction from White Gryphon, Ayshen. I have no doubt that you have not only granted our every wish, but anticipated needs we had not even thought of."

Darian, meanwhile, felt his mind slowly coming back to him. No wonder no one would tell him who his teacher was supposed to be! He'd have been so terrified he probably would have run all the way back to k'Vala, or even farther.

And Starfall was Firesong's father. Well, that explained a few things. How Starfall had managed to get someone as famous—or infamous, depending on your point of view—as Firesong k'Treva to come be the teacher of poor, lowly little Darian, for one. *Gods save me, how can I ever manage to be worthy of this kind of attention?* he thought in a haze of confusion that bordered on panic.

Just as he began to seriously consider that run to k'Vala, Firesong's companion dropped back from the rest.

"He mumbles in his sleep, you know," Silverfox said conversationally.

"He *what?*" Darian replied, baffled. *Where did that come from?*

"He mumbles in his sleep, he has a terrible weakness for candied yams, and he can never remember where he leaves things. He's human, Dar'ian. He's not a superior being, he's as fallible as anyone. I know that at this point, this doesn't seem likely to you, but I assure you, it's true." Silverfox placed his hand gently on Darian's shoulder, and Darian felt himself relax, despite his anxieties. "I can also promise you that in spite of all of his protests to the contrary, he was quite eager to come here and teach his father's cherished protégé. Firesong just likes to be coaxed."

"I—I'd think that after everything he's gone through, he deserves coaxing, sir," Darian replied shyly and was rewarded by Silverfox's dazzling smile.

"And I agree with you entirely." Silverfox chuckled, patting Darian's shoulder. "I would agree with you even if I were not understandably prejudiced on his part. Don't fear him, Dar'ian. Listen to him, learn from him, but do not fear him."

The strange white bird floated down to land on Firesong's shoulder; he reached up absently to scratch its crest, and it climbed down from its perch to nestle in his arms, head tucked blissfully under his chin, crooning. *A firebird*— Darian now recalled. *Firesong's bondbird is a firebird.* The horrid painting that had been on Justyn's wall flashed into his mind, and the blob on the painted Firesong's shoulder that everyone in Errold's Grove had thought was a chicken or a goose.

A good many things now made perfect sense—the special arrangement of heated pools, for instance. Everyone knew that the reason Firesong wore masks was because he had been terribly scarred at the end of the mage-storms. Presumably, he was shy about exposing those scars to anyone but the closest of companions—and you couldn't wear a mask to soak in the pools, you'd ruin it. Silverfox might well feel more comfortable in a ground dwelling, especially in a storm when the tree would sway and toss—hence the extra rooms below.

And both of them were giving up a considerable level of luxury to come here, only for the purpose of teaching Darian. Under other circumstances, it would have been perfectly reasonable for Firesong to insist that Darian be sent to him. No wonder so much effort had been spent on building his *ekele*!

And of course, who *wouldn't* want to impress the fabled Adept Firesong with the finest *ekele* it was possible to build? No matter how poor it was, compared to what he had left, at least it would be clear that they had *tried*.

But when Firesong came to the new *ekele*, he stopped, and turned to his father. "Surely this is not ours—" he began.

His voice reflected surprise, not disdain.

"It is," Starfall replied, a hint of satisfaction in his voice. "We may not have a fully-charged Heartstone, or a Veil to hold back the weather, but we have power enough and skill enough to give you comfort. You will find your own pools here below, a bathing room, a steam room, and a room for Silverfox to receive clients."

"I am mostly retired, but I still do take massage clients," Silverfox said smoothly, as Firesong choked. There had been something implied that Darian didn't understand, but he had a good idea that Kel could tell him—and would.

"I have well-insulated the *ekele*, Adept Firesong," Ayshen said diffidently. "I do not think you will find any chills or drafts this winter."

The Adept seemed charmed, pleased, and just a little surprised. "I am not sure what to say," Firesong replied at length. "Except to thank you, thank you all. You have more than made us welcome."

"Oh, I am certain that you will find plenty to complain of," Starfall laughed. "But until you do, I hope you find your new *ekele* satisfactory! And on that note, we will leave you to settle in."

As Darian was about to leave, Firesong turned to him and summoned him with a crooked finger. "Come up with us," the Adept said. "I would like to talk with you a little."

Darian swallowed, felt his mouth go dry as old snakeskin, and obediently followed the two into the ground-level of the structure. They paused long enough for a glance around the pool room; Firesong nodded as Silverfox exclaimed in pleasure.

"When the plantings get their full growth, this will be enchanting," Firesong observed warmly.

"I cannot believe that they have gone to such trouble for us," Silverfox replied, shaking his head, then he laughed. "Well, perhaps they have heard tales of your famous plaints when you lived in Valdemar, and had none of the niceties of a Vale at your disposal!"

"That could well be," Firesong agreed, with as much humor as Silverfox. He found the staircase and began climbing it, with his partner and Darian close behind.

Darian had not seen the *ekele* since the furniture was moved in; as he entered behind the other two, he saw that not only had furnishings been put in place, but there were beautifully woven rugs on the floor and hangings on the walls.

Silverfox went briefly to the window, then looked back at Firesong. "I think I will see the chambers on the ground first. If there is a storm, I still do not care for being in the boughs of a tree."

"Only one who was raised in a tree could, *ashke*, so if there is a storm, I can understand," Firesong chuckled. "For that matter, if there is a storm, you may find me joining you below!"

Silverfox saluted them both and then descended the stairs noiselessly, and Firesong gestured to Darian to take a seat. Gingerly, Darian sat down on a chair woven of willow withes, and Firesong took another just like it, placed opposite him. The Adept leaned back in the chair, relaxing as the withes creaked, settling beneath his slight weight, but Darian remained sitting straight upright, back and shoulders staff-stiff. He had no idea what to expect, and wondered desperately what Firesong expected of him. He couldn't look away from those silver eyes.

"So," Firesong said, after he'd watched Darian carefully for a time. "Being a mage, becoming an Adept—was this your idea, or someone else's?"

"If I'd had a choice, you mean?" Darian hazarded. "In the very beginning?"

Firesong nodded.

"If I'd had a choice *originally*, I'd just be a trapper, like my parents," Darian said softly. "After my parents died, I was apprenticed without anyone asking me what I wanted. I'd rather have been apprenticed to the village woodcutter. I didn't want to be a mage, I didn't want anything to do with magic. I couldn't see any use for it."

To his great surprise, Firesong burst out laughing so hard that he started to cough and had to get control of himself before he could talk again. "You couldn't see any use for it!" he rasped out at last, shaking his head, and dabbing at his eyes with a silken handkerchief. "Well, at least I won't have to disabuse you of dreams of easy glory! But I forget. You never saw any really powerful magic, did you?"

"Not with my original master," Darian replied truthfully. "Once the mage-storms began, I don't think he could do much of anything; he certainly couldn't change, steer, or even predict the weather, and that might have impressed me that magic had some uses. That was Wizard Justyn—"

"Justyn, Justyn . . ." Firesong muttered, eyes intent as he concentrated. "I think I may have met him once. Name sticks in my mind." He closed his eyes, then opened them again. "I think I have it. It would be right after the end of the Ancar-Falconsbane debacle, I think. Mercenary-mage, got a head wound doing something ridiculously heroic, lost most of his powers and got talked into using what he had as a Healer out where they didn't have one. Someplace in the middle of nowhere—very nice nowhere you have here, by the way. I love what you've done with the place. He was part of a group of similarly retrained folk, not a big group, though. Darkwind,

Elspeth, and I met with them before they got sent out to new posts. Your Justyn wound up out here, obviously. Am I right?"

Darian's mouth fell open; he couldn't help it. Firesong had just told him more about his own master than he himself had known! He could only nod in astonished confirmation, and felt embarrassed that he had known so little about Justyn.

So he really did *meet the people he claimed he had! And we never believed him.*

"How did you know?" he asked. "How could you remember after all this time?"

Firesong shrugged. "I can't help it; I almost never forget a face or a name, but I can't remember where I left my boots. Well, at least I won't have to disabuse you of any grandiose schemes for becoming a Wizard-King; that's a relief anyway. Tales notwithstanding, I'm afraid there aren't many kingdoms going without claimants. What have you done and learned while you were with Adept Starfall and Mage Firefrost? How have they been educating you?"

Darian told him as succinctly as he could; it really wasn't difficult since he and Firesong shared the same kind of magical education. Firesong listened, nodding from time to time, and said at the end, "You've had a good, solid education, but that's to be expected with my father teaching you. You said that originally if you'd had the choice, you wouldn't have chosen magic. What about now? If I could remove it from you, is that what you'd want?" Then he said something else that shocked Darian. "I can, you know. That's one of the things a Healing Adept can still do, and I suspect that's one of the reasons why Father wanted me here. If having this power really bothers you, still, I can take it away."

Once again, Darian was caught off-guard by the unexpected question, and answered without thinking. "Ah—no, not now. It seems as if it's something I should do." He shook his head, unable to come up with anything that sounded right. "I guess I haven't thought about it, about having a choice, I mean. There didn't seem to be one."

"There is a choice," Firesong said somberly. "And I want to give you one. An *informed* choice. There's something more I want to show you, before you make that choice."

Before Darian had any idea of what the Adept was up to, Firesong had reached up—and removed his mask.

Darian blinked, but did not turn away or lower his eyes. In many ways, the scar-seamed face behind the mask was not as horrific as it could have been. It certainly wasn't *pretty*, or rather, the fact that it was the ruin of something that had once been handsome was actually painful to think about. The silver eyes looked out of a randomly patterned set of shiny, tight patches divided by thick, red scars, something that was nearly another mask. It wouldn't give nightmares to children—

Not screaming nightmares, anyway. Maybe bad dreams, though.

"There is often a price to wielding great magic, Darian," the scar-twisted lips said. "This was mine. Envoy Karal paid with his sight. Two more of our party paid with their lives. I was very, very lucky, when it came down to cases. I could easily have died as well, had I not been protected by one of those who did. I had—thanks to the gods, who sent Silverfox—learned that there were far more important things than having a pretty face, and losing it didn't destroy me. I was beautiful." The scarred lips smiled. "I still am. I don't wear masks for my own sake, but the sake of others, so that they need not feel pain that I myself no longer experience. But, Darian, had I not learned things about what is important by then, this minor price could have been a very major one. Have you thought about that, the possibility that you, too, might be asked to pay a great price for power?"

While Darian sat in silence, Firesong put his mask back on again.

"What about *not* using it?" he asked finally. "There's a price for inaction, too. The trouble is, usually other people get caught in paying it as much as you do. At least, if I keep this Gift and use whatever power I have, I'll be making the choice to act instead of just standing by and wringing my hands."

Behind the mask, the eyes closed for a moment. "That is a good answer—and, I might add, one I've not heard before. It should have been obvious you aren't the kind of young man to choose inaction."

The silver eyes opened again, and there was a smile in the voice. "Young Dar'ian Firkin k'Vala k'Valdemar, you have passed my test. I will be quite pleased to have you as my student and to teach you all I can, until you have achieved everything possible within the limits of your Gift, or you drop from exhaustion. Have I passed your test as well?"

Slowly, Darian nodded. "I think . . . you won't be an *easy* teacher, but you'll be a good one. I think . . . we can get along."

Firesong chuckled. "You'd be surprised at how few people realize that is important for teacher and pupil! One more thing, before I let you go for the day. If ever there is something that you are afraid to tell me, do not hesitate to confide it in Silverfox. That—in part—is his profession, to be a trustworthy confidant."

"I will, sir," Darian replied, knowing a dismissal when he heard one. He stood up, and as he was about to leave the room, Firesong motioned to him to stay.

"Dar'ian, I have one request." He sighed, and Darian wondered if he'd done something wrong already. "Do me the very great favor of never calling me 'sir' again. Don't call me 'Master' either. Call me Firesong." His eyes grew mournful. "Being called 'sir' makes me feel so *old!*"

"Yes, s— Firesong," Darian replied quickly. "But I've come to respect those who are wiser than I am, and I only meant it as a compliment."

"Hmm. Well, in that case, I'll let it pass, once in a while." Firesong replied.

Darian went out the door and down the covered stair, unable to tell if Firesong was serious or had been teasing him.

He decided to walk at the edge of the small lake that lay just beneath the cliff housing Kel's aerie and Snowfire and Nightwind's home. Darian was so preoccupied with sorting out his thoughts that he practically walked into Snowfire and Nightwind.

"Dar'ian, wake up!" Nightwind called, startling him into looking up. She smiled at him, and he smiled back sheepishly.

"Sorry," he said, coming over to join them; they were dangling their feet in the water like a couple of youngsters. "I was thinking. I was just—well—I was talking to Firesong, or he was talking to me, I mean, and I have a lot to think about."

"Hmm. I should imagine!" Nightwind replied. "I know Silverfox, of course—a very fine *kestra'chern*, by the way—but I'd never met Firesong. I must admit to you that when I heard who your teacher was going to be, I was *not* anticipating being as impressed as I was."

"You, too?" Snowfire said with astonishment. "I knew his reputation, and I rather thought he'd be something of a pain. I figured he'd have a tantrum when he saw his *ekele*, and as for training Dar'ian, no matter what Starfall said, I thought he'd be very haughty about it."

"He's not like that at all," Darian began.

"I agree, I agree!" Snowfire replied hastily. "I agree completely! I don't know what's happened to him since he made that particular reputation, but he certainly doesn't deserve it anymore."

"I know what's happened," Nightwind replied, with a cynical half-smile. "Silverfox is what happened. He could humanize a monster."

A step behind Darian, and Nightwind's sudden blush, made Darian look around. Silverfox had just stolen up upon them in time to hear that last remark, and his grin at Nightwind's embarrassment was full of mischievous charm.

"So, do you have any monsters you need tamed?" His grin widened. "Less of that is my doing than you might think, my dear," he said genially. "Behind all those exquisite masks is a very real and generous man whose *humanity* has never been in doubt. He simply had to reconcile himself to the fact that he didn't have to wear the masks on his heart, only his face."

"Come here, you wicked creature," Nightwing replied, leaping to her feet and holding out her arms. "Give me a proper greeting!"

"So little Nightwind still wants a hug from Uncle Silverfox?" the *kestra'chern* teased. He did go to her and give her the greeting hug she wanted, though, and then clasped hands with Snowfire.

"I am very pleased to meet *you*, may I add," he went on. "We stopped long enough at k'Vala that I managed to hear of your joining with my old friend, and I was quite anxious to meet the fellow capable of swerving her from her childhood vow never to wed anyone at all!"

"Silverfox! I was only twelve!" she objected, laughing.

"You seemed quite serious at the time, my dear," Silverfox replied, and turned back toward Darian, who was edging away, thinking that he was intruding. "Please, Dar'ian, come join us. I had come specifically to talk to you a little more."

"You're sure I won't be in the way?" he asked.

Snowfire and Nightwind both beckoned, and Silverfox smiled. "Not at all. A great deal of what I wanted to discuss with you concerns these two, as well, since I am told they are your oldest friends here. And it is about Firesong. I should like you three to know more about him, as he will be a part of k'Valdemar for some time to come. Perhaps longer than even *he* anticipates."

Snowfire raised a quizzical eyebrow. "You think he might stay?"

Silverfox only shrugged. "I cannot predict. I can only say that until a reason for him to leave should manifest, he will remain, and if none does—"

"Interesting." Nightwind found another soft spot on the bank to sit, and invited Silverfox to take her earlier perch. "So what is it that has turned your Firesong into a paragon?"

"Time, trials, and being forced to work with a fraction of the power that he was used to having," Silverfox said casually. "No more Great Magics for him or for anyone; every bit of magic has to be carefully planned to gain the maximum benefit from the minimum of power. That has forced him to be patient, careful, restrained. He can no longer afford to act on impulse—almost a shame, since he had turned impulsiveness into an art form."

"In short, he grew up," Snowfire snorted, then blushed. "I'm sorry. That was entirely uncharitable."

"Not entirely wrong, but *very* uncharitable," Silverfox agreed. "I ask you to try to recall that his reputation was made in the days when he could afford to send up a Gate just because he preferred not to ride a single day's journey. And no small part of that reputation was caused by his own insatiable urge to tweak the noses of others—so to speak."

Silverfox trailed his fingers in the water meditatively, then added, "He still has that sense of humor, but he has learned to express it in ways that are more—humorous."

"I detect your delicate hand there," Nightwind chuckled. Silverfox's only response to that was an odd look.

"I told him that I thought we'd get along all right, sir," Darian offered. "I still do, and I think I like him, too."

"Good! That was what I was hoping to hear you say," Silverfox applauded. "Have you any questions?"

"Ah—one." Darian decided to just come out and ask it. "What exactly is a *kestra'chern*, and why did Firesong choke when Starfall mentioned your clients?"

Nightwind suddenly developed a fit of coughing; Silverfox quelled her with a look.

"A *kestra'chern* is predominantly one who comforts, Dar'ian," Silverfox said, taking care with his words. "That is the profession. The least that a *kestra'chern* does is to supply ease, a distraction, and an absolutely trustworthy confidant. The *best* of us are in part Healers—Healers of the mind and spirit, rather than of the body, although we have some skills there, and are often asked to help Healers when they are shorthanded. Sometimes that leads to some very intimate contact, for sometimes it is easiest to lead someone to open his heart when he has been intimate in body. That is not always, or even often, the case; it truly depends on the *kestra'chern*."

Darian was perfectly capable of reading between the lines; but he also thought about Lilly, how she had used her crude skills to keep the barbarians occupied with *her* and away from the village girls—and he made a mental note to tell Silverfox about her at some point.

"As for why Firesong choked—" Now Silverfox grinned. "Starfall initially had a—how shall I put this?—a somewhat narrow and distorted view of my profession, and said some misguided things about my relationship with Firesong."

"Starfall nearly had a litter of kittens," Nightwind said rudely. "And what he *said* doesn't bear repeating. Needless to say, several of your k'Leshya compatriots had some choice words with him when we found out."

"Oh—*oh*!" Now Darian understood Firesong's reaction—

hearing his father go from disapproval to calmly mentioning a room for Silverfox's *clients*—

I think I'd have choked, too.

Snowfire snickered. There was no other word for the sound he made. "Don't misunderstand me," he said, "I admire Starfall immensely, but he has been known to get pig-headed about some things."

"So you will recognize the same trait in the son," Silverfox said smoothly. "I am glad, however, that there are no misunderstandings now; we have a full plate, which will be fuller yet if those threatened barbarians should appear."

They all nodded, but it was Darian who broke the silence that followed that statement. "I've put it off long enough, I guess," he said, mostly to Snowfire and Nightwind. "I'd better take care of one last thing before I discover I haven't got the time for it."

"What's that?" Snowfire asked.

Darian made a face of distaste. "Tomorrow I'd better put in an official appearance in Errold's Grove."

Lord Breon's Keep

Nine

Keisha kept herself busy, trying not to miss Shandi too much. Midsummer Faire came and went (Keisha stayed away, except for a single trip around the traders' booths), with no further signs from the mysterious Hawkbrothers and the absent Darian Firkin except for the frequent overhead flights of gryphons, sometimes bearing burdens, sometimes not. Lord Breon's son came to the Faire representing his father, "selected" the wedding-shawl that had been especially made for him (with no indication that he realized his selection had been carefully steered). Valan of Kelmskeep assured everyone that, yes, the Hawkbrothers were in the process of setting up their settlement, and yes, Darian Firkin was with them. As to when he would reintroduce himself to Errold's Grove, that, Val didn't know. He *had* seen them, met with them on several occasions, even been to their settlement, so he could at least testify to that much.

Keisha didn't much blame Darian for not showing up immediately and putting himself at the disposal of the village. If *she* were in his position, she'd give them a great deal of time to settle themselves down before she came to visit. The village of Errold's Grove was entirely too keyed up about the return of their peregrinating son for her liking.

Fortunately, the excitement of Midsummer Faire, with Val in attendance, twice the usual number of Hawkbrother-traders, and several entirely new traders up out of the south, gave the villagers plenty to spend their excitement (and money) on.

Keisha wouldn't have stayed so much away from the Faire, but after the first few candlemarks, she discovered that she couldn't tolerate the press of people. She retreated to her workshop, discovered during the excitement of the games and contests that even that wasn't far enough, and removed herself to the woods until the contests were over. Increasingly, Keisha suffered from headache, upset stomach, general nervousness when she was around two or more people—and she had no idea how to make it stop. Her best shelters were her workshop and the forest, and of the two, she preferred the forest, for in her workshop she was easy to find, and during the Faire people seemed to think it was their duty to coax her to attend.

She kept away from her family, too, as much as possible. In fact, even the outwardly peaceable Fellowship folk were something of a trial to be around, for beneath their placid exteriors lurked a stew of complicated emotions. Evidently there were some members of the group for whom a placid life and an absence of outward conflict was more of a trial than arguments would have been! Fortunately, she could get her meals without having to stay at the table.

She salved her conscience by providing her family with food instead of her physical help—greens and herbs from her garden, other foodstuffs from the bounty given her by her patients. *They* seemed to fear that now that she was on her own, she was in serious danger of starving to death. Every day saw a rough, temporary container plaited of green reeds or made of giant leaves stitched together left on her doorstep, containing something to eat—a loaf of fresh bread, a round pat of fresh-churned butter, fresh-picked vegetables, a meat or berry pie, a half-dozen eggs—if it was edible, it generally ended up in a basket on her doorstep. Sooner or later the bounty would probably dry up, but while it continued, sharing it with her family soothed the pangs of conscience for "deserting" them.

It was just that at the moment, it was harder than ever for her to be around them. Two of her brothers were trying to court the same girl, which led to a great deal of masculine head-butting, snorting, and prancing around the dinner table. The youngest two were in the stage of adolescent revolt, which meant a great deal of conflict with her father. Her

Mum was worried because they'd gotten only two letters from Shandi, and both were very brief. Keisha wasn't at all surprised, considering the daily round of chores and classes Shandi described! Shandi wasn't spoiled, but she'd *never* had to work this hard in her life! There seemed to be a great deal of book-learning, too, which was not Shandi's strongest suit.

Be fair, Keisha. She's not a dunce either. She would just rather do handiwork than bookwork.

At least they'd done the wisest thing at that Collegium, so far as Shandi's chore-assignments went, and put her to work on sewing and mending for her share of the daily work. By now they had probably discovered that with Shandi's nimble fingers on the job, they didn't need to assign anyone else the sewing tasks!

Mum worried, though, and that made Keisha's stomach ache, which made it impossible for her to eat, which made Mum worry more, and—well, Keisha began to look for reasons to be away from the dinner table.

It certainly is convenient how many little accidents occur around dinnertime.

In fact, it was getting so she could find those little accidents before anyone came to fetch her—granted, though, she *was* looking for them. But when it came to baby's colic or mother's burned hand, brother's tumble from a tree, father's work-related blisters or sister's bad sunburn, Keisha had never been so attentive to the needs of the village. Small wonder she was getting little gifts left on the doorstep.

In the afterglow of mingled pleasure and exhaustion that followed the Faire, the only topics of discussion among the villagers were Val's betrothed, the pledging of two of the village couples, and the resounding success of trading. For the moment, they had forgotten to fret about Darian and the Hawkbrothers, the weather, the harvest, or the level of the river. All of these were safe enough topics not to cause argument, and laden with contentment rather than worry; Keisha woke on the third morning after Midsummer, looking forward to a few more days without headaches.

She was out in her garden when the unusual sound of hoofbeats on the path behind her made her look up—to find herself staring up at a strange, deerlike animal with long, curved horns and a Hawkbrother on its back. She gaped at him stupidly, her mind gone blank.

"Heyla!" the rider said, cheerfully, in very good Valdemaran. "I am looking for someone of authority in Errold's Grove to deliver a message to. Some children sent me here."

That, at least, brought her out of her daze. She stood up, wiping her hands on her garden-smock. "The Mayor is probably checking the irrigation mill," she said, thinking out loud. "I know the priest is visiting a sick farmer. Will I do? I'm sort of the Healer."

"Assuredly," the Hawkbrother replied. "It's simple enough. We of k'Valdemar Vale are finally settled in, and I was told to say that the Elders of the Vale and Mage Darian will come tomorrow to present themselves as new neighbors to you. They told me to tell you that there is no need to make a great event of this, or special preparations. We waited until after the Faire so as not to disrupt your celebration."

She stared at him for a moment, before stammering a reply. "Ah—that will be fine, wonderful!" she managed. "I'll go find the Mayor and let him know right now! Who shall I say gave the message?"

The rider had already given some subtle signal to his mount; it was ten paces back up the path before she got out the last word of her reply. The rider called back over his shoulder.

"I am Wintersky k'Vala—and thank you for taking the message for me!" His beast leaped into a gallop, and he vanished into the forest.

She didn't wait any longer herself; the Mayor needed to hear this right away. She tore off her smock and left it in the middle of the garden, pelting down the path toward the river as fast as her feet could carry her.

She intercepted the Mayor and the blacksmith on the path leading to the river. They were their way back from their weekly inspection of the mill that kept the vegetable fields nearest the village irrigated—the ones on the other side of the river, being at a lower level, could be watered naturally. She waved her arm wildly at him as soon as she saw him and increased her speed; he stopped immediately, a look of worry jumping into his eyes.

She might have been running, but not long enough to be the least winded. She didn't wait for him to ask what was wrong. "A message came from the Hawkbrothers, sir!" she called, as she came to a halt on the path in front of him. "The new ones, the ones with Darian Firkin! They're coming here tomorrow to meet you!"

The worry changed immediately to pleasure. "Finally!" he exclaimed. Then the worry returned. "But tomorrow? How can we make proper preparations with such short notice?"

"The Hawkbrother—he said he was Wintersky k'Vala— said he was told to tell you that this isn't a formal meeting, that you aren't to make a big fuss over it—" But she saw she might just as well have been talking to a wall and stopped trying. The Mayor was off in a tangle of plans and preparations, and probably wouldn't believe that the Hawkbrother had said any such thing. In fact, he broke into a trot, heading straight for the village square, probably with the intention of gathering every person of importance in Errold's Grove to see what they could put together for a "proper" greeting committee.

The blacksmith was right behind him, too, but heading for his home. The news was about to spread through the village by the fastest means possible. *He* was going to tell his wife, who would promptly start the news going in all directions. Wives were better than Heralds and Companions at getting any news of any kind spread.

Which meant that Keisha could go back to her garden with a good conscience.

I only hope it'll continue to stay my *garden,* she reflected, worried. *Darian can't possibly want the cottage back. No, surely not. He's living with the Hawkbrothers.*

Everyone in the village was awake before dawn. From the great oven of the village baker (who was also the miller) came the scent, not only of bread, but of roasting meat. From dozens of hearths rose equally appetizing smells. From the other huge oven at the threshing barn came the aroma of cake and pie. Errold's Grove was going to give a feast for Darian and his Hawkbrothers whether they wanted one or not.

As soon as the first dawn light pierced the morning sky, groups of children streamed past Keisha's cottage, heading for the forest, their voices shrill with excitement. They came back within a candlemark, laden with boughs of greenery and bunches of long, trailing vines. Keisha followed them and joined the older children in decorating the square with the greenery, while all the tables and benches that had just been taken back into houses after the Faire were brought back *out* again and set up in the square itself.

By midmorning, most of the preparations were complete; food that didn't need to be warm had been brought to the Temple for later serving, the bowers and decorations were up, banners and flags flew from windows looking out on the square, and a small boy, giddy with pride at his important assignment, was up in the Temple tower, watching for the first sign of the Hawkbrothers.

Keisha's only symptom so far was a knotted stomach and a faint headache; those she could bear easily enough, so she remained with the rest of the village, waiting in the square. After two false alarms, at midmorning the shout went up from the tower.

"They're coming!" the boy shrilled. "Oh, there's a *lot* of them! And they're riding on deer!"

Keisha's stomach lurched, and she faded back into a doorway, while the Mayor gathered up his cronies and hustled them up onto a low platform left over from the Faire at the end nearest the Temple. Moments later, the visitors rode into the square.

A spontaneous cheer burst out, making their mounts start. The visitors seemed pretty startled, too, at least to Keisha's eyes, but they kept their composure in spite of all the noise. She saw two of the ones in the lead—a thin, but good-looking young man about her own age and a dignified, craggily handsome older man with long, silver-white hair—put their heads together for a quick consultation. The young man gestured discreetly at the platform, the older man nodded, and they led the entire group toward the waiting Mayor.

The Mayor stood nervously clasping his hands as they approached him and his group. The cheering died down when the visitors dismounted and made the last few steps afoot.

The Mayor had probably memorized a grand speech, but his efforts were entirely set at naught, for the first words out of his mouth were "By Haven, Darian! Is that really *you*? You're—bigger!"

The younger man laughed and held out his hand, clasping the Mayor's firmly. "Boys have a habit of growing up, Lutter," he replied, his warm, deep voice very amused. He shook the Mayor's hand. "What are you, Mayor now? Good for you; I'm not surprised. Congratulations!"

Mayor Lutter flushed, and plainly made the decision to discard his planned speech, since the atmosphere of great dignity and importance he had been trying to establish was spoiled anyway. "Good to have you here again. Now, who are these fine folks?"

Darian introduced them, and Keisha took careful note of their names. The older man was Starfall k'Vala, an Adept, clearly one of the men in charge, and dressed in a tunic and breeches of exotic color and cut. A fellow who was dressed like the Hawkbrothers she was used to seeing was identified as Snowfire k'Vala, and a lady with night-black hair and sharp blue eyes as his mate, Nightwind k'Leshya. *She* was given the title of *trondi'irn*, whatever that was. But the next two to be introduced had every eye in the village fairly popping from its socket, Keisha's included.

"This is Healing Adept Firesong k'Treva, and the *kestra'-chern* Silverfox k'Leshya," Darian said proudly, gesturing to the pair. Silverfox would have startled almost anyone in Errold's Grove with his appearance. His black, silver-streaked hair was so long it touched the back of his knees, and he wore it unbound, flowing as loose as a maiden's. His elaborately brocaded, sleeveless vest of green and teal could only be silk, as were the emerald shirt with its wide sleeves, and the matching, tight-fitting breeches. Keisha yearned to examine the silk brocade more closely, and his leather knee-boots fit so smoothly they must have been tailored to his legs alone.

But Silverfox paled in comparison with Firesong . . .

Firesong's silver hair was just as long as Silverfox's, but

he sported a braid on either side of his face, with strands of crystal beads, silver chains, and tiny bells braided into them. His shirt of emerald green was embroidered all over in a pattern of blue, green, and silver feathers. Its pendulous sleeves reached down to his knees, and it was held in close to his body with a silver belt in the form of two birds, whose tails flowed together at the back and whose beaks hooked together in the front. He wore loose-fitting silk breeches tucked into green boots with silver ornaments down each side. But the crowning touch, the object that set him apart from everyone else, was the mask that he wore, completely covering his face.

It seemed to be of metal, and yet it was far too flexible to be of that substance. Patterned in glittering silver, with touches of shining emerald and sparkling sapphire, its ornamentation echoed the feather-embroidery of his tunic, giving him the look of a fantastic bird.

It was the mask that did it, that told her that this was *the* Firesong, the famous Adept who trained Princess Elspeth, who helped save Valdemar in the Great War, who then helped save it again from the mage-storms. . . .

"I am quite pleased to visit this place," Firesong was saying, pretending to ignore the fact that he was the center of *everyone's* gaze. "I understand that the wizard who helped to save your village was someone I had the honor of meeting a very long time ago. Justyn, wasn't it?"

Keisha wondered why that casual remark would make Mayor Lutter pale, but the man regained his composure after a moment of coughing. "Ah, yes, Wizard Justyn—he was young Darian's first Master—that's his statue, there, facing the bridge, you know—seemed the most appropriate place—least we could do to honor his memory—"

Mayor Lutter pointed, and naturally everyone turned to look, in spite of the fact that most people here were as familiar with the statue as they were with the members of their families. Of course, from this angle, all anyone saw was the *back* of the statue, but at least it was evident that the statue was a pretty good one. It should be, considering it had been done by the same artist who made all the religious statues hereabouts, and not by the fellow that Mayor Lutter originally wanted to hire, a dauber who usually carved and painted inn signs. Lutter had been overruled by nearly everyone. Keisha saw Darian nod to himself, with a pleased little smile.

Mayor Lutter still seemed shaken. "Ah—you sent word not to make any special preparations—but we couldn't—you know—we've prepared a feast in your honor—" he stammered. The women waiting near the Temple took that for an order, and started bringing out dishes. Things were a bit confused for a moment, then the Mayor's wife Mandy took charge and got everything set to rights and organized. Tables and benches placed on the platform were quickly covered with clean white cloths, and the visitors were guided to their seats. Everyone else scrambled for seats down below, as the young women and wives appointed as servers began bringing out food.

Keisha would have taken this opportunity to slip away, but Mandy Lutter wasn't having any of that.

"There you are!" said the reedy voice as Keisha tried to ease her way out of the crowd. Nandy's thin, hard hand seized her arm, and the Mayor's wife pulled Keisha up toward the platform. Keisha *wanted* to jerk her arm free and run off, but that would have been unbearably rude, so she allowed Nandy to hustle her up onto the platform and into a seat.

"This's Keisha Alder, our Healer," Mandy proclaimed. "I'm afraid she's a bit shy." Keisha moved to protest, but was stilled by Mandy's sharp glance.

Keisha looked cautiously about, and discovered she'd been seated between two of the visitors; Darian was on her right, and the lady with the black hair was on her left. And curiously, as she got control over her *own* nerves, she realized that the nausea and headache she'd been suffering from ever since she woke up were—gone!

"—Kel will be arriving a little later," the woman was saying to the Mayor. "He wanted to run his morning patrol before coming here, and that seemed like a wise course to us."

Keisha wondered who "Kel" was, but she didn't get a chance to speculate, for Darian addressed her just as the woman went on to talk about the bondbirds.

"I've been told that you have the old cottage that I used to share with Justyn," the young man said, with a friendly enough smile. But immediately Keisha worried. *Did* he want it back?

"Ye-es," she replied carefully. "No one was using it—you don't mind, I hope?"

He chuckled, and his eyes crinkled at the corners. "Why should I mind? It's nice to know it isn't sitting empty, or worse, fallen into a ruin. I just hope you've managed to make more of it than we did."

"People fixed it up for me. They fixed the walls, the roof, everything," she told him, and hesitated a moment. "I don't suppose you'd want to see it, would you?"

His face lit up with his smile. "Actually, yes I would, quite a bit. I was trying to think of a way to ask you if I could."

"I will—if you'll let me see the gryphon up close!" she said, suddenly thinking of a way to achieve her own wish.

Now Darian laughed. "Let? Havens, when he comes in from patrol, you'll have a hard time keeping him away! If there's one thing that Kel loves, it's an audience."

That led her to questions about gryphons in general and Kel—or "Kelvren" as his name really was—in particular. Darian was perfectly willing to answer them, and while *he* was talking, *she* didn't have to.

Darian was a vast improvement over her brothers, both in manners and appearance. He never interrupted, passed platters without being asked, offered food to her before taking some himself, and never heaped his plate with the best cuts. He used knife and fork properly, didn't wipe his mouth on his cuff, and didn't make sarcastic or cutting remarks, even when Mayor Lutter was holding forth with great pomposity on things he obviously knew nothing about. When that happened, he just exchanged *looks* with others of his party, and hid his smile by turning his head.

As for appearance—well, Keisha didn't blame the rest of the girls for competing to serve him, nor did she blame them for their posing, their flirtatious glances, their outright adoration in some cases. He was really one of the best-looking young men she'd ever seen, and the leather Hawkbrother clothing with its fringes, beadwork, and tooling only gave him an exotic touch that was very attractive.

He seemed completely oblivious to their attempts to catch

his eye, though. Mature and self-possessed, he managed to pay attention to Keisha's questions and to the discussions that the Hawkbrother Elders and the village officials were having at the same time. She was used to having to listen to more than one conversation at the same time, since she often had two or more people babbling at her about an illness or injury, but she'd never known anyone else to have that gift.

Well, maybe he's too busy with that to pay any attention to the girls. Or maybe he's used to admiration. At least he doesn't seem vain about it, if he is.

"The bondbirds are mostly in the trees around the edge of the village right now," he said, in answer to her last question. "No reason to call them in, and too many strangers make some of them nervous. Firesong is enough strangeness for all of you to handle, I think!"

"You have a bird, don't you?" she asked.

"Of course! I couldn't be a Hawkbrother without one!" he laughed. "His name is Kuari, and he's an eagle-owl. He's fledged of Snowfire's two birds. When we've got lots of space, I'll call him in if you'd like to see him. He is really far too big to call into a crowd."

"What's it like, having a bondbird?" she asked curiously. "Is it something like having a Companion?"

"Huh. A bit, I'd guess. The bond strengthens with time; in the beginning, you have to work to talk to them, but after a year or so, they're always in your head and you'd have to work to keep them *out*—assuming you'd want to." He raised his eyebrows. "I can't imagine why anyone would want to, though. They're so different from humans that it isn't like having someone eavesdropping on you." He warmed to his subject. "Their needs are very different from a human's, and their interests—it's only because they are bred to be extremely intelligent that they have much in common with us at all. Have you ever been around ordinary birds of prey at all?"

"Not really," she admitted. "In fact, the only raptors I've ever seen up close have been a couple of bondbirds, the ones that come with Hawkbrothers who've brought things to trade." She offered a slow smile. "I really like Steelmind's buzzard, he's so calm."

He chuckled. "You haven't missed much with ordinary

raptors. Oh, they are beautiful, graceful, and amazing to watch, but there isn't much room in those heads for anything except hunting, breeding, and survival skills. They're very focused. That's the way Nightwind puts it. Bondbirds are less focused, but they *do* have intelligence and the ability to socialize, and not just with us. They play games and socialize with other bondbirds, and not just of the same breed. They *have* to be able to do that, or they couldn't work together—and too many of them would be on the dinner menu for the biggest of them, if they *didn't* have that ability to tell friend from food!"

She stifled a laugh. "I never thought about it that way."

"Believe me, it's quite true." His attention wandered for a moment, as he caught part of one of the other ongoing conversations. It was only for a moment, though, and it came right back to her. "When you see the size of Kuari, you'll understand. Honestly, I'm not strong enough to hold him for long without something to help support his weight."

That candid remark surprised and charmed her. She couldn't imagine any of the young men she knew admitting they weren't strong enough to do something.

By this time, the meal was just about over; the last of the dishes were whisked away to make way for bowls of fruit and pitchers of wine. "Would you like to see the cottage now?" she asked, and when he hesitated, she assured him, "There won't be any serious talk going on yet. Mayor Lutter won't want any real discussions of anything happening in front of the whole village." She listened a moment to the Mayor's current topic, the past Midsummer Faire. "He's on the Faire. The next thing will be the harvest, and the number of traders he expects. He'll be priming your people for suggestions later about what they might bring to trade on a regular schedule. You can see the cottage and be back before he gets onto the next thing."

"That sounds fine, let's slip off." He rose from his seat at the same time that she did. He set out in exactly the right direction, and it took her a moment to remember that he *had* lived here for years, so of course he would know where the cottage was!

"Well," he exclaimed, as they approached the workshop.

"You were right about people fixing it up. It certainly never looked this good when I lived here."

She felt a bit of pardonable pride, for it *was* a neat little place now, with the stone walls scrubbed and morning glories and moonflower vines climbing up the trellises she'd built on either side of the door. The thatch had been patched and freshly trimmed last fall, too, and this spring she'd painted the shutters white.

"Show me around the outside first," Darian urged. Always happy to show off her garden, Keisha took him around to the back.

"Oh, *this* is good," he exclaimed, as the garden came into view. "What have you got here?" Without waiting for her reply, he walked carefully around the beds, identifying plants aloud. "Feverfew, wormwood, basil, thyme, lobelia, comfrey—" Keisha was impressed, for she would never have thought he'd have any knowledge of herbs. "I must say, I'm glad Justyn didn't have all this."

"Why?" she asked, startled.

"Because then I wouldn't have had so many excuses to go out into the forest," he replied with perfect logic. "Keisha, you've done some remarkable things here. This is wonderful from the point of view of having supplies at hand."

"And to trade," she pointed out. "I'm able to get some things by swapping with traders that come here. Perfume oils are popular, and dyes, of course."

"Of course." He took another long look around the garden, nodding. "So, why don't you show me what you've done with the inside?"

His grin as soon as he entered the door made her flush with pride, and she was very glad she'd cleaned everything thoroughly last night. "Good job. *Really* good job. You've made this place into a fine home *and* workshop."

"I had help," she began shyly, but he shook his head.

"I see *one* person's hand everywhere," he began, but a tap on the doorframe interrupted him.

The Hawkbrother woman—Nightwind—stood there. She said something quickly in the Hawkbrother tongue; he nodded and turned back to Keisha.

"Nightwind says that Lutter wants to speak with me, and

she wants to have a word with you," he told her. "Right now, she says—while things are still quiet."

"Me?" she squeaked, surprised once again. "Why?"

He shrugged helplessly. "I suspect that's to be between Nightwind and you. I'll see you later, when Kel comes in."

With that, he slipped past Nightwind, who entered and closed the door behind her.

"You need not look so apprehensive," the woman said, in slow, careful Valdemaran. "I think that this may be a very welcome conversation for you."

Keisha swallowed, and recalled her manners. "Will you sit down? Can I offer you something to drink?"

"After that feast?" Nightwind laughed. "Thank you—but no. I shall sit, however."

She took one of the two chairs at the cold hearth; warily, Keisha took the other.

"I have spoken with Healer Gil," Nightwind said, with no warning, and Keisha stifled a groan. "Nay, do not look so stricken! *I* am a kind of Healer, as is Adept Firesong; we believe that together we can supply the teaching that you lack."

Before Keisha had time to react, Nightwind went on. "You do not know how close you came to turning into a hermit," she said soberly. "You have been feeling unwell around others, have you not? That is because you have never learned to shield."

"Shields? You know what that means?" Keisha was too excited by this to be annoyed and embarrassed now. "I haven't been able to make any sense out of what was in the books, and I *knew* it was important, but Gil couldn't explain and—" She stopped herself, took a deep breath, and told herself to calm down. "So that is why I get upset when other people are upset?"

"Exactly." Nightwind relaxed just a trifle. "And you will be getting your first lesson from me, right now. I put a shield around you at the feast; now you will learn to make your own." She studied Keisha's face. "I think you will learn quickly, and it is a good thing that you are a Healer, rather than an Empath. You already are grounded and centered."

Those were two more terms that hadn't been explained in

the Healers' texts. "What does that mean?" she asked, determined to indeed begin her lessons at once.

"When you are working here, when you are in the forest—you feel a strong connection to the earth, do you not?" Nightwind asked, and Keisha nodded eagerly.

"I've never even dreamed of flying," she confessed. "I dream about being a tree, a really huge tree, with roots going all the way down into the heart of the earth."

"Empaths must learn to ground and center themselves, to *create* that connection to the earth," Nightwind told her. "Healers—those with the Gift—are born with it. They just have to learn to identify it, strengthen it. So—first, I will take the shield from you, and I wish you to do just that. Find that tie and wait a moment. I will touch your mind with mine, and show you the strength of the earth about you, and how to pull that strength into yourself."

Keisha was too excited now to be apprehensive; she had always enjoyed learning, and now she was about to be given the keys to mysteries that had frustrated her for years. She closed her eyes and sought that still, deep place within herself where her tree-dreams came from. It was easy enough to touch, but a moment after she did so, something strange happened.

There was something—someone?—there as well. Something that wasn't *her*.

:*Good,*: she heard, startled, inside her head. :*So you have exactly the sense of self that you need already! And you are hearing me in words?*:

Cautiously, she tried to form her reply in the same way she "heard" it. :*Yes. What is this?*:

:*This is Mindspeech, so besides being a Healer, you are also a Mindspeaker. That is not always, or even often, the case. It will make things easier for both of us. Now, let "me" come closer, and touch "me" so that you see through "my" eyes.*:

Keisha forced herself to relax as the alien presence somehow moved closer to her, and then—

"Oh, my!" she exclaimed involuntarily; her eyes flew open, and she felt disoriented, seeing things in the strangest kind of double-vision, herself looking at Nightwind looking at herself—

She didn't have to be told to close her eyes again; she squeezed them shut as her stomach churned. Nightwind also closed her eyes, making things easier.

Nightwind waited patiently until her insides settled, then opened her own eyes. *:Now, see what I am seeing? This is just the surface of the world.* This *is how a Healer sees it, with the OverSight.:*

The world was suddenly alive with light, all colors of light; to Nightwind's eyes, Keisha had a halo of emerald green, the seedlings growing on the window ledge had a similar halo of light, though weaker. Keisha had a sudden flash of memory. She *had* seen the world like this before, but she had rejected it as an hallucination.

"Let me try by myself!" she demanded, and Nightwind pulled away. She opened her eyes and, with a mental twist, brought this new kind of vision into focus.

It worked! With a gasp, she saw the world about her as a web of light and energy. She got up and went to the window that overlooked her garden; it was unbelievable! And not only could she see the light, but—

"I can tell which plants aren't doing well!" she exclaimed.

"And if I were ill, you would see that," Nightwind agreed. "Now I want you to touch the place where the light is strongest—no, with your mind, not your hand! Touch it, and bring it into yourself. Here, watch me."

Obediently, Keisha used this new sight to watch her teacher; it took some time before she caught the trick of what Nightwind was doing, but when she tried it tentatively, she had yet another surprise.

Not suddenly, but slowly, gently, a warmth and well-being began to fill her, in a way that defied description. The closest was to sitting by a warm fire on a cold night, or in the sunshine on a spring day after a long, hard winter. It was not a rush of feeling. This was more like the easy misting of a good, soaking rain, permeating the thirsting earth. It filled places she hadn't known were empty until now.

Nightwind said nothing, waiting as Keisha sat with closed eyes, very nearly in a trance. Finally it was Keisha herself, feeling that she had been "filled" to capacity, who opened her eyes and spoke.

"What did I just do?"

"What every Healer does; you replenished yourself from the earth," Nightwind told her. "Now, the next thing you need to know, and urgently, is how to shield. This will put a barrier between you and other people. If you are going to stay sane, you will have to make this as much a part of you as breathing, and only let it down when *you* want and need to, in order to sense what is wrong with a patient. Now—here I put an artificial "edge" around you. See it?"

It was a "thickening" of the glow around her, as thin as a piece of paper. Keisha nodded.

"Now take your own energy, and put it *there*. Make it into armor—make it tough, flexible, and strong. Concentrate! Make it tough enough to keep *me* out of *you*. I will begin pushing on it, and you must keep me out."

Impossible to describe in words, except the ones that Nightwind had just used—but very real and very palpable— Keisha "felt" the barrier she was creating. As she made it stronger, she "felt" something outside of it, pushing on it; in response, she poured more of her energy into it. She sensed it trying to tear a hole in the barrier, she responded by doing something she couldn't even have described, making the outside slippery, too slippery to catch hold of. The presence outside changed tactics, hammering blows on barrier; rather than hardening it, she responded by making it elastic, giving under the blows and absorbing the force.

Nightwind laughed, and the force vanished. Keisha waited.

"That was very good for a beginner," Nightwind said, tossing her hair over her shoulder. "In fact, I suspect that you have been doing *something* all along, learning how to partially shield just under the pressure of the people around you. That would also be typical for a partly trained Healer. Leave the barrier in place, Keisha. You need it."

Keisha had been about to try to make the barrier go away, and obediently left it alone.

"Now drop your OverSight; just look at the world again."

Keisha had to close her eyes to do that, but after a moment of effort, when she opened them again, the world went back to looking normal. Nightwind smiled cheerfully.

"This will be much easier than either of us thought," she

assured Keisha. "So—pack up enough for a trip of a few days. You will be coming back to k'Valdemar Vale with us." She actually grinned as Keisha's mouth dropped. "Oh, you are about to receive some very *intense* training! And do not worry about your village; we will make certain that if you are needed, we will have you here in time to help. And this is a better compromise, I think, than sending you far away to the great Collegium. Yes?"

Keisha could only nod dumbly. After all, hadn't this been what she wanted? Now she would actually get the training she needed without having to leave the area.

But going to live with Hawkbrothers— She could hardly imagine it. And what would the villagers say?

Mum is going to have a litter of kittens.

"I am going to rejoin the rest of our group," Nightwind told her. "I will inform your Mayor and so forth that you will be coming with us when we leave."

Well, at least I won't have to!

"I will tell him that this is also at the orders of Healer Gil and Lord Breon," Nightwind added, and her eyes twinkled with suppressed laughter. "I suspect that will put an end to any objections before they start. Pack carefully. Take only what you think you most will need and will not find in our Vale. We will take care of most everything, even clothing, if you like. I will come get you when we are ready to leave."

With that, Nightwind rose and left, leaving Keisha feeling as if a real wind had blown in, turned everything upside down, and left again.

But, oh—it felt so good!

Nightwind and Kelvren

Ten

Keisha decided that the most important things to pack were her books—the ones that had baffled and frustrated her for so long. Hopefully Nightwind would be able to explain them as well as she had explained shielding. She wrapped them carefully, then packed up enough of her clothing for a few days, and as an afterthought, added her workbasket. She doubted that she'd have any time to do any fancywork, but if she found herself with time on her hands and nothing to do, she'd be angry at herself for not bringing it.

That didn't take very long, and she looked around for anything else to take with her. Plants? Seeds? Presumably the Hawkbrothers had plenty of medicinal plants of their own—

The Herbal. We can compare notes, and if they don't have some of my plants, we can get young plants out of the garden when they bring me back.

So into the bag of books went the Herbal, and she considered bringing a gift with her. After all, that was the only polite thing for a guest to do, bring a guesting-gift. But what *could* she bring that they didn't already have, and plenty of it?

The scarlet dye! After all, everyone liked a good, strong scarlet, and she had a brand-new cake, bought at a very generous discount, besides the ample portion left from her experiments. She wrapped the cake carefully in paper, then in a scrap of cloth, and tucked that in with the rest.

With nothing more that she could think of, she went out to set up the garden to take care of itself for a few days. She and the potter had an arrangement. All of the big storage jars that came out of the kiln with hairline cracks became hers, and she tested them to ensure that the leaks were very slow indeed. Then she moved them into the garden and placed them at intervals along the rows of plants. Normally she kept them covered and empty, but if she knew she was going to be busy for several days running, she filled them with water and left them. The slow leaks would drip water into the ground, keeping the plants watered without her needing to ask someone to tend them.

Tedious as the job was—well, it was time to fill the jars, then transplant all the seedlings she had in the cottage into the garden. At least it would fill the time and keep her from chewing her nails, waiting.

The jars were full, and she was mindlessly arranging and rearranging her shelves when Nightwind finally tapped on the door again.

"Are you ready?" the woman asked as Keisha turned to face her. Keisha licked dry lips and nodded.

"It's almost sunset. Are you really going to travel in the dark?" she asked, not quite certain of the journey ahead of her.

"Darkness doesn't make much difference to the *dyheli*," Nightwind replied, as Keisha took up her bundled belongings and hurried outside.

"Are we going to follow *dyheli*?" Keisha asked, right on Nightwind's heels.

"No, dear, we're going to ride them," the woman said, managing somehow not to sound patronizing. Keisha halted abruptly when she realized that the entire group was right at her doorstep, patiently waiting for her. Her usual hesitation around strangers came back redoubled.

She felt too frozen to move with all those eyes on her, but Darian came to her rescue, taking the bundles from her hands before she could drop them, smiling encouragingly at her. "Come on, I'll introduce you to your *dyheli*," he said, taking her hand and giving it a little tug to get her moving. As soon as she took the first step, he dropped her hand again, as casually as he had taken it. She followed him to one of the horned animals, who looked at her with interest from intelligent brown eyes. "Keisha, this is Meree," he said, exactly as if he was introducing two people. "She'll be taking you to k'Valdemar Vale."

:You have a quiet mind,: said a clear voice in her head. *:I shall enjoy bearing you.:*

Keisha felt her eyes widening. "She talks!" Keisha blurted without meaning to.

Darian, bless him, did not laugh at her. "Just like a Companion," he said cheerfully, "though *dyheli* talk to anyone that they choose to, and Companions normally only talk to their Heralds. You'll like Meree, she's very interested in herb-Healing. You might know some things growing around here that she doesn't, and vice versa. You'll have plenty to talk about as you travel, at least."

The notion of trading herb-knowledge with a deer almost made her laugh nervously, yet she kept it back. But after all, why not discuss herb-knowledge with someone who happened to have four feet instead of two? Certainly she ought to warn Meree about the sheep-sorrel fungus.

Darian made a cup of his hands, and boosted Keisha up into the saddle; there were stirrups, though they were loops of leather rather than metal, and she had a little trouble getting her feet into them. He fastened her belongings behind the odd saddle; the *dyheli* did not have a bridle or reins, only a kind of handle at the front of the saddle for her to slip her hand into. She hadn't ridden enough to feel comfortable even on so familiar a creature as a pony, so she did just that, immediately.

Darian swung into a saddle on a handsome stag with such effortless grace that she felt embarrassed that she had been so clumsy. But after all, she consoled herself, *he's been riding around Valdemar for four years; he ought to be good at this.*

:Don't worry, child,: Meree said sympathetically into her mind. *:Tayledras are masters at making people feel self-conscious. They don't mean to, it just happens.:*

Oddly enough, the remark made her feel a bit better, and she settled herself, trying to get the feel of the saddle.

That seemed to be the signal to move out; Darian hadn't even settled into his saddle, and the entire group launched off with a great leap, at a pace that left her hanging on for dear life. She'd expected an easy amble. Instead, it was a bounding lope that bounced her backward and forward, throwing her alternately toward the *dyheli's* rump, then toward the wickedly dangerous horns. *This—can't be comfortable for either of us—*

:Move with me,: came the patient voice in her head. *:Here. Like this.:*

This was unlike the way that Nightwind had simply touched her mind; the *dyheli* seized her mind in a gentle but implacable mental grip, and she found her body moving under someone else's control for a few moments. It happened too quickly for her to panic; she took note of the way her body now felt, how it moved—for she could feel, even if she didn't have control—and just as abruptly, Meree released her.

It took a few moments for her to get herself properly coordinated, but once she got the knack of it, everything fell into place and she began to enjoy herself. She was going far faster than she herself could run, with the wind of their passing in her face and hair, the forest all around her. She felt the *dyheli's* powerful muscles moving under her legs and hands, and the thought came to her that Meree was far stronger than she looked.

By the time she was comfortable with riding, they were well into the forest, far enough that she didn't immediately recognize exactly where they were. They might even be past the areas she was familiar with by now. It was already dusk beneath the trees, a thick, blue dusk with a flavor of its own, of old leaves, crushed evergreen needles, a touch of damp and the scent of sap. Overhead was the sound of wings; as she looked around, she saw that many of the riders had a perch built onto the fronts or backs of their saddles, and their birds perched there, taking the movement of the *dyheli* as easily as the movement of a branch in the wind. If they weren't asleep, they were comfortable and relaxed.

So if the bondbirds were down here, with their riders— what was flying above?

:Kel. The gryphon,: Meree answered. *:He's the one you hear. There are three owls as well, but you won't hear them; owls fly silently.:*

"Can you hear everything I think?" Keisha asked, feeling a little nettled at this intrusion on her thoughts.

:You aren't shielded, so of course I can. I'll stop if you want

me to.: Meree sounded perfectly indifferent, as if such a thing wouldn't matter to the *dyheli*, but maybe that was just Keisha's own shading on the answer.

Good question. *Would* it matter? Meree was unlikely to gossip about Keisha's innermost thoughts, after all.

:Your innermost thoughts are of very little interest to me. Now, if you were a member of k'Valdemar herd, it would be different, but gossip about humans is, at the most, not even entertaining for one of us.:

Keisha had a vision of a pair of *dyheli* with their heads together over a back fence, kerchiefs tied over their horns, gossiping like a pair of Errold's Grove matrons, and giggled. That destroyed any annoyance she'd been feeling, and she attempted to frame her answer in thought, rather than speech.

:What about "gossip" about plants? Do you know about the fungus that grows on sheep-sorrel?: Speaking this way was easier than she had thought. Instead of having to say "sheep-sorrel," and then attempt to describe it and the fungus, she found she could just picture them clearly.

:Sheep-sorrel, yes, but what of this fungus?: Meree replied, and they were off, with both Keisha and Meree becoming more and more animated as the ride progressed. Keisha learned about half a dozen plants that she recognized, but hadn't known uses for; Meree learned even more from Keisha. Meree referred to things not only by how they looked but how they tasted. Keisha wished she had her Herbal handy. She wanted badly to make some notes in the blank pages.

:We can go over this later, when you can write and draw,: Meree promised. *:You will have the time, I will see to it, and I will not forget what you want to record.:*

Keisha realized she had learned more about the Gift of Mindspeech in a few hours conversing with Meree than she had gleaned in all the books sent her by the Collegium. For instance, along with that simple statement came attached information, that the *dyheli*, as a species that had no way of recording information, relied entirely on trained memory, so much so that Meree literally *could not* forget unless she chose to, or a stronger mind took the memory from her. That another race, the *kyree*, also trained their memories in the same way. This extra information just tagged along with the rest, like lambs behind their ewe, but just popped up in Keisha's memory as she examined the statement.

The idea made Keisha dizzy; imagine having entire libraries of knowledge right in your mind, instead of having to look things up! How could anyone manage all that? How did Meree keep it all straight?

:Look and see,: was Meree's reply, and she obligingly opened her mind to Keisha without a second thought. Keisha could only bear a few moments, but it was fascinating, with all the information neatly arranged in a flexible web, so that many trains of thought would lead to a particular bit of knowledge, each bit led to others that were related, and new bits could be fitted in without stress.

Like game trails in the forest, she thought, dizzied, as Meree closed off her mind again.

:Very like,: Meree agreed, *:Now, have you come across anything as a cure for wet-tail?:*

By that time it was so dark that Keisha couldn't see anything, and she allowed herself to trust to the Hawkbrothers around her and not worry about what might lie out there under the cover of shadows. The conversation with Meree was fascinating enough to keep her attention, so much so that the time passed without her noticing how long the ride had been, until Meree said, *:If you look ahead, you will see the beacons atop the two rock spires that mark the entrance to k'Valdemar Vale.:*

She rose a little in her stirrups to look past the rider ahead of her—and sure enough, there were two blue-white lights in the distance, shining beneath the branches of the trees, with huge clouds of bugs swarming around them, winking in and out of sight as the light reflected from their wings. Now and again, something larger flashed through—a bat, taking advantage of this insect feast. As they neared, she saw that the lights were not as bright as she had thought; they only seemed that way in contrast to the darkness. Nearer still, and she realized that they weren't lanterns or any other sort of light that *she* knew; they were round balls, about the size of her fist, perched somehow on the tops of two rough-hewn pillars of rock about three times the height of a man.

This was certainly *nothing* like Errold's Grove!

The *dyheli* slowed as they neared the pillars, until they were moving no faster than a walk. *:You will soon see* hertasi, *so do not be alarmed,:* Meree warned, and the image of the *hertasi* came to Keisha along with the name. She was glad for that warning, for she would certainly have been alarmed otherwise! A manlike lizard with rows of sharp, pointed teeth that walked on its hind legs would qualify as a monster by Errold's Grove standards, and probably a dangerous one at that. But when the little lizard-people crowded around the arriving riders at the entrance to the Vale, she managed to smile at them, albeit a little nervously.

Darian joined her as soon as Meree stopped moving, and helped her to dismount. She completely lost her nervousness in the unexpected pain of her legs as she swung her off-side leg over the saddle and tried to slide down to the ground. Her legs absolutely refused to bear her weight, and they *hurt.* Only hanging onto the saddle and Darian's support kept her from ending in a heap on the ground.

"Ooooh!" she groaned indignantly. "What happened? I thought I was in *good* shape!"

"You are," Darian said with sympathy. "You just aren't a *dyheli*-rider yet." He held her steady as her legs wobbled under her, and she took a couple of tentative steps away from Meree.

"I guess I'm not any kind of rider," she replied, as one of the lizards took her bundles and the *dyheli's* tack, and Meree moved off. Finally her legs stopped rebelling—though they were still horribly sore—and she was able to hobble without assistance.

The lizard whispered something musically to Darian; he replied in the same language, and it scampered off with her things before she could stop it.

"I'll take you to the guest lodge," Darian offered. "That's where the *hertasi* is taking your bundles."

"It has a bed, I hope," she groaned. There must be wonders all around her, but at the moment she was in no condition to enjoy them.

He laughed. "I think you need a soak in hot water more than a bed."

The idea of a hot bath was heavenly—but—she thought she

remembered something about the Hawkbrothers and communal bathing, which did not appeal to her at all.

"I have an offer for you," he said, interrupting the thought. "My home is nearer than the guest lodge—and *you* aren't used to the customs of our hot pools. I'll set you up with a private bath and go on to the lodge and see everything is ready there for you. Then I'll come back and get you."

Disrobing in a stranger's house and taking a bath there? And not just a stranger, but a strange *male?* Her mother would be scandalized, but again, this wasn't Errold's Grove. The promise of a hot bath—and the state of her sore muscles—decided her.

Besides, even if I were as pretty as Shandi—which I'm not—at the moment I'm sweaty, dirty, and staggering. That's hardly enticing.

"Thank you! You are the most considerate person I have ever met!" she said fervently.

"Oh, you should meet some of the others before you say that," he replied lightly. "Here, come this way."

Other than the two pillars, so far she hadn't seen any signs that this place was inhabited. As she followed him up a twisting path, she still didn't see any kind of housing, though the path itself was man-made and very ornamental, with a sparkling little stream crossing it several times, all manner of fragrant flora, and baroque lanterns hanging from carved posts.

"I thought you were settling here," she said. "Where is everyone?"

"Up there," he pointed, and she looked upward toward the trunk of the tree he indicated.

"There's a house up there!" she exclaimed involuntarily, stopping and staring in fascination. Warm rounds and rectangles of light betrayed windows, and through the branches she glimpsed bits of walls and floor, and a stair spiraling around the trunk.

"An *ekele,*" he corrected. "Almost everyone has an *ekele;* Hawkbrothers prefer to roost." He grinned. "The exceptions are the *hertasi,* who'd rather burrow, the *kyree,* who like caves, the k'Leshya Kaled'a'in like Nightwind, who like homes built into the sides of cliffs, and me."

She was relieved to discover she wasn't going to have to

climb one of those twisting staircases. With the way her legs felt, she wasn't certain she'd be able to make the trip!

"And here we are," he announced just then, gesturing grandly at a tall mound of leaves—a mound with windows glowing warmly beneath the leaves, that is. He opened an otherwise invisible door, and they stepped into one of the oddest, and yet most inviting houses Keisha had ever seen.

There wasn't a single straight line in it, though, and that was a bit disconcerting. "One of the *hertasi* designed this place," he said, as he led her through the first room (which was so neat and clean she could hardly believe it belonged to a male), a second (obviously a bedroom, and a bit more cluttered), and into the third. There was a single oil lamp turned low, hanging from a wall-sconce; he turned it up, and busied himself with a metal spout in the wall.

The whole room was tiled in white, pale blue, and pale green ceramic; even the ceiling (what there was of it) was tiled. Most of the ceiling was actually a window! And around the four sides of this window were boxes with vines growing in them.

Sunken into the floor was a tile-lined bath tub; Darian had just turned a spigot and put a plug in a hole in the bottom of it, and water poured in. Clear, clean, and very chilly looking, the spray made her shiver.

Darian watched as the water filled the tub, and turned the spigot again when it was within a thumb-length of the rim. But then, before Keisha could ask him how the water was supposed to be heated, he held his hand out over it.

Something was happening, something she felt, rather than saw, until she closed her eyes and did that little trick with vision. Then she saw light-energy moving from Darian to the water, but what did that mean?

Wait, it was getting warmer in this little room, and more humid! A moment later, she knew where the heat was coming from, for the water in the tub had started to steam.

"Try that with your hand and tell me if it's hot enough," Darian said, just as she blinked, and lost the OverSight. She knelt at the side of the tub and gingerly put her hand in.

A little more and it would have been *too* hot. "Definitely," she told him. He grinned.

"I like it a lot hotter, but I'm used to the Hawkbrother pools. Now just wait a moment, and I'll bring you something to wear when you get out."

He ducked into the bedroom, and came back with a loose, gauzy shirt and breeches of the same materials. "You can keep these, they're too small for me now." He opened a wicker-work chest next to the tub. "Clean, dry towels are in here." He turned and pointed to a series of stone boxes at the side of the tub. "Gourd sponges are in there, a scrub brush, and soap; there's a couple of different scents, so you've got a choice. I'll be back in a while."

He didn't wait for her reply; he just left, and she heard the outer door close after him. She peeked out, just to make sure that he'd really gone, but the little house was absolutely empty except for herself.

Well, there was no point in letting the water cool! She stripped to the skin and eased gingerly down into the hot tub, which was long enough for her to stretch completely out and deep enough that the water came up to her chin. Immediately, the heat eased the sore muscles of her legs, and she sighed and relaxed against the sloped, tiled back of the tub.

If anyone had told me about what this place was like, I would never have believed them. Would she be too spoiled by this Vale to want to go home again?

I could put some comforts together with help. A bathing room of her own, for instance, wouldn't be too difficult to add to the cottage. The potter could make the tiles. *If I built an oven underneath the tub, instead of sinking the tub into the floor, I could heat my own water. A rainwater cistern on the roof would give me water for the tub, or I could tap into the irrigation system. Or I could pump it from the well at the sink and carry it.* The cistern would be the least work. *That would be a good way to warm someone up who was badly chilled, too. A reasonable excuse for me to ask for help building it.* She grinned to herself. No, she probably *wouldn't* be so spoiled she wouldn't want to go back, not as long as she could figure out ways to reproduce the aspects of this place that she liked!

When she'd soaked long enough that she thought she'd be

able to move again without moaning, she finished her bath
with rosemary soap, and allowed the water to drain. Darian's
old clothing, lightly scented with juniper, was a bit big on
her, but it was so good to put on clean clothes that it didn't
matter. She rolled up the waistband and arms, so she didn't
look too much like a child playing dress-up.

She decided to wait for him in the outermost room, and
bundled up her old clothes and took them with her. When he
arrived, he looked pleased to find her there. "Your room is
ready in the guest lodge, and the *hertasi* are bringing you
something to eat there, in the morning. That will be easier
for you than trying to find our dining hall right off. You can
leave your clothes here, if you'd like," he added. "The *hertasi*
will clean them and bring them back to you by morning."

"I could get to enjoy having *hertasi* doing everything," she
sighed, as she laid her clothing to one side.

"It's a good trade for them, and for us," he agreed, as she
followed him out onto the dimly lit trail. "They get safety,
protection, and share our food and supplies, and we get their
service. Out there they wouldn't have a chance; cold slows
them down, they'd make prime prey for the slave trade, and
they'd wear their little lives away trying to grow enough food
to stay alive. In here, they don't have to worry about any of
that. We even have a festival twice a year to thank them,
where we take care of them and give them gifts." He grinned.
"They are very tolerant of our cooking, but twice a year is all
they can stand."

"How *are* you getting food and supplies?" she asked
curiously.

"Trade and hunting," he replied promptly. "There are some
things we grow for ourselves, but staples we trade for; it
makes more sense for us to grow very exotic and rare things
than to try to cultivate acres of wheat. We've already set up a
pact with Lord Breon, for instance; he's quite pleased to be
getting some of our goods in trade for flour and so forth. And
here is the guest lodge."

They had just gone around a twist in the trail, and there,
beneath the shade of an enormous tree that supported an
ekele around its trunk, was a building similar to Darian's
little home, with rounded walls and a tiled roof.

The main difference seemed to be that this place was not screened by a growth of vines, and that it looked to be bigger than Darian's. Young vines at the base of the walls promised that soon this building would be camouflaged, too. "There are six rooms here for now, though you're the only guest," Darian told her. "We went ahead and put you in the first one." He opened the door as he spoke, and ushered her into a kind of common room, lit by another oil lamp, with several doorways radiating from it. The nearest was open, with a light inside. "There will be more lights around here when Lord Breon gets our lamp oil to us. Nightwind or Firesong will send someone for you in the morning."

She yawned hugely, covering her mouth in embarrassment. "I was going to ask you to introduce me to the gryphon and your owl, but I don't think I can stay awake that long."

"That's what the morning is for," Darian replied genially. "You go get some sleep; after your first *dyheli* ride, I'm sure you need it. Sleep as long as you need to."

He left her alone in the building, which now seemed much larger than it had a few moments ago. She entered the lit room, and found that her things had been unpacked, the clothing hung neatly on a bar mounted to the wall, or folded and set in a basket beneath the hanging clothes. The books were all stacked on a table next to the bed with a quill pen, ink, and paper; the only other thing on the table was the lamp. Her workbasket waited beside the table. It was all rather spare, compared to Darian's home, but then this was only supposed to be guest quarters.

The bed, however, looked soft and inviting, and she climbed right into it without undressing to find it was as comfortable as it looked. She thought about getting up and changing into a sleeping shift, but it was too comfortable; she didn't want to do anything but blow out the lamp, and fall into dreamless sleep. So that was precisely what she did.

When she awoke the next day, it was with a feeling of excitement and anticipation that was enhanced by an aroma so mouth-watering that her stomach growled loudly and insisted she *must* get up and get dressed to investigate the source. Light filtered in through the gauze curtains of the window over the head of her bed. She leaped out of bed, and changed out of the clothing she'd borrowed from Darian (which had been wonderfully comfortable to sleep in) and into one of her Healer-trainee uniforms. That was mostly what she had packed for this trip; she felt a little self-conscious about them, but they were the best clothing she had (bar her festival clothes), and she really *was* a Trainee now. Still brushing her hair and barefoot, she opened the door to the common room, and on a table was the source of the fragrant aromas; three rounds of bread that, by the scent, were stuffed with something. Beside the plate of bread rounds stood a cup and pitcher of cold, sweet tea.

The first roll she bit into was still warm and stuffed with onion-and-sage spiced sausage, the second with rosemary-spiced vegetables, and the third with berry jam. She ate every crumb, and drank half the tea. When she had finished her meal, she noticed a familiar-looking pile of neatly folded fabric on a chair near the outer door; sure enough, it was yesterday's clothing, clean again.

Now what? she wondered, and finally brought out her workbasket, opening the outer door to let in some fresh air and signal that she was awake and ready to go to work. She was left in peace for a little, and had come to the end of a pattern when a faint scratching sound made her look up.

One of the lizard-creatures stood in the doorway, and it nodded when it saw that she had noticed it. Now in the daylight, she saw it more clearly; with its huge, expressive eyes and intelligent look, it was unexpectedly appealing.

In fact—it's awfully cute, she thought, softening toward it.

She put her work away and stood up; the lizard beckoned with an outstretched talon, and she followed it out into the Vale.

She was glad that Nightwind had sent a guide; the place seemed to be a maze of little paths. Eventually the trees ahead thinned out and disappeared, and they emerged on the edge of a small lake with a cliff on the opposite side. The lizard vanished, and Keisha looked around in confusion.

"Over here!" Nightwind called, waving from atop an expanse of rock. Beside her lounged the gryphon.

Keisha walked toward them, slowly, taking it all in. The gryphon was perhaps the most stunning creature she had ever seen, barring Firesong. His head had a definite eagle look to it, though he had a pair of real, feather-tufted ears. His feathers were a gleaming golden brown, with gold markings, and he was *huge*. His bright gold eyes were fixed on her as she approached; they were like enormous rounds of tiger eye stone come to miraculous life.

"Darian reminded me that you wanted to meet Kel," Nightwind said as she neared. "So, this is Kelvren, our resident senior gryphon. Kel, this is Keisha Alder, the Healer of Errold's Grove."

"I am pleasssed to make yourrr aquaintancsse," the gryphon said politely, bowing his head.

"And I, yours," Keisha replied, with a little genuflection of her own.

"My title, my job, is *trondi'irn*, which means that I primarily take care of and Heal those who are not human," Nightwind went on. "Especially the gryphons. Kel and I have been partners in that way since we were both accepted into the Silver Gryphons. In a small group like this one, I also Heal the humans—when we grow larger, we will have separate Healer and *trondi'irn*, though they will both be expected to work together and assist each other."

Keisha nodded, but couldn't think of a response. Nightwind patted the rock beside her, inviting Keisha to join her. Keisha climbed up and sat down, with the gryphon within touching distance of both of them. There were long, stiff feathers, much like guard hairs, around the nostrils and eyes. The great beak was polished or waxed, gleaming in the sun. Like a raptor, he had double eyelids, the inner one probably to protect his eyes during a fight or a kill. He had a spicy-sweet scent to him, a hint of ginger and cinnamon, which rather surprised her. He wore jeweled ear studs in each ear, and the shafts of each crest-feather had been decorated in jewel tones and gold leaf to match the ear studs.

"You aren't maintaining your shield," Nightwind observed. "You are going to *have* to get into that habit; any time you think about it, make sure it's there! If you're checking it a hundred times each day, that's not too many. Use a mnemonic if you have to; associate the checking with something you see a lot of—fallen leaves, stones in the path."

Already feeling guilty, Keisha put her shield up, and Nightwind nodded.

"That's better. Now, I'm going to ask you some questions, because I suspect that you have already done some things with your Gift that you aren't really aware of doing, and I want to find out what they are." She began to question Keisha closely, asking her all sorts of odd things. Had she ever known what was wrong with a human or animal by just looking? Had she ever found herself knowing that she had given a human or animal enough medicine without measuring? Had she ever felt drained and tired after helping someone, even though she hadn't done a great deal of physical labor?

The list of questions went on and on, some seemed quite senseless, but others were surprising, because Keisha *had* felt, or done, those things and hadn't known how or why.

Finally, Nightwind was through, and she looked down at the notes she had taken with a waxboard and stylus. "You're using your Gift with animals, rarely with children, never with adults," she said. "You're using it mostly to determine what *exactly* is wrong with them, and what dosages of medicines are sufficient. You are not using your Gift to Heal without medicine. That's about normal, for someone who's untrained, but who is developing a powerful Healing Gift."

She seemed to be waiting for a response. "It's nice to know that I'm normal in something, at least," Keisha replied dryly, and Nightwind laughed.

"I've asked Kel to help me this morning, in part because I'm intimately familiar with him, and in part because the way he's put together is going to give *you* some surprises." She raised a brow, and Kel chuckled. "Remember how I touched your mind, and you saw through my eyes yesterday? Lower your shield, and we'll do that again, but this time we'll be looking at Kel using Healing OverSight."

So began the most intense morning that Keisha had ever spent in her life. She learned that there were many kinds of OverSight, many ways of using it, and how to use all the kinds that she had. Specifically, she began to learn how to use it to discover what was wrong with someone, whether it was injury or illness.

"But I'm mostly treating either familiar animal diseases, or humans who can *tell* me what's wrong," she protested.

Nightwind raised that eyebrow again. "Oh, indeed? What about someone who is unconscious? Someone with multiple injuries who isn't aware of all of them? A child too young to talk? Do you *always* treat just the obvious symptoms without looking for anything further?"

She dropped her eyes and had to admit that this was exactly what she had been doing.

"That's acceptable for a beginner, for a Trainee, but you can't stay a beginner forever," Nightwind said, softening her rebuke. "At some point you're going to have to function as a full Healer, and the sooner that can happen, the better."

By the end of the morning, Keisha had a dull headache unlike anything she had ever experienced before, and Nightwind called a halt to the lessons. "For this afternoon, I think you should go through your texts and see if *now* you understand some of what confused you before," her teacher told her. "The headache you have now is due to using that part of your mind and Gift that you haven't exercised before—rather like riding muscles!" Keisha giggled a little at that, and Nightwind smiled. "So this afternoon should be devoted to your books, and when your headache eases, I'd like you to start examining people and creatures around you in this new way. Stop when it starts to hurt again, but the more exercise you give this talent, the stronger it will become, and the easier to use. And remember to keep your shield up otherwise!"

Keisha felt dizzy with all the orders, but nodded anyway.

"Now we'll go get something to eat; I'll show you the common dining hall." Nightwind slid off the rock; Keisha followed her. "Kel, thank you, we're done with you. Go fly your patrols."

"Happy to be of ssserrrvicsse," the gryphon said genially, then took straight off from the rock in a thunder of wings that sent dirt and bits of debris flying in all directions.

Nightwind also gave her the clue to following the paths—
which turned out to be absurdly simple, once you knew it.
Paths leading to the entrance had reddish markers which
were often colored stones beside the path, paths leading to
private residences had black markers, paths leading to the
water had greenish ones, paths leading to the buildings housing the common areas—dining hall, kitchens, laundry, baths,
and soaking pools—had gray markers. The paths themselves
were made up of substances reflecting their "key" colors—
bark, pebbles, sand, and so forth. "Just follow all the gray
paths, and eventually you'll come to what you're looking
for," Nightwind told her. "The guest lodge is on a gray path,
too." Where paths met, there were marker stones in the appropriate colors, so sooner or later, no matter how lost she
got, she'd eventually be able to straighten herself out.

The dining hall turned out to be one of the few wooden
buildings in the Vale, a long, low structure that was nothing
like Keisha imagined it would be inside. One single room,
with the ceiling supported by slender pillars; there was no
real sign of what the room's function should be, it could have
been used for any purpose required. Instead of rows of tables
and benches, there were a few tables with stools, a great
many cushions, some couches, and some individual chairs.
Part of one corner had been built up with three raised tiers,
also covered with cushions. At the far end, food had been laid
out for people to help themselves, which they did, then taking their choices to sit however they chose to eat.

"There is almost always food here, even between meals,
but hot food is only served at mealtime," Nightwind told her,
as she directed Keisha in getting a wooden platter and helping
herself. "Things tend to happen in a Vale that upset sched-
ules, so there are plenty of folk missing the regular meals
who need feeding at any given time."

They found seats—Keisha felt much more comfortable eating at a table—and Nightwind began asking her questions
about herself. Keisha discovered that she and the *trondi'irn*
had more in common than she would have guessed. Both of
them had a swarm of male relatives to put up with—in Nightwind's case, it was a horde of cousins, rather than brothers—

and both had younger sisters that they liked and missed enormously. "Though Nightbird may come here anyway— but not until her training is finished."

Both of them seemed to have the same slightly cynical outlook on life as well. Nightwind had a better sense of the absurd, though, and Keisha wished she had Nightwind's ability to see humor in things. It looked to her as if Nightwind got more enjoyment from things by not taking them too seriously.

"I have to get back to work," Nightwind told her, when they'd finished eating and put their platters in the bin for dirty dishes. "Keep following this gray path, and you'll eventually come to the guest lodge." She frowned slightly. "At some point in the next couple of days, I'll have to get Tyrsell to give you our language; the *hertasi* for the most part don't understand Valdemaran. If you see Dar'ian and your headache is gone, tell him I said that."

"I will," she promised, though she couldn't imagine how she was to learn a language on top of everything else. She wandered the gray path, enjoying the sights, and eventually did come to the guest lodge. With a sigh, she went inside and obediently got out her texts.

To her delight, a large part of the things she had not understood *did* come clear, although the texts often used slightly different terms for things than Nightwind did. OverSight, for instance, was called Mage-Sight or Healing-Sight. Now that she knew some of the basics, though, she was amazed at how much the texts actually told her, occasionally explaining things better than Nightwind had.

She became so absorbed in her studies that she barely noted the passage of time until she found she was straining to read, looked up, and realized that it was growing dark. More than that, her foot was asleep, and she was starving. She put the book down, and decided to get some dinner on her own.

She walked to the dining hall through a dusk lit softly by lanterns and scented with the perfumes of night-blooming flowers. A different sort of fragrance coming from the dining hall made her move a bit faster, though, and she shyly took her place amid a tangle of strange Hawkbrothers to get her platter and fill it. With a little searching, she found a quiet corner out of everyone's way, and sat there, watching and listening to the strange music of their unfamiliar tongue.

She was just about to leave when she (almost literally) ran into Darian. He caught her by the elbow as she passed him, with a contagious grin for her when she realized who it was. "Working hard?" he asked, with a wink.

She made a face. "Hard enough to get a headache," she replied, sighing. "I wish I'd known this was going to be so difficult."

"Well, that's good, it means you're stretching new talents," he told her, without a hint of pity. "Almost everything worth doing is hard, at least at first. Do you still want to meet Kuari?"

"Absolutely!" She remembered then what her teacher had told her. "Oh, and Nightwind said to let you know if I saw you that she wanted—someone—to give me the Hawkbrother tongue."

"That would be Tyrsell," Darian identified, nodding, so that a wisp of hair dropped into his eyes and he brushed it back with an absentminded wave of his hand. "Tyrsell is the king-stag of the *dyheli* herd; he's the one I was riding yesterday."

A *dyheli* teaching her a language? "That doesn't seem right. They don't *talk*, I mean, not aloud," she responded, with a frown. "How can he do that?"

"Oh, you'll understand soon enough—still have the headache?" he asked, and she shook her head. "Good; let me bolt something down, and I'll take you to the *dyheli* meadow. The sooner you have Tayledras, the better. The *hertasi* mostly don't understand Valdemaran."

"That's what Nightwind said." She followed him as he got bread rounds that looked very like her breakfast this morning, and waited while he inhaled his dinner.

"Sorry about my manners," he said between bites. "I got used to eating quickly, because things are always happening quickly around a Vale." He grinned again. "Maybe that's why we take our leisure so *seriously*, because most of the time we're madly scrambling to get things done. You've got to keep a balance in life, so that you can enjoy your pleasures completely, and then go and enjoy your work completely. Heyla, when you rest well, you work better, right?"

She nodded.

He led her down another series of twisting paths, coming out into a moon-gilded meadow full of the horned *dyheli.* One was patiently waiting for them where the path met the meadow. He wasn't all that much bigger than the rest, but there was a sense of power about him that Meree hadn't had.

:Darian has told me that Nightwind wishes you to have Tayledras-tongue,: rang a solemn voice in her mind. *:Will you lower your shield for me?:*

She'd been diligent in remembering to check that she had it up, and lowering it was a little like relaxing her grip on something. She sighed as it came down, feeling something inside her head relaxing as well. *Will I ever really do this without thinking about it?*

Tyrsell stood over her, a silver statue in the moonlight. *:Now sit, please. This will not take long.:*

Obediently she sat down on the grass. A moment later, she found herself looking up at Darian from a prone position, with her head aching all over again and no notion how she'd wound up lying down when she'd been sitting just the heartbeat before.

"Sorry about that," Darian said apologetically. "If I'd warned you what was going to happen, you'd have tensed up, then it would have been harder on both you and Tyrsell. I know *exactly* how you feel right now—this is how they gave me the language years ago."

It took her a moment to realize that he was speaking in the Hawkbrother language—and she understood it.

"How does he *do* that?" she asked, sitting up, and rubbing her head. "How can he shove a language into my head when he doesn't actually speak it?"

Darian shrugged. "I don't know exactly how; being able to take over someone's mind like that is a special *dyheli* Gift. The king-stags use it to control the herd if they panic."

"It feels like he ran the whole herd through my head!" she complained; Darian chuckled, and she got the sense that Tyrsell was amused as well.

"I know; I remember all too clearly how I felt after my turn, and it took me months to get comfortable with all the new concepts that showed up in my head along with the words. Come on, I'll show you back to the guest lodge and get a *hertasi* to bring you a headache-potion." He helped her to her feet; she had the presence of mind to turn to the *dyheli* before they left.

"I hope I didn't seem ungrateful. Thank you very much, Tyrsell," she said carefully. "This is going to make things endlessly easier for all of us."

:You are welcome, and thank you *for your courtesy; it will serve you well with my people,:* the stag said. Then he turned and walked calmly off into the moonlit meadow, just as if he hadn't just worked something very like a miracle.

"How are you coming with your studies?" Darian asked her as they turned back onto the path.

"The good news is that I haven't got anything to unlearn," she replied, one hand to her aching temple. "The bad news is that I have a lot to learn in a short time. From what the books say, I think it was a good thing Nightwind made her offer. I would *never* have worked this out on my own."

"You might have," he offered, surprising her. "After all, *somebody* did. There had to be a first Healer."

"I suppose so." The books had also told her just how close she had come to losing control of her Gift, and what that would have meant. No wonder she had thought longingly of becoming a hermit! She had very nearly been forced to do just that, in order to stay sane!

"Nightwind is awfully kind, and a lot more encouraging than I thought she'd be," Keisha continued. "And the best thing is that Nightwind says that I was right all along to say I couldn't go to the Collegium. She says that even untrained, I was doing things that Gil can't, and that my primary duty was to the people I take care of."

"I can see that." The lights of the guest lodge appeared ahead of them, and just as Keisha noticed them, a *hertasi* also approached them on the path. "Do you want to make the request?" Darian continued, "Or shall I?"

"I'd like to," she decided. When the *hertasi* neared, it seemed to sense that she was going to say something, and stopped, waiting attentively. "If you would be so kind, I have just been given this tongue by Tyrsell the king-stag, and my head hurts dreadfully," she told it. It hissed with sympathy.

"I know just the thing, Keisha-Guest," it replied. "Shall I bring it to the lodging?"

"Please," she replied with gratitude, and it whisked away so fast it almost seemed to vanish.

"Very good!" Darian applauded. "You're going to make a Hawkbrother yet!"

She thought about that, after Darian left her and the *hertasi* had come and gone with her headache medicine. She hadn't really considered "becoming" a Hawkbrother, but Darian had, so obviously outsiders could. Could she come to serve both the Vale and the village as a Healer, in time?

It was at least as intriguing as becoming a Herald, like her sister.

Eldan and Kerowyn

Eleven

Kuari roused all his feathers with a full body shake, then tucked up a foot and closed his eyes. *He* knew Darian wouldn't be going anywhere for a while.

"Well, what do you think of our little Healer?" Nightwind asked Darian as they gathered to meet with Lord Breon and Val. The Valdemarans had taken to coming over with the wagons full of trade goods rather than asking the Tayledras to come to Kelmskeep. Darian had a notion that this was as much because both Lord Breon and his son were fascinated with the new Vale as it was to save the Tayledras the inconvenience of making the trip.

"I think she isn't 'little' at all," Darian responded, deciding that Nightwind was fishing, and he wasn't going to take the bait. "She's the same age as me."

Nightwind laughed. "Point taken. *I* think she's going to be quite competent, she's easy to get along with, and I wish I could persuade her to live here instead of Errold's Grove. We could certainly use her."

"I don't think there's any way you could get her to forsake the village," Darian replied thoughtfully, pulling his hair behind his ears. "She takes her responsibilities awfully seriously."

"Oh, I didn't mean she should give up tending the villagers," Nightwind corrected, shaking her head. "I just don't think they need to have her there to handle every hangnail and black eye. She could get there from here within a candlemark by gryphon-carrier, and for anything less than serious she could visit once or twice a week, easily enough."

He had to laugh at that; Nightwind sounded as if she'd already decided for Keisha, and if he understood Keisha at all, he doubted she cared for anyone making up her mind for her. "I don't know; you'd have to persuade her first. At least they're taking her more seriously than they did Justyn, and they're treating her quite well."

"Having to do without can make people astonishingly appreciative," Nightwind said dryly. The conversation might have continued in the same interesting vein, but at that point, the voices of several people in discussion drew nearer, and in a moment he and Nightwind were joined by the rest. Bondbirds flew in to roost ahead of their bondmates; Hweel and Huur took perches near Kuari and began preening each other, while Aya joined Starfall's bird, who had been there all along. As Aya settled himself, the rest of the group entered the garden.

They met in Starfall's garden beneath his *ekele*, a miniature version of the various garden spots within k'Vala Vale except that all of the plants here were cold-hardy, either evergreens, or plants that would have a leafless, dormant period during the winter. Right now, of course, they were flourishing mightily, coaxed into accelerated growth and quick maturity by Steelmind and some of his apprentices. Tough vines had been woven and trained to form the frames for comfortable seats, holding cushions stuffed with dried grasses and fragrant herbs. Canopies of more vines shaded the occupants, while tall shrubs, climbing plants, and young trees gave the place privacy. A tiny waterfall plunging into a pool filled with young fish sent cooling spray into the air and lent the soothing music of falling water to the setting—though thanks to some of the bondbirds, the pool had to be restocked regularly. Yet, with that art that was the hallmark of the Tayledras, all of this carefully contrived work of man seemed to have been magically wrought by nature.

By common consent, most meetings with Lord Breon were held here. The *hertasi* provided anything in the way of refreshment that might be needed, shade and water cooled the air, and no one really wanted to be inside on days of good weather. Meetings weren't held in bad weather, because a delay in the arrival of the Valdemaran trade supplies meant nothing, and if the weather was going to be bad, why risk the chance of accident or spoilage? With so many mages here in k'Valdemar, it was a simple matter to read the weather, then make certain that Lord Breon got warning of any storm that could not be delayed or hurried on.

It was a pity that the discussions here in this oasis of tranquillity had little to do with peace and growth.

"I have word back from the capital," Lord Breon said, when they were all seated. Besides Nightwind and Darian, the usual participants from k'Valdemar were all in attendance; Ayshen, Kel, Starfall, Snowfire, Hashi, and Firesong. "They are sending us the small force we asked for, under the direction of a Herald with experience in diplomacy."

Two *hertasi* made the rounds, offering cool drinks, and vanished when everyone had been served. Starfall nodded, and his face betrayed the relief he felt. "I am glad to hear that, the more so because of what Kelvren saw on his patrol this morning. Kel?"

"Ycsss." The gryphon took up the thread, sitting up very straight, intense and serious. "I have ssseen the barrrbarrriansss. They arrre at the farrrrthessst point in my patrrrolsss. They continue in theirrrr patterrrn."

This was no news to Darian or Nightwind, who'd heard it directly from Kel before the meeting. Ayshen had no expression, Snowfire looked resigned, and behind his mask, there was no telling what Firesong thought.

Lord Breon nodded; after all, he had probably been expecting to hear this for some time. "That would be, making a fortified camp, remaining until the hunting and grazing are down, then moving on?"

"Exactly ssso," Kel agreed, bowing his head in Lord Breon's direction. "And asss rrreporrrted, they do have childrrren, women, old people. Even babesss in arrrmsss, and prrregnant women. Not what I would call an arrrmy."

Lord Breon frowned as if this wasn't altogether good news. "But it *is* an invading and occupying force, especially if they are sending out scouts ahead of the main group, and intend to keep the noncombatants in a protected camp while the fighters deal with any resistance."

He does have to think of these things, Darian reminded

himself, and took note for the future. Some day, presumably, so would he.

"It's also the pattern of nomadic herders, like the Shin'a'-in," Snowfire pointed out, to cover all possibilities. "They may not even know there is a settlement anywhere near. It simply could be that they've depleted their old grazing grounds too much to recover in a single season—or that all the magical weather disruption of the past decade has caused a drought in the north."

Lord Breon nodded. "Also true—but really, we can't have them coming into Valdemar or the Pelagirs and establishing new grazing grounds without asking permission first. It *is* our land, after all. The Crown says that in accordance with our long-established tradition, *if* they are peaceful and agree to settle, we are to welcome them, but they will have to follow the law!"

"True enough," Snowfire agreed. "If we ignore them and let them proceed as they wish, we simply send a message that whoever else wants to flood down here will meet no resistance and no law! If we choose to let them remain here, it *must* be by treaty, with agreed-upon limits, and on our terms."

"I think we ought to fight them!" Val burst out. "Why should we let them just wander in and take over? Why should we even tolerate them *near* our border? They're barbarians! Why should we want them here at all?"

"We don't intend to let them wander in and take over; haven't you been listening?" Darian suppressed impatience with an effort. "Look, I have the most reason of any of us to want to fight these people. Remember what they did the last time they came here! They hurt and killed people that I *knew*, people I cared about! If it were up to my feelings, I'd lure them all under a cliff and drop it on them, pregnant women, grandmothers, babies and all. But those feelings should have nothing to do with this—and there are women and children at least in that group that had nothing to do with what happened the last time and certainly don't deserve to be judged by me. For all we know, this isn't even the same tribe. They may know nothing about what happened years ago. They could be peaceful. They could be running away from the same lot that overran us!"

Val cast a glance at him that was part contempt, part incredulity, but since the rest were all nodding agreement, including his father, Val said nothing more. Darian had the feeling that the subject wasn't finished, though, and he'd hear more from Val about it.

Starfall let his gaze rest on Darian, but Darian had the feeling his words were meant for Val. "The greatest leaders in both our histories were always those who understood the motivations of those they faced," he said. "When you understand why they move, then you know what to offer, and what to withhold."

The discussion continued as if Val's outburst had never occurred. "I think we ought to first contact them in a way that impresses them," Firesong said thoughtfully. Today his mask was of thin, pale doeskin that fit like a second skin—giving a more uncanny impression, somehow, than any of his more elaborate masks. "A show of strength of all kinds, if you will. We should make it quite clear that we can handle anything they have, with ease."

"I tend to agree," Lord Breon said, looking keenly at Firesong. "Quite. I assume you mean a display of magic will be included in this?"

"That, and the bondbirds—perhaps some of our other allies." Firesong turned toward Snowfire. "Didn't you say that these tribes have totemic animals? If we include apparently wild animals in the display, it might gain us a great deal of respect spiritually as well as physically."

"As far as I know, they do, and they attempt to imitate the behavior of those animals. Bringing the birds—even the *dyheli* and *kyree*—could very well impress them. The last lot had a bear-totem, and their shaman had managed to partially Change them to match that totem." Snowfire's eyes took on the sharp look that meant he was thinking quickly. "If they have another such, we will need to get the upper hand magically at once. Creating Changechildren in these days—"

"Or he managed to partially control the Change within a Change-Circle," Firesong pointed out, and both Snowfire and

Starfall looked startled, then slowly nodded. "That could have been simply a matter of caging bears in the same Change-Circle as the warriors he wanted to Change, and hope that a melding took place. Just because he had specifically Changed people doesn't imply great power or control. Master Levy is still taking a survey of the Circles to discover if there is a pattern there, one as to which Circles were exchanges of territory, which created monsters, and which simply melded the animals that were already within them. It wasn't," he added dryly, "a priority at the time they were occurring to find that kind of pattern, but it might have occurred to others to look for one."

"But if there *was* a pattern, and the barbarians noticed it—" That was Ayshen.

"Or they simply took their chances, and it worked *once*," Darian put in. "Given the behavior that we witnessed with the last lot, that wouldn't be out of character. The shaman didn't seem too worried about wasting lives. He'd have been perfectly happy with a single success, and one success would be all he'd have needed to impress the rest."

"There is that," agreed Starfall, as the rest who had been involved in that confrontation seconded Darian's observation. He sighed. "And it is an interesting thought, but it doesn't explain why this lot has women, children, and oldsters along. Oh, *why* won't these people stay home?"

"Because we have something they want," replied Firesong, with inescapable logic. "And they think they can just take it away from us. They're not interested in challenging us to a game of riddles to win it, or a Bardic contest, or paying for it. That's why we call them barbarians."

The rest chuckled, though the attempt at humor was a little strained, and so was the response. Even Val laughed uneasily.

"Now, we don't know yet whether they'll challenge us, or offer us something in trade, or give tribute," Ayshen pointed out. "Still—better we be more careful than less."

"The main thing now is to delay them if they come too close, I think," Lord Breon offered. "Which brings us back to Firesong's show of strength. Once the reinforcements arrive, we'll have a better idea of what *their* tactics will be, and exactly how forceful we'll have to be in order to impress them."

"And just how large our reinforcements will be," added Snowfire. "Hopefully, we'll be able to back our show, and not have to resort to bluff. Bluffing makes me very nervous." He shook his head. "You know what the Shin'a'in say: 'Bluffs either cost you half or twice.' Kel, tomorrow I want you to do a thorough count, if you can. Noncombatants, people who *might* fight, real warriors, and what their herds are."

Kelvren nodded, hissing agreement. "It will delay me. I will not rrrreturrn until nearrrrly ssssunsssset."

Snowfire waved that caution away. "That's all right, if you can manage to accomplish it. We need those counts to make reasonable decisions."

Kel snorted contemptuously. "*If* I can manage? I am not one of thosssse elderrrly layaboutsss at k'Vala, you know! Fearrr not, I ssshall have yourrrr countsss, and they will be acurrrate in everrry detail!" He paused. "I will be sssseen, howeverrr. Fly high though I will, the sssize and body-ssshape will differrr frrrom a merrre eagle—asss it sssshould be."

Darian's lips twitched, and he watched Nightwind hide a smile. *Oh, gryphons! How dull life would be without them!*

"Now, just to change the subject briefly," Starfall interjected, before anyone could laugh at Kel and hurt his feelings. "How is our trade balance with you, Lord Breon?"

"Dead even, with this load." His face relaxed, but Val took on a look of boredom, rolling his eyes upward. It was obvious that Breon's son and heir would *much* rather have been discussing possible battle plans. "Is there any way we could get some of that patterned silk from you?"

Starfall pursed his lips, thoughtfully. "We aren't set up to *make* any here yet, but if we don't have what you want in stores, I don't doubt we can get it made up from k'Vala. What did you have in mind?"

"It isn't me, it's my lady." He looked sheepish. "The wedding, you know. She's got a notion that we should all have new wedding clothes in the same patterned silk, but different colors. I don't think she cares *what* pattern, but I'd look damned silly in flowers."

Val groaned, his attention recaptured. Darian didn't blame him; it was *his* wedding, after all, but his mother was obviously arranging it to suit her liking, not his. Poor bride! It obviously didn't matter what *her* taste was either, for Val's mother was making all the decisions. "*Not* flowers! And not rabbits or cute little baby *anything*, or—"

"How about a simple geometric?" Nightwind interjected before Val could wax eloquent on the subject of what he didn't want. "Or water patterns? Or leaves? Feathers?"

"Feathers would be good, or leaves, or water patterns," Val told her, relief suffusing his features. "As along as it doesn't make a girl squeal, 'Oh, that's *adorable*,' it'll be all right."

Oh, dear. Obviously some of the arrangements have been getting that response. After taking part in the joining-ceremony and vetoing a few such arrangements himself, Darian had sudden sympathy for poor Val.

Nightwind laughed. "I think we can manage," she promised. She studied Breon and his son. "I think, a rich golden brown for your side of the wedding, and—what's the bride's coloring?"

Val started to get a love-struck look in his eyes, and Breon caught it. He interrupted swiftly before Val could go into a flowery description. "She's brown-haired, fair. Pinkish fair."

Val looked indignant at such a callously abbreviated depiction of his beloved, but Nightwind sailed on, settling the question of color for the benefit of trade.

"Blue, then, for the bridal party. We've got good silk dyes for both those colors, and both are popular with us. If we don't have something here, k'Vala will have it in stores. Silk is light, especially silks for a warm-weather wedding; I can ask for a gryphon to fly them straight to Kelmskeep. It will be a good excuse for Kelvren's lady-friend to fly in for a visit." She cast a sly look at Kel, who contrived to look as if he hadn't heard her, but twitched his tail and shifted his hips. "Tell your good lady she'll have her fabrics in a week at the very most."

No one mentioned that in a week they might be facing off against the barbarians.

Worry about that when we know what we're facing; no point in getting ahead of ourselves. Besides, taking care of wedding arrangements will keep noncombatant minds off the barbarians.

"And you'll want—what?" Breon asked.

"Same as the last time. Our needs don't change much. Have your seneschal or factor negotiate with Ayshen for the price," Starfall said offhandedly, and Breon nodded with satisfaction. Since k'Valdemar had already presented Breon with the Vale's official wedding present (an exquisite set of colored glass goblets in sufficient quantity to allow the young couple to hold a reception for the Queen and her entire Council, brought for the purpose from k'Vala) he wasn't looking for anything but a reasonable trade.

"Right. Now, barring a war with barbarians, we've got Harvest Festival coming up at the same time as the wedding. What had your people planned to bring to the Faire?" This was the signal for a far more mundane discussion, and Kel excused himself—and so did Val and Darian. Darian chose a direction at random, and Val followed him.

I think I'm about to hear more from the would-be warrior.

Val's thoughts had obviously turned back to the barbarians, and he accosted Darian as soon as they were out of hearing of the adults. "Say, Darian—you've *fought* before, right?"

Darian made a sour face. "Fought the barbarians the first time around, and had some skirmishes with bandits in Valdemar. That's fighting *people*—we took out some Changebeasts in Valdemar, too, but that isn't what you meant, is it?" He continued walking, and Val kept right up with him.

"No, I meant combat. Real fighting. The clash of sword on sword, the thrill of meeting man to man, facing your enemy and bringing him down—" The cliches poured from Val as his face grew more and more animated. He obviously suffered from a surfeit of heroic ballads and tales. Darian decided to quash him. It wasn't that he disliked Val, that was far from the truth. If anything, he liked Breon's heir too much to let him go down that particular path of delusion.

That path leads to an early grave, given bad odds.

"I've done that," he said flatly. "You want to know what it's like?"

Val nodded eagerly, his earnest face alight.

"All right. Here, sit down." They'd come as far as the lake

while talking, and Darian gestured to a boulder. He took his seat on another, and gave careful thought to exactly how he was going to say his say. "First off, this isn't a duel, it's a combat. No rules. Do you know what that means, at all?" When Val shook his head, he continued. "It means that the enemy is going to try to kill you *before* you can get close to him, so he'll be flinging mucking great rocks at you, shooting at you, doing everything he can to keep you from getting close. He would much rather kill you from a distance, given the choice. If you get stuck with an arrow or knocked out by a rock, he's going to rush at you and try and whack something off while you're down and helpless, because it's easier to kill you then. If you don't get taken out by flying objects, every fellow on the other side is checking out the people coming at him, and he's going to try to make sure that *he* is bigger than *you*. If you've got fancy armor or weapons, he's going to want them, too, so his best bet is to cut a leg out from under you or whack off an arm and leave you lying there, screaming and bleeding to death. The other thing is that he's a greedy bastard, and anyone who looks even slightly important is going to have a *lot* of people coming at him, all at once, all trying to be the one to get that fancy sword and armor. If he can't manage to cut off a limb, or at least cut it half off, he'll try to bash in your skull because that's the second easiest way to kill you. There's no fancy swordwork going on; there's no room for it, you're mashed in with a bunch of other people, all whacking away. Meanwhile, as you're trying to keep him from doing awful things to you, and trying to do awful things to *him*, you're stepping on and stumbling over all the poor beggars who didn't manage to keep that from happening. They're bleeding, screaming, and dying; if they don't have fancy armor, their guts are spilling out and you're stepping right in them. Some of them are people you know. Some of them are friends. Some might be relatives. And you'll be seeing them as nothing more than things you don't want to fall over."

Val's face had gone rather sick, which Darian was extremely grateful for. Breon's son—thank all the gods!—was intelligent, and had imagination. That was probably why he'd gotten all caught up in the idea of adventure in fighting in the first place. That imagination would save him from his misguided notions of honor and glory, if Darian had any say in the matter.

"When it's all over, if you're on the winning side, you're absolutely sticky with blood, ready to drop with exhaustion, and every place on your body aches. Hopefully the blood you're covered with is other people's; if some of it's yours, this is when you realize just how much even a little wound *hurts*. If you got a big wound, if you aren't on the ground already, or you aren't dying, you generally fall down when everything's over, screaming with the pain. You could have broken bones sticking *through* your skin, and you're seeing parts of the inside of yourself you never wanted to see. If you are really, really lucky, someone recognizes that you're an important fellow and gets the Healer to you in a hurry. If not, you'll be lucky to get yourself to the Healer's tent somehow to wait for candlemarks while he works his way down to you. This is also when the excitement and fear and so forth that carried you through wears off, and you start to remember that you stepped in your cousin's face, you saw your uncle's head caved in, and you're not sure if your best friend is still alive. There's stuff besides blood on you that used to be parts of people. That's when you look around, see all the dead, dying, and wounded, and you throw up. Practically everyone else who never fought before—and some who have—is doing the same thing. That's what real combat is like." He stopped for a moment. "Oh, and after a fight, Healing takes second place to wound closure, so you may wait days or weeks before that wound in your leg that was cauterized closed—burned closed with a red-hot poker—gets properly Healed up." Val licked his lips, which were just a shade greenish.

"It's not like that in— I mean, I've never heard anyone talk about it like that." He seemed shaken, but not inclined to doubt Darian's word. Darian was quite glad he'd made a point of never exaggerating in front of Val; this was turning out as he'd hoped.

Darian shrugged and tried to look weary and worldly-wise. "That's because no one wants to remember those parts, but ask your Weaponsmaster, and let him know you want to know what it's *really* like on a battlefield, before, during, and after the battle. If he's honest, he'll tell you the same things I did." He thought of something else. "If you want, I can get one of the *dyheli* to give you the memory. They were in on the forest-battle four years ago."

"Oh." Val remained silent, looking out over the lake for a while. Darian let him stew things over; he needed some time to get his mind wrapped around Darian's blunt description. But Val had, out of incredulity, gotten a *dyheli* to give him a memory of k'Vala Vale. He hadn't believed the descriptions he'd heard of it, until he'd experienced Tyrsell's memory, and he knew that Darian would never have offered him access to a memory of combat if it wasn't as vivid—or more so—than Darian's own description.

Actually, given that the dyheli *aren't predators, their memory is going to be a lot nastier than my description. Bloodletting offends every instinct they've got.*

"I wondered why Father, and you—" Val shook his head and looked mortified. "I came very close to making a serious mistake. I have to apologize to you."

"Thought I was a coward?" To Val's obvious surprise, Darian grinned. "I'm not offended! I used to think the same things that you did about fighting. Honor, glory, adventure, fame, all that stuff. Probably everybody does, until he does it himself. Maybe a mercenary's children know better, and probably anyone who's had a fight go over his land does, but unless you've seen it for yourself, how can you know?" His grin turned cynical. "Well, think about it, how could they get us bone-headed youngsters go out to get bits hacked off if they didn't make it sound glorious?"

Val managed a sickly sort of smile himself. "You've got a point." He blinked, as if something had just occurred to him. "Now that I think about it, battles almost never happen in empty land, do they?"

"Not unless somebody manages to force it that way, no," Darian replied. The fellow was thinking, all right! "Obviously, we're going to try to choose the ground ourselves, but we may not get to make that choice."

"So Father isn't going to want something like that rampaging through the village, or over the crops, ruining them—"

Darian decided on a final ghoulish touch. "Imagine trying to *eat* crops that came up the next year in a field where people died! Crops fed on *blood*!"

Val shuddered. "I'd—rather not."

"So we bluff them, or negotiate with them, or—well, Firesong, Snowfire, and your father have a lot of ideas, I expect. They've all fought before, and they've got all the reasons in the world to make peace first, if it can be done without making a bad bargain." It was Darian's turn to look pensively out over the lake. "Believe me, if it were up to me— These people, or ones like them, killed Justyn right in front of me. They hurt a lot of people I knew, and killed a couple. They tried to kill *me*, twice, and they nearly managed it. I'm the last person to want them to get off easy, but—" He shook his head and looked back at Val. "If we force them to fight, things will almost certainly be bad, and more people I know will be dead or hurt. I don't want revenge half badly enough for that."

You know, I think Justyn would be very happy to hear me say that.

Val nodded, very slowly, and Darian decided to change the subject so that they could part on a good note. "So, tell me about this girl you're marrying! When does she get here? What is she like? How did you meet her?"

Since Belinda was obviously a subject Val could wax eloquent on for hours, this was the best thing he could have done. Until Lord Breon came to fetch his son for the trip home, Darian heard so much about Belinda that he suspected he could write a book—or at least several pages—about her many virtues. Val was completely smitten.

When Breon *did* come to get Val, though, the handclasp Darian got from the younger man, coupled with the thoughtful look and the nod they shared, let him know that Val had not forgotten the earlier subject. As Breon and his son rode off on the trail back to Kelmskeep, Darian felt quite proud of himself.

Firesong came up beside him at that point. "You look like a cat that's gotten into the cream," he said. "What have you been up to?"

"Convincing Val that fighting in battle isn't the way the Bards sing about it." He glanced sideways at Firesong to see how the mage would react.

Firesong laughed aloud, crossing his arms over his chest. "Good for you! I knew you had more sense than he did about that particular subject, but I didn't know you'd take it on yourself to talk to him."

"Somebody had to. I'd as soon not see his bride become a widow, you know?" He turned to Firesong, and grinned. "I'd have felt responsible."

"Good," Firesong nodded. "You *are* responsible. It's when we stop feeling responsible for each other, for the people we know we can affect, that we become the barbarians."

Firesong waited, and Darian sensed that there was another Talk with his Teacher in the offing. On the whole, he didn't mind those, except when Firesong seemed to expect an unreasonable level of magical expertise from him, given how short a time he'd been studying with good teachers. One of those had been just yesterday, in fact. Firesong had shouted impatiently at him, and he had left the lesson abruptly rather than lose his temper.

Firesong cleared his throat, and Darian put on an attentive look. If there was any chance his teacher would actually apologize, he wanted to encourage it.

"Silverfox gave me a bit of a lecture this morning, before the meeting," Firesong finally said, actually sounding sheepish. "When you do something that is exceptionally mature, like taking on young Val and disabusing him of the notion that battle equals painless glory, I start thinking of you, not as a student, but as a potential peer. I get both of us in trouble when I do that, because then I *expect* a similar level of skill in mage-craft. I expect that's what happened last night."

He glanced at Darian out of the corner of his eye, and Darian just nodded, warily. He didn't quite trust himself to actually say anything yet, but this was certainly a promising start.

"I got very impatient with you last night, and that was wrong of me. Silverfox very properly reminded me that you are someone who has not had the benefit of working with unlimited energy, and that you are a real youngster, not an adult like the people I'm used to training. You *act* like them, but you simply haven't got experience." He tossed his hair back over his shoulder, a habit Darian noticed he had when he was nervous. "The Herald-Mages I've trained have almost all been in their twenties, or even older. I keep forgetting that you're only eighteen, and at the same level of teaching I was when I was only twelve or fourteen."

Now Darian gingerly cleared his throat. "One year with poor Justyn, and four years working with teachers who are not Healing Adepts doesn't equal the kind of education you had, no. But you are right in that sometimes I just am not grasping what's going on. You were wrong in thinking it was because I'm too stubborn to admit my way is wrong; what you expect me to do simply doesn't occur to me." He flushed, thinking about how angry he'd gotten; the accusations still stung because they were so unjust. "You're supposed to be my teacher, and it isn't fair to force me to guess answers I can't possibly reach! I think it might be because I'm not really Tayledras, and I'm not used to thinking and seeing things as so intimately interconnected. Hellfires, your entire *religion* is built around that!" He scratched his head and managed a sheepish grin of his own. "Maybe that's why I got so hot and walked out of the lesson. It wasn't until I cooled down that I was able to figure out what you were saying, and put it to use."

"Maybe you should wear a crest of Valdemar on your forehead to remind me," Firesong suggested facetiously.

He snorted. "Don't tempt me, if wearing one would prevent another dressing-down like last night! Teach me, or don't, but don't play guessing games with me! That's all I ask."

Firesong's posture conveyed a certain amount of discomfort—possibly because Darian had hit on several of the things Silverfox had evidently chided him about. "Silverfox has promised to sit in on our lessons if you don't mind, and throw things at my head if I start getting unreasonable. And I wondered if you'd mind if we included that little Healer for the next couple of days? Having her there will keep me on better behavior, I suspect—and according to Nightwind, she could do with some of the same lessons you're getting."

"Having both Silverfox and Keisha there is all right with me," Darian said instantly, hoping he could keep himself from betraying the fact that he would welcome Keisha there for more reasons than just sharing the lessons. He was more than a little interested in Keisha, yes indeed, and he wouldn't mind the opportunity to see more of her at all!

"I'd also like to get the two of you working together now, so you can mesh your skills under *my* eye and not have to try it on your own," Firesong continued, at last looking more at ease. "I work with Healers all the time, but the first time you try is often full of pitfalls. It's like trying to do the *kyanshi* couple-dance when all you've ever done is children's round-dances." Darian sensed a sudden grin behind the mask. "Just thought you'd like to know what you're in for."

He rolled his eyes. "Thanks," he said dryly. "All I *have* ever done magically is children's round-dances, you know! And now you want me to attempt a fiendishly complicated display piece that not one couple in a hundred ever tries!"

"Nonsense," Firesong dismissed. "Neither the magic nor the dance is as complicated as they look, which is part of the problem. Don't worry, that's why I want you to do it under my eye. I'll walk you through it, and you'll be amazed how quickly you pick it up."

"I'll take your word for it," Darian replied dubiously. "I suppose you'll want to try this tonight?"

"Not tonight. Maybe tomorrow." Firesong clapped him on the shoulder. "Tonight I plan to go over what I attempted to hammer into your thick skull *last* night, since you so obligingly told me you'd gotten the trick of it."

Oh, hellfires. Now I'm in for it, and I don't have any excuses. "Yes, Firesong," Darian sighed. "I'll be at the workcircle at sunset."

It was morning, but there was no real reason to leap out of bed, and Darian liked having the leisure to lie in the dark, thinking and listening to the birds twitter in the vines. After the magic lessons of last night, shared with Keisha, he had a lot to think about.

She'd been attentive, very careful, with a fine, delicate mental touch. Much to Firesong's amazement, they had meshed powers almost at once, with the same surety of mental "hand" reaching for "hand" as long-time partners.

Firesong had at least been polite enough to keep his comment of :*Oh, so you like girls, do you?:* strictly Sent to Darian, but he hoped that Keisha hadn't noticed his sudden blush.

He'd been impressed—and although Keisha had not shown any such emotion on the surface, Darian could tell that beneath her calm exterior, she had been very close to tears of relief and joy.

Well, she's spent a long time not knowing how to use her Gift, and not only being able to use it, but to know she can ask someone else to augment her power, must be just exhilarating.

He stretched and turned over on his side, with the scent of fresh linens and herbs tickling his nose. He could not imagine why other people had told him that Keisha was prickly. Serious, yes, and maybe too serious, but she'd had responsibility shoved at her for so long that she probably hadn't learned how to have fun. But prickly?

Yet, so far, Val, Nightwind, Healer Gil, and even Lord Breon had warned him that Keisha was touchy, difficult to get to know, and held people at arm's length. He just didn't see any of those things in her—unless, if by "touchy," they meant that she didn't have any sympathy for fools, if by "difficult to get to know" they meant that she didn't talk about things she wasn't sure of, and if by "keeping people at arm's length" they meant that she was shy. She was certainly *shy*. That seemed a little odd in someone who had such a mob of siblings, but maybe she'd learned to be very self-contained because of that.

People in Errold's Grove respected her, but she didn't have any suitors. She didn't even have anyone he would have called a close friend. The young men of the village didn't even seem to think of her as a *girl*.

All the better for me. If they can't see how pretty she is, that's their problem. On the other hand, maybe it's a bit difficult for anyone to think romantically about the person who's patched you up after doing something really stupid, and threatened to hold your nose and pour medicine down your throat when you've had a sick stomach.

He grinned into the dimness. He could just see Keisha doing that, too!

His pleasant thoughts were abruptly interrupted by the uncharacteristically rude entrance of a *hertasi,* who burst in through the front door. "Dar'ian! You are needed!" it cried as soon as the door flew open.

He thrashed his way free of his covers, and flung himself out of bed. "Where?" he asked, stumbling into the room. "What's the matter?"

"The outsiders come! The Vale pillars—the others wait there—" it said, and whisked out the door again, presumably to rouse other folks.

The outsiders come? Well, it can't be an enemy attack, or there would be a lot more shouting going on outside. Besides, I don't think even a hertasi *would refer to an enemy attack as "the outsiders come."* With that in mind, he took some care in dressing, though he did so quickly, and left his weapons behind.

When he reached the two pillars at the entrance, there weren't too many of "the others" waiting; just Kel, Nightwind, and Snowfire. "What's going on?" he asked, combing his hair with his fingers and confining it with a headband. He'd combed it properly before he left, of course, but all his efforts at looking neat had been destroyed when he ran.

"Kel spotted an armed force with a pair of Heralds leading it heading this way as he started out on patrol this morning," Snowfire said, as Kel nodded. "He came back to tell us, and I sent *hertasi* around to wake you all up." To Darian's chagrin, Snowfire looked as if he'd been up for hours, and had gotten the *hertasi* to give him a complete grooming while he waited for folk to muster out. *How did he manage to do that?*

"So our reinforcements are here? Why are they coming here, instead of Kelmskeep?" Darian asked, attempting to neaten himself up.

"They're *coming* from Kelmskeep; at a guess, they overnighted there, and Lord Breon sent them on to us this morning," Nightwind hazarded. "We'll find out soon enough."

A drowsy-eyed Firesong joined them at that moment, yawning behind his mask, followed by Starfall. Firesong had thrown on a loose robe, and was still in the process of belting it about his slim waist. His hair showed signs of having been hastily braided, and his eyes still looked sleepy. "Ugh,"

Firesong said with distaste. "Military types! Why on earth they should think that it's admirable to shake everyone awake at dawn or before, I can never understand!"

"The forrrce isss larrge enough to sssatisssfy you all, I think," Kel put in, ignoring Firesong's complaints with amusement. "I counted overrr a thousssand."

"I hope Breon sends some supplies with them," Starfall said thoughtfully. "That is a lot of hungry mouths to feed. Well, we'll manage, we generally do."

"I suspect that would be why he isn't bivouacking them at Kelmskeep," suggested Nightwind, with one hand on Kel's neck and the other on Snowfire's arm. "Well, we have room; I'm sure they brought tents, and we can camp them out here if there isn't enough room in the Vale itself."

"For one thousand to fifteen hundred?" said Ayshen, who with Tyrsell and Hashi was the last to join them. "No problem." He turned with a flourish of his tail, and issued orders in the hissing *hertasi* language to another of his kind that had trailed deferentially along behind him. The other bobbed an agreement and scampered off.

Hweel raced in beneath the branches, heading straight for Snowfire, who extended his arm and braced himself for the weight as Hweel landed. 'They're within sight," Snowfire reported, while Hweel transferred half his weight to Snowfire's protected shoulder.

And so they were. Darian peered out into the forest. The first of the reinforcements, tiny in the distance and further dwarfed by the giant trees, came into view on the road. They were easier to see, perhaps, because in the lead were two Heralds, white uniforms and white Companions making them doubly visible.

They moved at a brisk pace, which showed that they were in good shape. As they neared, just at the point where Huur was visible as an escort, flapping lazily along just above the heads of the leaders, Firesong suddenly laughed out loud.

"What?" Starfall asked sharply, casting a glance at his son.

"Nothing to worry about," Firesong replied, his voice overlaid with humor. "I just recognized someone I know very well." By this time, the group was within calling distance, and he stepped forward.

"I might have known you'd be unable to resist a fight, you terrible woman!" he shouted. "If you were a Hawkbrother, we'd name you 'Fire-eater.' Aren't you ever going to retire?"

"Not while things stay interesting!" the righthand Herald called back, a woman with a long blonde braid streaked with silver, whose easy grin matched her light words. "Firesong, you useless popinjay! What are you doing here?"

"Corrupting our youth, of course," Firesong replied, backing up a pace and clapping his hand on Darian's shoulder. "I'm tired of perverting Hawkbrothers, I thought I'd start on Valdemarans. This is Dar'ian, my latest victim."

The Companions halted, the mixed troops behind them came to parade-rest, and both Heralds dismounted from their saddles with agility that gave the lie to the silver in their hair. The woman clasped Firesong's hand first, followed by the man.

"My friends, permit me to introduce you to the redoubtable Herald-Captain Kerowyn and Herald Eldan," Firesong said, waving his free hand at them.

Darian's mouth dropped open. First, the famous Firesong, and now the equally famous Kerowyn? Who would show up here next? The Queen herself?

"Heralds, these are the Elders of k'Valdemar Vale," he continued. "My father, Starfall k'Vala, *dyheli* king-stag Tyrsell k'Vala k'Valdemar, Eldest *hertasi* Ayshen k'Leshya, *kyree* envoy Hashi, Scout-Captain Snowfire k'Vala, *trondi'irn* Nightwind k'Leshya, Silver Gryphon Kelvren, and my pupil, Darian Firkin k'Vala k'Valdemar."

Kerowyn saluted them all. "A very great pleasure, which, in spite of what Firesong implied, I hope remains a *peaceful* pleasure. These are your Crown reinforcements." She waved at the waiting troops behind her—not all men, Darian saw; at least half of the mounted fighters were women. "I bring one mounted company of two hundred seasoned fighters out of my own Skybolts, and two green companies of regular Guard infantry at five hundred each. That's twelve hundred fighters in all, with three full Healers and their six apprentices, and supply wagons and support personnel."

Some faint worry lines eased from Snowfire's face. "If twelve hundred fighters can't keep things under control here, we'll need an army, not reinforcements. And if Herald-Captain Kerowyn can't get the most out of every trooper she has, then you can stew my boots and serve them to me for dinner."

Kerowyn laughed, and shook her head. "Oh, I'm no miracle worker, but I think we'll do all right, provided we use our heads. Have you a place where we can pitch camp?"

"Bring your people with me, Herald-Captain," Ayshen spoke up. "I'll show you where to camp, and the amenities that you and your people can share with us. We can discuss other arrangements on the way."

"Good, thank you." She nodded at Eldan, then made a hand signal. The troops snapped to attention. "I'll see to the troops. Eldan will meet with you now, and you can brief him."

"I had bessst get to my patrrrol," Kel said instantly. "I will make hassste and bring you the latessst intelligence."

He made good on his word, leaping into the air and clawing his way into the sky with tremendous wingbeats. None of the Valdemarans was startled, though several watched him with admiration; They might be green, yet they must be from some area where they had seen gryphons before now.

Eldan and his Companion joined the Elders, while Kerowyn mounted hers and took her place at the head of the troops. Darian and the rest all moved off the trail to allow the troops to file past. Darian watched them, thinking how odd it was, that under other circumstances, he might have been one of them. *If I'd run off, or if the village had sent me off to Lord Breon instead of apprenticing me—that could be me, carrying a pike and my pack. Huh.*

"Are you getting on all right?" Eldan asked Firesong in an undertone. "We haven't had any news of you more recent than last summer."

"Actually, not at all bad," Firesong said lightly. "We get along, Silverfox and I. You and the lady look well."

"Couldn't be better; we've got four perfectly capable Weaponsmasters now, and she didn't see any reason why they couldn't take the trainees without her looking over their shoulders. Karal's teaching some classes, if you can believe it. Things are so calm between Valdemar and Karse that his diplomatic skill is scarcely needed, so he's teaching Karsite culture and language."

"Wonderful! He must love it." Firesong sounded genuinely pleased. "An'desha is up to his eyebrows in shamanistic business, and I've never seen him happier. I left him in Kata'shin'a'in, helping to weave a new history-tapestry." He straightened, and looked about. "Well, we can catch up later; now we should deal with business." He bowed a little to Eldan. "So, Herald Eldan, would you and your Companion care to join our council for an explanation of what's going on?"

"That I would, Healing-Adept Firesong," Eldan replied, with the same odd mingling of seriousness and humor that Firesong displayed. "Lead on."

Lord Breon

Twelve

It took most of the day to get the reinforcements settled in their encampment. They were entirely self-sufficient, having their own cook, tents, and supplies, but everyone agreed that being able to use the Vale's facilities made their camp seem downright luxurious. They were not in the least shy about stripping and plunging into the hot pools, men and women together, and at any hour of the day or night one was as likely to encounter a clutch of Valdemarans there as a group of Tayledras. Most often, the two groups mingled; the so-called "green" troops were green only in the sense of not having seen real combat, for they had trained and bunked with the Skybolts, and had Skybolt senior officers. Those who couldn't handle the accepting and flexible manners of Kero's troopers had long since been weeded out. Tayledras and Guards got along very well, with the troopers holding to the attitude that, once on someone else's home ground, you played by *their* rules and not by what was called "good manners" and "appropriate behavior" at home. "Stay polite and respectful and ask before you touch," was the watchword in the camp, and as a result, everyone got along remarkably well.

The next day Lord Breon and Val arrived for a real council of war, bringing with them their Weaponsmaster, who was Lord Breon's second-in-command. With a storm threatening, they met in the common dining hall, taking up roughly a third of the available space. By common and unspoken consent, since this was hardly a secret council, anyone of the officers of sufficient rank who cared to listen in could do so as long as they stayed quiet.

"What's this Captain Kerowyn like, personally?" Lord Breon asked Firesong, as the assembled council waited for Kero and Eldan, who were the last to arrive. Today Firesong's mask seemed to be made all of fresh green leaves. Tayledras and a few of Kero's officers lurked around the periphery of the group, and Darian saw a couple who were clearly Skybolts smile at that question.

"You'll like her," Firesong promised him. "Kero can be counted on not to jump to any conclusions and not to fight unless she has to. She's very straightforward, never hedges her answers or gives you the answer she thinks you want unless it's also the true one. She's got—oh, decades of practical experience; before she came to Valdemar and was Chosen she was a mercenary captain with her own company in Rethwellan—the Skybolts, the same group that came up here with her. So, like most mercenary captains, she doesn't believe in wasting her limited resources, her fighters. She plans things, she doesn't just charge in and hope for the best."

Darian saw nods of agreement from the Guards, and heard a great many murmurs of approval from the Hawkbrothers.

Lord Breon also nodded and seemed satisfied, at least to Darian. "That's exactly the kind of person we need for this situation. Now, I take it that Herald Eldan is more of the diplomat?"

"Yes; they make a good team that way." Darian definitely heard good-humored affection in Firesong's voice. "Kero's too blunt to make a good diplomat. They've been together since Kero was Chosen, and Selenay prefers to keep them as an official team, since Kero would probably find a sneaky way to accomplish the same thing without actually disobeying orders. You'll like him, too."

Just then, Kerowyn and Eldan showed up, but only Eldan was wearing Whites. Kero had changed into something of the same cut as a Herald's Whites, but it was all of gray leather, well-worn and practical, but not white, by any stretch of the imagination.

"I thought you were a Herald!" Val exclaimed, obviously without thinking before he opened his mouth.

He really has a problem that way, Darian noted. *Does he ever think before he speaks?*

"I am. I'm also officially on war-duty as of this moment, and I am *not* wearing one of those 'oh-shoot-me-now' outfits while I am in the front line. Eldan gets to be the obviously important person—he's the diplomat, and he *won't* be in the front line of fighting as long as I am in command unless he changes into something inconspicuous first." She cast Eldan a significant glance, which Eldan ignored. This was evidently an argument of long standing between them. "I'm the one in charge if there's fighting, and I'd better stay hard to hit if I'm going to stay that way." She managed a very thin smile. "If this outfit is good enough for Weaponsmaster-Herald Alberich, it's good enough for me."

"That doesn't sound very . . . heroic." Val was either oblivious to the effect his blurted comments were having, or today he was just letting his thoughts go straight to his mouth without pausing to examine them. He wasn't usually *this* clumsy. Darian winced inside, waiting for the rebuke.

But Kero actually softened a little. "My dear boy, I have been fighting for all of my adult life. I don't have anything to prove anymore. I never did when I was a mercenary; if a merc doesn't live, he doesn't get paid. Heroics are for the young with nothing to lose." Then she raised an eyebrow and added dryly, "When it comes down to cases, Eldan's job is more important than mine. Diplomacy is much more economical than combat, unless you just happen to have a lot of people and no food to give them. Think about it, son. Think about it in terms of these green and fertile fields, and all the people who live on them—and the possibility that these new people are very, very hungry."

Distant thunder growled, and it grew darker in the dining hall. *Hertasi* went about quietly lighting lamps.

Val finally figured out that he had been very rude and inconsiderate—and worse, perhaps, from his point of view, he'd exposed himself as inexperienced and immature. He blushed a brighter scarlet than Darian had ever managed and looked down at the table.

So much for Val's love affair with heroic ballads. What I didn't kill, Kerowyn flattened. But Kero was already getting down to business, and Val quickly got caught up in the plans along with everyone else.

"All right then, gryphon—Kel, right?—Kel, give us the numbers, then we'll have something to work with." Outside, thunder rumbled, warning that the storm was upon them. The first drops of rain hit the roof heavily.

"Of rrreal fighterrrsss, five hundrrred and twenty-two. Of old men, old women, youngsssterrrs old enough to take a weapon, and women without babesss, fourrrr hundrrrred and eighteen. Of ssssmall childrrren, babesss, nurrrsing and prrregnant motherrrrsss, and crrripplesss, two hundrrred and forrrty-one." Kel sounded very sure of himself and added, "I counted in many passssesss, until the numberrrsss alwayssss came out the sssame."

"Good for you—wait, did you say *cripples*?" Kerowyn stared at the gryphon incredulously. "Are you serious? There are crippled people among them?"

Kelvren had to wait as a flash of lightning followed immediately by an enormous peal of thunder drowned out any attempt at discussion. The rain began in earnest, drumming down on the roof with the promise that this would not be a mere cloudburst.

"Yesss. Mossst arrre childrrren, but sssome are adultsss." He scratched an ear-tuft slowly and thoughtfully. "I thought that sssseemed odd, myssself."

"Most barbarian societies that *I've* ever heard of wouldn't allow their cripples to live, much less cart them along on a cross-country trek," Kero said, tapping her lips with one finger. "Unless, of course, the cripple had a special skill that was vital to the tribe but didn't require mobility. Obviously, no child would qualify to live in that way. What's going on here?"

Darian decided to speak up. "That doesn't sound anything like the first lot of barbarians that came here. They killed their own wounded."

"In-ter-est-ing." Kero drew out the word, intoning each syllable as if it was a magical incantation. "Well. What else can you tell me, Kel?"

"That the way behind issss blocked. The ssstorm we have now isss jussst the firrrsssst of many to come—ssso sssay the weatherrrr sssignssss and the weatherrr-watcherrrrsss among the Tayledrrrasss." Kel nodded at Snowfire who gave silent confirmation. "The rrriverrrsss to the norrrth arrre flooded. The tribe cannot rrrretrrreat."

Darian listened to the rain on the roof, and thought about hundreds of people trapped by rain-swollen rivers. How were they handling it?

"That is not good; we can figure that if these people aren't desperate now, they will be when we confront them with no way to retreat." She looked around the table, making certain that she met everyone's eyes. "They'll not only be desperate, but trapped. *If* we fight them, we can count on them fighting to the last man, woman, and child. We'll win, but it will be expensive, and we'll end up with a gaggle of barbarian children and cripples to take care of afterward. This is, of course, assuming that the mothers don't kill the children to prevent them from falling into our hands, which is very likely. Think you can handle having to sort through and bury a lot of dead babies?"

Darian felt his stomach lurch, and everyone else looked rather grim. Val was white, probably his imagination working again.

I don't like these people, but I don't hate them that much.

Kero nodded. "I thought not. Good, we will pursue diplomacy until there is no chance whatsoever that we can make it work. Fighting will be the last of a very long list of choices. Are we agreed? Aye for those who are."

There was no dissension, and when Darian checked the expressions of the onlookers, there wasn't any discontent there, either. Some of the Tayledras, and a couple of the Guard, looked dubious, but no one disagreed. More thunder rolled outside, and the windows lit whitely as lightning passed somewhere above.

Now I see why Kero didn't mind having people listen. This is better than having rumors running wild through camp.

"Eldan, I yield the table to you," she said, sitting back in her chair, with her arms folded comfortably across her chest. "If I've got anything to say, I'll just raise my hand like the rest."

Eldan chuckled, as if this was a joke only he and she

understood. "Right enough, Kero. The first step in a diplomatic meeting is the first contact. Does anyone have any ideas there?"

Lord Breon cleared his throat. "We talked about it some, already. Figured we'd come in looking strong enough to squash any offense without thinking about it, but holding our hands to give these people a chance to speak for themselves. Show of magic, show of strength, even bring in the birds and the nonhuman allies to impress 'em with our totem animals."

"That's a good plan; I think anything subtle is a waste of time," Eldan replied, with an approving glance around the table. "There is one thing I *would* like, as a 'just in case.' I'd like to evacuate the village—" he consulted a paper, "—ah, Errold's Grove. I'd like to send the evacuees to Kelmskeep for safety."

Lord Breon protested in alarm. "Wait now, in the middle of growing season? There'll be things that need harvesting soon—and herds—and—"

"Whoa!" Eldan held up his hands, cutting Lord Breon short. "I didn't say *everyone*. Evacuate those who are too frightened to stay, children, women with babies, the elderly. Basically, anyone who can't move in a hurry or will panic if trouble comes. *This* time we have warning, and we'll have time enough to clear the rest out *if* there's fighting and *if* it looks as if it will move in the direction of the village. All right?"

Lord Breon frowned, but agreed grudgingly. "I don't think you realize how much work *everyone* has in growing season, though," he grumbled. "This is going to leave my farmers and small-holders mightily short-handed."

Darian saw Kero and Eldan exchange another look, and Eldan's slight shrug. "I think your farmers and small-holders will be grateful that their families are somewhere safe, my lord," Eldan soothed. "And if you are worried about the harvest, perhaps some of our fighters could pitch in to help. They won't be doing anything here but drill, and some of them might appreciate the change of pace."

Darian thought of something that might be an incentive. "There must be twenty pretty girls in that village with no husband-prospects, and there's a perfectly good inn there as well."

Kero grinned and winked at him.

"There, you see?" Eldan spread his hands. "We'll take our volunteers from those who grew up farming. At that rate, you can even have the mothers with young children as well as those with babies evacuate. In the event that the whole village needs to be cleared out, we'll have a rearguard in place to hold the road behind!"

Lord Breon sighed heavily. "All right. It's a damned good idea, and I've no doubt m'lady can keep the whole lot of 'em busy helping with wedding froufraraw."

"Kelvren, can you fly a long sortie tomorrow?" Kero asked, as if struck with a sudden thought. "I'd like you to see if there's any pattern to the barbarians' migration."

Kelvren slapped his foreclaw to his chest in what Darian thought must be a salute. "Cerrrtainly."

"Right." She looked around the table. "Can anybody think of anything else for now?"

"Only that we should make this meeting a daily one," Snowfire said, and smiled apologetically at Lord Breon. "Sorry, my lord, but unless you prefer to let us deal with this without your opinions or wishes, your lady will have to do without you for a while."

"My lady told me to pack my bags," Lord Breon replied and grinned. "She reckoned Val and I were in for an extended stay. Gods forbid that fighting comes that far, but she can command my personal troops as well as I can, and as for setting up for refugees and a siege—she's as good or better than I am. That's one reason why I wed her in the first place." Val looked startled, as his father bowed to Starfall and Snowfire. " 'Fraid I'm going to have to beg quarters from you, gentlemen, and campspace for my men."

Keisha felt as if she had somehow fallen into someone else's life. Here she had gone along for years, with nothing more serious than sick sheep and broken bones to take care of, and nothing more worrisome than trying to work her way through those damned indecipherable texts. . . .

And now?

She was living in a Hawkbrother Vale, taking lessons from one of the most famous mages in the world—well, in Valdemar, anyway—learning how to do things that weren't even in those texts. And if that wasn't enough, now there was an army in residence, with no less than three full Healers and six apprentices, all perfectly willing to give her extra lessons and advice if she thought she needed it. She had seen more new people at once in the last few days than all of the people she'd ever seen in her life added together.

"Not that you really need much advice," observed Gentian Arbelo, the most senior of the three. He was also the oldest, bald as an egg, and the thinnest healthy man Keisha had ever seen. "You have all the basic herb-knowledge so solidly there's no point in questioning it, and you could teach *us* a few things about the local cures. As for using your Gift—" he shrugged. "It's more a matter of practice and getting comfortable with it than needing any advice or lessons. Still, if you want to sit in when any of us work, we'll be happy to link minds with you so that you can see exactly how we do things."

"Please," Keisha responded immediately, hoping she didn't sound as desperate as she felt. "Please. I need experience, and I'm horribly afraid I won't have much time to get it."

"There is that," agreed Nala Karcinamen, the junior Healer. "If there's fighting, well, we're going to wish we had double our number."

The middle, a robust and cheerful man, of middling height, brown hair, eyes, and beard, who called himself Grenthan Miles, made a face. "Piff! This is Captain Kero we're talking about! If there's a way to get this settled without crossed swords, she'll find it, her and Eldan both. Meanwhile, this *is* an army, they're always beating on one another, and that means bruises and cuts. Likely, there'll be at least one serious fight with a broken bone if we sit about for more than a fortnight. We'll have hangovers, upset stomachs from overstuffing, all manner of minor troubles. There's nothing better to practice on, m'dear, and if you botch it up a bit, there's no serious consequences." He grinned first at Keisha, then at his two colleagues. "We'll take her on the rounds and let *her* use her Gift on 'em with us as safety. She'll get practice, we can use the time for some full exams, and that'll keep every mother's child in this mothering army up to strength. What do you say to that?"

Nala looked dubious, but Gentian nodded. "Good idea. In fact, it would be a good idea for all the apprentices." His grin, buried as it was in a bright red beard, was doubly infectious. "By the gods, we'll spoil those soldiers, though! They'll think this is how we should always treat 'em!"

Keisha flushed, her cheeks hot, and Nala gave her a penetrating look. "Have you something you'd like to say, Keisha?" The plump and motherly gray-haired woman looked more like someone's grandmother than a Healer who'd followed armies literally all her life. She seemed to understand Keisha's shyness, and how hard it was to volunteer information.

"Just that—I do know some remedies you may not, mostly for common things—and they don't *all* have to have— *painless* Healing." She flushed even more, her cheeks so warm they were painful. "You want to discourage people from pretending to be sick, right? Or complaining of truly trivial problems? The medicines aren't very pleasant, but they are very efficient."

All three Healers burst into delighted laughter, lessening her blushes. "She'll do, she'll do!" Gentian crowed. "Oh, yes, she'll do!"

"You're sure you want to be here?" Kerowyn asked Keisha as they reached the outskirts of Errold's Grove just after suppertime—a time chosen when everyone would be home from the fields.

"They know me; you're outsiders. They know I wouldn't say anything that can be ignored. If I'm here while you tell them the bad news, they won't be so inclined to try to pretend it isn't true." Keisha really *didn't* want to be there, but she knew she had to be; among other things, she figured she might as well get the inevitable confrontation with her parents over and done with. They were going to want her to evacuate with the others, and obviously she couldn't do that.

"The best thing to do is to ring the bell in the square," Keisha went on, thinking out loud. "If we ask Mayor Lutter to assemble everyone, he'll try to find some way of putting it off—or worse, he'll only assemble people he thinks are important." She gave Kerowyn a helpless shrug. "He's good enough at arranging Faires, but I wouldn't trust him to make *any* decisions in a case like this, much less make the right ones. He'll think first of how to keep his own status high and keep getting appointed Mayor, and not concentrate on anything useful. My guess is that he's been keeping the fact that the barbarians were coming this way a secret. The only ones who probably know are the town council members."

Kero snorted and looked absolutely disgusted. "Politicians! Always butting in where leaders are needed! No fear, I know the type, and I can handle him easily enough."

Just ahead, people wandered the village paths in the late-evening sunlight. Some were women, gathering to trade gossip, some were young people, mostly couples, and children played in the yards as they rode in, Kerowyn on her Companion, and Nightwind and Keisha on *dyheli*. Kerowyn had changed back to her Whites—grudgingly, but Eldan had said severely that her authority as a Herald might be needed to get people to act instead of dithering. There would be no difficulty with riding back after darkness fell, since the *dyheli* and Kero's Companion had excellent night-vision, and there was going to be a full moon.

As soon as the children spotted Kero, they ran back to their houses, shouting with excitement. *Gods, this is an awful lot of excitement for Errold's Grove. People are going to be talking about this year for decades,* Keisha mused, as folk began to gather beside the road, their faces full of expectation. "Maybe we won't have to ring the bell, after all," Keisha ventured, seeing the number of people appearing on their own.

"Good; I want to alert people, not scare them witless." Kero's Companion Sayvil stopped, and Kero stood up in her stirrups. "Listen, people—I want everyone in Errold's Grove assembled in the square, right now! You littles—yes, you and you and you—go to all the houses and fetch everybody."

The children she pointed to ran off, squealing with excitement at being given an important mission by a *Herald*. "The rest of you, follow us to the square, unless you know of someone the children won't likely find."

Kero took the lead, followed by Nightwind and Keisha and a parade of chattering, excited people. *The noise alone will probably bring people out,* Keisha thought, as the crowd behind grew larger with every step they took.

The square had been cleaned out since the "reception" for Darian and the Hawkbrothers. *How long ago was that? Just days, maybe a fortnight, but it seems like a year.* There was nothing in the way of structures there at all, except the Hawkbrother bower near the Temple.

"Don't dismount," said Kero, as their three mounts halted, with Kerowyn between Nightwind and Keisha. "We'll use the height to our advantage. Anyone want to bet how long it takes for this Mayor of Keisha's to appear, demanding that we go through him?"

"He's not *my* Mayor," Keisha protested, and at that exact moment, Mayor Lutter appeared at the edge of the crowd, face red, shoving his way through to the center.

"What's going on here?" he demanded, as he came up to the nose of Kero's Companion, Sayvil. "What's the meaning of this?"

Sayvil looked down her long nose at him, and deliberately sneezed wetly in his face. As he jumped back (as far as he could, given the crowd), wiping his face with his sleeve, Kero's lips twitched. "The situation with the approaching barbarians the Hawkbrothers told you about has escalated, Mayor Lutter," Kerowyn said, loudly enough to be heard clearly by at least a third of the crowd. "I'm here to give Crown orders for Errold's Grove."

That set up a buzz, as the folk in the front exclaimed in alarm, those in the back asked what had been said, and those nearest Mayor Lutter seized on *him*, demanding to know why he hadn't told them about approaching barbarians. This kept him very busy trying to make up an explanation, as Kero had probably intended.

People continued to collect, as Kero waited patiently. When it appeared that no one else was going to join them, she stood up in her stirrups, surveyed the group with an impassive face, then abruptly signaled for silence.

Amazingly, she got it; even the increasingly agitated cluster of people around Mayor Lutter quieted down. The Mayor, glad enough for the respite, mopped his sweating face with his other sleeve.

"I am Herald-Captain Kerowyn, commander of the Sky-bolts," Kero announced. As a murmur again rose, she continued, ignoring the sound. "I see some of you recognize me; those of you who do can make your explanations to everyone else later. Apparently your Mayor has not passed on some information he received some time ago, so I'll repeat it in brief. Northern barbarians have been approaching this area for some time; at first it was unclear whether they were going to stop short or continue until they came to Errold's Grove, but they show no signs of stopping, so we are assuming they *will* come here."

Interestingly, although Kero's words were practically guaranteed to cause panic, no one moved or even said anything. It might have been Kero's stern gaze; it might also have been that she had some rudimentary Empathic control over the crowd. Or, if she didn't, perhaps Sayvil did. At any rate, no one ran off, or even moved much.

"There are some significant differences between this group and the last," Kero continued. "The most important of which is that this group contains women, children, old people, and even cripples. That suggests that they are not a conquering army, but rather migrants, nomads, or even refugees; people of that nature can be negotiated with. Nevertheless, the Crown is taking your safety very seriously, and I am in command of three companies of Guard troops that include some of my own Skybolts, who will make certain that you are protected."

A spontaneous, and very relieved, cheer arose, which Kero permitted to continue for a moment before raising her hand again. As before, she got silence.

"Meanwhile I have advised Lord Breon to let everyone who wants to evacuate Errold's Grove. I suggest that mothers with infants and small children do so, all children below the age of fourteen, all older folk, and anyone else who doesn't feel safe. I realize that this will cause some hardship, so since we wanted some troops stationed here anyway, those troopers will help out in the fields to replace people who evacuate."

She allowed her gaze to travel across the crowd, slowly, so that she at least gave the illusion of meeting each and every eye. "There you have it. Lord Breon has agreed to accept the evacuees at Kelmskeep, and whatever you want to bring with you, go ahead and do so. This is *not* an emergency evacuation, and you can take as much time to pack up and move out as you need to, within reason. I'd say four or five days is within reason."

"Do *you* think the barbarians will come here?" shouted one of the Fellowship folk.

Kero shook her head. "To be honest, not really. However, I want all possibilities covered, and if my judgment proves to be totally wrong—and it could, the gods know it's happened before—I don't want anyone here who is unable to run like a rabbit if trouble shows up. *My* recommendation is basically that the able-bodied and healthy can stay, but everyone else should go."

Keisha chose this moment to speak up. "I've been at the Vale, which is where all the news is coming. This is real, and if it were my family that had a grandma or baby, I'd not only tell them to go, I'd help them pack and escort them to Kelmskeep. Since my folks can all not only run like rabbits but can bite when cornered—" she noted several weak grins in the crowd, and stronger ones from her brothers," —I'd say it's safe enough for them to stay until the Herald-Captain tells them otherwise."

Anyone who might have been wavering until then was convinced.

Kero waited a moment, then asked, "Anyone have any questions?"

"Only of Mayor Lutter," said one voice, with a decidedly grim note in it. Murmurs of agreement followed.

"Right. You *will* have several more chances to ask me things, myself, or one of my lieutenants. There'll be an officer stationed with the men who come here to help out, and if he or she doesn't already have orders that cover any question you might have, they'll have authority to make a decision." She took a slow, deep breath, and looked satisfied with the results of her speech. "Carry on, decide who's going, take your time. I'll send the first batch of men over tomorrow, and if you don't feel confident about getting to Kelmskeep by yourselves, some of them will provide an armed escort over. This isn't an emergency. Yet."

At this point, the only excited and agitated people were the ones around Mayor Lutter; Keisha felt rather sorry for him, but he *had* brought his troubles on himself.

But she saw her mother and father making their way toward her, moving slowly through the crowd with determination on their faces, and she braced herself for what was to come.

"You *are* going to Kelmskeep," stated her mother, as soon as she was close enough, in the tone that warned she would accept no other answer from her daughter.

But it wasn't her daughter who sat the back of a *dyheli*, not here, not now. It was the Errold's Grove Healer, who knew that there was a perfectly good Healer at Kelmskeep, but if she left, there would be none at Errold's Grove at a time when one would be needed urgently. Furthermore, the Errold's Grove Healer knew that if it came to a conflict, her place was with the other Healers caring for injured fighters, not huddling behind walls of stone, far from any conflict.

So— "No," said the Healer of Errold's Grove, just as firmly.

Her mother and father simply stared at her. *No wonder. I may have disobeyed, but never in anything major, and I've never refused them to their faces.* Keisha hardened her shields as well as her resolution; no matter what they said or did, she had no intention of being dissuaded.

"What do you mean, *no?*" demanded Ayver and Sidonie in chorus.

"I believe it's my duty to remain either here or at the Vale, where I am needed, and not in Kelmskeep, where I am not," Keisha replied, in a level and moderate tone. "So I will not be going to Kelmskeep." She was deeply grateful that Kero told them all to stay mounted; the height-advantage she had gave her an advantage in authority as well.

Her father began to get a bit red in the face, himself. "No daughter of *mine*—"

"I am your daughter only *after* I am a Healer," Keisha

countered, hoping that she sounded calm and reasonable.
"My first and most important duty is as a Healer. Once she's
a full Herald, you wouldn't even think to tell *Shandi* to stay
out of danger, would you?"

The trouble is, I'm afraid they would. . . .

Even through shields, she could tell that she had just set
the spark to the tinder. There was going to be a very ugly outburst in a moment; she braced herself, cringing inside.

"Pardon," Nightwind said, stepping in before either parent
could send down thunder and lightning. "But Keisha is eighteen, is she not?" At Sidonie's automatic nod, the *trondi'irn*
continued. "Then by your own laws, she is two years past the
age when she can legally make her own choices."

"That she is," Kero said cheerfully, bringing her own formidable personality in on Keisha's side. "She can marry, be
apprenticed, take on business or a debt, choose whatsoever
profession she wishes, no matter *what* your desires are."

"But she's a *child*!" Sidonie wailed. "She can't possibly
make any kind of rational decision!"

"By your law, she ceased to be a child two years ago," said
Nightwind quietly. "By *our* law, she ceased to be one four
years ago. And by demonstration of responsibility, she ceased
to be one at least that long ago." She smiled, a smile full of
pity and sympathy. "Lady, your child is in no sense a child,
and has not been so for years. She was simply too dutiful to
remind you of that fact, but now her higher responsibilities
have forced her to that point. Don't force her to hurt you just
to prove she's long since grown up."

Suddenly Sidonie's face crumpled, though at least she
didn't burst into tears. Keisha swallowed, with the revelation
of how difficult it must be to let children grow up; it was
all there, in her father's shocked and stricken look, in her
mother's heartsick eyes. She began to waver; was she wrong
in standing against them?

But Kero was not going to let the situation decay. With a
wicked gleam in her eye, *she* stepped in again. "I must remind you," she said, in a voice as devoid of pity as Nightwind's expression was full of that emotion, "I *am* in charge
of this situation, and in my opinion you would be seriously

interfering with the best interests of Valdemar by trying to persuade one of my Healers to cravenly abandon her post. It could even be construed as treason," she added thoughtfully.

"Oh," Ayver said, his face blank with shock. Sidonie took a few moments more to see what Kero was getting at, but when she did, her expression went just as blank as her husband's.

Now it was Kero's turn to soften, a little. "You've been good enough parents to raise not only a child Chosen but another who sees her duty as a Healer as more important than her own wishes. Now be good enough parents to let that child live up to her potential."

Ayver was the first to recover. "Just promise that she'll be taken care of!" he said to Kero, with the fierce glare of any thwarted father.

"I am Herald-Captain Kerowyn, and I *always* take care of my people," Kero told him with supreme dignity. "You have my leave to inquire from any of my people how they are cared for."

There seemed nothing more to say at that point, and with that bee in their ears, they beat a hasty retreat. Dusk had faded into darkness, and they were swallowed up by the night before Keisha could call them back.

Keisha let out the breath she'd been holding in, and looked at both Nightwind and Kero with gratitude. She couldn't believe how quickly the confrontation had ended, although she wished with all her heart that it had been less painful for her parents. "This isn't the first time you've held off angry parents, is it?" she asked Kerowyn, who laughed.

"No, it's not," she agreed. "And you should see them when their baby-child is going to go hit people with sharp things, instead of Heal them of the aftermath!" She shook her head reminiscently. "Hate to do it, but a child has to grow up sometime in their parents' eyes, and better they should blame me than their own flesh and blood."

"Well, thank you, thank you both," Keisha sighed. "I almost gave in to them; I probably would have, if you hadn't helped."

They all turned their mounts away from the dispersing gathering, and headed back toward the Vale just as the full moon appeared above the trees, gilding their path with silver.

"I don't think you would have," Nightwind said, after a long silence that took them right to the edge of the night-darkened forest. "But don't feel ashamed that they made you feel as if you were going to." Now Keisha heard the smile in her voice. "Parents always know what strings control your heart and soul. After all, they are the ones who tied them there."

Shandi and Karles

Thirteen

This was, of course, not the first time that Darian and Snow-fire had gone scouting an enemy encampment. The easiest way was the path they had chosen—through the treetops. The easiest way was also the safest; getting themselves into a tree near the barbarian encampment, and letting the owls make overflights while they used their owls' eyes to observe. Snowfire sent out both of his birds, but Darian only had Kuari to keep track of. This, of course, meant that Snowfire had twice the work of Darian, but Snowfire might have been happier if Darian hadn't insisted on coming along in the first place.

He had only agreed because they had a limited time to work in, and needed as much information as they could get.

Darian put his back up against the curiously smooth bark of his tree, and concentrated on the noncombatants, the women, girls, and young children, who were gathered around their own fire. Snowfire sent Huur and Hweel to single out those who seemed the most important in the clan, and to look for a shaman or mage. Darian didn't know what Snow-fire was seeing, but from his point of view, much as he hated to admit it, these people were nothing like the arrogant bar-barians of years ago.

As Kuari actually perched no more than a few feet above the heads of a gathering of women and children, he took note of a wealth of details through the owl's sight. For instance, there was one decoration repeated over and over in their clothing and ornaments—a cat. It was some sort of great hunting-cat, and the colors it was portrayed in were whites, grays, and blacks, giving it a ghostlike appearance. Decorations included stylized cats in profile in every conceivable position, cat faces, cat eyes, and cat paw-prints. As ornaments, he counted cat furs, cat teeth, cat skulls, and cat claws. This, then, was probably their totemic animal.

So much for the decorations of their lives. Now for the substance.

In this much, this batch of barbarians was similar to the last—the sexes were strictly segregated. Women, girls, and small children below the age of puberty grouped around one campfire, sharing one meal, the adult males crowded around another, sharing a different meal, with more of the choice cuts of meat. Snowfire was concentrating on the adult males, so Kuari and Darian ignored them.

Whatever dinner the women had was long since eaten, though the men were still chewing away; the only signs of it were the cracked and gnawed bones in the fire, the two pots filled with coals to burn out the residue of food left in them. One thing did surprise him. The women did not seem particularly cowed or slavish; they chattered among themselves, scolded rowdy children, sewed hides into articles of clothing or decorated the finished clothing. If this isolation was an indication that they were considered inferior creatures by the men, there was no sign that they were kept that way with beatings and brutality.

As Kel had reported, though, there were several people, mostly children, who seemed afflicted with a curious paralysis or wasting disease. These victims lay quietly on furs beside the fire, occasionally rubbing emaciated limbs as if to ease a constant ache. An arm might be afflicted, or a leg— never both legs or both arms.

On the other hand, how could a child survive long with such a profound affliction in a nomadic clan? Even in Valdemar, people with paralysis had difficulty in simply staying alive. He had the sense, gained mostly from the way that women would look at the afflicted children and sigh, that there had been other children who had been stricken worse than these—and had not survived.

He gleaned all he could, noting that not all the women were making or decorating new garments. Some were working on weapons, fletching arrows, fitting heads to spears. Yes, those things could be used for hunting, but they could also be used for war. Just how many spears and arrows did the tribe need for hunting, anyway? *A nomad tribe can't afford to carry much; why make so many weapons when there are hectares of raw materials all around them?* He could understand stockpiling spear tips, arrowheads, but not whole weapons. Spears in particular were clumsy and hard to transport for people who had no wagons; why bother making entire bundles of extras?

Because they expect conflict, that's why. Can't stop to fletch arrows or fit a point to a shaft in the middle of a fight.

Finally he figured he had gleaned as much information as he could from simple observation, and called Kuari back in. As the great eagle-owl landed on the limb beside him, a huge branch wide enough for two people to walk side-by-side on it, he looked over to the next branch to see how Snowfire progressed. Huur was already there, sitting quietly beside her bondmate, and from the look of it, Hweel would not be far behind. Darian began carefully stretching muscles and getting ready to move out.

It wasn't long before Snowfire whistled the quiet signal that meant it was time to retreat, and Darian followed the scout's lead through the upper limbs of the trees, moving along the branches of the great trees as surely and silently as if they traveled forest paths. Where limbs crossed, they used their climbing staffs to hook the branch of the next tree, either to pull themselves up, or lower themselves down. Even in Valdemar, Snowfire had drilled his "younger brother" in this tree-walking, and no matter that the trees there were no more than a tenth of the size of those in the Pelagiris. A Hawkbrother was as at home in a tree as any Valdemaran was on the ground. That was the real secret of their ability to move invisibly through the Forest, though to Valdemarans it might as well have been magic.

They didn't descend to the earth again until they were far from the encampment. Two *dyheli* waited impatiently in a clearing to carry them further toward safety. With the moon on the wane, the *dyheli* were only moving shadows below to Darian's eyes, but to Kuari's, the thick darkness made no difference. With Kuari to guide him, Darian followed Snow-fire down to the ground; the *dyheli* (not Tyrsell, but a swift runner all the same) was at his side as his feet touched the moss. Faster than thought, Darian was in the saddle, and the *dyheli* bounded away, no more than a pace or two behind his herdmate.

There was neither the time nor the leisure for either of them to talk, not with the *dyheli* at full gallop. Darian hung on, most of his attention with Kuari, who scouted the back-trail, watchfully making certain that barbarians had not somehow detected them. Huur and Hweel scouted ahead, serving as their guides as the moon set and the darkness thickened further.

Darian had made so many similar rides in the last four years that his senses were keenly attuned to the signals that meant *real* danger. He no longer started, hand to weapon, at every little sound. The farther they got from the encamp-ment, the more he relaxed—insofar as it was possible to do so. The mission had only begun; it would be a very long night before it was over.

We got away with our spy-out; that's a decent omen. So far, so good.

The war council wasn't waiting for their report in the Vale. Tonight was *the* night of confrontation, and the barbarians weren't as close to the allies as *that*. Their own war band had an encampment of their own, near enough for an effective strike at the barbarians, but hopefully far enough away that the barbarian scouts wouldn't detect *them*.

The *dyheli* slowed to a walk as they neared the periphery of the camp. With Darian just a pace behind him, Snowfire an-swered three low-voiced challenges before the *dyheli* brought them to a shallow cave in the hillside facing away from the barbarians, and into a circle of firelight reflecting off faces that looked up at their approach. This cave was the only spot safe enough for a fire and offering enough privacy for the war council.

Once they were out of the saddle and settled in among the rest, taking seats cross-legged on the soft sand floor, Darian reported his findings first. Snowfire listened as intently as the others, although, except for the identification of the clan-totem, there wasn't much real information there. "I'm sorry I can't tell you more," Darien ended, on a note of apology. "But at some point we've *got* to get hold of one of their people—maybe a child—and get their language. There's too much I missed by not understanding their conversation."

Snowfire then made his own report. "I didn't see a mage or a shaman anywhere among thc mcn, nor did I see a special tent, or any of the sort of equipment and paraphernalia that a shaman or mage would require," he said, eliciting a nod from Firesong. "From the little of their speech that I understood, I believe that they call themselves the "Ghost Cat" clan. If what I *heard* is true, they believe their totemic animal actually led them here. I also understood that they are terrified of the ChangeCircles, and will make any detour to pass around them, and that corresponds with what Kel has observed. They don't seem to be aware of the existence of Errold's Grove or k'Valdemar Vale; as far as they are concerned, this is completely unknown, probably empty territory. I saw *some* preparation for fighting, but not what I would expect if they planned a major assault. In my opinion, they are ready to fight, and will if they see the need to attack or defend, but it did not look to me as if they planned to go to war."

Kero nodded, and looked first into Sayvil's eyes, then nodded at Eldan. "Then we should go ahead with our plan. We come in, show superior abilities, and try to awe them. I'll have the Skybolts in place as backup for the contact party, but they won't show their faces unless the contact party has to be rescued. Sound right to everyone else?"

Darian followed Kerowyn's glance around the circle; there was no dissension, but he didn't expect any at this point. After all, they'd been over and over this plan so many times that they had, he hoped, worked any flaws out of it.

"Let's do it," Firesong said. "Before I lose my nerve."

He's joking, Darian thought as they all stood, and shivered. *I wish I could.*

Now it was time for Tyrsell to join the group, but as Firesong's mount, not Darian's. Darian would remain with the Skybolts as advance scout, ready to mount a rescue, should that become necessary. This did not make Darian feel any better; he could not help thinking about all those well-made arrows he'd seen being fletched, and imagining his friends facing a hail of them.

Kerowyn would *not* be with the contact party either; that was Eldan's place. Like Darian, Kero had a different place to fill. She would be with her troops, waiting in hiding, hoping she wouldn't be needed.

She isn't any happier about that than I am. Kerowyn hadn't said anything, certainly hadn't *done* anything, but there was no doubt in Darian's mind that she would gladly have accepted any excuse to get Eldan out of the contact party.

But there were only two Heralds, and Eldan was the diplomat of the two; it was, as he had gently reminded Kerowyn, *his* place to be conspicuous, at least for the moment.

Kelvren, who was so excited by his part in this that his hackles were up, was to be the crowning piece of the display. Whether or not these people were familiar with gryphons from afar, they could never have seen one up close, and to have Kel come swooping in out of the dark would be a considerable shock.

With Eldan and his Companion in the lead, Snowfire and Firesong flanking him riding *dyheli,* and followed by a good-sized escort of mounted Skybolts, the party's size should be enough to surprise the barbarians. Appearing suddenly and unexpectedly out of the night was a time-honored tactic of the Hawkbrothers; it worked as an effective way to intimidate interlopers more often than it failed.

Darian hoped that tonight would not be counted as one of the failures.

Lord Breon had wanted badly to be included as one of the party, and had only been dissuaded from his intention by Kerowyn. The Herald-Captain had pointed out that it was her duty to protect him, not the other way around, then added that she didn't know the territory around Kelmskeep half so well as its Lord; if it came to a running fight, she needed his expertise. So Lord Breon was also going to be an observer, and probably would be fretting inside as much as Kero or Darian.

The darkness was their friend, not the barbarians'. With the aid of the three owls, they moved into position without dis-

turbing the few sentries, much less the sleeping camp. The
barbarian sentries were posted within sight of the dying
campfire anyway, too close to the camp to be an effective
ward against a force like theirs. As Kero arranged her own
fighters, positioning Darian and Kuari as lookouts, the others
moved closer still, just barely out of the barbarians' sight, as
near as they dared.

Darian stayed where Kerowyn had placed him, in another
tree, halfway between her people and the camp. It wasn't
as safe a perch as it might have seemed; one of the things
that the contact party was going to produce was a *lot* of light,
and he would make a tempting and easy target if anyone spotted him.

In a situation like this one, the Gift of Mindspeech was all
the more valuable; everyone knew when everyone else was in
place and ready, with no clumsy signals that might be mis-
heard or not heard at all. Without that warning, he might
have been so startled as to lose his balance when the contact
party made their initial move; as it was, he winced involuntarily when the group revealed their presence.

It must have been a hundred, a thousand times worse for
the barbarians.

For them, there was no warning. In one moment, they slept
peacefully, the forest sounds of crickets and frogs, the occasional bird call, no different than any other night. In the next,
it must have seemed as if the heavens and earth opened up at
once.

With a great flash of light and a corresponding blare of
horns—supplied by Kerowyn's people—the contact party "appeared" out of the dark as if they had suddenly burst through
a Gate or were conjured by some other magical means. With
mage-lights burning fiercely above them, with the owls flying
at head height on either side of the group, they galloped up to
the very edge of the camp. At the last moment, Starfall and
Snowfire held up their hands, and the owls landed neatly on
the gloves. The whole camp was roused, of course, but very
few had the temerity to burst out of their tents, and fewer
still to brandish the weapons they'd seized.

Giving them no time to recover from the first shock, the
second descended from the dark sky—Kelvren, in full panoply,

his wings providing a thunder of his own as he landed in front of Eldan.

Darian had to give the barbarians credit for bravery; they were shaking, as pale as snow and plainly terrified, but they stood their ground.

Yes, but can they stand the third shock?

A deep and angry "voice" shouted inside Darian's head—and in the heads of every other creature present that hadn't shielded against it. Darian had put up just enough of a shield to keep the voice from being painful, but he wanted to hear what Tyrsell said. For this was Tyrsell's contribution, his ability to Mindspeak to anyone and anything, and if the barbarians weren't familiar with Mindspeech, this might well be the most frightening shock of all.

:Who are you, invaders? How dare you intrude on us?: Tyrsell demanded. *:Why are you here? What excuse have you for invading our lands, stealing our game, devouring our grazing? Why should we not destroy you at this moment, and leave your bones to lie in the dust as a warning to others?:*

There was no telling how the barbarians would take this—how they would even "hear" it and interpret it—but this was the best that any of them could come up with, providing equal parts of threat, intimidation, and opportunity for explanation. Firesong produced appropriate stage-dressing as Tyrsell Mindspoke, sending up fountains of light on either side, as his firebird made a similar entrance to Kelvren's. Aya plunged down from the treetops, showering false sparks as he flew, then coming in to land on Firesong's outstretched hand.

Darian held his breath, watching the barbarians for dangerous behavior. When it was apparent that the contact party was waiting for an answer—waiting *angrily*, but still waiting and holding their hand—people ventured from tents, milled around a little, talking nervously, then centered all their activity on three men in particular.

As the contact party continued to wait, standing as rigid and unmoving as a group of statues, those three men walked cautiously to the edge of the camp, clutching their weapons.

No eclipse-amulets! That was something Darian had been

watching for particularly—the mage (or shaman) who had led the first barbarian invasion had worn one, and Darian had gotten the impression that it was worn by the leaders of a rather nasty magical cult, even by barbarian standards. If he'd gotten even a glimpse of another one like it, *he* was going to call a retreat!

But no; the three leaders—a wiry man with grizzled hair and beard, and two younger, much more muscular fellows— had donned quite a bit of jangling jewelry before they ventured forward, but anything like an amulet was cat-headed or cat-shaped.

The one with the gray hair spoke loudly and slowly, with a great many gestures that didn't mean anything to Darian. Meanwhile, the other two shook rattles and brandished, not weapons, but brightly painted rawhide shields.

:He asks if we are demons of the darkness, and if we are, says that the other two are powerful shamans who will drive us away.: There was no doubt of Tyrsell's grim amusement with this situation. *:Firesong, why don't you be your theatrical self while I answer him?:*

Firesong raised Aya over his head while Tyrsell stepped up beside Kelvren. The firebird threw off a veritable waterfall of false sparks, which rained down on his bondmate, as Firesong conjured another mage-light in the palm of his other hand.

:Fools! Demons of the darkness shun the light, not court it!: Tyrsell "shouted" contemptuously. *:We are the keepers and guardians of this land, and we demand that you answer to us for your invasion!:*

Nervously, the two would-be shamans dropped their painted shields as ineffective, and took up spears instead. The leader, however, waved them back, and addressed the party again.

:He says that if we are not demons, then he demands that we meet him in daylight.: Now Tyrsell's mind-voice held a grudging admiration. *:Pretty brave fellow, to stand up to us like this.:*

Whatever the answer was from the contact party, Darian didn't hear it; he only got Tyrsell's third (and final) announcement.

:Because we are just, we give you leave to defend your

actions, and time to choose your words with care,: Tyrsell said sternly. *:Look for us by dawnlight.:*

The party backed up, one slow step at a time—then there was another explosion of purposefully blinding light and blare of horns—and when silence and darkness descended again, the party had "vanished." At least, they had as far as the barbarians were concerned.

In actual fact, of course, they simply rode or flew away, but with their eyes dazzled and ears ringing, the barbarians wouldn't have seen that.

Darian waited until the allies were safely behind the Skybolts' lines before making his own move—which was to return to the barbarian camp to see if he could make out what their reaction was.

Although he couldn't understand a word they said, some things were clear enough. The children and most of the women were absolutely terrified, but not all. Several hardy souls among the women rallied—and railed at—their more timid sisters, suggesting to Darian that the older ones had seen magic before and knew the difference between show and substance.

And they aren't afraid of magic, which means . . . what? That it's never been used successfully against them?

Among the men, only the younger ones were cowed; virtually all the males of Darian's age and older had gotten over their shock and gathered around the three leaders, deep in a council of their own. And once the hardier women had calmed the rest, *they* joined the council circle as well!

It was possible for Darian, watching through Kuari's eyes, to infer some things—most notably, a sense of caution, in the intonations of those who spoke, in the postures of those who listened. Finally he decided that he had seen and heard enough, and retreated behind his own lines.

"They're not as scared as we'd like," he reported, as he dropped down out of the tree into the midst of his own war council.

"But not aggressive either?" Kero asked quickly.

"Not aggressive, at least not at the moment," Darian confirmed. "They've seen showy magic before, I'd bet on it."

"On to the next phase, then," Snowfire said. "We approach at dawn, and see what they have to say for themselves." He looked up at the tree branches above his head. "Dawn isn't that far off; we won't have long to wait."

In the mist and still, pale gray of dawn, the contact group approached the barbarian camp once again—this time without the lights and noise. They stopped a bit further away, however, just out of arrow-shot range, where Kelven joined them.

A cautious deputation approached from the encampment, but not immediately. From the haggard faces and dark-circled eyes, it appeared that the barbarians had gotten no more sleep than the allies. Once again, Darian was in the tree branches, but hidden better this time, and without Kuari. The eagle-owls had no advantage during daylight, except for show; Darian was here to satisfy his own restlessness, not as a primary scout. That duty had gone to Wintersky, Ravenwing, and their bondbirds.

It appeared that at least they were going to be treated as important enough for the barbarians to put on their best finery, for the deputation jingled and clattered with every approaching step. *In their own way, they are impressive,* he thought, peering through his screen of leaves. The oldest man—possibly the chieftain—had donned a fur cloak of the pelt of a huge cat, with the fully preserved head of its original owner acting as the hood. Their leather tunics and breeks were as well-constructed as Tayledras scout gear, and though they jangled with amulets and jewelry, and their decorations were a bit garish for Darian's taste, they were no worse than the Shin'a'in, who had never seen a color they didn't love. But they weren't wearing armor, and there was still no sign of that eclipse-amulet Darian recalled only too well. Unless they were supposed to be sacrificial lambs, they weren't expecting to meet with physical force in this parley.

This time, the allies intended to wait for the barbarians to speak first, so they waited with expressionless faces, still mounted, as the strangers approached. They, in their turn, stopped well short of the contact party; the leader cleared his throat ostentatiously when no one spoke, mind-to-mind or otherwise, and began what sounded, from the measured cadences, like a prepared speech.

:This is the Clan of the Ghost Cat,: Tyrsell interpreted, and with that name, images—of a huge, fierce, and reclusive predator, and of something else, a fleeting shadow by day, a call in the night, a trusted presence that guided. . . . *:They claim their totem animal led them here, and by that sign from their gods, they say it is their right to stay. I must admit, as a defense, it has the benefit of being unique and probably unprovable.:*

After a pause to confer, Tyrsell replied. *:Whether or not that is true, you are in* our *land, where* our *gods hold sway, and* our *laws decree the measure of what is and is not to be.:*

This time the leader went on at some length, with many broad and flamboyant gestures. *:He wants to know by what right we claim this land; says that there are no boundary markers, no claiming poles to show that we speak the truth. If* this *land was ever settled by the hole-dwelling people and diggers-of-dirt—that is us, by the way—it has been abandoned for decades and should belong to anyone for the taking.:* The leader's voice grew bolder, possibly because the contact-party hadn't struck him down. *:He has no idea that it is me doing the talking, by the way. He thinks it is either Firesong or Starfall. Kelvren impresses him, but he thinks Kel is something we've tamed.:*

Kel remained unruffled, fixing the speaker with his unblinking gaze.

:Now he tells us how huge and strong his clan is, how many warriors they have, how many battles they fought.: Tyrsell paused a moment. *:This is partly a bluff; something— a disease—drove them out of their own lands, and they ran rather than face a foe they had no hope of beating.:*

This time Darian heard Starfall's reply. *:Tell him his own numbers,:* the mage said, with grim humor. *:Let's see how he reacts to the fact that we know his strength down to the last baby.:*

Tyrsell did just that, and Darian had the satisfaction of seeing the barbarian leader shaken. But he recovered quickly, and spoke again. *:Now he says that we should know that* *even the babies of his Clan are fighters, that if we come against them and try to force them out of the place their totem has brought them to, even the babies will take up bows and swords and slay our men.:* Tyrsell pawed the ground, roused in spite of himself. *:There's no doubt; he means to stay, and he'll make it cost us dearly to be rid of him. His people are desperate, and that's dangerous.:*

Darian hadn't needed that last admonition; he knew for himself just how dangerous a desperate person was.

:We do not need to use the spear or the sword to rid ourselves of pests,: Tyrsell replied loftily, and Darian sensed Firesong's hand in his phrasing. *:As any should know who once had the misfortune to dare the Killing Trees of the north. We had hoped that the foolishly bold and suicidal had learned to keep a wary distance from our lands by now.:*

The leader barked an artificial laugh, and made his counter. *:He says that the so-called Killing Trees did not prevent his passage, and implies that this means his magic is stronger than ours.:*

There was a stirring in the distance, and for a single moment, Kero's troops showed themselves before blending back into the shadows and undergrowth. This *did* affect the barbarian leader; he had not gotten long enough to count heads, for Kero had timed the moment so that all he had was an impression—an impression of great numbers.

:You managed to avoid the Killing Trees by passing to the west, and your boast is hollow as an old reed. Magic is not our only weapon,: Tyrsell said with great boredom, *:It is only the easiest to use.:*

The leader remained silent now, as his underlings whispered urgently in his ear.

Tyrsell did not wait for them to formulate a reply, not when the negotiations had just turned in the favor of the allies. *:Here are our fighters, our magic, and our gods barring your way—but we are a generous people, and compassionate to those who are willing to serve. These lands have no current tenant, it is true; what have you to offer us in return for leave to remain?:*

If anything, that startled the leader even more than the presence of the troops. His posture full of confusion, he made an abrupt gesture, spoke a few words, and retreated with his party.

:He wants to go discuss this with his people,: Tyrsell said uneccessarily.

Back in camp, with Wintersky spying on the barbarians and Kero's sentries keeping careful watch, Tyrsell gave them a fuller account of what he had read in the barbarians' thoughts.

Darian fought back a yawn, clamping his jaws on it. It seemed an eternity since the last time he'd slept, and with his excitement and fear wearing off, he felt a bit light-headed with weariness.

:You all know, of course, that without taking his mind in such a way that he would know *I had done so, I could only read what came to the surface of his mind?:* Tyrsell began, as a preamble.

"If we didn't before, we do now," Kero replied logically. "So, what information came along with those surface thoughts?"

:This Ghost Cat—I am forced to believe it is either a very powerful hallucination, or it is very real.: Tyrsell shook his head in irritation as a fly buzzed around his ears. Darian fought another yawn. *:I am* quite *serious; and I am inclined to think that it would be difficult to hallucinate such a thing during the course of a migration lasting moons.:*

Firesong and his father exchanged sharp glances, and Kero and Eldan did the same. "That puts an interesting kink in our plans," Kerowyn ventured. "But until this Ghost Cat shows itself to me, I'm leaving it out of the calculations for now. What else?"

:The disease I mentioned. The three of us managed to get bits and pieces of the whole story.: Tyrsell sounded proud of himself and his underlings, as well he should be; that would be a difficult proposition to read from the surface thoughts. Darian wondered about this Ghost Cat; Firesong had told him about the two Avatars that helped his friend An'desha—could this Ghost Cat be something like them? And if so, then what did *that* mean for the Tayledras and Valdemar? *:There was a tradition of an annual gathering of clans and septs of clans*

every Midsummer, and the last year it ever took place, it was held in Ghost Cat territory. Just as a matter of caution, they *always avoided Change-Circles, but as we know, other clans don't. Someone from Blood Bear Clan found a Circle and went into it—and came out with more than he'd expected.:*

"The disease," Snowfire stated, without surprise. "We were afraid something like this would happen, and we took precautions against it—"

"Obviously they didn't," Kero said dryly.

:Exactly so. It ran through the assembled clans like a wildfire. They call it "summer fever," since it disappears in winter, though they don't know why.:

"Is this disease the cause of the crippled children?" Snowfire asked.

:It is. It begins as coughing, sneezing, chills and fever, then becomes a wasting disease. It kills more often than not, as the chest muscles waste away and breathing becomes impossible, or as full paralysis sets in and the victim is helpless to keep up; only the very lucky survive.: Tyrsell was uncharacteristically sober; evidently he found the images that had come with that knowledge to be disturbing. *:Usually death from disease comes to the old and weak or the young and helpless. This death does not pick and choose in that way. Enough fighters died in the first sweep that every clan feud was called off, but new outbreaks have occurred every summer since then.:*

Darian wasn't sleepy anymore; whether he was picking up images from Tyrsell, or his own imagination was working hard, but he *had* seen those children lying beside the fire. . . .

"All right, but why come here?" Firesong asked.

:Their shaman was one of the victims, but before he died, he told them that a sign would lead them to a place where they would find healing and an end to the sickness. And after he died, the Ghost Cat appeared, and led them south. That was when their lore-keepers recalled that we of the south reputedly have many powerful Healers.:

"Oh, really?" Eldan's eyebrows rose, and he turned to Starfall. "Was this Cat a revenant, do you think? Or an avatar?"

Great minds follow the same path, Darian thought.

"It could be," Starfall said cautiously. "But we shouldn't discount either. Well, now we know why they avoid Change-Circles."

:*Before he died, their shaman declared that their own gods and magic were helpless against this "plague from outside" and that "they must look outside for help." They aren't down here purely by chance, following the Ghost Cat. They've heard of the Valdemaran-style Healers, as I said, and have come looking for some. Their initial intentions were to kidnap some and coerce them into helping, if they had to.:*

"Huh," Kero snorted. "They don't know Healers very well, do they?"

Darian had to agree with that.

:*However, confronted by our strong force . . . that doesn't seem like too good an idea anymore.:* Tyrsell's sides heaved with an enormous sigh. :*And that is all I can tell you.:*

"I think we'd better bring the Healers in on this," Darian put in, with visions of more crippled children in Errold's Grove. "How do we know *we* won't catch this fever?"

"We don't, and that is a damned good point," Kero responded. She rose—but halfway to her feet, was interrupted.

"Captain! Visitors!" One of the Guards entered the cave and saluted Kerowyn smartly. "Two to see you, urgently, Captain!"

"I didn't send for anyone," Kero began crossly, as she straightened. "And I'm certainly not *expecting* anyone."

"I know you aren't, Captain Kerowyn," said a high, young, female voice. "I came here on my own."

Around the edge of the cave stepped a young woman dressed in Heraldic Trainee Greys, and trailing her was her Companion—who had a distinctly hangdog and guilty look about him. Darian cast a quick glance at Kerowyn's Sayvil, who was glaring at the new Companion with much the same expression that Kero was using with the Trainee.

Darian knew an incipient explosion when he saw one, and he was quite glad that he wasn't standing in the footprints of either the pretty young woman or her Companion.

There was something about the girl that was naggingly familiar to Darian, even though he was certain that he had never seen her in his life.

"I also brought my sister," the girl continued, undaunted. "And since you just now mentioned Healers, I can't help thinking that my premonition was accurate."

She beckoned, and around the same edge of the cave, looking nervous and determined at the same time, stepped Keisha Alder.

Keisha hadn't had a moment to think from the time that Shandi scooped her up until the moment they both intruded on the war council. Much to Keisha's relief, Darian rose and worked his way over to her, and both of them escaped from the council as quickly as they could. The fierce interrogation that Kero was putting Shandi Alder through was also an extremely uncomfortable and public grilling. No less public—though silent—was the similar set of coals that Shandi's Companion was being hauled over by Sayvil.

"Your sister must be crazy. I can't *believe* she ran away from the Collegium," Darian said, shaking his head.

Keisha just sighed. "I can't either—though to give her credit, she didn't exactly run away."

Darian gave her a quizzical look. "So what did she do?"

He found a place for them both to sit. Keisha was only too glad to sink down onto a cool stone and stretch her aching legs out. Riding pillion, even on a Companion, was about as uncomfortable as riding a *dyheli*.

"She bullied them into letting her come back, if you can believe *that*! She said she had some sort of premonition, and since she obviously wouldn't take 'no' for an answer, they gave in!" Keisha thought incredulously about the Shandi who had left Errold's Grove, Shandi the peacemaker, Shandi the gentle, and shook *her* head with disbelief. "I hardly recognized her—"

"Start from the beginning," Darian interrupted. "I want to hear this in sequence."

Keisha took a deep breath, and began at the beginning—just after dawn this morning. "I was in Errold's Grove. Nightwind told me to spend half my time there since I'm supposed to be the on-station Healer now, and I'm supposed to take care of anything that happens to the volunteers, now that most of the other Healers are here with Kerowyn. I'd just checked the camp at morning call for anyone sick—no one was, but I always check—it was just about dawn. Then one of the sentries reported a Herald coming. We expected Eldan, of course, so I stayed to see what had brought him there. Obviously, we thought something might have happened out here. And out of absolutely *nowhere*, up comes Shandi, acting as if she had every right to be there and not at the Collegium where she belongs!" She couldn't keep her indignation to herself; it crept out and colored her last sentence.

Darian cocked his head to one side. "Are you aware of how much you sound like your mother?" he asked dryly.

She flushed. "I suppose I do; well, being someone's big sister tends to make you feel that way. Anyway, she somehow managed to bluff the lieutenant into thinking she had orders to find Herald-Captain Kerowyn. She found out where you all were, and before anyone could question her about anything, she just scooped me up and kidnapped me! She *says* she had a premonition that she and I had to be here for some reason, and that was why the Collegium let her go."

"Do *you* believe her?" Darian asked.

She hugged her knees to her chest, and rested her chin on them. "I don't know," she confessed. "If it was anyone else—but it's hard to think of Shandi as—as having premonitions I'm supposed to believe in." She rubbed the side of her head, easing the ache in her temple. "I mean—Shandi, of all people! She never showed any signs of anything like that before!"

"People often don't, not until they're Chosen anyway," Darian reminded her.

"She says her Gift is ForeSight, but that it isn't properly trained yet, so all she gets is bits and pieces. I just don't know." Keisha rubbed her tired eyes, and wished that this had happened to anyone but her.

"Can you think of any *other* reason why she should come pounding up here?' Darian asked, reasonably. "And can't you think of a lot of reasons why she would avoid doing so if she could?"

Keisha had to smile at that. "Well," she admitted, "now that you mention it. If Mum and Da got word she was here, they'd have a worse fit than they did over my staying. She'd *never* hear the end of it. And as for the Captain—" she shuddered. "—I'd rather die than have to explain something like *this* to Captain Kero."

Darian spread his hands. "There you have it. I'd trust that premonition, personally. Everything she told you sounds perfectly logical to *me*. I don't think her Companion would have gone along with this if she had been making it up, do you?"

Keisha nodded, slowly, and felt a little better. "You're right. You're absolutely right."

The only thing is, she said her premonition involved me. *I don't like the sound of that. . . .*

Darian interrupted her worrisome thoughts. "Now, would *you* like to hear what we've been finding out, since it seems that you're going to be involved?"

Keisha nodded, and when Darian was done, she remained silent, thinking everything he'd told her over carefully. "This Summer Fever," she ventured. "I don't like the sound of it. *It* sounds more dangerous than the barbarians."

"Why?" he asked, puzzled.

"They've had a few years to get used to it—I've never heard of anything like it down here," she told him, feeling a little chill in her heart. "If it got loose here, it could go through *us* like a wildfire."

"We have Healers," he objected. "Surely they can do something first."

"You have to know what you're up against, how it works, before you can fight it," she pointed out. "Otherwise it's like fighting an enemy blindfolded. Sure, you can flail around with a sword and hope you hit something, but you're more likely to get hit yourself first."

He winced. "I see your point."

"That's not all that bothers me, but it's the main thing," she continued, wondering if he would understand how she felt. "I think you aren't going to like this, but I think we have to help them."

As he'd described the children with their withered limbs, she'd felt that old familiar tug, that insistent call to *do* something. The only difference was, now she had the tools to act on that call.

"What do you mean by that?" Darian asked sharply.

"I mean, I'm a Healer now, in everything but the robes. It's part of the vow. I *have* to help where there's need, and you can't deny that these people need help!" She watched him closely, begging with her eyes for his understanding. "Don't you see? That's why Healers are what we are. We don't take sides, we just help, no matter what!"

She watched strong emotions flit over his expression, watched him fight down an immediate retort and give his anger a little time to cool. "I know it sounds crazy, even disloyal, but you can ask any of the others, and they'll tell you the same," she said softly.

"I don't doubt you," he said brusquely, "But *I* think it's madness." He smiled crookedly. "Maybe that's why I'm not a Healer. Still . . . you did say that in order to deal with this sickness, you have to know what it is you're fighting and how to combat it, right?"

She nodded.

"And *I've* never heard of a fever or a plague that would stay politely in one place or attack only certain people—no matter what some priests would claim. So if you're going to be able to battle it when it finally decides to jump to *our* side, I'd rather you did your flailing around on patients that aren't Tayledras or Valdemaran." He turned his hands palm-upward and shrugged. "Chauvinistic of me, but there it is."

"It's a point," she agreed, relieved that he had conceded the potential conflict. She already had the germ of an idea in her head, but for it to succeed, she would need him. She stood up. "First things first, though. Let's go see if Captain Kero left anything of Shandi. I want to know more about this premonition of hers than she told me on the ride."

Firesong

Fourteen

They spotted Shandi, *sans* Companion, walking toward them through the camp as they returned to the cave. Keisha was glad that the Herald-Captain hadn't significantly damaged her sister; in fact, Shandi was remarkably composed for someone who had just faced the redoubtable Kerowyn on the wrong side of a situation.

Nevertheless, she was clearly glad to see Keisha and Darian, and equally glad to be taken off to Darian's campsite. "Whew!" she said, collapsing on Darian's bedroll and stretching out flat, both eyes closed. "I've faced off against Cap'n Kerowyn with a weapon, and I *never* wanted to do that again, but getting a dressing-down from her is a hundred times worse!" She opened one eye and looked up at both of them. "Whose bed am I taking up anyway? Yours? You're Darian, the half-Hawkbrother, I presume?"

"Right on both counts," Darian said, his mind still clearly elsewhere, but his tone quite cool and unimpressed with Shandi's casual attitude. "And I presume that the Herald-Captain has informed you just how dangerous this situation is that you've casually barged into without so much as a 'by your leave'?"

Keisha was astonished; she had *never* heard a young man take that tone with her sister! They usually couldn't keep themselves from near-servility, but Darian had just done a little dressing-down himself, had come within a hair of sounding *angry* with her, quite as if she were his little sister and not Keisha's! There was no doubt that the comment was intended as a rebuke, and Keisha hadn't *ever* heard a young man rebuke her sister since Shandi had turned ten!

Shandi sat straight up, also taken aback by Darian's tone. "She did," she replied, nettled. "She also gave me leave to remain, on the basis of my premonition and the Collegium's acceptance of it, as long as I understood I was under her orders, absolutely and without exception or excuses."

Darian leveled a look at the Trainee that was just as severe as Kerowyn would have wanted. "She means it, and we'll back it," he told her flatly. "If you're ordered out of here, you *will* go, even if I have to knock you out and tie you onto that Companion of yours. And don't think you can hide somewhere if you're ordered out either; you can't hide from the eyes of our birds or the noses of our *kyree*, no matter where you go or how cleverly you think you can conceal yourself."

"I've no intention of disobeying orders!" Shandi snapped back, eyes flashing and her temper beginning to show. Keisha stepped in before it turned into a quarrel.

"I've got to know more about this premonition," she said earnestly. "You didn't give me anything to make any kind of judgment on."

"I don't have that much myself," Shandi replied in irritation, still annoyed with Darian and giving him a dagger-laden glare. "All I got was a few flashes and a feeling—a flash of me, one of you, one of *him*, though I didn't know who he was at the time, and a very, very strong feeling that I had to be where the Captain was, so strong that I was halfway to Companion's Field to get Karles before I came to my senses. That's it."

"That's *all*?" Darian asked incredulously. "And on that basis the Collegium gave you leave to come to a battle zone? Are they crazed?"

"So far I've had a grand total of four days of training in my Gift," Shandi said tartly. "It's not exactly under my control, all right? I have to make do with what I get. It was good enough for the Senior Herald at the Collegium."

"Now why am I so certain that the Senior Herald at the Collegium didn't even know that we'd contacted the barbarians yet?" Darian shook his head in disbelief, but didn't challenge her any further, which made Keisha grateful. Shandi didn't lose her temper often—at least, the Shandi *she* knew didn't—but when she did, the results were often spectacular. At the moment, that was one spectacle she'd prefer not to witness.

Darian took a deep breath, closed his eyes a moment (probably counting to ten, or invoking patience), and then opened them again. "You're probably tired," he said. "You must have ridden like a madwoman to get here as quickly as you did. Why don't you get some sleep while I make sure someone gets a billet set up somewhere else for me? A bed's a bed, and I don't care where I sleep."

Shandi heaved a great sigh and lay down again. "Thanks. Sorry to be so sharp—I am pretty tired—"

She closed her eyes, and didn't so much fall asleep as pass out; she did it so quickly that Keisha realized she must have gone without sleeping—except in the saddle—for her entire journey. Darian obviously realized it, too; he managed a little smile, and took Keisha by the elbow, leading her silently away through the rows of tents.

"You're the only one of us that looks like she got any sleep last night," he observed, when they were out of earshot.

"I probably am," she replied, noting with concern the deep shadows under *his* eyes. "That was awfully good of you, to give up your bedroll to her."

He waved the compliment aside. "It's just a bedroll, the *hertasi* can move my things elsewhere, and they will as soon as I— Heyla!" He interrupted himself, as a *hertasi* poked its snout out of a larger tent. It waited expectantly while he hissed something at it, bobbed its head, and ran off.

"There," he said with satisfaction. "I've got *myself* a new bunk with Wintersky, and *you* one with the Healers—which I'd better take you to, so you can all get your heads together over this Summer Fever thing."

"Thank you," she replied, feeling more confident than she had since Shandi carried her off this morning. "Maybe I'm wrong, but it seems more important to *me* than the barbarians fighting with us."

"And maybe you're right," was Darian's thoughtful reply. "After all, there's always the tactic of bottling them up in their camp and starving them into submission, but a line of fighters isn't going to keep a plague inside their pickets.

Listen, I hope you weren't offended by the way I treated your sister, but—well—" He scratched his head, then shrugged. "I'm not impressed. She strikes me as used to getting her own way a lot, pretty immature, actually. Honestly, she hasn't half the brains and good sense you have."

"She's probably so tired that half her brains aren't working," Keisha pointed out. "Besides, she's not used to boys who treat her like—like—"

"Like a brat who's getting away with something she shouldn't?" Darian offered, with a half smile. "Like a spoiled village princess who expects fellows to melt just because she looks at them with those sweet, brown doe-eyes? Oh, please!"

Keisha was so surprised by his answer that she simply stared at him for a moment. "Well—she *is* so very pretty—"

"Not prettier than you," Darian said bluntly. "And you have a great deal more than being pretty, if you'll pardon my saying so. A Hawkbrother could turn a mud-doll into a beauty; we aren't that impressed by prettiness alone." For all his bluntness, he started to blush as he said that, and looked quickly away as she continued to stare at him in further astonishment.

"Right, *here's* the Healers' tent," he said quickly, waving at the large tent pitched at the end of the path they were on. "You go right on up. The *hertasi* will have told them you're coming. I'll find Wintersky's billet and get a nap myself, before something else happens."

Still blushing, he left her and made a sharp turn to the right, as she watched him hurry away with bemusement.

Then she shook herself into sense, and made straight for the Healers' tent and business. Granted, it was entirely a new and rather delightful feeling to have a young man tell *her* she was pretty, and blush over her, but this was neither the time nor the place to get moonstruck.

When she got within earshot of the tent, she heard the debate already going on inside; she pushed open the flap, and was greeted immediately.

"Keisha!" Nala called with relief. "Good, we need all the minds on this that we can get! What do *you* know about this wasting disease?"

The Healers had arranged themselves in a rough circle in the middle of the large infirmary tent—which at the moment had no patients in it. Nala and her apprentices squeezed over on the bench they were using, and Keisha took her place beside them. She detailed everything that Darian had told her, and then added, "Tyrsell the king-stag is the one who had direct contact with the chieftain's mind; would you like him to come give us everything *he* got?"

"That would be extremely helpful," Gentian said thoughtfully, not at all disturbed by the notion of having the *dyheli* dump a basketload of mental images directly into his mind.

Keisha turned in time to see a *hertasi* coming into the tent with what must be *her* bedroll. In Tayledras, she asked it if Tyrsell could be invited to the tent, and why.

"Easily done, Healer," it answered, with a bow of profoundest respect, and left the bedroll on the tent floor to answer her request personally.

"I believe that we must assume that this illness is both contagious and a grave danger to us," Nala said, as Keisha turned her attention back to the group. "Remember the description, that it first went through the barbarians like a wildfire? *Now* we can expect them to have built up some immunity, but we have no such protection at this point."

Grenthan mopped his brow and the back of his neck with a kerchief. "You surely know what the villagers and even Lord Breon would insist on, if we let it be known that we consider it very dangerous," Grenthan said reluctantly. "They'd want us to surround the camp and burn them and it down to the ground."

"That's unacceptable!" Gentian snapped, rounding on his fellow Healer as if Grenthan were an enemy. "We cannot condone anything of the kind!"

"I *don't* advocate that," Grenthan protested, his hands up as if to ward off a blow. "I'm just telling you what Lord Breon would say!"

"But we have no cure, no treatment," Nala pointed out. "We don't even know what we're facing. Where does the Oath put us? Are we to serve everyone, or the greatest good? Are we to try to save outsiders at the possible expense of unleashing a plague on thousands of our own, innocent people?"

"I don't think that there is any doubt that we are to serve everyone, friend and enemy alike; the Oath is crystal clear on that point," Gentian replied stiffly. "I can't imagine how you could interpret it otherwise."

"You can't serve *anyone* if you're all dead," Keisha said slowly, and shook her head. "We don't even know how this thing spreads. You could all be infected by now; for all we know, Eldan and the rest brought it back with them from their parley, and it's only a matter of time before we all get it."

Instantly, their faces all went blank; she waited while they searched within themselves for signs of infection of any kind. It didn't take very long, they were so used to doing so, and the looks of relief told her that at least *that* fear was groundless.

"So it isn't instantly contagious. Still—" She let the sentence hang in the air, not needing to add, "it could have been." She let the thought sink in, then continued. "I can't see how we have the right to expose our own folk just so we can treat these strangers."

"We won't get anywhere by *not* treating it," Nala said, at last. "The question is, *how?* From what you told us, these barbarians would welcome us if we just marched straight into their village!"

"And they might equally slit our throats if we couldn't provide instant cures," Grenthan countered, fanning himself with his sleeve, as the air inside the tent became close and warm. "Yes, I agree, we must act, but I don't relish the notion of putting myself so completely at their mercy, which might well be nonexistent. Look, I *do* agree with the Oath in principle, but I have serious reservations about applying it to a pack of folk who eat their meat raw!"

At that moment, the *hertasi* returned, with Tyrsell at its side. Keisha quickly explained what she wanted, and the king-stag readily agreed.

:Do brace yourselves, please,: the *dyheli* said calmly. :You are unused to this, and it will be something of a shock to your minds.:

The experience wasn't anywhere near as traumatic as getting the Hawkbrother language, but the "lump" of memory-images hit each of them with a palpable impact, much as if they'd been struck by a stone, leaving them reeling for a moment. Keisha managed to stammer thanks; Tyrsell nodded gravely in return and left the tent without a word, giving them all the peace to sort out the jumble of sights and sounds, emotions and visceral sensations that came with the memory fragments.

The three experienced Healers actually sorted things through a lot faster than Keisha would have thought, possibly because they were all used to sorting through the chaos of a battlefield. Of the six Healer Trainees, three felt unwell and had to go lie down, and the other three sat blinking owlishly and a little stunned during the rest of the discussion. Keisha had been ready for the experience, and was the first to recover, waiting for the rest to make what they could of what they'd been given.

"This definitely isn't anything we've seen before," Grenthan acknowledged. "At a guess, it spreads through direct contact, the way a cold does."

"I think it might be less contagious than a cold," Nala added thoughtfully. "Otherwise, everyone would have been struck down when it first appeared. And I think that low temperatures, winter-chill, probably kills it, or at least makes it dormant—after all, these people spend their winters in tents in a chillier climate than we have—did any of you get that memory? Of the way they go from fall to spring without ever once getting out of their fur clothing, not even to couple? They must smell to high heaven, but that might be why they don't catch the disease in winter. It can't spread through the frigid air, and there's nothing I'd call physical contact during the cold moons. It could spread through flea-bite, I suppose. Fleas hibernate, when the cold doesn't outright kill them."

"I did get those memories," Gentian seconded, and shuddered. "The cleanliness of these people leaves a great deal to be desired, at least in winter."

"Well, given how cold it gets, I can't see that I blame them," Grenthan said diplomatically. "It's also beside the point, which is the question of what we are to do."

"I'll tell you what you *won't* be doing," said a wrathful

voice from the open tent flap. "You *won't* be marching into a barbarian village, giving aid and comfort to plague carriers, not while *I'm* in command here!"

Kerowyn strode into the center of their circle, and glared at all of them with impartial impatience. "What's more, if any of you try, I'll personally have you bound hand and foot and tied to a tree to prevent you from going anywhere! Dear gods, *why* am I being saddled with a wagonload of idiots? Where is your *sense*? Where is your loyalty?"

"Our loyalty is to our Oath, as it *should* be," shouted Gentian, who had gone red in the face with anger as Kerowyn spoke. "Captain, I might remind you that it was a Healer who stuck to *his* Oath many years ago who kept you from becoming a cripple!"

"Healers don't take sides," Nala seconded, with a little less volume, but no less force, and a glare just as fierce as Kerowyn's. "That's the Oath, and a good thing, too!"

"Damn you, people, what about the rest of us?" Kerowyn shouted right back, her eyes so cold with rage that they sent chills down Keisha's spine. "Just what are we going to do if you all get sick and die, and the barbarians decide to make a fight of it anyway? What are we supposed to do if they decide you aren't trying hard enough to cure them, and figure to encourage you with a bit of creative torture? Or slit your throats, because you couldn't help the ones already crippled?"

"What idiot would assume *all* of us would go into the camp?" Grenthan countered with derision. "Great Lord, since when have Healers *ever* abandoned a post they'd been assigned to?"

"The same idiot who heard you discussing just that would naturally make that assumption," Kerowyn snarled right back.

"*Whoa!*" Keisha shouted, jumping to her feet, and bringing the entire shouting match to a halt. When they all turned to stare at her, she fought down the impulse to run out of the tent, swallowed, and sat down.

"We can't go into the camp, Herald-Captain," she said in a more normal tone of voice. "We'd already decided that. We don't know these people or what they'll do, we don't know their language, customs or superstitions, and we have no way of predicting anything *they* might assume. All we *do* know is that they have legends of Healers, and as we are aware, legends are difficult things to live up to."

"Not to mention that not even an idiot puts himself completely into the hands of people who already considered kidnapping and coercion," Gentian said gruffly. "Cap'n Kero, some of us have been with you for a very long time, and the very last thing we'd do is leave you in the lurch. What we *do* agree on is that our Oath demands that we try to help these folk, and that the Oath comes first, even before our loyalties. And *you* wouldn't have it any other way. There've been plenty of your people who've been cared for by the Healers on the side opposite yours, and you know it."

"The other thing we agree on is that this disease is enough of a danger to Valdemar that we don't dare ignore it and hope it sticks to the barbarians," Nala said stiffly. "Whether you like it or not, we *can't* leave until we've found a treatment, and we can't do that without treating the barbarians."

"Even burning the camp and its occupants might not stop it," Keisha put in, softly but shrewdly. "Since we don't know how it spreads at all, some of the biting insects might well be carrying it now, and it will be only a matter of time before it spreads to us. We really do have to find a cure, or at least a palliative."

Kerowyn looked very sour indeed, but conceded their points. "Just promise me that you won't do anything until after you've consulted me," she added, with a look that told Keisha that if they didn't agree, she would follow through on the threat to truss them up like dinnertime fowls.

She got that promise—from everyone but Keisha, and Keisha could hardly believe it when she didn't seem to notice the omission.

"I hope it spreads by fleas," sighed Nala when Kerowyn had left. "Dear and gracious gods, I *hope* it spreads by fleas, the way Boil-Plague does. Fleas, we can do something about, but who can stop the air from flowing?"

Keisha got up for a moment and took a quick peek outside the tent. Then she returned, as the others watched her curiously. "I actually have an idea," she said diffidently. "If you want to hear it."

"Go right ahead," Gentian urged. "At the moment, we're dry."

"If we could get the barbarians to send one of the sick people *out*, one of us could go into quarantine with the sick person. That way no one would be at risk except a single Healer." She swallowed, then continued. "I figured I'm probably the best one to do that; you can't send an apprentice, and you know that. You all say I have a really strong Gift, you all agree that I'm as good as any of you with herbs and medicines. I'm the obvious choice because I'm the easiest one to replace."

That started another argument entirely, with all three of them coming up with whatever they could think of to deter her from any such idea. The strongest argument against her plan was that she didn't have experience in using her Gift, especially not against something deadly. "Oh, I agree that you've done very well so far," Gentian half-scolded, "but that was against tiny infections, colds, belly-aches! Not against a fatal illness, not against something no one has ever seen before!"

Keisha shrugged, pretending indifference. "Diseases work the same whether they're mild or serious," she pointed out. "A tiny infection and a rotting limb are the same. It's just a matter of degree."

"The idea does have merit, though," Nala said, after keeping her own counsel while the others argued. "It would keep infection from spreading to the rest, and it would keep the Healer out of the hands of the barbarians. I'd be willing to try treatment on that basis. I've survived plenty of plagues before this; what's one more?"

"And just how are we going to get a volunteer barbarian?" Grenthan asked shrewdly.

"We could ask?" Keisha suggested timidly.

No one laughed at her, although she more than half expected them to.

"Well, the barbarians have obliged me by falling in with my second choice of tactics," Kerowyn sighed, as Darian belatedly scrambled into his place in the council-circle, feeling much better for a good, long sleep. "Your Hawkbrother scouts reported that they were building up walls around their camp and fortifying them; I sent a deputation out to them to see what they'd do. They *didn't* meet my people with arrows, but they also didn't show so much as the tips of their noses."

"Grand," groaned Lord Breon. "We've frightened them, and now they aren't going to move one way *or* the other."

"Not without a visitation from their miraculous Ghost Cat, is my guess," Kerowyn agreed, and ran her hand along the top of her hair. She cast a speculative eye at Firesong, who shook his head.

"Don't even start on what you're thinking," he warned. "I wouldn't create a Ghost Cat illusion for *anyone* under circumstances like this. Firstly, *I* don't know how it's expected to behave, and secondly, what if it *is* an Avatar? Are you willing to risk the anger of a god? I'm not! Not even one who's working outside his own lands!"

"It was a thought," she replied wistfully.

"A bad one," he countered, leaving no room for further argument. "Why don't you just set up a siege and hold them in place until they give up and surrender?"

"They do have to eat, so they are going to come out at some point, but a siege under these conditions is far from ideal," she responded. "It certainly wasn't what I had in mind. And only their gods know what they're planning in there; it could be anything. Remember, only a third of our troops have seen combat. *All* of theirs have."

There's that sickness of theirs, too; what if part of their plan is to somehow spread it to us? What are we going to do then? Darian was worried, and he wasn't the only one, for he heard Lord Breon confide to Eldan in a whisper, "I wish I could just pour oil on that entire nest of vipers and burn them out."

"Perhaps we're pushing them too hard," Eldan said aloud, in reasoned, measured tones. "After all, these people have been through a very great shock in meeting us; they've had their lives threatened, and they've seen that we have animal spirits of our own. We meant to intimidate them; we may actually have intimidated them so completely that they feel they are in a corner. What we should do, I think, is to give them time. We need to cultivate patience in dealing with them. In fact, I think we ought to pull back all our visible troops, and leave only the birds as sentries." He smiled thinly. "They've seen that we have birds who might well be totemic spirits with us; the birds standing sentry alone should be enough, because now they will never know when a bird is one of ours or just a simple forest creature."

Kerowyn shot him a strange glance, as if she hadn't expected that from him, began to open her mouth, then closed it again, looking very thoughtful. "That's got some merit," she said, after a moment. "What do the rest of you think?"

Darian kept *his* mouth shut; he had an idea of his own, and he wasn't going to broach it. What he didn't reveal, he couldn't be forbidden to undertake.

"Personally, I think that's reasonable," Starfall spoke first. "It's not as if we're under an arbitrary deadline to get this solved. We can afford to be patient with them."

"If they bottle themselves up, their own Summer Fever may solve the problem for us," Snowfire added.

"Harsh," Starfall said, "but true."

"Maybe *you* aren't under a deadline, but I've got Harvesting coming up, and my lady has a wedding planned. She's going to take it poorly if it's got to be delayed because we're playing nursemaid to a lot of greasy, fur-wearing barbarians," Lord Breon muttered, but he made no further objections.

"They've come out of a terrifying situation, and just when they thought themselves safer, were met by more frightening people." Eldan spoke as if he had thought this over already. "If we meet them with mercy, who knows how they will react? They could become the best allies Valdemar has ever had! *Our* ancestors were refugees, just as they are—and who knows, maybe our own forefathers were closer to being greasy fur-wearing barbarians than to us, their descendants." He cast a glance at Lord Breon who had the grace to look a little ashamed. "We have never refused a refugee because he came with a burden of powerful enemies, and even though the enemy this time is a disease, I don't see why that should change our attitude."

"Give them at least three or four days," Firesong urged. "That's my council. Who knows, but maybe they've bottled themselves up to invoke this Cat Spirit of theirs, and if it is the Avatar of any reasonable deity, it *should* tell them to be sensible and go along with us!"

"Oh, surely!" Kerowyn replied, with more than a touch of sarcasm. "I don't know how many gods *you've* had to deal with in your time, but being sensible has not been on the agenda of many of the ones *I've* come across."

"Perhaps not sensible according to your needs and desires, Captain," Snowfire said with absolute politeness. "But I'm certain it was sensible to those who worshiped those gods— always providing, of course, that the ones interpreting the gods' will were honest. Case in point—Karse before Solaris."

"Huh. Good point." She sat down and looked all around the circle. "So, pull back and patience it is. Anybody have any objections?"

Clearly there were none that anyone thought worth mentioning, so Kerowyn declared the meeting at an end, and she and Snowfire left to meet with their respective troops and scouts and give them their new orders.

The debate in the Healers' tent had gone on for most of the day, and showed no signs of stopping. Nightwind had joined them, as the only representative of the Hawkbrothers, and she had concurred with the consensus that *something* would have to be done about the Summer Fever and quickly, before it crossed to the allies.

"It's summer *now*," Keisha pointed out. "What if another outbreak starts among them? What do we do then?"

"We'd have to impose some sort of quarantine, I suppose," began Grenthan.

"That could be difficult if we're in the middle of armed conflict with them," Nightwind said dryly. "Just how would we enforce it? Insist that only healthy people be allowed on the battlefield? Hold inspections for fever and sneezes before anyone can fight?"

Keisha choked back an involuntary laugh at the absurd image *that* conjured up; no one else seemed to find it funny, except perhaps Nightwind herself.

"I wonder—" she started to say, then stopped.

"What?" asked Gentian, who had become the default leader at this point.

"Well, I just wonder why these northerners don't have any real Healers of their own?" she continued, flushing, thinking that it was probably a stupid question. "I mean, the shaman seems to have done herb-Healing and that sort of thing, but no one uses the Gift. . . ."

Apparently no one else thought it was a stupid question, because a wary silence descended on the group. Finally Nala cleared her throat uneasily.

"In Karse, before Solaris, they used to test children for the Gift of Healing and sacrifice them if they were too old or too strong-willed to be indoctrinated into the priesthood," she said slowly. "You don't suppose that these barbarians do the same thing, do you?"

"In Karse they also sacrificed children with Mindspeech, on the grounds that it was a mark of demons," Gentian reminded her. "But the use of Mindspeech didn't frighten these people. And I have very clear images from Tyrsell's gleanings that the shamans have never used the Healing Gift in the way we do. I suspect that Healing is a Gift they either don't possess or don't recognize."

"If they thought it was an evil thing, they wouldn't be looking for Healers," Nightwind added. "No, I don't think this is a case of doing away with children showing the Gift. Anyone with an untrained, unused Gift of Healing would just go off by himself to get away from the things he started to pick up from everyone else, and that's hardly unusual behavior among these folk. From what I've gleaned, people split off from their clans all the time, either because of feuds, or jealous protection of a good hunting range, or basic dislike of others in the clan."

One of the apprentices cleared his throat; this was a young man Keisha would have picked for a scholar, not a Healer. "It makes more sense in a society like theirs for people who don't fit to go off on their own. They'll never find a mate, and dissension weakens the group."

A scholar's reasoning if ever I heard it, but he's right.

"Still—wouldn't at least a few of them learn what the Gift meant?" Nala asked. "I've known plenty of self-trained Healers."

"But those self-trained Healers knew not only that there

was such a thing in the first place, but what it meant and what signs to recognize it by," Nightwind replied. "Not only that, but think of what their lives are like, *particularly* now! With that much pain and illness all around them, children with the Gift might well shut themselves down completely just out of instinctive self-defense. They'd probably do so long before any other real signs manifested. It's happened that way before, and if you don't know that the bad feelings you are getting are coming from other people or that they mean that you can actually help those other people, you'd welcome anything that made them go away."

"There are times when I'd welcome it now," Nala put in wryly.

At that point, Darian arrived, with a message that made all of their debate moot, at least for a few days. "May I interrupt you?" he asked, poking his head inside the tent, and bringing with him a breath of cooler air.

"Be my guest," Gentian responded. "You aren't interrupting anything that hasn't been talked to death by now. We're arguing in circles."

"The barbarians have shut themselves up in their camp, and the war council has agreed to pull back and let them settle for a couple of days anyway." He joined the circle, squeezing in next to Keisha, who obligingly moved over for him. "The thought is that maybe we were a bit too good at giving them a scare, and that they may need some time to stew things over and figure out that we don't want to wipe them out. Well, some of us don't. Anyway, no one is going to do anything for the next day or two, or even three. Thought you'd want to know."

"That gives *us* some breathing room," Gentian said with obvious relief, then looked around the circle. "Go think about these things, and we'll talk them over tomorrow. Maybe a little sleep will give us a new direction."

Keisha already *had* a direction in mind, but she was going to need Darian's help to make her plan work. She waited while the others went their separate ways, then said, before Darian could leave, "I'd like to get your opinion on something. May I borrow a little of your time?"

"Of course!" he agreed, eagerly enough to give her a little

thrill of pleasure. "Let's collect some dinner, and we can talk while we eat."

At that point she realized that the *chava* and vegetables that had been passed around the Healers' conference had worn off a very long time ago, and she was only too happy to follow his lead.

He seemed to want real privacy as much as she did, for he found a place near the brook that supplied water for the camp, practically on top of a set of fist- and head-sized water-rounded rocks that broke up the flow, where the babbling waters effectively masked low-voiced speech. "I have an odd feeling that our minds are running along the same lines," he said, managing to get his dinner eaten while avoiding talking with his mouth full. "So, what did you have in mind?"

She stared at the water for a moment, phrasing her plan in her mind. "I think we ought to try and catch a barbarian," she replied. "First of all, we need to be able to talk to them in their own language. We can't do *anything* by just going through Tyrsell, not really. Maybe they've experienced Mindspeech before, but talking to them in their own language would make them feel more comfortable."

"You are either reading my mind, or we're reasoning along exactly the same lines!" he exclaimed, with muted surprise. "And you are absolutely right, that's precisely what we need to do. I had it in mind that we weren't going to really learn what's going on in their camp unless our watchers knew their tongue. But you have something more in mind than that, don't you?"

"We need to find out directly whether or not this Summer Fever is in their camp, and just what they expect a Valdemaran Healer to be able to do about it," she told him firmly. "At that point, we'll have a basis for negotiations, don't you think?"

"Negotiations or not, we *do* need to know if there's anyone that can spread the Fever to us, absolutely." He toyed with a bit of bread, his expression so opaque that Keisha couldn't read it.

"We aren't going to get any of that from the leaders; they probably have some stupid code about fighting honor, and they'll *certainly* have their status tied up in warfare. We'll have to catch someone ordinary, someone who isn't a fighter, who'd be perfectly happy if there wasn't a battle, or at least wouldn't be looking to start a fight," she continued. "An old man, or a woman, perhaps."

"Or a child." He mulled that over, while she held her breath, hoping that his answer would be the same as hers. "Whatever, it should be someone who'll sneak out of the camp alone, so with you, me, Kel, and Tyrsell at most, we can overpower him long enough for Tyrsell to get the language."

"Exactly!" She beamed at him. "I guessed you'd be clever enough to see that—and willing to have me along to help!"

"Willing? Havens, I can't see trying this without you. Kel can subdue someone, but we're going to have to immobilize our man, and Kel's claws aren't dexterous enough for that." He grinned back. "Now *this* is just what I meant about you having good sense, with courage to match it!"

She flushed and looked down at her stew bowl, eating very rapidly while she tried to subdue her blushes.

"When do you want to try this?" she asked. "And—I know you're not enamored of her, but I think we ought to bring Shandi in on this, too. She's very clever, and she's another set of hands."

"What about that Companion of hers?" he replied, skeptically. "I'm sure she wouldn't give us away, but what's to stop him from tattling to Kerowyn's Sayvil?"

She covered her mouth with her hand, embarrassed at her own stupidity. It was just so alien to think of Shandi with a Companion! "Oh, I completely forgot about him— No, you're right. We shouldn't bring her into this. Karles would have to tattle to Sayvil, especially after the way that Sayvil dressed *him* down. And what Sayvil knows, Kerowyn will soon find out. Companions are pretty bad about keeping any secrets but their own."

"Well, as to when—we can try tonight, have Kuari keep a watch on the camp and let us know if anyone from the women's fire sneaks out." He scratched his head, thinking. "My guess is, the women will probably try to get out under cover of darkness to fetch water, and some of the older children might have some snares out in the forest they'll want to check. With our people withdrawing, they aren't going to be quite as willing to do without fresh food and water when there's no apparent danger. I know I was perfectly capable of running snares when I was only seven or eight; I can't see why they wouldn't be able to. During a siege, every little bit of food is valuable, and a boy might well get manhood status by daring to go outside the palisade to bring in rabbits."

She considered that; although she didn't like the idea of trying to run about in the dark, she could see that this would offer the best opportunity. "We'll have to catch our quarry far enough away from the barbarian camp that help won't be able to come," she said cautiously. "It'll have to be so far that even if our prey raises a fuss, she won't be heard, for there's no point in taking the chance that someone would mount a rescue. It could get touchy when someone vanishes out in the forest, you know."

"With any luck, the barbarians will think that a forest monster caught her," Darian replied, with just a touch of callousness. Then he looked faintly apologetic at his own attitude. "Oh, I know that sounds bad—it's just that I still can't help but think back, and want *some* kind of revenge."

She nodded, fully able to understand his feelings. "Revenge doesn't get you anything productive, though. And it tends to breed more of the same."

"Yes," he sighed. "You know, sometimes it's an awful lot of trouble to be a civilized, reasonable, passably good person."

She thought back on all the times when she'd been tempted herself to just lash out at the world—the things she could have inflicted on poor, stupid Piel, for instance—and nodded. "I know," she replied, with profound understanding. "Believe me, I know."

"If we're going to keep doing this, we've got to get a *kyree* on our side," Keisha whispered to Darian, as they crept, slowly and with many pauses for Darian to check with Kuari, through the undergrowth near the barbarian camp. She had made it very clear to him that she had no intention of climbing through the trees, and with some reluctance, he agreed that she was probably justified in refusing. She didn't have the skills, the practice, or even Kuari to lend her his sight; she'd be going blindly, depending on Darian, and hoping she didn't make a fatal false step. The tree route would be extremely difficult by daylight, but impossible for her at night. No matter how much she trusted Darian's competence, she didn't trust it *that* much.

Kel was with Kuari in the trees above, Tyrsell trailing along with them below. *And thanks be to all the gods, Shandi is still sleeping like a bag of rocks, or she'd have found out what we were going to do, I just know it.*

Keisha had thought she was used to moving through the woods, but it was a different proposition in this thick, damp darkness. Sudden noises startled her, twigs caught at her clothing and her hair, and she couldn't seem to go three steps without making noises that sounded very loud to her. Darian was able to slip through the undergrowth as easily and noiselessly as a bit of mist; by contrast, she blundered through everything in her path like a blind calf.

Nervous sweat plastered her hair to her scalp and her shirt to her back, and it was a tremendous relief when Darian's hand on her wrist signaled a halt, and they crouched in the shelter of some bushes. "Kuari says there's someone sneaking out of the camp right now," he whispered. "It's not a warrior, so this might just be our best chance at getting what we need. It looks as if he's coming this way, so we'll just stay where we are and let Kel ambush him."

He? Well, as long as it isn't a fighter, it should still be all right. We should still be able to handle him if Kel takes him down.

She nodded, hardly able to believe their luck. She'd assumed that they'd have to spend many nights like this—that this one was probably going to be nothing more than a rehearsal for an opportunity to come. But she reminded herself not to count on anything, and suppressed the nervous excitement that made her hands tremble and stomach clench. They didn't have a captive yet.

"I don't believe this—" Darian whispered a moment later. "He's still coming straight for us!" He paused, and puzzlement crept into his voice. "He's following something. Kuari can't quite see it, but there is something there. Maybe a pet escaped and he's trying to catch it?"

"A hunting dog, more like, too valuable to get away,"

Keisha suggested. But out of nowhere came a strange shiver of premonition, a certainty that of all things, a dog was definitely *not* what was out there.

But Darian seemed satisfied with that explanation—or if he wasn't, he didn't say anything to her. "If it brings him this way, it's fine with me," he said fervently. "He's already too far from their camp for anyone to hear if he yells; a bit more, and he'll be so far out that the bondbirds watching the camp won't notice anything either."

"Even better!" That was something that had worried them both, that they'd give their plan away the instant Kel made his capture, and they'd be in trouble with their own side before they got a chance to see their plan through.

"In fact," he added, with growing excitement, "it looks like Kel is going to be able to bring him down practically at our feet!"

Try as she might, there was nothing to really see in these dark woods except variations in the degree of darkness. She already knew that she could peer out there until she got a headache, and still see nothing. As time crawled as slowly as the ant making its way up her leg, Keisha swatted at insects and tried to be as quiet as possible while doing so, straining her ears for any sound that might signal the approach of this stranger. But when such a sign came, it wasn't a sound but, much to her astonishment, a sight.

Out beneath the trees, out on the edge of vision, she saw light. Something out there moved lithely from bit of cover to bit of cover; something very large, and very pale, shimmering with a ghostly iridescence so faint that for a while she was half certain that the effect was nothing more than her own imagination or eyestrain. The only reason she noticed it in the first place was its movement. It certainly wasn't human, nor was it a dog, or any other beast Keisha recognized. She didn't get a good look at it; either it was adept at hiding itself, or it changed shape from moment to moment.

Was *this* what their quarry was stalking? If so, they owed it a debt—

Just when it seemed that the creature was getting near enough that she'd be able to identify it, it faded into a wall of shadow, and vanished completely, while the hair on the back of her neck stood up in atavistic alarm.

But it had been visible long enough for the young barbarian following to get exactly where Kelvren wanted him.

From somewhere up above came a blood-curdling screech; the slight shadow making his way carefully through the undergrowth in the wake of the ghostly light froze, still balanced on one foot. Then he made a break for it, but it was too late.

Everyone had told Keisha that seeing Kelvren make an attack was one of the most thrilling spectacles imaginable. It was too bad that it was far too dark for her to see anything except a pair of shadow-wings for a fraction of a second, followed by a tremendous crash in the undergrowth.

"I have him!" Kel crowed happily, over the sound of hysterical screams. "Now come and tie him up!"

Darian conjured a mage-light in one hand, and stared into the sullen eyes of their captive. He looked to be just around Darian's own age, perhaps a little younger. He was angry, frightened, and Darian would not have given a copper bit for their lives if he got a weapon in his hands.

Physically, he was a little shorter than Darian, with weathered, scratched skin that would be pale beneath his tan, and a shock of unwashed, tangled black hair. His eyes were as black as his hair, and his teeth, clenched in a grimace, had the canines filed to points. They'd tied his hands behind him, and his feet together, and sat him up against a tree trunk while they moved on to the next part of the plan.

He wasn't going to cooperate in any way whatsoever, not that Darian cared. *He doesn't have to be cooperative in order for Tyrsell to get his language.* Darian looked up at Tyrsell, who had watched the entire proceedings with intense interest. "Are you ready?"

:I am. I rather doubt that he is, however.: The *dyheli* snorted. *:And you, Healer, are you ready?:*

"As much as I can be." Poor Keisha looked horribly nervous; this must have been so foreign to her, even though she had already undergone the process once.

"I know it's no help to say this, but if you can relax, this should be relatively easy for you," he told her with as comforting a smile as he could manage. "The first time is always the hardest; you're used to it now, and you've had lots of practice in Mind-Gifts. It's generally the fact that you're resisting something so entirely new that you instinctively fear it that gives you the worst headache."

She blinked at him as if that hadn't occurred to her. "Oh," was all she said, but as the hostile eyes of their prisoner went from him to her and back again, she visibly relaxed.

:Well done,: Tyrsell said with approval, and then they were both lying flat on their backs, staring up at branches and leaves reflecting the mage-light, as Kel and Tyrsell watched them with interest. Darian didn't have more than a touch of headache this time; he hoped Keisha had fared as well.

Her first words seemed to indicate that she had. "Forty-one words for *snow?*" Keisha exclaimed in disbelief. "Why would anyone need all those words for different kinds of snow? Snow is snow!"

"All I care about is the words for 'what the hell do you people think you're doing here?' " Darian replied as he sat up, pleased to discover that he still had no more than a vague ache behind his forehead to show for this latest language acquisition.

The young man had not fared so well; he was still out cold. *:I took the liberty of giving him Tayledras, but not Valdemaran,:* Tyrsell informed them loftily. *:That way he will understand some of the negotiators and can act as a translator, but you will still have a language he does not know so that you can speak freely before him. Besides, it was a useful way to keep him from getting into mischief until you awoke.:* The king-stag wrinkled his nostrils with his head high, testing the air. *:If you have no further need of me, I will be off.:*

"No further need, but we couldn't be doing this without you. Thank you, Tyrsell," Darian replied with feeling.

:You are most welcome. I hope that your plan succeeds.:

Tyrsell slipped away into the darkness, leaving them alone with the young barbarian who was just waking.

"What did you do to me?" he demanded angrily, his face contorting with the pain of his headache. "Is this some demon-born torture you've worked on me?"

"No," Keisha said, "it only feels like one." As the young man's eyes widened to hear her speak his own language, she continued. "Our magics enable us to take what we wish from your mind, and it seemed useful to have command of your tongue. So, as you can see, there is nothing that you can keep secret from us, but taking your knowledge exacts a toll in pain from you and we would spare you that; you can suffer more of this, or you can answer our questions. The choice is yours."

"Personally, I'd answer her," Darian added sternly. "Or you're likely to wish someone would kill you to be rid of the pain in your head. The more we take, the worse it will get."

His face paled, and he appeared to wilt—and without that sullen, defiant expression, he looked several years younger than Darian.

"What do you want to know?" he asked, defeat written large in his expression.

"Your name, first," Keisha said.

"Hywel, son of Pedren, son of Hothgar the Ugly, son of—" he began, obviously quite prepared to recite a lineage back to the beginning of his tribe.

"That's enough!" Keisha interrupted, stopping him. "Hywel will do."

"So, Hywel, why have your people fortified their camp?" Darian asked, keeping his stern expression. "We offered to treat with your people, but they are rejecting our offers with apparent hostility."

"Because we are not fools!" the youngster retorted. "You threaten us, you come upon us with magic and warriors. Are we to simply lie down and allow you to slaughter us? Why are you so hostile to us? We had heard that the peoples of the south were hospitable and welcomed strangers!"

"You mean 'soft,' don't you?" Darian asked cynically, and the young man flushed, then paled. "Well, you've found out differently. We've seen your kind; we know what to expect from *you*. Four years ago, one of your clan war parties came down here, looting and killing, making slaves and worse out of my folk, ruining what they didn't steal! Why shouldn't we meet you with fighters and magic? We *should* have met you with fire and the sword for what you did the last time!"

He started to warm to his subject, but the young man interrupted *him*, with a curious look on his face. "Why do you say it was my people who did this to yours?"

"You're from the north," Darian replied stubbornly, anger burning in the pit of his stomach. "You look the same, barring a few decorations."

"There are *many* Clans and tribes in the north, and most of them look the same to an outsider," Hywel retorted, eyes flashing. "Nevertheless, they are not all the same. *My* people have done nothing to yours. It was not my people who put yours to the sword. *My* people," he added proudly, "do not trade in, keep, or make slaves. Our fighters do not make up war parties to loot the wealth of others. I do not know which of the marauding tribes brought harm to you, but we are not them."

That simple statement brought Darian to a halt; it had never occurred to him that the tribes of the north could be as different as, say, Valdemar and Karse.

"My Clan is Ghost Cat," Hywel continued, with such pride that Darian was surprised. "And we are very like our totem. We are solitary hunters, we have our own herds. Our fighters are not thieves—they serve and protect the Clan from those who would steal our wealth. We prefer being unseen, like the Cat. None fight more bravely when we must," he continued with bravado, "But we do not seek conflict. We walk by ourselves, seek our own path, and all places are alike to us." He tilted his head to one side, looking at Darian curiously. "What totem did your enemies follow?"

"A bear," Darian replied, wondering how much of Hywel's speech to believe. "And the shaman bore the sign of the eclipse."

Hywel's eyes nearly popped with surprise. "And you *drove them off*? Indeed, you are either lucky beyond belief or god-touched! That is Blood Bear, and they live for battle; when they can find no enemy, they fight among themselves! Most

Clans avoid them at all cost; they have even violated Midsummer Truce in one of their rages!" He dropped his voice to a whisper and looked anxiously from side to side. "Some of their warriors gained the aspect of the Great Bear itself, by venturing into the Forbidden Places with their shaman. This I know, for I saw some of the Bear Warriors, when I was still at the women's fire. It is said that they are the ones who brought the Summer Fever out of the Forbidden Places, which they dared to enter in their madness and their search for further unnatural powers and monstrous servants."

That seemed to clinch it; the entire speech rang of the truth, for Darian hadn't mentioned the half-bear warriors, or the lizardlike creature that had served as one of the leaders. Further, the youngster could not possibly know that *they* knew about Summer Fever and how it began. That brought Darian to a momentary standstill, at a loss for what to ask next, his anger running out of him.

Keisha, however, was fully prepared to take over.

"What brought you out here in the darkness?" she asked sternly. "Why were you skulking about like one who would do ill? Were you planning to steal from us?"

"No!" Hywel said indignantly. "We are Ghost Cat, not thieves! I would not soil my honor by theft!"

"But if your people had closed themselves into their camp, why were you outside the walls, and at night?" Keisha persisted. "Did you mean to spy upon us?"

He stared at her, stubbornly, but with fear at the back of his eyes.

"I can, and will, take the knowledge from you," she threatened. "Do you give it to me freely, or would you care to have your pain redoubled and have me gain it regardless?"

He closed his eyes, and whispered miserably, "For my brother. I came for my brother. He has the Summer Fever, and I prayed to our gods to send me a sign, to send me a guide to find one of the Wise Ones who can cure all ills. The fever has taken two of my brothers already, and I think to lose Jendey would kill our mother. I prayed and fasted, and tonight, the Ghost Cat that has led us for so long appeared to *me*, and led me—here—"

Darian felt chill mixed with awe—for there *had* been that strange, ghostly shape leading the boy, and it had vanished utterly just before they caught him.

And what if this is the hand of their god, leading him to us because of Keisha?

He exchanged glances with Keisha, and she changed to Valdemaran. "This is a little too spooky," she said, shaken. "I saw him following—something. Kuari saw it, too, didn't he?"

"I know. I guess you saw what I saw?" At her nod, he shivered. "Now what?"

"If a bout of fever has started in the camp, the odds are that it's going to cross over to us," she replied. "But—this might be what *I* was hoping for. Earlier today I suggested to the Healers that if we could get a single victim outside the camp, we might be able to find a treatment without being under threat ourselves." She shrugged. "What do you say about letting him bring his brother out, and letting me take a chance with him? I wouldn't be in their power, and *he* wouldn't dare hurt me, not after what we've done to him."

"We could just go back and let the Healers make sure we haven't caught it—" But that would be throwing this gift back in the face of the god, who clearly intended that he and Keisha should do *something*. He didn't think that would be a very politic move at this point.

"Besides," Keisha continued, with a grimace, "There're two more things going for this idea. First of all, this is a *child* we're talking about; not even Lord Breon would object to helping a child. Secondly, we obviously have to decide right now, and we can't afford to wait around to ask for permission. Hywel isn't going to have a lot of time to sneak in, get his brother, and sneak back out again—and this may well be the last time he *can* get out." The grimace turned into a crooked smile. "It's easier to beg forgiveness than get permission, so I think we ought to figure on begging forgiveness."

"You're sure you want to go through with this?" Darian asked dubiously, trying to think of good reasons to veto the notion, but fairly sure that anything he could think of, she'd have a counter for.

She sighed. "I don't *want* to, but I have to. I can't explain it any other way, except to say that this is something that I have responsibility to handle. I was given the Healer's Gift; it's my duty to use it."

But he already understood; hadn't he said essentially the same thing to Firesong?

He drew his knife, and Hywel tried to shrink back, clearly expecting that he was about to be murdered. But when Darian slit his bonds instead and stood up, he remained seated, staring up at Darian and rubbing his wrists.

"Go!" Darian snapped, gesturing with his knife. "If you want a Wise One for your brother, go now and bring him back here—just you and him, and no one else! We have a hundred eyes in the night, and if you bring anyone else, *we* will not be here, and your brother will die."

Hywel's expression changed, from fearful to hopeful and back again. "Is this true?" he breathed, "Do you mean this?"

"Do you believe in the guidance of your Ghost Cat?" Keisha asked softly. "I am a Wise One."

That was enough to decide him. He sprang to his feet. "You will never regret this!" he cried. "Never! I will serve you all my days, and my spirit will defend your children and your children's children after I am ashes!"

With that, he turned and ran off into the dark, running as surely as if his feet had eyes, and the eyes in his head were those of an owl.

Darian looked askance at Keisha. "Did we do the right thing?" he asked, suddenly unsure.

"Oh, yes," she replied, staring into the darkness after Hywel. "We did the only thing we could all live with."

The Ghost Cat Shaman

Fifteen

"**I** have an idea," Kelvren said, a few moments after Hywel had vanished into the darkness. "I hearrr the strream not farrr frrom herrre. Go therrre, and wait forrr my rrrreturrrn."

He took to the air, leaving the two of them alone. Darian listened for a moment, then moved off to the right, the magelight bobbing along over his head. Keisha followed him, and within a few moments, heard the sound of the stream herself.

Darian brought them to a spot on the banks of the stream, a larger version of the freshet beside their camp, which tumbled noisily over flat rocks in a series of small waterfalls. Here they found a place where moss made a thick, soft carpet beneath their feet, kept well-nourished by the spray from the stream. Keisha sat down with a sigh, and Darian did the same. "Are you sure you're up to this?" he asked, worried for her sake. "This isn't anything like you've done before."

She licked her lips, and stared off into the darkness for a moment, wearing an expression that suggested she was testing her own resolve. "I know. And I'm not *sure*. But the rest of you can't do without Nightwind, Gentian, Grenthan, and Nala, and the apprentices aren't even as far along as I was two years ago. I thought that learning to use my Gift was going to be hard, and it was at first, but only at first. It was a lot like riding; once I knew what to do and what it felt like to do it *right*, it was just a matter of exercising those muscles until they were strong and didn't hurt anymore—and I've been doing that a *lot*, as much as I could stand. Plus, I can talk to Jendey, and it's going to be scary enough for him to be handled by a stranger. It would be worse if they couldn't even speak to him. If not me, who else?" She made a face, as she thought of the endless wrangling in the Healers' tent earlier that day. "Besides, the others would want to debate this idea for hours, and all the time this little boy would be getting sicker. I need to stop this fever as early as possible."

Darian rubbed his tired eyes. "I wish there were some other way, but I can't think of anything."

"Neither can I." She cocked her head to the side, listening intently, as she heard the sound of labored wing beats. "Is that Kel?"

It was, and he carried a clumsily wrapped bundle. "I have prrrovisionsss, a tent, and yourrr herrrb-bag, Keisssha," he said smugly, once he was down on the ground. "Alssso, bed-rrrollsss. You can make a little Healerrr'sss tent rrright her-rre, and bessst of all, no humansss will know that thessse thingssss arrre misssing until you tell them, Darrrian."

"How?" Darian asked, staring at the bundle. "How did you manage to get all that?"

Kel looked even more smug, if that was possible. "I have my waysss."

Keisha hugged his neck, much to his pleasure, before seizing the bundle. Darian helped her untie it and get the tent and camp set up. It was a very small tent, barely big enough for two people, but if the weather turned it would keep Keisha and her patient dry and sheltered. It wasn't long before they had everything set up, with a tiny campfire to keep the mage-light company, and there was nothing more to do but sit and wait for Hywel's return.

"I wish I'd brought handiwork," Keisha sighed, fidgeting with her medicine-bag, pulling things out, looking at them, and putting them back in again. "Even mending. Something to keep my hands busy."

"You could ssscrratch my crrresst," Kel suggested brightly. "It isss verrry lucky to ssscrrratch a grrryphon'sss crrresst."

"Is that true? We're going to need plenty of luck," Keisha replied, as Kel stretched out his head in her direction.

"It isss well known," Kel assured her, as Darian kept back a laugh at Kelvren's bare-faced ploy to get a scratch. "A long and trrreasssurrrred trrradition." Kel's eyes glazed with pleasure as Keisha's dexterous fingers rubbed the sensitive skin under his feathers. "Ahhhh," the gryphon sighed. "Don't you feel luckierrr alrrrready?"

"We're going to have a chance to test that tradition," Darian said, jumping to his feet as Kuari alerted him. "Here comes Hywel with the boy."

Boy? Closer to a toddler, rather. When Hywel ran up to them, panting with exertion, the little one he carried in his arms could not have been more than five or six years old at the most. Keisha waved Darian away and took the fur-wrapped burden from Hywel herself.

"Don't come near us," she warned, before Darian could move to help her. "There's no point in two of us being exposed." She laid the boy down on one of the bedrolls. "How long has he been sick?" she asked Hywel.

"A day, no more." He stroked his brother's damp forehead with surprising tenderness. "You see, already he is lost in fever, and that is not good. It is those whom the fever takes hard and early—who—die—" The last three words came out sounding strangled, as Hywel choked back what could have been a sob. He rubbed his eyes fiercely, as Darian stood well off, feeling distinctly awkward and useless.

"Hywel, you stay with me; all I need is an extra pair of hands, and if Jendey wakes up, he'll be easier with you here." She looked up from the boy, and shrugged. "You and Kel might as well go back and tell them what I've done. I'm sorry to have to leave you that unpleasant chore, but you can always tell them that I did it before you had any idea what I was planning."

"Oh, and try to lie to Firesong and Starfall? Digging a well with my teeth would be easier, and a lot less painful." He smiled crookedly. "No, we're in this together, and I'd better get back and get it over with."

He wanted to ask if she was going to be all right and knew it was a stupid question. "Remember all that luck you just got," he said instead, feeling horribly helpless.

"I will," she said, as she put the child down on one of the bedrolls, but it was clear that her mind was on the boy and nothing else, and he was just distracting her.

He started to leave, then turned back. "I don't want anything to happen to you, Keisha," he managed, and stopped himself before he said anything ill-omened.

At that, she looked up and smiled with surprising warmth. "Thank you," she replied softly. "Now go, because I don't want anything to happen to you either. Don't let the Herald-Captain eat you alive!"

Knowing then the best way to help her would be to obey her, he left, but slowly, looking back over his shoulder until he couldn't even see the light from the tiny campfire anymore.

Oh, this is a very sick little boy, she thought, taking the child into her arms. He was so fevered that heat radiated from him. Keisha's first act was to unwrap the child from his bundle of furs, strip him of his sweat-sodden clothing, and wash him down with cool water to bring his fever down a little. Fever was a good thing in principle, but this boy's fever was so high that he was in danger of going into convulsions unless she cooled him.

She sponged him a second time with something that killed body-insects, wrapped him briefly in the furs so that the fumes would work on whatever bugs he carried, then unwrapped him and sponged him a third time with plain water. If fleas *did* carry the sickness, she'd just protected herself.

That done, she dressed him in one of her old shirts and bundled him into the bedroll. "Take those furs and things out of here and put them out somewhere to air for about five days," she ordered Hywel. "Either that, or, bury or burn them."

She heard a choked-off sound, as if he were about to object, then silenced himself. A moment later, he and the filthy furs were gone.

Only a day! I've never seen a fever progress so quickly. She waited impatiently for Hywel to return as she checked reflexes in Jendey's arms and legs. Whatever this illness was, at least the paralysis and wasting hadn't set in yet—or at least it hadn't set in so much that there was a noticeable difference from healthy reflexes.

Deep down inside, she was afraid, horribly, desperately

afraid—but she buried that fear in work. As long as she could keep working, she could keep the fear at bay.

Hywel returned as she checked Jendey's breathing. "When this fever kills—how does it do so?" she asked, frowning as she listened to the lung- and heart-sounds through a hollow tube she placed on his chest.

"It smothers," he said simply. "You fight for breath, but there is no strength in the chest, and it smothers."

Paralysis of the chest muscles? That would make sense. So what do these things all have in common?

Could the fever be attacking the network of nerves that told muscles when to move and how? That network came from the spine, even the newest Trainee knew that. There were fibers that were said to carry orders from the brain to the spine, and out to the muscles, as well as carrying sensation back to the brain, just as blood flowed from the heart out to the body and back. Accidents and wounds had proved that if you cut them, paralysis and loss of feeling was the result— so could this fever be killing or damaging them to get the same effect?

She seized a silverpoint and a notebook from her medicine-bag and wrote down her speculations. If what she tried failed, and if *she* succumbed to this fever—at least the next Healer would have a little more to go on.

"What are you writing?" Hywel asked, with awe in his voice.

"Spells," she said briefly, which seemed to impress him further. "Tell me all you know about how the Summer Fever started."

He didn't seem taken aback that she asked the question, and she made notes as he talked. "It was the Midsummer Gathering," he said obediently. "It was held that year in Ghost Cat territory. I was still at the women's fire then, so it was, oh, many cold seasons ago."

Oh many indeed, I'm sure, she thought, guessing his age at fourteen. *Three, maybe four at the most. Around the time the first lot came down here.*

"Blood Bear was there, and that was when I saw the Bear Warriors, who were as much bear as man," he continued. "Our fighters brought back tales that they had monsters at their fires also, some as slaves, and some among the warriors, and that there was boasting around the men's fire that they had brought only half their numbers, for the rest were out raiding. *We* shunned the Forbidden Circles, for the Ghost Cat had sent warning dreams to our shaman, but the Blood Bear shaman scoffed at our dreams, swore that such places brought power and strong spirits, and he and more warriors went ahunting Forbidden Places."

"So they brought back the Fever?" she asked, as she put down the silverpoint and selected carefully from among her medicines.

"Not at once, no," he told her. "They brought out strange animals like small, hairy people who chattered like magpies and howled like dogs. These, I did not see, but my father told me of them. They tried to make slaves out of the beasts, but the creatures were weak, acted sickly and odd, and soon died. A few days later, the fever began." He shrugged. "That is all that I know."

So this came from contact with sick animals from the Change-Circle! That makes a little more sense. She finished mixing her draught of medicines with juice and honey, and carefully raised the feverish boy, putting it to his lips. He was very thirsty, in spite of being mostly out of his head. He sucked at the cup eagerly and perhaps because of the sweet taste, drank it down to the last drop.

He's getting dehydrated; I have to get more liquid into him. She filled the empty cup with cool water and repeated the process until he turned his head, refusing further drinks. She smoothed back the damp, black hair from the flushed forehead; this child was so different from the littles of Errold's Grove, yet so very much the same, with a mother who would mourn his loss deeply, and a brother who loved him enough to do anything to save him.

She made him as comfortable as she could, finished her note taking, then turned to Hywel. "I am going to work magic to read his fever," she said sternly, fighting down panic that threatened to paralyze her. "You must not interrupt me—"

"Na, you go to the spirit-world, *I* know," he said wisely, interrupting her. "Just as our shaman did. If our shaman had not been struck down with the first to suffer Summer Fever, he would have chased the Fever-Spirits with the good spirits he brought back. I have seen him walk with the Ghost Cat in the spirit world, many times; I will guard you when your spirit travels from your body as the warriors did for him. Have no fear."

As good as explanation as any, she thought, when she recovered from the startlement she'd felt at his easy acceptance of what she was going to do. *At least he knows what to do.*

There was no time to put it off further; she had done everything she could for the boy with hands and herbs. Despite doubts and soul-numbing fears that she had hidden from both Darian and Hywel, she must rely on a Gift she had only recently learned to use. Now only her Gift could help him further; she settled herself at the child's side, and sank into Healing Trance.

She was aware at first only of herself, because she was still within the shields that she had managed to make second nature and automatic. To her own inner eye, she radiated a pure, clear, emerald-green light, contained within a skin of radiant yellow. Taking heart from this, she reminded herself that this was something she had done before; the job was larger, but no different than fighting simpler illnesses. She took the shield-skin inside herself, absorbing the energies, and fixed her attention on the living creature nearest her, the muddled and roiled energy-bundle that was the sick child. Even at this distance, it was obvious to her OverSight that the boy was dreadfully, dangerously ill. To examine the nerve-net she would have to sink deeper than she ever had before, and look more closely. Examining the surface would tell her nothing.

She moved herself to hover over the boy, then slowly let herself merge with him. Her awareness passed through the skin, a protective envelope of sickly pink energy, damaged here and there by the tiny scratches and cuts any active child could get in playing, and which also had its share of insect bites, which appeared to her as inflamed half-spheres, glowing a sullen red. There was no sign of major infection in the skin, however, and she passed on without soothing the insignificant hurts, saving her strength for a greater foe.

His muscles were next, muscles that were well-developed

for a child so young; tough and strong, flexible ropes that twisted and sent off sparks that meant pain as Jendey tossed in fever. There was something deeply amiss here, but it was not within the muscles themselves.

So far, I've guessed right. Just to be certain that she had not missed something, she did not sink further to examine the nerves quite yet.

Instead, she went to the torso as she had been taught, to make certain that the source of his sickness was not in the organs, and began with the heart. An infection of the organs *could* have been pouring paralyzing poisons into Jendey's blood, poisons that affected the nerve-net, but which originated elsewhere.

At this time, there was no sign of strain or irritation there either, nor in the gut—but the lungs *were* congested and irritated, displaying the sullen red glow of inflammation. But they were, as yet, no more serious than a bad cold.

But there was definitely something desperately wrong, for all the body's defenses were mobilized. All along the paths of the blood, the body's defensive armies swarmed, healing energies flowed, yet they traveled to no central battleground, as if they were confused and could not find a target.

Just as confused and desperate as I am. . . .

She shoved away the thought. Failure was not an option.

She turned her awareness to the spine, sank deeper yet, looking for the black miasma of damage, the sullen murk of attack.

Then she found it—and nearly withdrew, appalled at the magnitude of the problem she faced.

The enemy was tiny, tiny, but numbered in countless millions. It subverted the child's own body to create millions more selves with every passing moment. No wonder this fever could not be fought with herbs and medicines—it overwhelmed by sheer numbers, killing the child in the act of spawning more selves from his very substance!

But she had seen this kind of enemy before—just not so virulent, and not centered in the nerve-net and spine. At least she knew the enemy's face now—and she knew how to combat it, provided she had the strength.

She drove down her fear, fear that threatened to send her fleeing back to her own body, all her work left undone. She gathered her own energies, and lashed out at the enemy with lances and light shafts of purest emerald green. The enemy swallowed her energies and millions of attacking creatures perished—a little damaged, but only a little, and in the next moment, the multitude surged back to life and strength.

Now it didn't matter; now there was nothing but action.

This was the moment when she *should* have been afraid; she should have given up. But now the instinct of the Healer had her in a grip that drove everything else out of her mind; she was caught in the battle, and could not have pulled away if she wished it. She had been warned of this suicidal drive for self-sacrifice, the trap that the strongest Healers were all too prone to fall into, and if there had been another Healer there, he would have pulled her out. It was too late—

Thought had been squeezed into a tiny compartment cut off from action, crammed in with the terrible, icc-cold fear. Nothing existed for her but the enemy hordes—and the energies with which she lashed them, heedless of what the energy drain was doing to herself.

And more; energy drained from her faster than she could replace it. This was a battle she was doomed to lose—and when she lost it, the enemy would move to take her. But she no longer cared.

You know, this would probably be going better if we hadn't awakened the Captain out of a sound sleep.

One lantern illuminated the inside of the tent the two Heralds shared; birds twittered outside, expecting the dawn. Inside, Kerowyn made her feelings known, while Eldan had made himself vanish, in a sound diplomatic move.

"You did *what?*" Kerowyn shouted, with incredulous wrath, when Darian finished his report. Darian stood his ground, backed by the Valdemaran Healers, by Nightwind, and by Firesong; they made quite a crowd in Kerowyn's tent, but didn't quite spill out into the open.

He was backed by them, but he had insisted on doing his own talking. "I did this, and I'm not a coward who hides

behind other people when it comes to standing by what I did;
I can defend myself," he had told them, and had been rewarded
by the approval in the eyes of both Nightwind and Firesong.

He felt a little sorry for Kerowyn's officers, who by now, if
they had intended to sleep until true-dawn, had been denied
that opportunity by the shouting. And if it hadn't been that
he'd never been so sure in his entire life that he had done the
right thing, he might well have bolted.

"We had a tactical opportunity that wasn't going to come
along again, Herald-Captain," he said steadily, looking
straight into her eyes and refusing to be intimidated by her
fury. "Furthermore, you may be in command of the assembled fighters, but I'm *not* one of the fighters. I'm a mage, and
not one under your command. I'm a mage with four years
of field experience, as well, and I am accustomed to being
expected to think for myself. We had our primary objec-
tive. We've gotten the language, which Tyrsell can now take
from his own memory and give to anyone else. Keisha and I
took the opportunity that was presented to us precisely because, in terms of personnel, it offered a substantial gain—
versus, at worst, the minimal loss of a single noncombatant.
We had the boy in a vulnerable position, and a moment of
opportunity to extract a *single* fever victim, a moment that
was rapidly vanishing. Neither of us is a good enough Mindspeaker to contact superiors for advice. There wasn't time to
do anything but act."

Talk to her in tactical terms, was what Firesong had advised him. *Don't talk to her in terms of Healer's Oaths or humanitarian motives. Give her gains versus losses. I'm not
saying she won't see and appreciate the humanitarian motives, just that she's a commander first, and that's how she's
going to react. Once she finishes reacting to the insubordination, she'll move right into thinking and analyzing.*

Firesong was right; as she listened to him, the scowl faded
to a mere frown, and the frown to a grimace. Finally she
threw her hands in the air.

"All right," she acknowledged. "I can see that. I just thank
the gods that I don't have anyone else in my ranks who's got
the curse of thinking for himself."

"Yes, you do, Kero," Firesong said mildly. "You generally

make them into officers if they manage not to get themselves or anyone else killed."

"You can make yourself useful by finding that *dyheli* and having him drop that language into Eldan's skull," she replied sternly to Firesong. She waited for his nod and withdrawal from the tent, then turned back to Darian. "You are going to stay here and give me every single detail of what you saw, heard, and did."

"What about us?" Gentian asked, with a wink for Darian that told him he'd won this round.

"Back to your Healer business," she said, making shooing motions with her hands.

Everyone else spilled out into the gray light of false-dawn, wasting no time in putting some distance between themselves and their commander.

Nightwind stayed with Darian, and Kerowyn didn't object. When everyone else had left the tent, she wearily waved at them to sit; there were only three places to do so in her tent and she was already occupying the only chair, still dressed in the old shirt and hose she wore to sleep in, her hair coming undone from its braid. So he took a seat on a small campaign chest, leaving the stool for Nightwind.

He went back over the night's events in excruciating detail, leaving out nothing, not even the changes in Hywel's expression. He also did not leave out the alleged Ghost Cat, although his description was as vague as his own sighting of the thing had been. When he had finished, Kerowyn brooded in silence for some time, her fingers automatically undoing and rebraiding her hair. Despite the fact that Darian knew they had been right to act as they had, the tension in the tent built until he thought he couldn't bear much more. Granted, he wasn't under Kerowyn's direct command, but she *could* order him back to the Vale, and the Tayledras would probably enforce her orders.

Finally: "Dammit, you did right," she growled as she bound up the end of her braid. "I don't like it one bit, but you did right."

The tension snapped, replaced by the feeling that someone had removed the weight of a horse from his back.

"Captain, if anything had been different, if Hywel had been

less cooperative, if the victim hadn't been a small child, if that ghost—or whatever—hadn't been leading him out in the first place, we'd never have done what we did," he replied with feeling. "I swear."

"It's that so-called Ghost Cat," Kerowyn said, chewing her lower lip. "That's the thing that's— *Bothering* me isn't the word, it's a more spooky feeling than that. It's not like some shaman's trick or wishful thinking. It seems as if *every* time it shows up, it guides these people properly, and I have to wonder if it can—and will—do more than that. You say you saw it, Tyrsell says he thinks it's real—and whenever anybody so much as mentions it, I get a shiver down my spine that I can't stop. I've had that same shiver before. . . ."

"And?" Nightwind prompted alertly.

Kerowyn smiled crookedly. "Let's just say that it's a sign of one of *my* Gifts." She turned back to Darian. "It's a good thing that you aren't under my command, because even if you are right, this is *way* too close to insubordination for my comfort. However, you aren't, and that lets me out of having to find a way to discipline you for exercising your brains without orders."

"Yes, Herald-Captain," he said, and deemed it wise to say nothing more.

"Now you go make yourself useful and *try* not to get into any more trouble," Kerowyn ordered. "I'd like to talk to this lady for a bit."

Darian left, with the distinct impression he'd had a narrow escape indeed—but also with the nagging feeling, which grew with every moment, that there was something of critical importance that he had left undone.

He got no chance to think about it, for the situation that had been at stalemate just a moment before suddenly avalanched down around their ears, with no prior warning whatsoever.

"Oh, *hellfires*" came the exclamation from behind him. Kerowyn suddenly shot out of her tent as if her hair were on fire, followed by Nightwind who was moving just as quickly. She sprinted up the path and grabbed Darian by the elbow, startling him into an undignified yelp.

"I need you—now!" she said, as Nightwind grabbed his

other elbow. Before he could even blink, the white bulk of Kerowyn's Companion thundered down on them from out of nowhere, and Kero and Nightwind literally threw him up on Sayvil's bare back. A heartbeat later, Kerowyn was up behind him, and it was a good thing that he had automatically grabbed a handful of mane, because the Companion launched herself into an all-out gallop as soon as the Herald's rump touched her back.

He clung with hands and thighs, the wind of their passing whipping through Sayvil's mane until it lashed his face and eyes unmercifully, leaving tiny, stinging welts. He'd heard of the legendary speed of a Companion, now he got a firsthand experience, which would have been breathtaking, if it hadn't been so terrifying.

In a much shorter time than he would have dreamed possible, they were among Kerowyn's fighters and Kero slid down off Sayvil's back, leaving him still perched there in confusion. Just beyond the screening of trees and bushes, someone shouted in a voice torn by anguish, fear, and rage.

"What's the situation?" she demanded, as one of the fighters separated from the rest and saluted.

"Things were dead quiet, then all of a sudden there was a ruckus in the camp," the scarred and weathered veteran reported brusquely. "Lots of shouting, carrying on, women wailing. Then the men started raising hell over there, and the Chief comes tearing through the barricades and starts waving weapons around and shouting at us."

"You!" Kerowyn slapped Darian's leg to get his attention. "We're looking for Tyrsell—but until then, *what's he saying?*"

Belatedly Darian realized that he understood the shouting perfectly well, and paused to listen to it.

What he heard made his jaw drop.

"Well?" Kero demanded. *"What?"*

Darian licked dry lips. "He says we sent child-snatching demons into his camp last night, and he wants us to bring back his sons *right now*. Or else—"

"Never mind. I can guess the 'or else.' " Kerowyn swore softly. "And it's just our bad luck that your little friends happened to be the Chief's offspring—which obviously, the older one didn't bother to mention." She chewed on her lower lip, then turned her gaze to her Companion. "Sayvil, go take him back to camp, then get your tail back here; this is no place for him. By now Tyrsell's given Eldan this language, and we'll see if his silver tongue can lie us out of this mess when he gets here. And we'll pray that Keisha can come up with a cure, *fast*."

Sayvil didn't wait for Darian to object; she all but launched herself out from underneath him, and only a quick grab for her mane kept him from tumbling over her rump.

He had the presence of mind to slide over her shoulder as soon as she reached the edge of camp where his first tent still stood and slowed a little; he hit the ground running to absorb his own momentum and it was a good thing that he did. She didn't stop, not at all; she just pivoted on her hind hooves and galloped away again, leaving him panting in the path behind her, staring after her, absently recognizing that there was another Companion standing behind him.

Gods—now what do I do?

"What in *hell* is going on?" a voice shrilled behind him.

He whirled, to find Shandi, clad only in a knee-length shift and barefoot, staring at him out of confused and terrified eyes. Her sleep-tangled hair had fallen half over one of her eyes, and she shoved it out of her face with impatient fingers.

"The camp's gone crazy, Karles is frantic, and Keisha's gone and *there's something I—we—have to do with her!*" she exclaimed, sounding more than a little frantic herself. "What's happening? Where's my sister? What is it we have to do?"

As quickly and succinctly as possible, Darian explained the events of the last twelve candlemarks. He got a little shrill toward the end, himself, and Shandi stared at him with a blank expression, while her Companion fidgeted and pranced with anxiety.

She hit her forehead with the butt of her palm, muttering to herself. "You—me—Keisha. What do we have in common?" Balling both hands into fists and pressing them into her temples, she squeezed her eyes shut and her features contorted with pain. "What in *hell* do we have in common? Why am I here? Why do I *have* to be here?"

Gods! he thought bitterly, thinking that she meant that she

didn't *want* to be there. *Why couldn't she be another Healer?*
Then at least she'd have been of some use to—

From out of the thin morning air, the answer came to him,
in the dryly amused voice of his teacher, Firesong.

He ran to Shandi and shook her shoulders with impatience.
"Can you work with Healers?" he demanded. "Have you?"

Her eyes sprang open and she gaped at him. "Yes, of
course—"

As they stared into each others' eyes, they all but shouted
in unison. *"That's it!"*

For the second time that morning, Darian found himself
clinging to a Companion's bare back, this time with Shandi
behind him. Karles must have taken directions straight from
his memory, for the Companion wove his way through the
forest unerringly, and at speeds that would have guaranteed
an accident had he been anything but a Companion. He had
only time to call to Kuari

*.Find dyheli! Find Tyrsell! Bring him where we were last
night and quickly!:*

Then there was no time for anything but hanging on.

When they burst into the little glade where the tent was
pitched and flung themselves from Karles' back, Hywel
jumped to his feet with his dagger drawn, then stopped himself just short of attacking them. Darian paid the boy no attention. *His* eyes looked only for Keisha, and when he saw
her, he exclaimed in shock.

"Damn!" Shandi swore. "She's lost! Darian, link with her,
now!"

He didn't have to be told. Keisha was a ghostly white, she
trembled where she sat, and it looked as if they hadn't
reached her a moment too soon. She was caught, trapped in
battling a disease she couldn't conquer—if she'd had more
practice, she would know how to break free, but of course she
had never Healed a life-threatening illness before.

Darian flung himself down beside her and grabbed one
hand, as Shandi did the same on her opposite side; they threw
their spirits into linkage with hers as swiftly as if they had
done so every day for their entire lives.

There was a rude shock for a moment as they jockeyed for
position, and then they melded into a seamless whole. He

poured energies spun out of the life all around them into the fading Healer; Shandi did the same, but *her* energies came, not from around her, but from her Companion. Neither of them saw what Keisha saw and fought, but they felt the battle going on within the boy, and Keisha's renewed strength as she threw off the intolerable burden of exhaustion, gathered her resources, and flung herself back into the fight.

And for a moment, Darian felt her soul-tearing fear that even this would not be enough.

He willed more than energy into her; he willed courage, and the memory of that anguished voice crying out, demanding that his sons be returned to him.

Whether that was the reason or not, at that moment, the tide of battle turned. Keisha began to gain ground against the fever. Shandi and Darian held steady, and with a last desperate outpouring of power, Keisha broke the fever's hold!

Shandi dropped out of the meld; Darian held longer, as she chased down the last traces of the illness and burned them away. Only then did he separate himself from her, and return his focus to the ordinary world.

"We're still not done," Shandi said grimly, as he opened his eyes and caught Keisha as she half-collapsed against him. "There's a war about to start out there!" She turned to Hywel. "Your father thinks we've sent demons to kidnap you and your brother, and he's got every intention of cutting his way through us to get to you."

Hywel's mouth and eyes went round—and Darian's estimation of his intelligence took a giant leap upward. "Take Jendey!" he cried. "Take him up before you on the Spirit Horse! We will follow with the Wise One!"

Hywel placed one hand on Karles' forehead as Shandi threw herself on the Companion's back; Karles snorted and nodded vigorously. The young northerner bent and picked up his brother—sleeping deeply, too deeply to stir, but without the hectic flush of fever in his cheeks, and no longer tossing in delirium. Shandi reached down for the child, and cradled him in front of her, seizing a handful of mane to keep herself steady.

Karles shot off; Hywel leaned down to help Keisha to her feet. She was still coming out of Healing Trance, blinking at them with bewildered eyes, her legs as shaky as a newborn fawn's.

"Hywel's the Chief's son?" she murmured, proving that although she *looked* no more than half-aware, there was little wrong with her mind or her ears. Darian draped her arm over his shoulder, as Hywel did the same on her other side. "Why didn't you tell us?" she asked, turning her gaze on the young northerner.

"I did not think of it," was his honest reply. "For us, to be Chief's son is to be no different from any other man. It does not mean that I will be chosen as Chief. I am just another hunter of Ghost Cat."

"Obviously your father doesn't see things that way," Darian retorted.

The call of an eagle-owl rang out above their heads, startling all of them. *:Bondmate, they come!:* Kuari called in his mind, as the hoof-beats of several *dyheli* at the gallop reached their ears.

Tyrsell skidded to a halt on the moss, with Pyreen and Meree right beside him. Darian helped Keisha up onto Meree's back, then aided the slightly reluctant Hywel onto Pyreen. This was no time to worry about the mere discomfort of naked *dyheli* spines. "Don't grab the horns, grab the neckbrush!" Darian ordered, as he clambered onto Tyrsell. "And hang on tight!"

Dyheli weren't quite as swift as Companions, but they came a close second; they caught up with Karles and Shandi, who had inexplicably stopped at the edge of the cleared area containing the Ghost Cat encampment.

Then they saw *why* the others had stopped.

There were two heavily armed forces in that clearing, forces who had been about to face off against each other in a battle for blood. Both sides had weapons drawn, and there *should* have been a fight going on at that very moment.

The two reasons why that wasn't happening were planted in the clear space, separating the two groups of fighters and holding them apart.

Both reasons were white, one glistening in the sunlight, one ephemeral as fog. Both reasons stood side-by-side in unity, holding off the fighters loyal to them by a force of will so strong that it might just as well have been a solid wall a hundred feet high.

One was Eldan's Companion.

The other was a huge shape, faintly glowing, that could have been an enormous feline.

Just as Darian, Hywel, and Keisha arrived, lining up beside Karles, the ghostly feline turned to face them all. It regarded them with an unwinking gaze, as the faces of the northerners turned to see what it was looking at.

Stunned silence—then, with a roar of joy, the Chief flung down his ax and shield, and hurtled toward them, arms outstretched, his men a scant pace behind him, cheering themselves hoarse.

Only Darian continued to watch the Ghost Cat, so only he saw it wink at him, slowly and deliberately, before it faded entirely from view.

Three days later, the morning sun overtopped the trees and golden light illuminated a scene that could not possibly have seemed likely the last time Darian had been here.

Where two armies had faced off, an open-sided pavilion stood; within it, a table and two chairs, one holding Chief Vordon of Ghost Cat Clan, the other Herald Eldan of Valdemar. Around the pavilion, an impromptu festival was going on, as northerners and Valdemarans, Hawkbrothers and Lord Breon's folk cautiously mingled, slowly learning one another's languages. Those who had already undergone "torture by Tyrsell" acted as willing translators.

Darian finally felt as calm as he looked, and had actually managed to catch up on his lost sleep. It hadn't been easy, though; he'd been much in demand by Ghost Cat and Kero's forces both, though not nearly as much as Keisha. *She* was their heroine, their savior, practically their saint—right up until the point where she got tired of it all and tartly informed them that they were an affront to her nose, and if they really wanted to do something for her, they could all take baths, right now.

The subsequent rush for the stream had been something to behold—as were the newly-scrubbed Northerners, their skin bright red from being scoured so hard.

They still treated her with respect, but after that with less awe, which was something of a relief to everyone.

"—the Wise Ones cannot be disturbed on a whim, or frivolously," Eldan said as Chief Vordon nodded. "So the Sacred Houses of Healing will be secret."

"Of course," Vordon agreed, as if nothing pleased him better.

Well, we're making reasonable demands here. I bet Vordon would show a different face if we demanded all the first-born sons as hostages, say.

"The Holy *dyheli* will conduct the Wise Ones from their Sacred Houses to your camp," Eldan continued, after a glance at Tyrsell. "The Holy *dyheli* will carry your need to the Wise Ones."

"Naturally," Vordon replied, shaggy head bobbing.

"Did he figure this out in advance, or is he making it up as he goes along?" Darian whispered to Keisha as they stood solemnly on the Valdemaran side of the negotiation pavilion.

"Making it up, I think, with some help," Keisha whispered back. "Heralds are very good at improvising."

So far, Valdemar and the allies were doing very well out of these negotiations. Things were *particularly* advantageous for the *dyheli*, for the "holy" *dyheli* were getting the protection of Ghost Cat's warriors, shelter for the winter in barns that Ghost Cat pledged to build, and grain in the winter from Ghost Cat's stores. Virtually everything Eldan asked for, Vordon was agreeing with: care for the *dyheli* in exchange for access to the Healers; a set territory in exchange for alliance with Valdemar and the Hawkbrothers, with Ghost Cat guarding the borders against other northern clans. They even agreed to settle and learn to farm in place of their nomadic life of hunting and grazing.

They couldn't be more unlike the last lot in that. Blood Bear Clan would rather have slit their own throats than take up farming. First, though, they'd have done their best to slit ours.

There had been some disappointment when the other Healers had examined the survivors of the last bouts of Summer Fever, and had been forced to confess that they could not reverse what movement and strength had already been lost. That disappointment had been overpowered by the relief of knowing that Summer Fever would never kill or cripple again.

Darian kept a steadying arm around Keisha's waist, under the excuse that she was still weak and not entirely easy on her feet. She let him—under the same excuse. He didn't think he was going to miss Summerdance nearly as much as he had anticipated.

He had every intention of taking things slowly, though. This wasn't a Vale, and Keisha Alder wasn't Tayledras. *And I'm not stupid. Offend the local Healer? No thank you! What was it Nightwind said once? "The ones who know how to put you together also know how to take you apart!"* Besides, he liked Keisha's friendship; he didn't have nearly enough friends to risk losing one to bad manners.

The northerners hadn't even been the *least* reluctant about improving their bathing habits after Keisha's initial scolding; as it turned out, they had more wistful tales about a valley full of hot springs that they had been driven out of by a stronger clan, and traditions of steam houses that they hadn't been able to build in *far* too long. They knew all about flea-killing herbs, but since such things only came into their hands at the Midsummer Gathering by means of trade, they'd had to do without since the first attack of the Fever. Grenthan and several of the *hertasi* were already constructing a Valdemaran-style community bath house and steam house for them at the edge of the village, and Keisha's gifts of flea-bane and rosemary had been greeted with cries of joy from the women. In short, these barbarians, at least, were not nearly as barbaric as their appearance had led everyone to believe.

Even Kelvren was happy, for he had an entirely new set of humans to ooh and aah over him.

And we have this all settled before Harvest Faire and Val's wedding—which makes absolutely everyone happy! Darian felt full of warm contentment and dared to believe that k'Valdemar Vale was going to be hailed as an immediate success. *Which makes me look awfully good. And which should put Kel's status up a few points as well.*

Thinking of Kel, Darian took a look around for him—and soon saw him, the center of a group of awestruck women, who admired his handsome feathers and timidly touched the talons he offered for their inspection. Darian strained his ears—and discovered, with no surprise, that the gryphon had already gotten Tyrsell to bestow the Ghost Cat language on him.

But when he heard what Kel was saying to the women, he nearly choked, and had to work very hard indeed to keep a properly solemn expression, one in accordance with the gravity of the making of such an important treaty.

For Kel had some treaty ideas of his own.

"It isss good luck to ssscrrratch a grrryphon'sss crrressst," Kel told the enraptured group.

"It is?" said the boldest of the lot—Hywel's sister, if Darian recalled correctly. She reached out immediately and began gently scratching Kel's outstretched head.

"Oh, yesss," Kel sighed happily. "It isss well known; an old and trrreasssurrred trrradition!"